KT-447-879

Where the
Heart Lies

Where the Heart Lies is Ellie Dean's fourth novel.
She lives in Eastbourne, which has been her home
for many years and where she raised her three
children.

3019256B470

01925 234 070

Also by Ellie Dean

There'll be Blue Skies
Far From Home
Keep Smiling Through

Where the Heart Lies

Ellie
DEAN

arrow books

Published by Arrow Books 2013

10

Copyright © Ellie Dean 2013

First published in Great Britain in 2013 by
Arrow Books
Random House, 20 Vauxhall Bridge Road,
London SW1V 2SA

www.randomhouse.co.uk

Addresses for companies within The Random House Group Limited can be found at:
www.randomhouse.co.uk/offices.htm

The Random House Group Limited Reg. No. 954009

A CIP catalogue record for this book
is available from the British Library

Penguin Random House is committed to a sustainable future for
our business, our readers and our planet. This book is made from
Forest Stewardship Council® certified paper.

MIX
Paper from
responsible sources
FSC® C018179

Typeset in Palatino by Palimpsest Book Production Limited,
Falkirk, Stirlingshire

Printed and bound in Great Britain by Clays Ltd, Elcograf S.p.A.

This series of books is dedicated to the 'little battlers', the women who rolled up their sleeves and fought their own war on the home front. Strong and invincible, these women should never be forgotten for, without them, the women of today would not know such freedom.

Acknowledgements

I would like to show my appreciation here for all the help I received from Jane Hollings, who is a midwife, neighbour and friend. She cheerfully told me some of her experiences – some funny, some tragic – lent me textbooks and answered my many questions without making me feel completely idiotic. A great deal of this book couldn't have been written without her guidance. The wine is on the way, Jane!

Thanks also to Jo George who, as a military historian, delved into archives and asked the right people all the questions I needed answering. It appears there was no official order to 'Save Private Ryan', as the Americans did when several brothers were killed like Frank's sons – but unofficially, it was understood that the surviving son could be relocated to a somewhat safer post in such circumstances. Thank you, Jo. What a lucky meeting that was in Italy.

Once again I owe a great deal to my husband, who has to put up with the drama of living with an author who seems to spend every waking moment in another time and another world. He's my rock and my best friend, and I couldn't do this without him.

Thanks too, to Georgina Hawtrey-Woore, my editor at Arrow, and to the wonderful team at my publishers who make sure the books look enticing. And last, but never least, to my agent, Teresa Chris, who has done so very much for me over the years, and seen me through the good times and the bad.

Chapter One

1941

Julie finished the washing-up in the stone sink, tucked her short brown hair behind her ears, and helped her mother, Flo, stack the plates on the nearby shelf. Her few short hours at home were almost over and she would soon be on duty again, rushing about on her bicycle to help deliver the babies who always tended to arrive at the most inconvenient time of night.

Being a midwife in Shoreditch and the surrounding districts was always challenging, and, in the middle of a war, sometimes frightening, but ultimately it was very rewarding and Julie couldn't imagine doing anything else. But these short visits home to Stepney were a blessing, too, for they were a reminder of how lucky she was to have such a warm and loving family to always guide and support her.

She finished putting the few bits of crockery away and watched her mother bustle about while her father, Bert, sprawled in his favourite sagging armchair by the small range. This cramped room, with bare floorboards and damp patches on the walls, was the heart of the two-up, two-down terraced house. It might be

1

damp and rather ramshackle, but it was luxurious compared to the squalor of the nearby tenements.

The tiny black range stood in the chimney breast, heating the room nicely as the wind buffeted outside. A scrubbed table was in the middle of the room, surrounded by a collection of wooden chairs and stools, and a dilapidated dresser stood against the wall, covered in photographs, cheap china ornaments, ration books and shopping lists. The wireless was a new and much prized addition, and it stood proudly in a corner, the mahogany casing gleaming from Flo's industrious polishing. The heavily taped window above the ancient stone sink overlooked the tiny backyard, the outside lav, and the terraced houses beyond the crumbling brick wall.

The front room had once been used as a bedroom when all the family were at home, but now Flo used it to eke out her wages by doing a bit of mending and dress-making. Flo was an industrious little woman who could always find something to do. She was in her fifties, as skinny as a rake and inclined to chatter about nothing much in particular, but her kitchen was always open to her neighbours, her sense of humour rarely waned, and she had a terrific sense of fun. Her family adored her, and it was because of her that they'd had the self-belief to go out into the world and make something of themselves – but they always came home when they could, for this was where their hearts lay.

Julie had been born twenty-three years ago in the

big bed upstairs, as had all of Flo's six children, and although the war had been going on for more than a year now, and her eldest sister, Eileen, had long left home for the south coast, it still felt strange not to have everyone sitting round the table on a Saturday afternoon.

Flo Harris seemed to read her daughter's thoughts as she adjusted the floral scarf she had knotted over the metal curlers in her greying brown hair. 'It ain't the same without the three boys making their usual racket,' she muttered, her brown eyes trawling the room. 'Gawd knows I moaned enough about it when they was here, but I'd give me eyeteeth to hear 'em laughing and teasing and have 'em eating me out of 'ouse and 'ome again.'

Bert Harris shifted in the creaking armchair, his braces dangling loosely from the waist of his heavy-duty trousers, his shirtsleeves rolled to his meaty elbows. 'They'll get better rations than what we do, gel,' he muttered round the stem of his pipe. 'The army knows how to feed a man good and proper, never you mind.'

Julie and her mother exchanged a wise look. It had nothing to do with rations, but the longing to have things back to normal, to see the three boys home again, safe and well, and not to have to rely on heavily censored letters to get any news from them.

'The rationing hasn't seemed to affect you that much, Dad,' said Julie with a chuckle. 'The buttons are still straining on that shirt.'

3

He grinned at her. 'Less lip from you, my gel. I can't help it if I'm all muscle.'

'Muscle, indeed,' Flo snorted, swiping playfully at him with a scrap of tea towel. 'It's the beer what makes them buttons pop.' She turned to Julie. 'Him and his mates drink gallons of the stuff down at the Toolmakers' every night, but at least it fills 'im up so he don't notice how little there is on his plate when he comes home for his tea.' She ran her hands over the faded wrap-round pinafore and gave it a tug. 'I dread to think what would happen if that got rationed as well as everything else. A man needs a bit of pleasure after a hard day's work.'

Julie smiled lovingly at her mother. Nothing much got Flo down, and despite the endless bombing raids, and the terrible fires that had raged through London only two weeks before, she still seemed full of energy and fun. 'You sit down and put your feet up, Mum. I'll make the tea.'

Julie reached for the old brown teapot which had survived the seemingly endless bombing raids, and carefully spooned in the used tealeaves her mother had left to dry on a saucer. The tea would be as weak as dishwater, with no milk or sugar to give it a boost, but it would be warm, and somehow they'd all become inured to it.

'You're looking tired, Jules,' said Flo, as she lit a cigarette. 'That Matron's working you too hard.'

'Nothing much I can do about that, Mum,' said

Julie cheerfully. 'There's a shortage of doctors and nurses now they've enlisted, but that hasn't stopped the number of babies being born. I swear I've attended more births in the last year than ever before.'

Flo grinned through the curl of cigarette smoke. 'It were the same in the last war,' she replied. 'We all thought the world was coming to an end, and the only comfort we 'ad was when our men come home. How d'you think I ended up with so many kids?'

There was no real answer to this, so Julie concentrated on making the tea. It was funny, she thought, that she could spend her days and nights in the most intimate company of strangers, but she still found it embarrassing to talk about sex and babies with her mother. But nursing was all she'd ever wanted, a dream fulfilled only through her parents' sacrifices and her determination to break the barriers and have a career that, until now, had been thought of as middle-class. Unlike so many of her colleagues, she'd decided not to enlist, but to stay in the East End and do her bit among the people she knew and understood, and give something back to the community who'd nurtured her.

'I wonder how Eileen's gettin' on down in Cliffehaven,' muttered Flo round the cigarette, the ash threatening to fall in her lap. 'You ain't heard from 'er, I suppose?'

Julie shook her head. 'She wouldn't write to me,

5

Mum. We never really got on, what with her being twelve years older.' She saw the disappointment in Flo's face and knew how much it must hurt to know your eldest daughter wanted nothing to do with her family – even in these dark times. 'I'm sure she'll get in touch soon,' she soothed. 'Especially after the latest firestorm we had in London.'

Flo sniffed and tipped the ash in a saucer. Sticking the fag in the corner of her mouth, she picked up her knitting and determinedly changed the subject. 'I'm surprised Stan ain't been round,' she said, squinting through the smoke. 'You two ain't fallen out, 'ave you?'

'Of course not.' Julie put the cosy on the teapot and placed it on the table alongside the cups. Her smile was soft as she thought about Stanley Rudge, and the engagement ring he'd given her only three weeks before. Stan was big and brawny, with black hair, dark eyes and a way of kissing her that made her legs go weak. 'We went out dancing the other night. He's on duty at the police station today, that's all. I'll see him next week.'

'I don't see why you can't get married now instead of putting it off until he passes his sergeant's exams. We could all be dead tomorrow, and then where would you be?'

Julie laughed. 'Six foot under without a wedding ring.'

Flo took the fag out of her mouth and waggled a finger playfully at her daughter. 'You know what I

6

mean. I don't want no more little surprises – not after what we've been through with Franny.'

Julie handed round the tea cups and glanced at the clock on the dresser. 'Where's she got to, anyway? I thought she was only popping next door for a minute, and she's been at least half an hour.'

'You know how she and that Ivy rabbit on. She'll be back soon enough, I wouldn't wonder,' muttered Flo. She put down her knitting and eyed Julie solemnly. 'I'm that worried about 'er, Jules, really I am. She should never have got 'erself in the family way, married or not. You will take care of 'er, won't you?'

Julie was also deeply concerned about her youngest sister, but she merely nodded and patted her mother's hand. 'I've arranged it with the hospital, and she's going in next week, two weeks before she's due, just to make sure.' They'd been over this ground many times already, but Julie understood Flo's need for reassurance. 'I know it's a worry, Mum, but she'll get the best care, I promise.'

'Talking about me again?' Franny waddled through the back door and slammed it behind her. She gave them all a weary smile. 'Nothing like being the centre of attention, but there must be more important things to go on about than me and me bump.'

'Are you all right, Fran?' Julie asked, concerned at how pale her youngest sister was, and how laboured her breathing had become on the short journey from the house next door. Franny had always been delicate, an elfin little thing who'd had to struggle all her life to keep up with her more robust brothers and sisters – now she looked exhausted, her eyes dull, her shoulders drooping. Julie swiftly took her pulse, which was far too rapid.

Franny eased her wrist from Julie's soft grip, tucked her fair hair behind her ears and slowly lowered herself into a nearby kitchen chair. Apart from the distended belly, she was as thin and waif-like as ever. 'Don't fuss, Julie, I'm fine,' she said softly. 'But I'll be glad when this baby's born, and no mistake. It's getting more difficult to do the easiest things, and I feel as big and clumsy as the barrage balloons I have to make every blooming day.'

'It won't be long now,' said her mother comfortingly, 'and you've got your sister to look after you, so you don't have to worry.'

'Yeah, I know, but I wish Bill was 'ere,' Franny said wistfully as she reached for the cup of cooling tea.

'Shame 'e didn't put a wedding ring on your finger before he took liberties and went off to war,' muttered her father as he slurped his tea from the saucer.

'Don't start, Dad.' Franny's blue eyes glistened with unshed tears. ''E's promised to marry me the minute he comes home on leave. We neither of us planned this, you know.'

'You should've been more careful, gel,' he muttered, glaring at her from beneath his greying bushy eyebrows. 'The doctor said you wasn't to have kids on account of the rheumatics you 'ad. Yer 'eart ain't strong enough.'

'Well, it's a bit late now, ain't it,' retorted Franny with unusual asperity.

'It's all right, love,' soothed her mother. 'Yer dad's just worried about you living over in Shoreditch. You should be at 'ome with us where we can keep an eye on you.'

'I'm better off near Julie and the 'ospital, Mum – and you've 'ad enough flak from the neighbours already without setting their tongues wagging again. Bill sends me enough money to pay the rent and top up me wages, and if I go into labour, I got Mrs Bessell downstairs who'll run down to the phone box in the next street to ring Julie.'

'I wish Bill's family would put their 'ands in their pockets,' sighed Flo. 'You'd think they'd want to 'elp, seeing as this'll be their first grandchild. I thought they might even offer to have you up there in Yorkshire out of 'arm's way.'

'They don't want to know, Mum,' sighed Franny, finishing the tea with a grimace. 'I've written to them twice and had no answer, but Bill says they'll come round to the idea once 'e's 'ome on leave and we're properly married.'

'Funny lot, them northerners,' rumbled Bert. 'You're better off without them, gel.'

Franny and Julie exchanged amused glances. This was one of their dad's beefs – he'd taken quite a while to accept Bill, who'd come to London to work on the docks, for he didn't trust anyone who hadn't been born and raised in the East End. Yorkshire was a distant world inhabited by an alien race that couldn't be trusted, and he didn't like the thought of his youngest getting mixed up with them. Franny's pregnancy just seemed to confirm his darkest suspicions.

The day was closing in and, as Flo drew the heavy blackout curtains, Julie looked at her watch. 'We'd better get going soon, or we'll miss the train.'

Flo was lighting the last of the candles. The gas and electricity were being rationed now and had been off for hours. 'Can't you stay just one more night?'

'Sorry, Mum, but I have to be back at the hostel before ten. I'm on duty at midnight.'

'I do worry about you out there in the middle of the raids,' Flo replied tremulously. 'All them whizz-bangs going off, and you with only a tin hat to protect you.'

'I prefer that to sitting in the shelter under the tool factory,' Julie retorted. 'The thought of all that heavy machinery over me head makes me shiver. I wish you'd go down the tube.'

'The shelter's nearer, and it's all right once you get used to it.' Flo's weary face lit up as she smiled. 'Blimey, gel, I work there every day, it's getting to be like a second 'ome. Me and Bert have our own little spot, and there's always singin' and such to while away the time. It's a bit like 'aving a party every night.'

Julie hugged her mother and kissed her cheek. 'I'll look after Franny, don't you worry,' she murmured.

'I know you will,' said Flo, her work-worn hand gently patting her daughter's cheek. 'You're a good girl, Julie, and we're ever so proud of you, you know.'

'I couldn't have done it without you and Dad,' said Julie. 'I know how hard it was without me earning all the while I was training.' She slipped her hand into the pocket of her woollen skirt, drew out a half crown and pressed it into her mother's palm. 'Here's a bit of something to keep you going till next week,' she said softly enough so her father wouldn't hear.

Flo closed Julie's hand over the coin. 'We don't need it, love. Not now I'm working at the tool factory and your dad's staying with the Water Board. We've more than enough for the two of us to live on, and you need to be saving up for your wedding.'

Her mother said this to her every time and, as usual, Julie ignored it and put the coin next to the clock. Her parents had sacrificed a lot so she could qualify as a nurse and midwife, and now she was earning two hundred quid a year, a couple of bob a week would not only ease her conscience but bring a few extra treats into her parents' lives. God knew

11

they worked hard enough, for her father was sixty-five and had deferred retirement to continue working as a plumber for the Water Board, and her mother not only kept this house going, did her sewing and helped out with the neighbours, but stood for hours in front of a lathe making tools.

While Franny hugged and kissed their mother, Julie planted a kiss on her father's bald spot. 'Take care of yourself, Dad,' she murmured, 'and look after Mum.'

'I've been looking after yer mum long before you was born, gel,' he said gruffly. 'I don't need you telling me.' He eyed her sternly. 'It's you what needs to take care, gel. Out at all hours, rushing about in the middle of raids. You keep that tin 'at firmly on yer bonce at all times – you hear?'

Julie gave him a swift hug, aware that, despite his gruffness, he loved them all dearly. She pulled on the navy overcoat supplied by the Nursing Association and grabbed her overnight bag and gas mask. 'I'll be back as soon as I can, but I'm on duty for three weeks until I have another sixty hours off.'

Bert rose from his chair, adjusted his braces over his shoulders and fastened his top shirt button before reaching for his jacket. 'The pub's on the way to the station, so I'll walk down with you.' He rammed his cap over his receding hair. 'What about you, Flo? Fancy a port and lemon?'

'I could do with one, and that's a fact.' Peeling off her wrap-round pinafore, Flo yanked out the curler that poked from the front of her scarf and fluffed out her fringe, then pulled on her thin, rather worn overcoat. She blew out the candles and dampened down the fire in the range, then picked up her battered handbag and gas-mask box and linked arms with Franny.

As they headed down the narrow street it was almost like the old days when they'd set off for the pub on a Saturday evening. But the evidence of war was everywhere. Bombed-out houses stood in isolation where once there had been terraces, the pitiful remains of their furnishings open to the elements. Vast craters were overflowing with rubble and had become playgrounds for the children still living in Stepney who used them as a treasure trove to find bits of prized shrapnel. The pavements were almost impassable, and nearly every house had been shored-up, patched with bits of timber, scraps of metal and salvaged bricks. Front doors were scarred, windows boarded, chimneys taken down before they could fall and kill someone. Looming over it all was the tool factory, which filled an entire block and rose three floors above the terraced roofs. Dark and dingy, it had been a fixture in Stepney for as long as anyone could remember.

The journey that should have taken a matter of minutes lasted almost half an hour, for although most of their neighbours had popped in during the last two days, and the night was chilly, they still stood on their doorsteps, arms folded as they gossiped, wanting to have a bit of a chat with Julie before she left for Shoreditch.

Julie's qualification as a nurse-midwife had been the talk of the community, stoking both envy and pride in this sprawling, close-knit London borough, and, as the war had progressed and news had filtered back about how hard she worked and how much she cared about her patients, the pride had eclipsed the envy. She was one of their own – a girl who'd made something of herself against all the odds – someone to be looked up to and admired.

The Toolmakers' Arms stood squarely on the corner opposite the vast factory. Built at the start of the last century, it was two storeys of dirty red brick, with fancy green tiles running in a frieze above the ground floor. The rooms upstairs, which had once accommodated dock workers and sailors on shore leave, were now billets for evacuees. The stained glass windows had been boarded over to protect them from the bomb blasts, and the picture on the weathered old sign that swung above the door was barely discernible beneath the grime. Despite the reasonably early hour, the noise inside was reaching deafening point, and two drunks were already staggering home arm in arm, their singing cheerful but discordant.

Julie hugged her mother and squeezed her father's arm – he was not a man to want to show any kind of affection out of doors where someone might see him. 'Have a good night, and we'll see you soon.'

'You watch yerself out there,' her dad muttered.

'Let me know the minute Franny goes into hospital and I'll be over,' said Flo. 'They've got a telephone at the factory. You can ring me there.'

'I'll let you know when there's a bed free,' said Julie, giving her a kiss. 'Don't worry.'

'Take care of 'er, Jules,' said Flo, her voice unsteady as the ready tears glistened. She hugged her youngest daughter.

'Blimey, Mum, you don't 'alf go on. I'll be fine,' murmured Franny, giving her a kiss on the cheek.

'Come on, gel,' muttered an impatient Bert. 'Me throat's as dry as a parrot's cage, and we're wasting good drinking time.'

Julie and Franny waved them goodbye as they pushed through the pub's doorway, and then linked arms and hurried down the road towards the station. As long as the lines weren't up, and Gerry didn't decide to bomb them, they should be back in Shoreditch in time to hear the news on the BBC Home Service before Julie had to leave for the nurses' hostel and prepare to go on duty.

Almost a week had passed since Julie's visit to Stepney, and the weather had taken a turn for the worse, with sleet and snow to add to the misery of the continued enemy bombing raids.

The telephone call had come to the nurses' hostel just as Julie was hoping for a quiet night. It had been a long day, with countless air-raid warnings disrupting her mother and baby clinic as well as her rounds as district nurse. Now it seemed it would be an even longer night, for this particular patient had already suffered two stillbirths, and despite all her advice, and that of the doctor, had refused a hospital delivery.

'I don't fancy your chances out there, mate,' muttered her best friend Lily, who was sitting on her bed filing her nails in the room they shared with four others.

Julie grimaced. 'Not my idea of fun either,' she admitted as she fastened the soft white cap over her hair and straightened the folds that fell almost to the shoulders of the pale blue striped dress. 'Sadie's mum's bound to be there, sticking her oar in and filling the room with her fag smoke.'

Lily grinned with understanding. She too was from the East End and had volunteered as a VAD. 'Need an 'and with this one, Jules?'

Julie put on her navy coat and gloves and tightened the dark scarf round her neck. 'No thanks, I can handle Val Wickens,' she muttered. She reached for the black Gladstone nursing bag that was always to hand. 'It's Sadie I'm worried about.'

Lily shrugged. 'She might be only eighteen, but she knows the score. If anything goes wrong this time, it won't be your fault, Jules.'

Julie didn't agree but said nothing as she plonked the tin hat over her flowing cap and picked up her gas-mask box. 'See you later,' she murmured.

Hurrying out of the room, down the stairs and

16

along the corridor, she reached Matron's office and peeked her head round the door. 'I'm on me way.'

'Cut along then,' Matron replied, not lifting her forbidding gaze from the pile of paperwork on her desk. 'Good luck, Harris,' she added almost as an afterthought.

Julie ran down the stairs and out into the bitter cold of a winter's night that promised more snow. Once the precious bag was secure on the luggage rack at the back, Julie set off on her bike down the dark, deserted streets. She had no fear of being attacked in a neighbourhood where coppers patrolled in pairs and only the prostitutes dared walk the streets after dark, for her uniform protected her – brought respect even from the roughest kind.

The sirens began to shriek as she reached the narrow alleyway that led to the crumbling rows of ancient warehouses which had been turned into tenements on the southern edges of Whitechapel. It was one of the poorest districts on her vast round and had suffered badly during the bombing, but the inhabitants clung to it, for it was all they knew, and they would defend their right to stay there to the last breath.

Julie returned hurried greetings as a tide of people rushed past her to get to the nearest shelter. She knew most of them from her rounds as a district nurse and midwife, and from the clinics at the centre. She propped her bicycle against a wall and looked up. The searchlights were already sweeping across the sky, and above the wail of the sirens and the shouts of the wardens, she thought she could hear the ominous drone of approaching enemy planes.

She quickly took her large bag from the luggage rack, shouldered her gas-mask box and straightened her tin hat before switching on her torch and hurrying through the profound darkness beneath the high tenement walls. It was a hazardous trip, for she had to dodge the piles of rubbish and dubious puddles littering the alleyway. She tried to ignore the advancing roar of the enemy bombers but still flinched as the big guns boomed out and a huge rat shot out of the darkness across her path.

'Put that bleedin' light out and get down the bleedin' shelter!' The warden stepped out of the shadows right in front of her.

Julie's heart missed a beat. 'You scared the daylights out of me, Harry!'

'Sorry, love, didn't realise it were you.' He looked shamefaced. 'What you doin' here at this time of night, gel?'

'I've got a mother in labour. Sadie Smith, number fifty-nine.'

Harry saluted with an index finger tapping his tin hat. 'Right you are, Sister. Sorry to shout at you like that. Need any help?'

'I'll be fine,' she assured him, even though she wasn't at all sure what she'd find up in that poky little room.

'Goodnight then – and good luck.' He marched off and was immediately swallowed by the shadows.

Julie wove through the endless lines of washing strung across the courtyard, hurried past the communal taps and lavatory sheds which were the only sanitary provisions for the hundreds that lived here, and lugged her heavy bag up the endless flights of stairs, the torchlight flashing over crumbling plaster and broken banisters. Her footsteps rang out in the echoing, bug-infested building until she reached the fourth floor. The stench of those bugs mingled with that of urine, faeces and unwashed bodies, and was accompanied by the reminders of boiled fish and cabbage and the general filth of too many desperately poor people crammed into one building. But she was inured to it, knowing that despite their poverty, there was always a cheerful welcome for the midwife.

'Thank Gawd you're 'ere,' said the blousy, henna-haired woman who was furiously puffing on a cigarette outside Sadie's door. 'I didn't think you'd make it what with Gerry on the bleedin' way.' Dressed in her usual attire of short skirt, high heels and ratty fur coat, Val Wickens had clearly taken time off from the street corner where she usually plied her trade.

Julie smiled back. Val might work the streets, and think she knew it all when it came to having babies, but under that thick make-up and tough talk, she had a heart of gold when it came to her precious family. 'Hello, Mrs Wickens. How's Sadie doing?'

Val shook her head, the cheap earrings swinging back and forth. 'By the looks of 'er, she's pretty far gorn,' she muttered. 'Silly cow didn't say nothing when I saw her earlier, but she must've been on the boil even then.'

Julie and Val were old adversaries when it came to Sadie. Val had had eight children, all born in her dingy basement room, and considered herself to be an expert. It had been Val that had persuaded Sadie to follow the family tradition and not be delivered in hospital. Julie merely nodded and went inside.

The small cold room was lit by a single candle wedged in a saucer and was bare of anything to alleviate the hopelessness of Sadie's circumstances. Apart from the iron bedstead with its stained, lumpy mattress, there was a sagging chair, a battered chest of drawers and a scarred table which held a jug and bowl for washing and a frying pan and primus stove for cooking. A faded coat hung on the back of the door along with the rest of Sadie's few bits of clothing, and a pair of shoes sat in front of the gas fire which hadn't been lit – either because there were no tanners to feed it, or the very real possibility that it might blow up if a match went anywhere near it.

But despite the bare floorboards and the rotting plaster, the room had been swept and scrubbed determinedly into some order. A blackout curtain had been nailed over the only window, a photograph of Sadie's sailor husband had pride of place on the mantel, and one of the dresser drawers had been fitted out as a cot with a knitted blanket, a scrap of sheet, and a small pile of hand-me-down napkins and baby clothes.

Sadie was curled on the rumpled bed, groaning as another contraction ripped through her. As it waned, she gripped Julie's gloved hand, her eyes wide with fear. 'I ain't gunna lose this one, am I?' she pleaded. 'It ain't dead already, is it?'

Julie gave her a soft smile and patted her naked shoulder. 'There was a strong heartbeat when I examined you this morning, Sadie. Now let me get me coat off and set up me things so I can check you again.'

Sadie gritted her teeth as another contraction began, and the enemy bombers droned overhead.

The crumps of the first explosions were distant, but the echo of their blasts still trembled in the walls as Julie pulled off her gloves, coat and scarf and swiftly tucked them neatly away in the sturdy brown paper bag she always carried with her. It was wise in such circumstances never to hang things up next to patients' clothes or risk the horsehair-stuffed chairs and mattresses, for they were alive with fleas and bugs.

'I got clean sheets and a bunch of old nappies wot I used fer my lot. There's water an' all,' said Val, lighting another fag. 'But it ain't hot, 'cos I didn't have no money for the paraffin.'

Julie silently noted she'd had enough money for her fags but said nothing as she opened her bag, took the carbolic soap, nail brush and small towel from the outside pocket, and hurried to wash her hands in the icy water. Pulling on her rubber gloves, she bent over the sagging bed to listen to the baby's heartbeat through the metal pinard, and give Sadie a swift examination. At least she'd shaved Sadie this morning and given her an enema, which was a blessing, for things were going too fast to do anything now.

'Everything is going just fine,' she reassured a terrified Sadie. 'You're in the second stage of labour and your baby's pulse is strong and steady.'

Sadie burst into noisy tears and grabbed Val's hand. 'Oh, Mum. It's going to be all right this time.'

'I give her a fag and a drop of gin to ease the pain, like,' said Val from the other side of the bed. 'D'you think she could do with a drop more?'

Julie looked across at Val in despair. 'Gin and fags aren't the answer, Val. I've told you before.'

'They done me no 'arm,' said Val with a shrug.

Julie didn't even waste time replying as she covered Sadie with the grubby sheet and rough blanket, and tried to think of some way to get Val out of here so she could concentrate on Sadie. 'Could you find me some more candles, Val? I can't see what I'm doing.'

A bomb exploded close by and made the whole building shudder, bringing down a cloud of filthy plaster. Julie swiftly placed the lumpy pillow over Sadie's face to keep off the worst of the downpour, and held tightly to her tin hat.

Val merely ducked her head and continued to smoke. 'What you want candles for?' she shouted. 'You got yer torch, ain't yer?'

'I can't hold the torch and deliver a baby at the same time,' yelled Julie over the high-pitched scream of an enemy fighter plane. 'Just do it, Val.'

Val grumbled good-naturedly as she tottered off in her high heels for her basement room in the next block, and Julie quickly set out her instruments as the dogfights went on overhead and the bombs continued to explode. There were enamel bowls, a douche can, forceps for holding swabs or needles, a dilator to enlarge the cervical canal, cotton wool, gauze, a hypodermic syringe, umbilical tape, sulphanilamide tablets and scissors.

'I wish I hadn't listened to Mum,' groaned Sadie from beneath the muffling pillow. Despite the cold, she was drenched in sweat and writhing on the bed. 'Is it true they can give you something to 'elp with the pain in 'ospital?'

'It is, yes, but it's too late to worry about that now,' shouted Julie over the rattle and boom of gunfire. As she examined Sadie again there was a sudden gush as her waters broke. It was a good sign, for it didn't bode well if the sac burst too early. She managed to catch most of it in the rumpled sheet before it could soak the already stained mattress. 'I'm just going to roll you on your side and get rid of this wet sheet so you'll be more comfortable,' she murmured.

'It 'urts,' moaned Sadie, who was now panting hard.

'I know, lovey, but it'll soon be over.' Julie bundled up the sodden sheet and tossed it aside. 'Right,' she said, after she'd got Sadie on her side. 'Now I want you to draw your right knee up to your chin so I can see what's going on.' She switched on the torch. 'The head's crowning, Sadie,' she said as calmly as she could above the surrounding racket. 'Now, I don't want you to push just yet, but keep on panting.'

Sadie did as she was told as the walls trembled, the candle flickered and the dirt of decades sifted down with the plaster.

'That's it,' Julie encouraged. 'Good girl.' She adjusted her tin hat firmly over the flowing white nursing cap and made the sheet into a tent over them both so the baby wouldn't come into the world struggling to breathe through a cloud of dust.

'I gotta push,' panted Sadie.

'Not too hard,' said Julie firmly, her hand gently holding back the onrush of the head. 'Breathe deeply and just push a little so the head comes out slowly and steadily.'

Sadie groaned and panted, her expression one of deep concentration.

'That's fine,' mumbled Julie, who now had the torch in her mouth so she could see what she was doing. She waited for the contraction to end and gently eased the way for the crowning head, and then cupped it in her hand as it emerged, checking again on the foetal heartbeat which remained strong and steady.

She took the torch out of her mouth with her free hand. 'Well done, Sadie, you're playing a blinder,' she shouted as yet another bomb exploded nearby. 'Now the next contraction will have your baby born, so you can push as hard as you like.'

The tiny shoulders emerged just as Val returned with more candles. Seeing what was happening, she swiftly took the torch and held it so Julie had both hands free.

Julie held her breath as the tiny shoulders and arms were presented and then the baby's whole body slithered into her hands. Clearing the mucus and muck from its mouth and nose, she held the baby up by the feet to make sure it hadn't inhaled any of it. But the tiny scrap was floppy, the chest not rising and falling with a first breath. She tamped down on the dread and swiftly slapped its tiny behind, desperate to hear the wonderful sound of its first cry. To fail now would be too cruel.

'Why ain't it crying?' yelled Sadie as she threw off the pillow and tried to sit up.

'It's dead, ain't it,' muttered Val.

Julie prayed for a miracle and was about to massage the little chest when the tiny scrap let out a furious yell that almost drowned the roar of the overhead bombers. The tears came unbidden as immense relief flooded through Julie. 'You've got a girl, Sadie, and she's a right little fighter, with a pair of lungs to beat the band.'

'Ow, she's lovely, Sadie,' squawked Val, making the torchlight dance in her excitement.

Sadie reached out her hands. 'Give 'er 'ere. Let me see, oh, let me see.'

'Half a tick.' Julie swiftly dealt with the umbilical cord, then shook the dust from one of Val's worn nappies, wrapped it round the baby and unceremoniously dumped her on Sadie's soft belly. 'We've got to get out of here before the whole place caves in, Sadie,' she said, hastily retrieving her torch and packing her things back in the bag. 'Me and your mum are going to take you downstairs.'

Val and Sadie were cooing over the baby, seemingly unaware that the building was rocking on its foundations and that clouds of dust were swirling round them.

Julie pushed past Val and swiftly put her tin hat over the baby before covering mother and baby with the clean sheet, then struggled into her coat and scarf. With her bag perched next to Sadie, she slung her gas-mask box over her shoulder and grabbed the mattress. 'Get the baby clothes, Val, and then grab the other end,' she ordered.

Val picked them up and dithered. 'It ain't right,' she muttered. 'She ain't got rid of the afterbirth yet.'

'It could take up to half an hour,' Julie retorted, flinching and ducking as a very close explosion blasted the window in and sent a spray of glass shards ripping through the blackout curtain. 'There's no time to waste, Val,' she shouted. 'Grab the mattress and get them out of here.'

Sadie didn't weigh very much, but still it was an unwieldy burden as they struggled to get the mattress and its precious cargo through the door and down the many narrow, winding stairs. The building shook, plaster and dust rose in a cloud and the stairs seemed to shift beneath their feet as the explosions ripped through Whitechapel. In the pitch-black it would have been easy to miss their footing, and Julie just hoped those towering heels of Val's wouldn't trip her up and have them all plunging to the bottom.

Both women were sweaty and trembling from the effort as they finally made the hallway. The torch-light revealed the deep recess below the staircase to be filled with stinking litter as well as a pram with no wheels, and a collection of cardboard boxes and empty bottles. In silent accord, they put the mattress down on the filthy floor and quickly cleared enough space by dumping most of the rubbish into the pram and heaving it out of the way.

It was dark and noxious, the smell making Julie gag as she squeezed in beside them. This was their only hope, for the public shelter was three streets away, the tube station even further. They'd have to trust to luck that the tenement didn't take a direct hit.

'Bloody hell,' moaned Val. 'It don't 'alf pong in 'ere.'

'Have a fag,' Julie advised. 'It might make it smell

better.' She turned on her torch, concerned that Sadie had been so still and quiet during their arduous journey. She needn't have worried, she thought with a weary smile. Sadie seemed unconcerned as the bombs exploded and the walls of the old tenement shuddered, for she was rapturously breastfeeding her newborn daughter.

In the dust-laden air, and amid the thuds and crumps of exploding bombs, Julie finally delivered the afterbirth and wrapped it in some of the old newspapers that were lying about. But sitting out a raid in this disgusting black hole was hardly the most sanitary of arrangements, and she feared that infection might all too easily set in. She cleaned Sadie as well as she could with swabs soaked in Dettol, checked the suckling baby's heart rate, then dressed her swiftly in the worn baby clothes and kept both of them covered with the bedclothes. It was vital the baby didn't get cold.

She switched off her torch to save the batteries and they were plunged into utter darkness as the fury of war roared all around them. The old building continued to rock and tremble as it withstood the blasts, and every second they expected the walls to cave in and crush them. As they sat, cramped, cold and terrified, they were unable to make even the most mundane observations.

Julie discovered that Val used her gas-mask box as a handbag, keeping her fags, a small bottle of gin and a lipstick and powder compact nestled alongside the mask. She refused the offer of a slug of gin, while Val took regular sips and lit one cigarette after another. But as the time dragged by, Julie began to wish she could follow the other woman's example, for a nip of gin would buck her up no end, and perhaps quell her fear of cramped, dark hidey-holes.

When the all-clear finally sounded, Julie switched her torch back on and looked at the watch pinned to her apron. They'd only been sitting there for two hours. It had felt much longer.

'Blimey,' muttered Val as she crushed yet another fag-end under her shoe, 'I can think of better ways to spend the bleedin' night.' She eased back the sheet and looked fondly at Sadie and the baby and grinned as she realised they'd both fallen asleep. 'Lucky for some, eh? I wish I could sleep through that racket, and no mistake.'

'Come on, Val,' said Julie as she crawled out of the recess, eased her back and tried to get the blood flowing in her legs again. 'We need to get her upstairs and into bed.'

It took much longer to negotiate the many stairs on the way up, for there were bits of wood and lumps of plaster and concrete lying in wait to trip them up and block their way. Finally they reached the fourth-floor landing to discover that there had been no real damage to the old building and thankfully placed the mattress back on the bed.

The room didn't look much different from when they'd left, but the window was shattered and everything seemed to be covered with a coating of grey dust.

'I'll clean the place up, never you mind, ducky,' said Val. 'You see to Sadie and the sprog.'

While Val stirred the dust with a cloth and broom and gathered up the shattered glass, Julie eased Sadie into the overstuffed, sagging chair and shook out the dust from the once-clean sheets that Val had brought. She made the bed then poured the last of the water into the bowl. Having cleaned the baby with a damp swab, she dressed her again in the clothes that were far too big for such a tiny mite, and handed her to Val while she helped Sadie wash and change into one of her husband's old shirts that passed for a nightgown.

Once Sadie was back in bed, she gently placed the baby in her arms and looked down tenderly at the little girl she'd helped bring into the world. Like all the babies born in this part of town, this little one faced a tough life, but she looked as if she was well on the way to coping, for she was asleep still, which was quite remarkable considering the terrible noise she'd been born into.

Once mother and daughter were comfortably settled, Julie packed her things away again and reached for her coat.

'Thanks ever so, Sister,' said Sadie, her eyes bright with tears as she cuddled her baby, the tiny fingers wrapped tightly round her thumb.

'My pleasure,' Julie replied with a soft smile. 'I'll

come back tomorrow to check you over, and then every day for the next two weeks. Try and get some rest, and keep off the gin, Sadie. It will make your baby sick as you're breastfeeding, and you don't want that, do you?'

Sadie shook her head, her gaze darting to her mother who had given up on the cleaning and was having a surreptitious swig out of her gin bottle.

'It's fer me nerves,' Val explained. 'Don't you worry, Sister, I'll see 'er right, and once the rest of the family get 'ere, she won't 'ave to lift a finger.'

Julie knew that Sadie and Val came from an enormous family that spanned several generations of Whitechapel inhabitants who lived within shouting distance of one another, so she had no fear that Sadie would be left to struggle alone. 'I expect they're on their way now the all-clear has sounded,' she replied as she wrapped the scarf round her neck and pulled on her gloves.

'Yeah,' said Val, 'and Mum will make us all a cuppa. Sadie must be gagging for one by now.' She cocked her head. 'You will stay and 'ave a cuppa with us, won't you?'

The thought of a cup of proper East End tea, so strong and stewed you could stand a spoon up in it, was very tempting, but Julie shook her head. 'Sorry, Val, but I have to get back.' She turned to Sadie. 'Now, you've got the extra food and milk stamps, haven't you? You need to keep your strength up now you're breastfeeding.'

Sadie nodded and sleepily nestled down with her baby against the lumpy pillows as Val gently drew the thin blanket over her shoulders.

Julie's heart swelled. Every birth was a miracle, and even in these poorest of surroundings it was clear that Sadie loved her baby and would do her best for it. 'I'll see you tomorrow,' she murmured, and left the room, closing the door quietly behind her.

Chapter Two

The large Victorian building in Shoreditch had started life as a private house before becoming a hostel for the young ladies who worked as clerks and typists in the nearby office blocks. Now the downstairs rooms had been turned into a clinic, with examination areas, a vast kitchen and dining room, a sluice, a laundry and a locked storeroom which housed the precious medical supplies, replacement uniforms and spare parts for the many bicycles.

Matron's office was on the first floor, where she supervised and controlled every moment of the thirty nurses and auxiliaries' working day, for they were not attached to a particular hospital or clinic, and worked alongside doctors from many different practices.

Matron Irene Starkey was a stickler for rules, and she didn't put up with any nonsense from the young women who lived in the nurses' hostel, regardless of their age, background or experience. Uniform was to be worn except when off duty; everyone had to be in by ten at night unless out on call; rooms were to be kept tidy, beds made before breakfast, and nursing equipment to be in pristine order at all times.

However, Julie and the others had soon come to realise that Matron Starkey's strict code was in no way vindictive for – like all the other matrons they'd encountered during their careers – it was clear she merely wanted the best standards of hygiene and discipline to be upheld so her nurses and volunteer aides could work with pride and efficiency, their patients safe in the knowledge they were getting the very best care.

Matron Starkey might run the place like a sergeant major, but she was a wise old bird, for she never allowed her nurses to work in the same area of squalor for more than three months at a time. Her reasoning was that they'd all learned during their hospital training to be proficient and knowledgeable on different wards. In the same way, each district exposed them to all types of homes and families and invaluable new experiences.

Julie's initial training had taken four long years of battling prejudice and low expectation from those in charge before she'd qualified. But by the time she'd taken the six months' midwifery course at the City of London Maternity Hospital in Islington, she'd learned to soften her Cockney accent and had become accepted. After a short time working there, she went on to complete another six months' training as a Queen's Nurse. She'd passed her exams with flying colours the previous September, becoming No. 16,988 on the Queen's Roll, and could add QN to her SRN qualifications and earn a very decent salary. She now proudly wore a Queen's badge on her cap and another on a cord at her neck. For an East End girl, she'd done extremely well.

Julie's time in the slums of Shoreditch, Whitechapel, Holborn and Bethnal Green, and indeed, her own Stepney background, had taught her far more than she could ever learn from a textbook. She'd become resourceful and versatile, learning to improvise and be resilient – and to listen to her patients and not treat them just as cases to be dealt with and recorded in her book. Her work often entailed washing hair, cutting nails and cleaning dentures, or teaching someone how to brush their teeth, get rid of head lice, and bathe properly, encouraging them to use the public baths more frequently to combat the infections that were rife in the slums.

Julie had been waylaid by Sadie's family after her delivery, and then by the warden who needed help with some of the casualties. She'd spent another two hours dressing wounds inflicted by flying shrapnel and falling masonry, and had then helped one poor, bewildered old man find his way back home. She'd returned to the hostel just before dawn and had wearily traipsed up the stairs and tiptoed into the bedroom to drag off her coat and cap, kick off her shoes, and collapse on her bed. She'd fallen asleep the moment her head hit the pillow.

Julie therefore wasn't feeling at her best as she and Lily clattered down the stairs the next morning in their ordinary clothes with their bags. She'd had very little sleep before being woken for breakfast, and despite the two cups of strong tea she'd had with her porridge, she still felt slightly disorientated and rumpled.

'I 'ate Mondays,' muttered Lily as she followed Julie into the deserted sluice. It seemed they were the first down for the Monday morning ritual of cleaning their bags and instruments.

They placed their bags on the scrubbed table and opened them before taking the soap, nail brush and towel from the outside pocket. 'So do I,' muttered Julie, as she joined her friend at the sink and vigorously washed her hands and nails in the hot water. 'I feel really uncomfortable asking people how much money they've got and how they spend it when it's clear they're struggling. Two and sixpence is a lot to pay, even if you are earning, and although some only have to pay thruppence for medical care, it can still make a big difference to the household bills.'

'I can barely look them in the eye when I go round with me receipt book and money tin.' Lily began to unpack her bag, setting the bottles, jars and tins and packets of gauze and sterilised dressings on the disinfected table.

'I'm always relieved when a new patient either has a provident scheme to pay the bill or simply ain't got two pennies to rub together,' replied Julie with a sigh. 'At least the very poorest don't have to pay – but it's horrible turning up on the doorstep rattling me tin after some poor woman's just collected her wages after a long week's slog in a factory.'

'I remember me mum scrabbling about for pennies when the district nurse called. Dad likes 'is drink, and she was forever going through 'is pockets when 'e'd passed out.' Lily grinned. ''E never knew, and never found the tin she'd hidden up the chimney, neither. There was only ever a few coppers in it, but they was a lifesaver most weeks.'

Julie nodded with understanding, although things had been very different in her house. Bert Harris always came straight home with his pay packet and handed it to Flo, who took what she needed and left him enough for his beer, pipe tobacco, and nightly copy of the *Evening Standard*.

They worked in silence for a while, scrupulously washing all their instruments in hot soapy water before replenishing the stocks in their bottles, jars and tins, and changing the white cotton lining in the bag for a clean one. Then, when everything was neat and tidy, they set to work polishing the black leather bags with Cherry Blossom boot polish until they shone.

'How's your Franny coming along? She looked about to pop when I saw her the other day.'

'I called in on her yesterday morning, and yes, she's got a couple of weeks to go, but she's not doing badly considering. She's had to stop work, 'cos she's finding it too hard to stand up all day at the factory. But I've been promised a bed at the hospital

37

tomorrow, so I'll be getting her in there before lunchtime.'

'It must be worrying for you, what with her 'eart and everything.'

'It is,' Julie replied, the thought of everything that could go wrong still uppermost in her mind. She determinedly blocked it all out. 'Franny's tougher than she looks, and as long as there are no complications, I reckon she'll do all right.'

Julie watched as Lily set her bag aside, washed her hands and carefully patted her shining blonde hair. With her heart-shaped face and big blue eyes, Lily always managed to look glamorous, even in an old jumper and skirt and with no make-up to speak of, and Julie felt a touch of envy. No one would ever think of Julie Harris as being glamorous; she was too thin, her hair was an indeterminate brown and fell as straight as a poker, and her nose wasn't half as elegant as Lily's. But her brown eyes were her saving grace; Stan had told her how lovely they were the other night when they'd gone dancing at the Regency.

She smiled softly at the memory, finished polishing the bag and went to wash her hands again. The engagement ring would stay on the chain around her neck until she was next off duty, for it would only get damaged with so much washing, and diamonds, no matter how small, could tear a hole in a rubber glove as quick as blink.

'I'm on duty in less than an hour and I haven't

ironed me spare uniform, so I must do it before Matron goes on the warpath.' Ruefully, Julie eyed the crumpled dress and apron she'd brought down with her, and which now resembled something dragged from the bottom of a laundry basket. 'I'll catch up with you later.'

'Right oh,' said Lily cheerfully. 'I'm off to learn the joys of how to take out sutures and clean leg ulcers and boils with Nurse Bradley today, so I probably won't see you until tonight.' She strolled off just as several other nurses and volunteers bustled into the sluice and the noise level rose as taps were turned on and delicious gossip was exchanged.

The thirty women who lived at the hostel came from diverse backgrounds and experience, ageing from between eighteen to mid-forties. Among those in the sluice this morning was little Doris who came from Camden, Ida from Camberley, and the posh Clarice, whose family owned half of Mayfair, but could muck in very happily no matter how unpleasant the task. Maud and Jane were spinster sisters who always worked side by side and were old hands at nursing in the roughest areas of London.

And then there was Alison, the liveliest of them all, and the usual source of any mischief. A country girl who'd come up from Cornwall to train as a midwife, Alison had never quite lost the wholesome creaminess to her skin, the rosy apples in her cheeks, or the sparkle in her eye – neither had she lost her West Country burr, and it was often a source of bewilderment and amusement amongst her East End patients as well as her colleagues.

'You came in late last night, me luvver,' she said as she washed her instruments. 'Must have been cabby out there with thar raid on.' She grinned. 'We'm, clucky down in the shelter, proper vitchered we'm, not getting to work dreckly. You'm go in across for a gaddle tonight?'

Julie grinned back as she mentally translated what Alison had said. It appeared she'd spent a frustrating night huddled in the basement shelter and was asking if she fancied going for a drink tonight. She liked Alison very much and there had been many a time when they'd broken the rules and sloped off with Lily for a couple of hours to a pub that was well away from the hostel and out of Matron's sight. 'Sorry, Ali, but I can't tonight. I'm meeting Stan.'

Alison shrugged and carried on scrubbing her forceps. 'See you dreckly, then,' she said cheerfully. 'I be 'aving no sprawl m'self by tonight, more like.'

Julie realised she meant she'd be as knackered as everyone else at the end of the day and probably wouldn't risk it. She nodded in agreement as she glanced at her watch. She would have loved to stay and gossip, but time was of the essence if she was to get her clothes ironed and herself ready for her shift, so she reluctantly left them to it and hurried into the laundry.

There were usually two women working at the tubs, wringers and steam-press, but it was still too early for them to arrive – unlike the cook, who lived in one of the attic rooms. Horace, the caretaker and general handyman, was probably sneaking a crafty fag in his shed while he kept a wary eye out for Matron and tried to avoid doing anything too strenuous. A bit of an old rogue, Horace appreciated a pretty face and could easily be coaxed into mending bike punctures or greasing chains, but he really preferred to be left in peace to drink his tea, smoke his fag, and catch up on how his favourite team, Arsenal, was doing in the lead-up to the Football League Cup which would be played at Wembley in May.

Julie peered through the window overlooking the vegetable plot in the back garden, saw the wisp of cigarette smoke curl from the gap at the top of the shed door, and knew her suspicions were right. 'I don't know what you're paid, Horace,' she muttered, 'but it's too much.'

She eyed the flat irons already lined up neatly beside the vast range that was never allowed to go out, and which provided the hot water so necessary for all the washing and sterilising. Selecting two, she placed them on the hot plate, dampened down the dress and apron, then went to fetch the ironing board which she had to wrestle to get unfolded and steady. She just hoped Matron would be too occupied checking everyone's bags to come in and catch her. Not ironing your uniform the night before was a heinous sin – probably punishable by death.

However, there was something rather satisfying and soothing about sweeping a hot iron over damp cotton and hearing the hiss of steam and seeing the creases melt away. Ironing had never been a chore to Julie, and she'd looked forward to Tuesdays after school, when her mother had a stack of clean washing awaiting her attention. She finished the dress, sprayed some more water over the creases in her starched apron, then began to press them out carefully.

With everything put neatly away, she noted Horace was still in his shed and shook her head disapprovingly before carrying the bag, dress and apron back upstairs to the room she shared on the second floor.

It was a large square room with a high ceiling and a big bay window which overlooked the street and the Mothers' Laying-in Hospital on the other side. In the summer the sun streamed through the criss-cross taping of the window, but on this cold, blustery day it gave no cheer at all, and the leafless branches of the nearby tree tapped plaintively against the glass.

Julie eyed the six iron bedsteads, each of which had a wooden locker and an uncomfortable chair beside it. The beds had been made neatly, the crisp sheets and rather rough brown blankets tucked in so tightly a penny could be bounced off them. There was nothing really homely about the place, just a few photographs, hairbrushes, books and tiny dishes of cheap jewellery on the tops of some of the lockers. Their clothes had to be hung in the two vast wardrobes, their shoes neatly placed in the bottom, hats and handbags placed on the shelf at the top. Everything else had to go in the lockers, and it was not permitted to put pictures on the walls, or personalise the beds with colourful quilts, eiderdowns or pretty pillows. It was like all the nurses' homes she'd lived in since leaving Stepney, and she suspected it probably wasn't much more comfortable than the cells in Wandsworth prison.

She smothered a vast yawn, placed the bag on her chair, and hung the freshly ironed dress and apron on a hanger over the wardrobe doorknob. Time was disappearing fast and she needed to get changed. With the others all downstairs or out on their rounds, she had the room to herself for once – not that it mattered a jot, she was used to undressing in a crowded room, for she'd shared with her two sisters until Eileen had suddenly left home.

Pondering on why Eileen had gone, she pulled off her warm skirt and sweater. She'd been very young at the time and hadn't understood much of what was going on, other than that Eileen and Mum and Dad were having a terrible row that morning. She'd wanted to listen in, but her mum had caught her earwigging and sent her off to buy a loaf of bread. By the time she'd returned home, Eileen was gone, along with everything she'd owned.

Julie now suspected it had something to do with the man Eileen had been seeing, for she could remember her dad going on about how he wouldn't trust him to tell him the time of day. Perhaps Eileen had run off with him and didn't dare show her face again?

'It's all old history,' she muttered. 'I don't expect I'll ever really know the truth of it, and Mum certainly ain't telling.' She shook her head as if to put these idle thoughts aside, and got on with changing.

Slipping out of her camisole and dainty panties, she fastened her suspender belt round her waist and then pulled on the enormous and much-reviled regulation knickers that were jokingly – and aptly – called 'blackouts'. Made of sturdy black material, they eclipsed everything from hip to midriff and were as ugly as sin. Fastening her regular issue brassiere – which was just as much a passion-killer as the knickers – she then carefully rolled on the thick black stockings which she'd had to darn painstakingly more than once.

Stockings were fiercely rationed by Matron and therefore had to be treated with great care and respect if the owner was not to incur her wrath. But the nature of the work meant they were often snagged or laddered, and it was the very devil to keep them looking respectable.

The blue striped, shapeless dress fell to regulation length below Julie's knees, and it felt fresh and crisp as she did up the buttons, adjusted the soft white collar and fastened the matching belt. Slipping on the sturdy black shoes, she tied the laces and gave them a swift dust with her dry flannel in the hope

Matron wouldn't spot the fact they hadn't been polished this morning.

Once her hair had been brushed and held back with combs, she put on her apron, pinned her watch to the bib front and reached for her cap. It wasn't one of the neat, rather flirtatious little white caps worn by the nurses on the hospital wards, but rather resembled something the army troops might wear in a desert storm. Tight to the head, the starched linen was pulled severely back over the ears, then hung in folds over the nape of the neck – it was obvious why it had earned the nickname of 'storm cap'.

Julie eyed her reflection in the wardrobe mirror as she pinned the Queen's badge on her cap, slipped the cord holding the second badge round her neck so it hung between the edges of her collar, and then made sure her stocking seams were straight. She still got a thrill from knowing how much she'd achieved since leaving home, and would never take the honour of being a highly qualified nurse lightly or for granted.

She gave herself a cheery smile before reaching for her overcoat, blue scarf and gloves. Suitably clad to meet the world outside the hostel, she picked up her bag, tin hat and gas-mask box and went down to Matron's office to discuss her schedule for the day.

As Julie cycled on her rounds through the narrow streets and alleyways of Whitechapel, she was greeted cheerfully by the women who stood gossiping on their doorsteps, fags stuck to bottom lips, curlers glinting beneath their headscarves. The men working to shore up the crumbling buildings or heading for their work at the docks tipped their hats, and the young boys who were eagerly searching for pieces of shrapnel among the rubble gave her cheeky grins. These treasures were carefully guarded, especially if the finder had been lucky enough to discover an enemy belt buckle or badge, or a piece of parachute, and could be used as barter for cigarette cards or comics.

Julie cheerfully waved back, stopped and admired the babies and the latest pieces of shrapnel, and joined in the usual moans over Gerry's bombing campaign, the rationing and the weather. Having left Sadie and her new daughter, who'd been called Julie in her honour, she headed for the wider, tree-lined streets of Shoreditch and the terraced house where Franny rented a room.

None of these houses had an inside bathroom or lavatory, but it was a better area altogether, with tiny front gardens, tiled paths leading to the front doors and net curtains hanging at the windows. Bill was clearly making sure Franny was comfortable while she waited for him to come home, and Julie blessed him for it. The poor man had enough to worry about with fighting the Germans and Italians in North Africa, without having Franny on his mind all the time.

She was approaching Franny's place when she

recognised the young policeman hurrying across the road. Her pulse raced as she saw him wave and smile. He was so big and handsome, and so full of energy, that she felt quite small and helpless when he was around. At twenty-seven, Stanley Rudge was quite a catch, and Julie still couldn't believe her luck, for he could have had his pick from the girls who'd flocked around him down Stepney way.

'Stan,' she breathed, 'what a lovely surprise. I didn't realise this was part of your beat.'

'It's not usually, but I knew you'd be visiting Franny today, so I got the desk sergeant to change things about.' His dark eyes looked down at her from beneath the helmet as he reached for her gloved hand.

Julie felt her heart thudding fit to bust. 'That's nice,' she said softly, unable to think of anything much when he looked at her in that way.

'I want to kiss you,' he murmured, his expression becoming intent as he leaned towards her.

Julie blushed scarlet and looked away. 'Not here,' she hissed, stifling a giggle, 'and definitely not when we're both in uniform, Stan. You should know better.'

'Why not? It's a free country, ain't it?'

She gave the street a quick, nervous glance. 'Half the neighbourhood's probably watching behind them net curtains, and it'll get back to Matron and your chief inspector.'

'I don't care,' he said, his voice low and full of passion. 'There's nothing wrong with giving my girl a kiss if I want to.' He grabbed her chin and planted a kiss on her lips before she could reply.

Julie melted, her senses swimming for a moment before she drew back sharply. 'You'll get us both into trouble,' she stuttered, all of a dither, 'and you won't get your promotion.'

He shot her a cheeky smile. 'But I got me kiss, though, didn't I? Quite set me up for the rest of the day, it 'as.' He took another step towards her. ''Ow about another?'

Julie giggled and shoved him back. 'Get on with you, Stanley Rudge. I've got work to do, and so have you. I'll see you tonight, all being well.'

He gave an exaggerated sigh and tried to look woebegone. 'I suppose I'll just 'ave to wait until then, but a man could die of wanting, Julie,' he said, his twinkling eyes giving the lie to his demeanour.

'Your old flannel don't work on me,' she said, stifling the giggles again. 'Get on and catch a few criminals and let me finish me rounds. I'll see you at the Bull.'

'I'll be waiting, pining, me 'eart aching for the moment you walk through the door.' He rolled his eyes dramatically as he clutched his heart.

Julie burst out laughing. 'Blimey,' she managed, 'you don't 'alf go on, Stan. You should be on the flaming stage.'

She was still laughing as she cycled away from him, and when she reached Franny's place, she looked back to find he was still standing in the middle of the street. Giving him a wave, she took her bag and let herself into the house.

The neat square hallway smelled of furniture polish – and oddly, burnt toast. The landlady, Mrs Bessell, must be out, for she was usually watching from her window and would shoot out of her door the minute she heard the key turn. Thankfully, she wouldn't have witnessed that little scene with Stan, for if she had, it would be round the neighbourhood in a flash.

Julie could hear music as she ran up the carpeted stairs to the first floor, which had been divided into three small self-contained rooms. As the other two rooms were let to office workers, she realised Franny must be listening to the 'Workers' Playtime' programme on the wireless. She tapped on the door and pushed it open. 'It's only me, Franny,' she said softly.

Franny was lying on the bed, propped up by pillows, knitting and magazines scattered about her as she slept beneath the patchwork quilt their mother had made for her own bed many years before. The room was bathed in the weak sunlight that streamed through the window and glinted in Franny's hair, which lay tangled about her little face.

She looked like an elfin child, Julie thought fondly as she set her bag down on the small table by the bed and regarded the room. It was just big enough for the bed, table, chest of drawers and an armchair, and it had a gas fire and a two-ring electric hot plate to cook on. There was a box stocked with cans and packets under the table, along with a kettle, saucepan, frying pan and cutlery.

A chipped china plate and a cup and saucer sat ready by the kettle, which made Julie's heart ache for the loneliness her sister must be suffering. If only things had been different, she thought, and the gossips hadn't frightened her away with their nasty sharp tongues; Franny should have been with her family where she belonged, not living with strangers during the most difficult time for any woman. But that was the way of things in these times, and Franny would not be the last girl forced from her home because she'd made a mistake and a twist of fate had meant there was no wedding ring to give her respectability.

Julie sighed as she turned down the volume on the wireless. Her young sister had made the best of things despite it all, for the room was pretty with pictures of the family lining the narrow mantelpiece, embroidered cloths on the back and arms of the worn chair, and a collection of china ornaments she and Bill had found in the flea markets. There was a faded rug in front of the fire and Mrs Bessell had provided not only the rather posh wireless, but also the floral curtains, which had been studiously lined with blackout material.

Julie took off her coat, gloves and scarf and sat down. Franny was sleeping so peacefully it seemed a shame to disturb her and, as she didn't have to be anywhere for an hour, she could do with a bit of a breather after that encounter with Stan.

She rescued the knitting that was about to slide to the floor, then picked up one of the brightly coloured film magazines. It would be a treat to sit and do nothing but read a magazine – she couldn't remember the last time she'd done that, and rather hoped Franny remained asleep for at least another few minutes.

She had read all about Fred Astaire and his latest film and was flicking through the rest of the Hollywood gossip and glossy pictures of the stars when Franny stirred and opened her eyes.

''Ello, Sis,' she murmured sleepily. 'I weren't expecting you today. 'Ow long you been sittin' there?' She struggled to sit up and swing her legs over the side of the bed.

'Don't get up, love,' said Julie hastily. 'There's no room for both of us to be moving about in here.' She rose from the chair and gave her sister a hug and kiss. 'You've got a good colour today, Franny,' she commented as she took her pulse.

'I been resting, ain't I?' Franny replied with a sigh. 'And I'm that bored, Jules. There ain't nothing to do all day but knit and listen to the flaming wireless. I've read them magazines over and over until I'm sick of 'em, and Bill's letters are so creased I'm scared they'll tear if I read 'em any more.'

Julie grinned down at her. 'Anything's got to be better than standing all day at a factory production line,' she soothed. 'And you look much better for the rest.' She eyed the prodigious mound beneath the faded jumper and skirt. 'All right if I have a listen in?'

''Elp yerself,' replied Franny, 'I'm used to being prodded and poked by all and sundry, but it's a lively one, I'll tell you that. 'Ad me awake half the night with its squirming and kicking.'

'I'm your sister, not all and sundry,' retorted a rather put-out Julie.

'Y'know what I mean,' Franny said on another sigh.

Julie gave a wry smile. Franny was making the most of it, and who could blame her? Within the next couple of weeks she'd be a mother, with very little time to do anything much but care for her newborn and try to snatch much-needed sleep whenever she could.

Julie poured some water from the nearby jug into one of her bowls and washed her hands before warming the pinard and placing it on Franny's abdomen. Putting her ear to the other end, she listened to the reassuring beat of the baby's heart and smiled as the little one kicked quite forcibly and jolted the metal against her temple. 'Lively's about right,' she said cheerfully as she rubbed the spot with her finger.

'I did warn you,' giggled Franny.

Julie gently and methodically ran her palms over Franny's abdomen before palpating it with the pads of her fingers to gauge the size and position of the baby. 'The baby's got a bit more growing to do, but it's turned nicely, head down ready to be engaged, just as it should at this stage. Have you had any more practice twinges since I last saw you?'

Franny shook her head. 'Nothing much to write 'ome about.' Her cheerful smile faltered. 'It will be all right, won't it, Jules? They won't let me 'eart get too tired, will they?'

Julie perched on the bed beside her, took her hand and went through everything once again. 'You'll be going into hospital tomorrow morning and will stay there until the doctor decides your baby is ready to be born. Then they'll send you to sleep and take you into theatre for a caesarean section. You won't feel a thing, and your heart will be monitored all the while you're under, I promise. Then you'll wake up in the maternity ward with a new baby all washed and ready to get to know and love.'

Franny's little face puckered as she fought the tears glistening in her eyes, and Julie was struck by how young and vulnerable she really was under the brave façade she'd kept up over the months. 'I'm frightened, Julie,' she whispered. 'I should never 'ave got meself into all this. What if . . .?'

Julie quickly put her arms around her young sister and held her close. 'We'll have none of that, love,' she murmured. 'You don't want to upset yourself or the baby worrying about things. I'll be with you every step of the way, I promise.'

Franny drew back, the tears still streaming. 'If anything 'appens to me, Julie, I want you to promise you'll look after the baby until Bill comes 'ome. I don't want it taken to some orphanage, or raised by strangers.'

Julie was shocked by her sister's pessimism. 'Franny, please don't talk like that.'

Franny blew her nose and knuckled back the tears, her expression determined. 'I know the score, Jules. I ain't daft, and I need you to promise me you'll look after my baby.'

'If I do that, then it's as if . . .'

'Just promise me, Julie,' Franny said fiercely. 'I need to know it'll be safe.'

Julie could feel the prick of her own tears as she yielded. 'I promise, Franny, but you're being unnecessarily—'

'I'm being practical,' Franny interrupted. She slid down the pillows with a sigh. 'Thanks, Julie,' she said softly. 'I can rest easy now.'

'Oh, Fran. I wish I could convince you that—'

''Ow's about a cuppa?' Franny said firmly. 'Mum brought over a packet of tea yesterday, and I've even got a bit of milk and sugar and a digestive biscuit to go with it.'

Julie realised that Fran had decided the subject had run its course, and anything she had to say would be ignored. With a sigh of acceptance, she looked at her watch and gasped to see how late it was. 'I'll make you a cup, but I can't stay, Franny. I've got three more mothers to visit before I can go back to the hostel and attend clinic.'

Franny looked crestfallen for a while, but as she sipped the hot, sweet tea and rested back on her pillows, she recovered her spirits. 'This is the life, ain't it?' she sighed.

'Make the most of it, Frances Harris,' Julie said with mock severity. 'All this lying about drinking tea won't last once your baby's born and yelling for attention.' She smiled and softly kissed her sister goodbye. 'I'll see you in the morning bright and early. Make sure you have that case packed with everything I put on your list.'

Franny did a comic salute. 'Yes, Sergeant Major. All packed and at attention.'

'At ease, Corporal,' Julie replied with a chuckle. She blew her sister a kiss and closed the door.

Leaning against it for a moment to gather her wits and restore her spirits, she tried to dismiss the worrying promise her young sister had forced her into. Franny's heart was definitely struggling, but everything possible had been arranged to see her through a safe delivery. Yet, even though Julie had done her best to banish the dark dread that Franny wouldn't come through – that things might go wrong, despite all the careful preparations – it still lingered. She took a deep breath, closed her eyes and willed the fates to be kind to Franny, for she'd suffered enough.

On opening her eyes, she shook off the doubts determinedly and focussed on the positive. The baby was small, but the heartbeat was strong. Franny was young, rested and in reasonable health, and Mr Philips, the consultant surgeon, was confident all would be well. Feeling rather more cheerful, Julie snapped out of her thoughts, remembered how late she already was for her next appointment, and hurried downstairs.

Mrs Bessell was waiting for her. A large Jewish lady of indeterminate age, with dyed hair and too much make-up, Rebecca Bessell jangled with all the jewellery she wore. She'd appeared rather daunting on first acquaintance, but had proved to be in possession of an enormous sense of rather wicked humour and a generous heart – combined with her Jewish need to mother everyone and know their business, these attributes made her the perfect landlady for Fran.

'How is she, already?' she asked without preamble.

Julie quickly told her about the plans for the next day. 'You still have the number for the hostel, Mrs Bessell?' At her nod, Julie continued, 'It's only for emergencies, but best you keep it until she's in hospital.'

'Such a lovely girl,' said Mrs Bessell sorrowfully, 'and so tragic to be cast from her family at a time like this. I was saying to my friend Bella Weinstock only the other day—'

'I'm sorry, Mrs Bessell,' Julie interrupted quickly, 'but I have to see other patients, and I'm already running late.' She saw the crestfallen expression and patted the soft, plump arm. 'I'm so grateful to you for looking after me sister. She's very fond of you, you know, and admires you terrifically.'

Mrs Bessell blushed and dabbed at her eyes, careful not to smudge her mascara. 'Oy, vay,' she murmured. 'She is like a daughter to me, Julie – a daughter. I will take her some of my chicken soup and keep her company – she needs to eat, to be nourished, at a time like this. She's too thin, much too thin already.'

Julie smiled at her with affection. 'I'm sure she'd love that, now I really must go.' She hurried out of the front door and almost ran down the path. Once Mrs Bessell started with the tears and the chicken soup it was the very devil to escape. But bless her, she had a good heart and Franny was safe in her house.

Chapter Three

The mother and baby clinic had been chaotic as usual, with small children dashing about, babies wailing and mothers raising their voices to be heard as they exchanged views on the difficulties of trying to raise a family with a war on and their eldest kids gone off as evacuees to the other end of the country. They also tried to outdo one another with relish as they swapped horror stories about their pregnancies and deliveries.

Julie was used to hearing the reminiscences and knew they circulated the tenements and back streets, putting the wind up any poor young girl who'd just got pregnant with her first. These sorts of apocryphal tales did Julie's cause no good at all, but she was powerless to stop them and had to accept they were all part of the rich tapestry of life.

The elderly doctor had left as the last patient scurried out of the door into the unlit street, and Julie and the other nurses quickly tidied everything away before they went in for supper. Julie had eaten quickly, for she was starving after having cycled over eight miles during the day, and had missed lunch.

When the meal was over, she'd retrieved her engagement ring from the chain and put it on her finger and changed into her best sweater and skirt. Carefully rolling on a lovely pair of delicate stockings, she stepped into a pair of high-heeled court shoes and clipped on her earrings. There was nothing much to do with her straight, boring hair, so she pinned it back with two pink plastic combs that matched her sweater. A dash of lipstick and mascara and a bit of powder completed the picture. She wanted to look her best for Stan, even if they did only have a couple of hours together.

'I'll cover for you and leave a back window open, if you like,' said Lily, who was on call until midnight.

Julie pulled on her gabardine raincoat, which was marginally smarter than the regulation overcoat. 'Thanks, Lil, but I need a good night's sleep after the last two days. I'll be in on time.'

Lily giggled. 'Seems a shame when you could be tucked up somewhere with that 'andsome fella of yours. You wouldn't feel the need for sleep then, and no mistake.'

Julie blushed. She and Stan might be engaged, but she had no intention of letting him get his own way until there was a wedding ring on her finger. 'Like I said, Lil, I'm pooped and I need a proper sleep. I've got a busy day tomorrow.'

'Ain't we all,' Lily sighed. 'That Nurse Bradley seems to think she can work me like an 'orse, running about after her arse and doing all the dirty jobs.' She grinned back at Julie as she finished brushing her hair and adjusting her cap. 'Still, I suppose there is a bleedin' war on, and I'm only a volunteer. Can't expect much better, can I?'

'You're a very good volunteer,' said Julie as she gathered up her handbag and gas-mask box. 'Ever thought of taking the exams and becoming a fully qualified nurse?'

Lily shook her head and sniffed. 'Nah, not me, Jules. Ain't got a brain big enough for all that learnin'. After the war I'm gunna go back to me job at the Hammersmith Woolworths – if it's still standing – and if I ain't married by then.'

Julie thought Lily was wasting her talents, and she could only hope that by the time this war was over, her friend might realise there was more to aim for. 'I'm off then,' she said as she tied her headscarf under her chin. 'See you later.'

'Mind 'ow you go,' Lily replied gaily, 'and give 'im a kiss from me.'

Julie laughed. 'I'll do no such thing. Find your own bloke to kiss.'

Lily pulled a face, her eyes sparkling with fun. 'I would if I weren't on duty tonight – and that's a fact. I'm feeling quite frisky.'

'You're always feeling frisky,' teased Julie. 'They should put something in your tea like they do the soldiers.'

She was still smiling as she hurried through the dark streets towards the Bull, which was several long blocks away from the hostel. Lily had a string of admirers and was a terrible flirt, but she was a true friend and never poached from the other girls.

Stan was waiting outside, looking handsome in his good suit, crisp shirt and dark tie, a soft-brimmed hat pulled rakishly over one eye as he cupped his hands round a match and lit a cigarette.

She stood on the far corner watching for a moment, drinking him in as he threw away the dead match and leaned against the wall, the cigarette smoke drifting over his head like a halo. She loved him so much, and wished they could marry and set up their own place – but what with the war, her work and the necessity of him getting his sergeant's stripes before they could afford to marry, it could be some time.

She crossed the street. 'Hello, Stan,' she murmured.

He turned his head, his gaze seeming to penetrate to her core as he looked down at her. Flicking away the half-smoked cigarette, he opened his arms and smiled. "Ow's my girl tonight, then? Ready to kiss me now, are yer?' he teased.

Julie snuggled into his embrace and raised her face to him. 'Try me,' she giggled.

His kiss was soft at first, and sweet, then his arms tightened round her and it became more demanding, his tongue flicking over hers, his lips crushing. 'Oh, Julie,' he groaned eventually. 'Do we 'ave to wait, darlin'? I've such a longing for you, gel.'

Julie gently pulled away from him, her senses in a riot. 'I want to as much as you, Stan,' she said shakily, 'but we mustn't. Not until we're married.'

'But that could be ages yet,' he protested, reaching for her again. 'Come on, Julie,' he coaxed. 'I got a mate with a nice little room up Islington way. He promised to be out tonight, so we'd 'ave it all to ourselves.'

It was getting harder to resist him, but despite the longing to lie with him, to know him completely, resist she must. 'It's no good, Stan,' she said firmly. 'I'm not going anywhere tonight but in this pub. I've had a long couple of days and I could do with a drink, not a wrestling match.'

'Blimey, Julie,' he replied, tugging at his hat. 'You don't 'alf make it 'ard on a bloke – especially when you look so pretty all done up like that.'

'Pass your sergeant's exam and keep that thought warm,' she replied with a soft smile. 'Come on, let's get that drink. I have to be in by ten, and it's cold out here.'

The Bull was a popular, lively pub, the crushed mass of people happily singing along to the piano as the noise level rose and cigarette smoke drifted in clouds over their heads. Stan moodily elbowed his way to the bar while Julie tried to find some- where to sit. She was in luck, for two off-duty soldiers were just leaving, and she grabbed the space and sat down just as Stan returned from the bar with two pints of beer.

'Bottoms up, gel,' he said, raising his glass and swallowing half the pint in one go.

Julie giggled. 'I get enough bums in the air as it is,' she reminded him. 'Chin, chin.'

Stan still looked morose as he surveyed the room and nodded to several acquaintances. He sipped his beer, lit a cigarette and sat back. 'I don't know why we come in 'ere,' he muttered. 'I've arrested 'alf of 'em at one time or another.'

'We come because it's near to the hostel,' she said lightly. 'Blimey, Stan, there ain't a pub in London where you won't bump into someone you've nicked.' She smiled at him uncertainly, not used to him being so sullen.

'It ain't my idea of a good night out,' he retorted. He finished his pint and without another word headed for the bar again.

Julie watched him, knowing what was eating at him and unwilling to let him have his way. She could only hope he'd snap out of this mood, for it was spoiling the short time they had together, and she was beginning to wish she hadn't bothered coming out at all.

The sirens went off just as he returned from the bar, and everyone groaned as the lights were switched off and they had to hurry into the blacked-out streets for the nearby shelter.

'I should go to the shelter at the hostel,' Julie shouted above the ear-splitting screech of the sirens. 'I'll be late back if this raid goes on for more than an hour.'

'Don't be so bloody silly,' snapped Stan, who was obviously still in a dark mood. 'Matron will understand if you're late, and this shelter's nearer. Come on.' He grabbed her arm, and without so much as a by-your-leave, propelled her down the road.

His mood had soured the evening, and now his grip was a bit too tight for her liking, so she pulled away from him and ran on ahead. Reaching the shelter, she didn't wait to see if he was behind her and hurried down the steps to try and find somewhere to sit.

It was already crowded, and she had to wriggle through dithering women and old men, and dodge round the bags and parcels and bits of household treasure that some of them refused to leave at home during a raid. Babies were wailing and toddlers were grizzling, and harassed women were shouting across to each other in the gloom and damp of the shelter, which stank of stale sweat, fag smoke and old socks.

It was not the nicest place to finish a disastrous evening, and Julie was already feeling claustrophobia creeping up on her. She found a space close to the door and plumped down, accepting rather ungraciously that she was probably stuck down here for the rest of the night with a moody Stan and the beginnings of a headache.

'You might have flamin' waited,' Stan grumbled as he plonked down next to her. 'Why'd you run off like that?'

'It doesn't matter,' she replied, not wanting to start yet another argument.

Stanley lit a cigarette and grumpily surveyed their surroundings. The ceiling lights were flickering behind their wire cages and the warden was preparing to shut the door. The sound of the ack-ack guns could already be heard down by the docks as the RAF boys hurried to fend off the enemy approach in their fighter planes.

The door closed with a heavy thud that made Julie flinch. Listening to the muffled sounds of the battle being waged overhead, she hugged Stan's arm and tried to quell the terrible fear that was squirming and growing inside her. She hated being shut in, hated the thought of how deep they were below ground, and hoped to goodness the flickering lights didn't fail and plunge them into profound darkness.

It was a fear born in childhood after one of her brothers had locked her in the coal-hole as a lark. She'd screamed and screamed for what felt like hours before someone found her, and she'd had nightmares for weeks after. It was the only time she'd seen her dad take a belt to any of them, and Freddy had yowled and blubbered and said he was sorry, but it hadn't made her feel better, and she'd done her best to avoid tight, enclosed spaces ever since.

'Sorry, love,' Stan murmured. 'I know I've been a moody so and so all evening, but it's 'ard for a bloke, you know?'

She nodded against his arm, the smooth material of his sleeve feeling cool and comforting against her cheek. 'I know, Stan, but it'll all be worth the waiting. I promise.'

Stanley didn't reply but just continued smoking his cigarette.

Julie closed her eyes and tried to shut out the crush of humanity around her, and the bangs and crumps overhead. She and Stan would be all right, she thought. They were just tired and out of sorts, and everyone had their ups and downs. They wouldn't be normal if they didn't.

The enemy raid seemed to go on and on, and Julie's fear of being buried alive became almost too much to handle. She sat as close as she could to Stan, who'd managed, unbelievably, to fall asleep, and tried not to flinch or shiver every time a bomb went off, or the lights threatened to go out.

This was far worse than sitting it out under the stairs with Sadie and Val, for there had been no locked door barring her escape from the tenements. Now, in the bowels of the earth, she could feel the ground tremble under her feet, could hear the mortar shift and feel the dust drift down from the ceiling as the lights flickered and the walls shuddered. They were shut in here, with no avenue of escape. One direct hit, and it would all be over.

Julie determinedly pushed back these terrible thoughts and set her mind to the problems of her relationship with Stan. Perhaps she was wrong to wait – wrong to protect her virginity when all she really wanted was to make love to him – for she could die here tonight and never experience the mystery of all the things she'd read about and heard.

At last the raid ended, and within half an hour of the last enemy plane leaving, the all-clear went and the warden opened the door.

'I've got to get back to the hostel,' Julie said urgently to Stan, shaking him awake. 'Will I see you on Wednesday?'

He slung his arm round her and gave her a hearty kiss as they shuffled along with the others towards the open doorway. 'Wednesday it is,' he murmured, 'and I promise to be in a better mood, Jules.'

They emerged into a cold, damp night which seemed to be filled with smoke and ash and the ringing of ambulance and fire engine bells. It was after midnight, but the sky was orange with the reflection of the fires they could see raging near the docks and to the east, and evidence of bomb-blast could be seen in the shattered windows of the buildings opposite.

'At least the Bull's still standing,' said Stan with a grin. 'I'll walk you back to the 'ostel and then pop in for a pint. I know it's way past closing time, but the landlady keeps 'er side door open, and me throat's as dry as chalk.'

Julie tucked her hand in his arm and they hurried down the road, dodging fallen masonry, raised paving stones and the vast jet of water that was coming from a broken main. The maintenance crews were already out in force, and Julie wondered if her dad was out in Stepney doing the same hasty repairs.

Stan wrapped his arms round her as they stood outside the hostel in the darkness. His kiss was warm and tender, his hug gentle. 'See you Wednesday, gel,' he murmured, his hand cupping her cheek, 'and I'm sorry if I've been a bit . . .' He grinned and shrugged. 'Well, you know how it is, Jules.'

She gave him a light kiss on his lips and then nodded. 'I do understand,' she replied, 'really I do.' Not wanting to say anything that might lead him to believe she was beginning to soften to his persuasion, she turned away and hurried up the path to the front door. Blowing him a kiss, she slotted in her key and stepped into the hall.

'Thank goodness you're back,' said a breathless Lily, who'd come racing out of the dining room. 'There's been a telephone call from Mrs Bessell. Franny's gone into premature labour.'

Julie went cold. 'Oh God,' she breathed. 'Did she call the ambulance?'

Lily nodded. 'Franny was admitted over two hours ago and taken straight into surgery.'

Julie was already running up the stairs, peeling off her coat and scarf along the way as Lily pounded after her. 'Do you know what stage of labour Franny was in when she was admitted?'

Lily followed her into the bedroom, gathering up the discarded clothes Julie flung about as she frantically changed into fresh uniform. 'I took the call and tried to calm 'er down, but she was in a bit of a dither and wasn't making much sense,' she said. 'Apart from saying the waters had broken, she didn't seem to know anything.'

Julie was fully dressed in her uniform by now. She grabbed her overcoat and struggled into it. 'I'll be at the hospital if Matron asks,' she managed. The fear for Franny was making her pulse race and her head spin.

'They won't let you near 'er,' Lily warned. 'Relatives aren't allowed to treat their own.'

'I know that,' Julie replied, already halfway through the door, 'but the uniform will give me answers I won't get as a civilian. Thanks, Lily,' she called as she raced down the stairs and slammed the front door behind her.

The maternity hospital was across the road, and by the look of it had escaped any damage from the raid. A large pale-grey stone building, it took up most of the block and towered over the surrounding houses. Julie ran along the curved driveway and raced up the steps into reception.

'Frances Harris, brought in about two hours or so ago. I'm her midwife,' she panted to the rather startled nurse behind the desk.

'She was taken straight into theatre,' the nurse replied, eyeing Julie with barely disguised curiosity – most midwives didn't come charging in here out of breath. 'I don't know anything else, but she should be out by now and in the recovery ward on the third floor. You can go up if you . . .'

Julie didn't wait to hear any more but took the stairs two at a time, incurring more startled and disapproving looks from the other nurses she passed on the way. She stopped running as she reached the endless corridor and walked as fast as she could until she reached the recovery ward. Taking a deep breath and trying to calm her fears, she pushed through the swing doors.

The nurse on duty was at her desk, a reading light illuminating the charts and medical notes that were strewn across it. 'Can I help you?' she asked pleasantly.

'I'm looking for me sister, Frances Harris,' Julie replied, her gaze trawling over the numerous beds in search of her.

'She's not here, I'm sorry,' replied the nurse.

'But I was told she went into surgery over two hours ago, and she was only due to have a C-section.'

The nurse stood and patted her arm. 'I can tell you're worried,' she said kindly, 'but I really can't help. Why don't you go down to the ground floor and the ward next to the theatre? Someone there will know what's going on.'

Julie hesitated, unwilling to accept that Franny

had been kept downstairs. Her sister must be in deep trouble. 'You're sure she's not up here?'

The nurse shook her head. 'We have four wards on this floor and I have all the patient notes here. Frances Harris isn't among them.'

'Thanks,' Julie said briefly and shot out of the door, plummeted down the stairs and raced towards the theatre wing. If Franny was down here in the special ward, then it could only mean she was still classed as an emergency.

'Please let her be all right,' she muttered as she flew down the corridor. 'Please, please be all right.' She came to a skidding halt outside the door, her heart hammering, her fears making her tremble. She should have got Franny into hospital earlier – should have gone back to check on her instead of seeing Stan.

She stood there, afraid to go in. Eventually, her years of training and discipline took over and, realising she must look like a mad woman, she smoothed her hair, straightened her cap and apron and pushed through the doors.

There were only four other patients and when she saw Franny, she knew immediately that her worst fears had been realised. But as she headed for the bed which had an oxygen tank by its side, and numerous drip-feeds hanging above it, she was stopped by a warm, gentle hand on her arm.

She turned sharply and discovered it was the elderly and much loved surgeon, Mr Philips, who'd come out of retirement for the duration. 'What happened?' she breathed.

Mr Philips steered her out of the ward and gently pressed her into one of the chairs that were lined along the corridor wall. He sat down and took her hands. 'Julie,' he began softly, 'your sister's labour had already gone too far for me to do a caesarean section.'

'But she knew to tell Mrs Bessell the minute anything started. Why did she leave it so long?'

He shook his head, the silvery grey hair glinting in the bright lights. 'She didn't leave it long by all accounts. Mrs Bessell told the ambulance crew the pains started only minutes before she ran down the road to call them. They got to the house very quickly and, as you know, the journey isn't long. But her labour was extremely rapid, and she was already in the second stage and fully dilated by the time we got her into theatre.'

She regarded the elderly man she'd come to know so well during her time in Shoreditch, her tears unshed, the fear gripping her heart. 'Is she going to be all right?' she whispered.

His grip tightened on her hands. 'I'm sorry, Julie. Your sister has suffered an amniotic fluid embolism, and although we're giving her oxygen and a fresh supply of blood, her heart has been further weakened by the shock.'

Julie felt the icy dread creep into her spine. 'But that's so rare,' she breathed, 'and so deadly. Does she have any chance of coming through this?'

'I'm so sorry, my dear,' he said solemnly. 'There was an occlusion of the pulmonary vessels, and although she survived the pulmonary collapse, her already damaged heart simply cannot cope.'

Julie stared at him as his words and their meaning slowly penetrated. She couldn't believe it, didn't want to believe it when she'd promised her sister that everything would go smoothly. 'But she's still alive. Surely there's some hope she'll pull through?'

His expression left no doubt, his next few words confirming it. 'We've made her as comfortable as we can, but there's nothing else we can do for her. The end is close, Julie. I'm sorry.'

Julie burst into tears. 'I've let her down,' she sobbed. 'I promised her it would be all right only this morning. I should have got her admitted earlier, should never have gone out tonight when I could have been with her.'

'You mustn't blame yourself, Julie,' he said softly.

'But I do,' she rasped, 'of course I do. She's my sister and I should have been with her.' She scrabbled for a handkerchief and blew her nose, desperately trying to find some sort of calm and coherence of thought. 'Did I miss something? Is it my fault – was it a mistake I made that led to this?'

'No, my dear,' he said firmly. 'The sequence of so many tragic events is highly unusual and it could not have been spotted in advance. No one is to blame, Julie – least of all you.'

Julie's tears rolled hot down her face and she blotted them away. 'The baby?' she whispered. 'What about the baby?'

'He's a little premature but healthy enough, and although he should really be on the special baby ward, I've put him with his mother so she can see him and get to know him before she . . .' His words trailed away and he sank his chin to his chest and gave a deep sigh. 'Something like this touches us all, Julie. You have my deepest sympathy.'

Julie blew her nose again and determinedly scrubbed away her tears and the last of her mascara. The time for crying was later. She had to be strong and calm and able to think straight, and act professionally. 'Has anyone thought to ring Stepney? Me parents should be here.'

'We've tried the number you gave us, but the lines are down. Probably because of the raid, but we'll keep trying, Julie, never fear.'

But Julie *was* fearful. Her sister was dying and her parents should be here. Yet there was absolutely nothing she could do about any of it. 'Thank you for your kindness, Mr Philips,' she said shakily. 'May I see her now?'

'Of course,' he murmured. 'Stay for as long as you like. I'll be in my office next door should you need me.'

Julie felt as if she was living in a nightmare as she softly walked down the ward to Franny's bed. Nothing seemed real – but the horror behind that sense of unreality was too awful. She didn't know how long she could keep up this façade of calm.

Franny was almost as pale as the pillowcases behind her little head. Her breathing was shallow and irregular beneath the oxygen mask, but all her attention was on the tiny baby nestled in a blue blanket in her arms.

'Hello, Franny,' Julie murmured as she sat down on the chair by the bed and put a gentle hand on her sister's skinny arm. 'I hear you've got a son.'

'Isn't 'e beautiful?' panted Franny, never taking her eyes from the bundle in her arms. 'I've called 'im William Albert – after – 'is – father and – our – dad.'

'Don't tire yourself with talking,' managed Julie as she fought her emotions. She gently drew back the blue blanket so she could see Franny's baby. Her heart swelled with love and sorrow as she looked down at him. He was very small, with the tiny wrinkled face and blotchy complexion of all newborns – but much more special than any of the babies Julie had helped deliver because he was Franny's. 'He's lovely,' she murmured.

Franny smiled a sad, sweet smile beneath the oxygen mask. 'Remember – your – promise,' she panted. 'Look – after – 'im – Bill – 'ome.'

'Of course I will.' Julie fought to swallow the lump in her throat. 'But you'll get better, Franny, really you will and . . .'

Franny shifted the oxygen mask and looked at Julie with clear blue eyes and an expression that brooked no argument. 'I'm dying, Julie. Love 'im for me,' she gasped in a rush. Those few words seemed to take the last of her strength, and she began to cough, the spittle tinged pink with blood.

Julie hastily stepped back as the specialist nurse bustled over and pressed the emergency button on the wall above the bed.

'Hold the baby,' she ordered softly. 'I need some space.'

Julie took the bundle and held it close, but all her attention was on Franny as Mr Philips rushed to the bedside. Franny was struggling to breathe, doubled over with terrible pain in her chest as blood now trickled from her nose and mouth.

Julie wasn't one for praying or church-going, but as she watched Mr Philips and the nurse fight to keep Franny alive she sent up an entreaty to God to spare her sister.

But God couldn't have been listening, for Franny collapsed on the pillows and lay still, and with one last, laboured breath, was gone.

Mr Philips shook his head, and Julie sank back into the bedside chair, the baby in her arms almost forgotten as she reached for her sister's hand. 'Oh, Franny, love. I'm sorry, I'm so sorry.'

Tiny William seemed to sense that something was wrong, for he squirmed and bunched his little fists before bursting into a high-pitched, keening cry.

The nurse finished taking down the drips and turning off the oxygen. 'I'll take William to the special baby ward while you spend some time with your sister,' she said softly. 'You won't be disturbed.' She moved away, pulling the screens round the bed before leaving the ward with the baby.

Julie lost track of time as she sat there and hardly noticed the air-raid sirens howling outside, or the roar of the returning bombers overhead. She talked about their childhood, the pranks they played, the summer delights of hop-picking in Kent, and the dreams they'd shared in those golden days. She spoke of her love and her sorrow, and repeated her promise to look after Franny's baby.

She remained with her sister all through the crumps and bangs and the rattle of gunfire, scarcely aware of anything until the all-clear went for the second time that night. In the hush of the aftermath of battle she rose from the chair, stepped through the screens and approached the sister on duty.

'I'd like to lay her out,' she said. 'It's all I can do for her now, and I want her to look at peace when our parents come. Has anyone managed to get hold of them yet?'

The ward sister shook her head. 'One of my nurses has been trying to get through all night, but the lines are still down. I'm sorry.' She gave Julie a sympathetic smile and squeezed her hand. 'You'll find fresh linen and everything you'll need in the room next door.'

Julie's tears slowly rolled down her face as she lovingly washed her sister's pale, lifeless body.

Gently drying her with a soft towel, she then reached for the hairbrush and carefully teased out the tangles and arranged the shining curls so they framed her sweet face and drifted over her shoulders.

Franny looked more fairy-like than ever in the endless sleep that had so cruelly snatched her from those who loved her, but as Julie kissed her forehead and slowly drew the sheet over her, she knew she would always remember her this way – in peaceful, sleeping repose where the cruelties and struggles of life could never trouble her again.

She pulled the screens round the bed for the last time, thanked the sister and left the ward. She didn't want to see them wheel her down to the morgue – didn't want to think of her down there alone in the cold basement where she would remain until her parents came to see her in the Chapel of Rest.

The special ward for premature and sick babies was at the end of the corridor. Although it was now four in the morning, Julie pushed through the door. The room was hushed and dimly lit, with a line of small cots down the middle and two nurses and a VAD on duty.

The senior nurse must have been warned that Julie might come, for she left her desk and greeted her with a warm, understanding smile. 'William has been fed and doesn't seem to have suffered too much from the trauma of such a rapid delivery,' she said quietly. 'But he will have to stay with us for a few weeks as he's still very small.'

Julie followed the nurse to the cot and looked down at the tiny scrap lying there, unaware of the drama that had surrounded not only his conception, but his arrival. 'May I hold him?' she asked, her voice gruff with tears.

At the other woman's nod, Julie lifted William from the cot and rested her cheek on his tiny head, breathing in the sweetness of him. He was an intrinsic part of Franny, her final and most precious gift for the man she loved, and Julie was almost overwhelmed by the sense of responsibility for this tiny scrap.

William stretched and squirmed and pulled a face, his rosebud lips working as if he was dreaming of milk.

'We'll look after you,' she whispered. 'Me and Mum and Dad will keep you safe. I promise.' She kissed the peach-like cheek and held him close, knowing that no matter how hard it became, or however long it took, she and her family would protect and love him for Franny until Bill came home.

Chapter Four

Julie cycled straight to Mrs Bessell's after leaving the hospital. The sweet woman was clearly devastated by Julie's news, and they tearfully consoled one another before Julie plucked up the courage to go up to Franny's room.

Mrs Bessell must have made the bed and tidied up during her long, sleepless night, but Julie felt a sense of abandonment in the room as she slowly gathered up the family photographs, the few pieces of clothing and the blanket their mother had knitted so lovingly. She wept as she found the drawer filled with baby clothes, and the packet of letters from Bill which had been tied together with blue ribbon. Franny had had such hopes and dreams – and now this was all that was left of a life half lived.

With everything packed away in one of Mrs Bessell's spare suitcases, Julie closed the door softly behind her and went downstairs to say goodbye. Mrs Bessell stood on the doorstep, her plump, sweet face lined with sadness as Julie promised to bring back the case and let her know about the funeral arrangements.

Julie still felt as if she was sleepwalking as she fixed the case to the bicycle and rode away, but as the morning sun broke through the haze of smoke, she felt the chill of reality settle round her heart. Franny was gone.

It was after nine by the time she reached the hostel to report in. All the nurses and volunteers would be out on their rounds by now, which was probably for the best as Julie didn't have the strength or heart to talk to anyone. But as she stepped into the hallway, she could hear Horace and Mabel, the cook, having a furious row over his inability to do anything without making a mess of her kitchen.

Born and bred in the East End, they both possessed a wide, colourful vocabulary that included every swear word and insult known to man, which they used freely, and at the top of their voices. To those not familiar with the broad Cockney accent, their rapid-fire slanging match would have been unintelligible, but to Julie, already feeling heart-sore and infinitely weary after her terrible night, every angry, foul word cut like a knife as they tore into each other. It was the final straw, and she burst into tears, fleeing up the stairs, only to find her way blocked by Matron on the first landing.

'Go into my office,' the older woman said kindly. 'I'll deal with those two.'

She closed the door behind her and Julie put down the case and let her emotions finally pour out in a torrent of anguished tears. Her heart ached with the loss, and she was pierced by a sense of failure that she had not seen, not known that something was wrong with Franny when she'd last visited her. The regrets flooded in. She should never have gone out last night – should have checked on Franny and insisted she was admitted to hospital sooner.

Julie became aware of Matron's return, sensed her closing the door on the heavy silence that now pervaded the house, and heard the muted rattle of a cup and saucer as it was placed on the desk in front of her. She was embarrassed to be so distraught, and tried her hardest to stem the tears and gain some control over her emotions. But it seemed the trauma of the night's events had struck too hard and too deep, and she simply couldn't stop crying.

'Mr Philips came to see me,' said Matron quietly. 'I'm very sorry to hear about your sister, but you must not blame yourself. These things happen, unfortunately, and there is absolutely nothing you or anyone could have done to forestall it.'

Julie dredged up the last of her strength in a determined effort to pull herself together. She blew her nose, wiped her eyes and took a deep, shuddering breath. 'Mr Philips explained,' she rasped through her tight throat. 'He was very kind.' Her hands were shaking as she lifted the cup and gulped down the hot, milky tea in the hope the sugar might restore her senses.

'I understand no one has been able to reach your parents,' said Matron, her pale blue eyes regarding Julie with kindness. 'The bombing last night was rather severe, which would explain the lack of a telephone service. You may have the rest of the day off to go and see them, but you will remain in your uniform and carry your medical bag as you are officially still on duty until tomorrow evening.'

Julie couldn't really see the point of such a silly rule but didn't care enough to argue about it. 'Thank you, Matron,' she said, her spine stiff with the effort of maintaining some semblance of calm.

Matron's smile was warm and full of understanding. 'Cut along then, Sister,' she said softly. 'But you might find it easier and quicker to cycle to Stepney. I'm told many of the railway lines have been damaged, and the buses are having difficulties getting through.'

Julie nodded, thinking the interview was over, but Matron came round her desk and took her hand. 'Have you eaten since last night, my dear?' At the shake of her head Matron sighed. 'I thought not. Get Mabel to make you a sandwich. You won't be of use to anyone if you faint.'

Julie left Matron's office in a daze of weariness and grief. She felt grubby and rumpled and so tired she could barely put one foot in front of the other – let alone eat one of Mabel's indigestible doorstep sandwiches. She just wanted to go home – to see her mother and father and find comfort and consolation in the little house where she and Franny had been born.

Having stowed Mrs Bessell's suitcase in the wardrobe, Julie washed her face and hands and combed her hair, which made her feel a little more prepared to face her parents. Collecting her medical bag, she went down to the bicycle shed and was soon on her way to Stepney.

The cold air on her face revived her as she pedalled, but as she passed bombed-out houses and corner shops, and navigated the piles of debris littering every street, she began to fret. It was clear the East End docks and warehouses had taken a hammering last night, for everywhere she looked she could see gaps where familiar landmarks had once stood, and piles of rubble strewn across the once bustling roads.

The maintenance and heavy-lifting crews were hard at work on almost every street: shoring up houses, repairing gas and electricity mains, replacing telephone wires and demolishing those buildings which were too unsafe to leave standing. And all the while the dazed and confused residents stood watching, their hands grasping the few precious things they'd managed to rescue from the wreckage of what had once been their homes.

Julie pedalled harder as she reached the outskirts of Stepney. The cold, damp air was full of the thick smoke that came, not only from the hundreds of factory and house chimneys, but from the steam ships on the Thames, and the burning buildings. London was in for another pea-souper smog.

St Paul's church was still standing just off Cable Street, the presbytery and surrounding houses seemingly almost untouched by the Nazi bombers. But something dark and chilling settled round Julie's heart as she cycled towards Backhouse Lane, for in the swirling smog she could see that the landscape had changed.

She skidded to a halt as she reached the end of the street and stared in horror at the scene before her. Four entire terraces had been obliterated – shattered into a million pieces of concrete and brick, the dust still hanging above the wasteland like a pall. But most devastating of all was what had happened to the tool factory that had once towered above those surrounding houses and had provided the nearest underground shelter.

Julie froze, unable to hold a coherent thought as she stared at the enormous pile of smoking rubble, and the huge, heavy machines that lay scattered, as if cast by a giant hand to lie buckled and twisted among the debris. Gangs of men were working furiously to shore up the sides of the hole they'd dug to rescue those still trapped beneath that pyramid of broken masonry, misshapen pipes, tortured steel beams and shards of glass. They must have been at it for hours – the raid had finished by four this morning.

Julie was aware that she was not alone – that neighbours stood in shocked and disbelieving silence all round her – but she couldn't take her eyes from that smoking, deadly pile, which looked as if it might collapse at any minute and crush the rescue workers. Had her parents gone down there last night – or had they gone up west to celebrate their wedding anniversary? Dad had said something about seeing a show and having a pie and mash supper afterwards.

'Watch yer back, Sister. There's people wot need 'elp, and more to come if only we can get 'em out.'

Startled, she turned and stared at the man whose face was lined with weariness and blackened by soot. His warden's uniform was in tatters, his hair stuck in filthy, sweaty clumps on his head, and in his hand he carried a pickaxe and shovel. 'I'm looking for my parents,' she replied in a daze. 'Mr and Mrs Harris.'

'Sorry, miss. The area warden 'ad the list, but 'e copped 'is lot in Dock Road.'

'My dad's Bert Harris,' she said, on the edge of hysteria. 'He works for the Water Board. You must know him.'

'Sorry, miss. You'd be better off going to St Paul's and asking there. The priests are tending to the minor injuries in the church hall, and you bein' a nurse, they could probably do with an 'and.'

'Have they managed to get anyone out?' she asked fearfully.

'Just a few who were lucky enough to be near the

door,' he replied wearily. 'But there's probably over a hundred people still down there.'

Julie shivered and tried not to think of the horror of being buried alive. She watched the warden walk away and join the other men who were digging in quiet desperation at the rubble while the heavy-lifting crew struggled to move the toppled machinery out of the way without bringing the whole mass down. Two ambulances and a fire engine stood close by, the crews willingly joining in as inch by tortuous inch the rescue workers cleared the debris.

Julie searched amongst the people standing dumbstruck amid the ruins of their streets, hoping beyond hope she'd see her parents. But there was no sign of them, and her questions were answered with just a shake of the head. She stifled a moan of terror and headed quickly back to the church.

Father O'Neil saw her the moment she stepped into the hall and hurried towards her, his face ashen with weariness and concern. 'Thank the Lord, Julie,' he breathed, grasping both her hands. 'I've done me best, but 'tis a poor effort, for I know little of medicine.' He glanced across at the two younger priests, who were trying to help an hysterical woman who had blood pouring from a head wound. 'It is at times like these that I wish we had a convent,' he muttered as he ran his fingers through his greying hair, 'for the nuns would know what to do.'

'I'm looking for me parents,' she replied, her gaze swiftly trawling the huddled mass of people who took up every spare inch of floor. 'Have you seen them? Do you know if they got out, or if they were taken to the hospital?'

Father O'Neil knew every one of his parishioners, even if they weren't of the faith. He frowned with concern. 'They're not here,' he replied, 'and I've not seen them, but someone here might know where they are.'

Julie quickly found several neighbours and questioned them closely as she treated their cuts and bruises and made slings for broken arms and wrists. Then she came across Franny's best friend Ivy, who was huddled tearfully in a corner.

Ivy had lived next door to the Harrises with her aunt and uncle ever since her mum had left her as a baby on the doorstep – the identity of her father had never been known. As Julie took her in her arms and tried to comfort her, the girl sobbed out her terrible story.

'I were lucky 'cos I were sitting right by the door, and when it blew I went wiv it – right across the bleedin' street, straight into Ma Foster's scullery. I 'it me 'ead something awful on her bleedin' mangle, and was out cold when they lifted me out.'

Julie swiftly assessed her injuries. There was a nasty swelling at the back of her head which could cause concussion, the cut above her eye would need stitches, and Julie suspected she'd broken her wrist. Apart from that, Ivy had had a very lucky escape.

She wanted desperately to ask if Ivy had seen her

parents, but feared the answer, dreaded hearing the words that would only confirm her worst fears, so she remained silent as she cleaned the cut and bandaged Ivy's wrist. No doubt Ivy would tell her soon enough.

Ivy sniffed back her tears and looked at Julie with eyes shadowed by the fear and horror of what she'd been through, her pinched face streaked with soot and smeared with the tracks of her tears and the seep of blood from the gash on her brow. 'Have you been up to the factory?'

Julie nodded, the dread cold in her heart as Ivy shivered and wrapped her arms round her skinny waist.

'I'm sorry, Jules,' she sobbed, 'but Bert and Flo was right in the middle of the shelter playing cards with me auntie and uncle. Right under all – them – machines,' she stuttered.

Julie looked at her in silent despair, the words ringing like a death-knell in her head.

Ivy took a shuddering breath and smeared away the tears. 'I don't know what 'appened to any of them – but I've looked and looked, and can't find no one.'

Julie held her close until the tears subsided. With four floors of machinery above them, how could anyone survive? And yet she had to keep faith – had to keep believing in miracles. For if Ivy and these others had got out, there was a chance her parents would too.

With the dread threatening to overwhelm her,

Julie made a sling for Ivy's wrist, seeking comfort in the familiar ritual. 'You'll need to go to hospital to check on that bump on your head,' she murmured, 'and I think your wrist's broken, so you'll—'

'I ain't going nowhere,' Ivy blurted. 'Not till I know what's happened to me auntie and uncle. They's all I got, Julie. All I got in the world.'

Despite her own terrors, Julie put a consoling arm round Ivy and gave her a hug as the girl again burst into noisy tears. She wouldn't tell her about Franny. It would be too cruel.

Frantic now to get back to the bomb site, Julie waited for the sobs to ebb and then handed Ivy over to the stalwart ladies of the WVS, who'd just arrived to dispense tea, sympathy and blankets to the shocked survivors. Hurrying out of the hall with her medical bag, she cycled back to where the tool factory had once stood.

There was still a profound silence amongst the watching crowd as the rescue crews shouted to one another and continued to make the hole bigger and safer until it was deemed ready to enter.

Julie watched breathlessly as those brave, brave men wriggled and squirmed to get through the hole they'd managed to open up some way back from the original entrance. All digging had stopped now, and everyone listened as their muffled voices came back to the surface. They'd found survivors.

The crowd sighed as one and shuffled closer, drawn by hope.

With infinite care the hole was widened and the first of the walking wounded was helped out. She stood blinking and confused for a moment and then was gathered up by her joyous, tearful relatives. A small boy was lifted out, a man swiftly following him – then two women, and another three children with their distraught mother, all dazed from their ordeal. An elderly couple followed but they were so traumatised, they had to be carried to the waiting ambulance.

The crowd shuffled closer as each new bloodied and bewildered survivor emerged from what could have been their tomb. Hope was alive again.

Julie realised the crews were hopelessly short-handed and rushed to help assess the wounds and direct the patients either to the ambulances or to the church hall. But as each man, woman and child scrambled to freedom, she prayed that her parents would be next.

The size of the crowd had strengthened now, with people coming from every corner of Stepney to witness this miracle and lend a hand. The ambulances rushed back and forth, their bells clanging, and the fire crews continued to shore up the rubble and dampen down the little fires that kept springing up.

The air was full of noxious smoke and floating ash, the dust sifting down into the sulphurous smog and making everyone cough. But it was a small hardship and no one seemed to notice, for all eyes were on that escape tunnel – all hope concentrated on each and every person that was miraculously pulled out alive. If so many had managed to survive, then surely their loved ones would soon appear?

There was a long pause after an old man stumbled out of the hole and had to be helped to his feet. The crowd waited breathlessly and Julie's hope wavered as stretchers were carefully lowered into the ground. Were they for the seriously injured – or the dead?

The grim-faced bearers finally appeared. There were blankets covering the still forms they carried over the rubble and laid almost reverently on a cleared patch of pavement. These were the first of the dead – which meant they had found no more survivors.

The tortuous minutes dragged by and there were cries of anguish from the onlookers, and the sound of weeping filled the silence as more and more shrouded bodies were brought out and identified. The line of the dead now stretched along the pavement.

Julie glanced at each one, fearing the worst, but keeping that tiny spark of hope alive, praying that her parents hadn't been down there at all – that Ivy had been mistaken, that they'd . . .

She stared down at the strange, misshapen mound beneath the two blankets on the stretcher as the men carefully placed it next to the others.

'Best not to be looking under there, love,' one of the men said wearily. 'They was crushed, you see, crushed together like Siamese twins. It ain't a pretty sight.'

Julie's fragile hope died as the entwined hands slipped from beneath the blankets. She recognised the thin gold band and garnet engagement ring on her mother's finger, and the shirtsleeve above the watch her dad had been given by the Water Board in recognition of his forty years of service. Bert and Flo Harris had died in each other's arms, as united in death as they had been throughout their married life.

'No,' she keened. 'Please, no.' Julie sank to her knees, took the tightly clasped hands and held them to her heart. Sorrow and despair engulfed her as she kissed the hands that had cared for her so lovingly, her tears washing away the grime of their tomb as she held them to her cheek and rocked back and forth.

She'd lost all sense of time and was unaware of everything going on around her as she knelt there on the rough road she'd once played on as a child and tried to accept that her parents had left her, that she would never see them again, never hear their voices or feel the security and love they'd so generously given.

'Come, Julie,' said a soft voice at her shoulder. 'The ambulance is waiting.'

Startled, she looked up through her tears in bewilderment. 'I don't need an ambulance,' she managed.

'It's not for you, Julie,' the priest replied softly.

She didn't understand, but was unable to speak as his hands slipped under her arms, firmly drawing her to her feet. Her numbed legs threatened to buckle and she collapsed against him. Grasping his stained and dusty soutane, she felt his arms go round her and she leaned into him, desperate for a moment of comfort, longing to feel the solidity and warmth of another human being in this coldest, darkest hour.

But that brief moment of solace almost broke her – for these were not her father's arms, nor her mother's or sister's. They were gone, out of reach, never to hold her again. And the knowledge that she'd lost everyone she loved hit her like a hammer blow.

She clung to him, the agony of her terrible loss too great even for tears.

He held her, murmuring soft words meant to comfort her, but all they did was remind her of when her parents had soothed her childhood fears and tended her scraped knees.

Julie finally drew back from the priest and looked up into his kind brown eyes. 'Thank you,' she murmured.

His smile was soft and full of understanding. 'Can you walk, d'you think?'

She nodded. 'I certainly don't need an ambulance,' she replied, her voice rough with emotion.

'They are here now to take these poor souls to

the local undertaker,' he said gently. 'You'll be able to see them again tomorrow in the chapel of rest.'

Her head felt as if it was full of cotton wool, her thoughts sluggish and jumbled. She frowned. 'Tomorrow? But I have to be on duty tomorrow,' she muttered. 'And I must make arrangements for Franny.' She began to tremble again, the tears threatening.

The priest asked no questions but simply picked up her medical bag and carefully steered her across the rubble to where her bike lay. 'It's probably best you come back with me,' he murmured, setting it back on its wheels and securing her bag on the rack. 'You've had a terrible shock, and the ladies from the Women's Voluntary Service will give you a cup of hot sweet tea.'

She let him wheel the bike and lead her away as the ambulance clanged its bell and set off down the street towards the undertakers at the back of Ensign Street. 'I didn't tell them about Franny,' she stuttered, 'or about the baby.'

'Have no fear, Julie. They are with our loving Father who sees and knows all things.'

Julie gave a harsh cough of derision as he helped her up the church hall steps. She was grateful for his help and knew he was only trying to comfort her, but his loving Father had ignored her prayers – had turned His back on her and, in a matter of a few short hours, had taken away her home and everyone she loved.

The priest made no comment as he found her a

space to sit on the small stage and then hurried off to get her a cup of tea.

Julie sat on the edge of the stage and stared out at the mass of miserable and injured humanity who'd come here for solace and a kind word in their hour of great need, perhaps finding comfort in faith and prayer. In her agony of bewilderment and pain, she couldn't believe there was a God, for where the hell had He been when they'd all needed Him most?

She felt restored by that jagged knife of anger, more able to cope. She looked up at the priest as he returned with a mug of tea. 'Thank you,' she said, taking it from him and wrapping her cold fingers round it. 'I'll drink this and get out of your way.'

'You don't—'

'Yes, I do, Father,' she interrupted. 'I have to get back to the hospital.'

'Are you sure, Julie?' He frowned, his brown eyes looking down at her with such concern that it almost broke her resolve.

She looked away from him as she finished the tea. 'I have responsibilities,' she muttered. 'See to your flock, Father, and I'll take care of me own.' She knew she was being ungracious, but that couldn't be helped. If she didn't get out of here soon, she'd break down again and never have the strength to do what she knew she must.

It was mid-afternoon by the time Julie made it back to Shoreditch, and although she was almost asleep on her feet, and faint with hunger, she didn't go straight to the hostel.

The Mothers' Laying-in Hospital was quiet and warm, the smell of disinfectant and starch comforting after the chaos and devastation of Stepney. Julie caught sight of her reflection in the glass entrance doors but didn't care that she looked a fright – that her hair and face were begrimed and tear-streaked, or that her stockings were in shreds and her coat grey with dust. She was concerned only for William.

Ignoring the disapproving and startled glances of those she passed, she hurried up to the baby ward. Pushing through the swing doors, she stood for a moment in bewilderment, unable to remember which was William's cot.

'You look all in,' said the nurse tactfully as she took in Julie's grubby appearance. 'Have you been out with the ambulance crews to the bomb sites?'

Julie didn't want to go into long explanations, so merely nodded in reply.

The nurse gently steered her out of the ward. 'I'll show you where you can wash,' she said kindly. 'We can't risk infection – not in there.'

Julie suddenly realised how thoughtless she'd been and, with a muttered apology, followed her into the sluice. The nurse handed her a bar of soap and a clean towel and quietly closed the door behind her to give her some privacy.

Julie took off her coat, cap and apron, careful not to get too much dust on the pristine floor as she folded them into the big brown paper bag she always carried with her medical instruments. Having stripped off the ruined stockings, she threw them in the waste bin. There was nothing she could do about the grubby, blood-stained dress, so she filled the sink with hot water and began scrubbing her face, neck and hands.

Once she felt clean again, she stuck her head under the tap and used the carbolic soap to wash the dust and grime from her hair. Feeling marginally better, she rubbed her hair vigorously with the towel, thankful it was short and would dry quickly.

She took a deep breath, suppressing another tidal wave of sadness and exhaustion, and forced her weary legs to carry her back to the baby ward. She gave a wan smile to the nurse who was now sitting on a low chair, bottle-feeding a baby. 'Where's William?' she asked.

'We've transferred him from the oxygen tent, and he's now in the cot at the far end.' The nurse eyed her thoughtfully. 'You look about done for,' she said sympathetically. 'Would you like a cup of tea?'

'If it's not too much trouble,' Julie replied, already on her way to William's cot. He was crying, his little face red, his tiny fists waving above the blanket in fury.

'You can change and feed him if you like,' said the nurse. 'The nappies are in that cupboard and the bottles are all made up in the kitchen over there. They only need warming.'

In a stupor of grief and weariness, Julie changed his sodden nappy, and then went to warm the milk in the tiny, spotless kitchen that led off the ward. The young nursing aide handed her a cup of tea, and she gulped it down gratefully. It was weak and almost tasteless, with only a hint of sugar, but it helped revive her spirits enough to keep going.

William had stopped crying by the time she returned to the ward, and she took him from his cot and held him close. He didn't weigh much, but his tiny body was comforting and warm in her arms – a reminder that life carried on regardless of the horrors surrounding them. She breathed in his baby smell, her cheek resting lightly on his downy head as she sank into the low chair and settled down to feed him.

She watched his fingers flex and curl in delight, noted how his eyelashes were dark against his pale skin, and how greedily he sucked at the teat. His vulnerability and total reliance on her touched something within Julie, and she knew in that moment she would do everything in her power to protect him. For now all they had was each other.

As Julie left the hospital and wheeled her bicycle over the road to the hostel, the air was rent with the sound of Hurricanes and Spitfires heading for the coast. She took little notice of them, for she was pondering on the miracle of a love so strong it was an irrepressible force. She'd seen that love in the poorest of hovels when a baby was placed in a mother's arms for the first time – had witnessed it in acts of incredible bravery when a child was at risk, and in the unceasing, selfless care that a mother gave to her ailing little ones.

William was not her baby, but in the short while she'd held him, fed him and watched him fall asleep, she'd felt that love sweep through her. It was fierce and overwhelming; stronger than anything she could have imagined. But it was healing, too, for in caring for William, she'd found a fragile solace.

The kitchen was deserted, but there was a plate of food keeping warm on the range and Julie tucked into it, hoping it wasn't meant for someone else. The gravy had dried, the edges of the corned beef hash were crisp, and the cabbage leaves were brown and curled, but in her ravenous hunger she didn't care. There was a portion of apple pie left in the larder and she soon demolished it, washing her meal down with another cup of tea. Sitting back in the chair, she felt partially restored, the need for sleep not quite as urgent.

The clock on the wall ticked heavily in the silence and Julie was astounded to see that it was after five. Matron might have given her the day off, but she'd had a full case-list today. She just hoped they hadn't been let down.

Matron came bustling into the kitchen just as Julie was rinsing her plates. 'I gave your list to Nurse Preston,' she said without preamble, 'so you can be sure that all your patients have been well looked after in your absence.'

'I'll remember to make it up to her,' murmured a grateful and much relieved Julie. Poor Polly Preston had a big enough round as it was without shouldering Julie's as well, and she just hoped she hadn't run Lily too ragged during the day.

Matron reached for the kettle that always stood by the range and glanced disapprovingly at Julie's filthy dress and bare legs. 'I suggest you have a bath and go to bed. You can continue your duties in the morning when you're feeling more refreshed.'

'Thank you, Matron,' Julie said quietly, 'but I'll need some time off to make arrangements for the funerals.' She saw the older woman raise her brow in question and went on to explain about her parents.

'Of course,' Matron replied when Julie came to a stuttering halt. She gave her a soft, kindly smile. 'You've rather been through the mill, haven't you? Take time off until the funeral and then, if you feel able to cope, you can pick up your duties again.'

'Thank you, Matron,' she murmured, touched by this usually stern woman's kindness.

'I've already spoken to the Church Adoption Society,' continued Matron as she made another pot of tea and set out a tray with a cup, saucer and two digestive biscuits. 'The paperwork should all be through by the time your sister's baby is ready to leave hospital.'

Julie stared at her, aghast. 'William doesn't need adopting,' she said hastily. 'He has me, and when his father comes home—'

'I don't think you've considered your position,' said Matron, her expression not quite as kindly as before. 'You're not married and can't possibly raise a child on your own. Think of the scandal it would cause. And you certainly couldn't continue with your work and stay here. We have no nursery facilities.'

The cold reality of her situation slowly began to dawn on Julie. 'But I promised Franny I'd look after him,' she replied, her voice sharp-edged with growing concern. 'She specifically told me she didn't want him raised by strangers.'

'He could be fostered out, I suppose, but with so many families—'

'No,' Julie interrupted. 'He stays with me until Bill can get home.'

Matron's lips formed a thin line, and her eyes hardened. She clearly didn't appreciate Julie's tone. 'And what if this Bill doesn't come home? He and your sister weren't married – he might not want the responsibility.'

That had never occurred to Julie and she hesitated before replying. 'He loved Franny, and she trusted him. He won't turn his back on his son.'

'Let us hope your faith in him is justified,' said Matron. 'But that does not solve the problem of who will look after the child until he returns.' She gave a deep sigh and stared out of the window to where Horace was lethargically hoeing the vegetable plot. 'Bringing up a child takes every ounce of your energy and requires full-time attention,' she continued softly. 'That is why mothers don't go out to work unless they absolutely have to.'

She looked back at Julie. 'You're very young, Sister Harris, and although you're highly qualified as a midwife, you have no experience of the sheer effort and commitment it takes to raise a child. It would be impossible for you to care for William and fulfil your duties as a nurse without a family to support and guide you.' She eyed her sternly. 'I assume this Bill has a family – give the baby to them.'

Julie reddened and couldn't look Matron in the eye. 'They live in Yorkshire,' she murmured, 'and although Franny wrote to them about the baby, she never received a reply. I don't think—'

'I suspected that might be the case,' said Matron with a sigh. 'It's always very difficult for families to accept a child born out of wedlock – even if it is purported to be their son's.'

Julie didn't like the inference that Franny's baby might not have been Bill's, but she kept silent, not wishing to antagonise the woman further.

Matron stood deep in thought for a long moment. 'Do you have any other family who might help you?'

'There's me older sister, Eileen,' Julie said

doubtfully. 'But she moved down to Cliffehaven on the south coast years ago and we've lost touch.'

'Then I suggest you try and reach her. She could be your only hope.'

Julie doubted it very much. Eileen had made it pretty clear she wanted nothing to do with the family once she'd left. There had been no letters, no visits, not even a passed-on message, and Julie had no idea of whether she was married or not – or even still in Cliffehaven. 'I'll write to her and tell her what's happened,' Julie murmured. 'But it's an old address, and she might have moved on.'

Matron took a deep breath, her expression stern. 'Let us hope she is willing to take on the child,' she said, 'because if she isn't, and you decide to go ahead with this foolish plan to raise him yourself, you will have to resign.'

Julie's heart was hammering, her thoughts in a whirl. 'William won't be out of hospital for a few weeks yet,' she said in a rush, 'and I'll need time to try and make proper arrangements for us both. May I stay until then?'

'Of course,' Matron replied. 'We are short-staffed and your work here is invaluable. Perhaps those few weeks will give you time to rethink this wild plan of yours and help you to see that fostering, or adoption, is really the only answer.'

Julie watched her leave the kitchen with her tea tray. Her back was ramrod straight, her head erect, each step purposeful and unhurried. Matron Starkey's advice was valid, her common sense practical and wise, but Julie could not – would not – break her promise to Franny.

And yet, keeping William posed a legion of problems which hadn't occurred to her in that rush of grief and love. Now, in the cold reality of Matron's concise assessment of the situation, they appeared to be insurmountable.

Chapter Five

Julie hadn't thought she would sleep after that conversation with Matron, but once she'd bathed and climbed into bed she knew nothing more until the lights were switched on at six the next morning.

'Hello, sleepyhead,' murmured Lily. She perched on Julie's bed in her brother's striped pyjamas, which swamped her tiny frame. 'Matron told us all what 'appened, so there's no need to go through it all again,' she said softly. 'How're you feeling?'

'Like I've been run over by a bus,' Julie groaned as she struggled to sit up. 'I ache in places I never knew I had.' She drew the rough blanket to her chin, shivering in the cold that had iced the inside of the windows and whistled under the door. 'I'm sorry you got lumbered with extra work yesterday,' she said, taking her friend's hand.

'You'd've done the same for me,' Lily replied lightly. Her wide blue eyes regarded Julie with sympathy. 'I hear Franny 'ad a little boy,' she said. 'That must be some consolation, I suppose.'

Julie drew up her knees and sank her chin onto them. 'He's beautiful, Lil,' she sighed. 'So tiny and sweet, but with such a strong will to live. You should see him feed.'

Lily frowned. 'I'm sure 'e's all those things, Julie, but you gotta remember he ain't yours. Don't go falling in love wiv 'im. It'll only make it harder when you 'ave to give 'im up.'

'I'm not giving him up,' Julie replied firmly. 'I promised Franny to keep him until Bill comes home.'

Lily gripped her hands. 'Julie, you ain't thinking straight, gel. What if Bill gets killed? What if he decides he don't want the baby after all? You'll be stuck good and proper.'

'I can't afford to think like that,' retorted Julie stubbornly.

'I think you 'ave to,' Lily murmured. She inched up the bed and put her arm round Julie's shoulders. 'I don't want to be unkind, Jules,' she said softly, 'but you ain't thought this through proper. What about your job – how would you support yerself and the sprog, and where would you live?'

'I'd manage somehow,' Julie muttered, 'and then there's me sister down in Cliffehaven, she might take us in. We'd be safer there, away from the Blitz anyway.'

'What about your job 'ere, and all yer mates? Then there's Stan. I thought you was getting married? Are you willing to turn your back on all of us?'

Julie didn't really want to leave her work here in London, and she certainly didn't want to leave Stan and all her friends. She regarded Lily for a moment and, as her thoughts swirled, an idea began to form. She grasped Lily's hand. 'If Stan and I get married straight away, then we could look after William together. We could find a cheap place to rent and I could work part-time.'

Lily eyed her solemnly. 'That sounds good in theory, but before you get too excited, don't you think you ought to talk it over with Stan?'

'I'll do it today,' said Julie, throwing back the bedclothes. 'We weren't supposed to meet up till Wednesday, but he comes off night duty at two. I can catch up with him at his lodgings.'

Lily stilled her as she reached for her dressing gown. 'Mind how you go, Jules. Men can be funny about this sort of thing. They don't like bein' rushed into making decisions and such, and Stan might not want—'

'Stan won't let me down,' Julie interrupted, invigorated by the certainty that she'd found the answer to her problems.

'If you're sure,' murmured Lily, but she still looked doubtful.

Julie gave her a hug and rushed out to use the bathroom. The day no longer stretched before her in an endless cloud of sorrow and anxiety.

Julie had left the hostel after breakfast, dressed in her smartest woollen dress and shoes, a soft beret covering her hair, the regulation overcoat keeping her warm against the blustery day. She'd visited

William for an hour, had changed and fed him and given him a cuddle as he fell asleep, then stood and watched him for a long while before quietly leaving the ward.

Cycling towards Stepney, she breathed in the clean fresh air that had come in with the wind off the Thames, and felt the sting of its chill on her face and in her heart. She dreaded returning to the street where she'd lived all her life, but knew she must, for there might be some remnants of the lives they'd lived there amid the rubble.

She stopped for a moment in front of St Paul's. The doors were open and somehow they seemed to beckon her. She rested the bicycle against the wall and hesitantly went inside. Her family were not Catholics and regarded churches as useful only for christenings, weddings and funerals, and, at a pinch, the occasional midnight mass at Christmas. She therefore felt a bit of an interloper as she slowly walked past the stone bowl with its holy water and down the aisle.

The church was hushed, the sunlight pouring through the stained-glass windows in rainbows of colour. The smell of incense was strong, and candles flickered on the altar and sparked in the brass candlesticks. Above the altar was a figure of Christ on the Cross, and the ancient stone walls were hung with paintings of His journey to Calvary.

Julie quietly tiptoed to a nearby pew and sat down. There were several people kneeling in prayer, their mouths moving silently as they threaded rosary beads through their fingers. She felt the tranquillity enfold her, and the gentle ghosts of generations of believers soothed her as she sat in this ancient place and tried to make sense of it all. She didn't pray, she didn't really know how, but she closed her eyes and remembered those she'd lost, and found a modicum of comfort.

She left the church feeling a little more confident about things, and was about to cycle away when Father O'Neil came hurrying along the path, his soutane billowing around his ankles.

He held out both his hands to her and smiled. 'Julie, 'tis a pleasure to see you in my church,' he said by way of greeting.

'I was just passing and thought I'd look in,' she replied, easing her hands away. She didn't want him to get the idea she'd taken up religion.

He nodded, the silver in his hair glinting in the sunlight. 'I've spoken to Mr Simms the undertaker,' he said solemnly, 'and I'm sorry, but it won't be possible to view your parents. Their injuries were . . .'

'It's all right,' she hurried to assure him. 'I wasn't going there anyway. I prefer to remember them as they were.' She shot him a tremulous smile. 'Now, if you don't mind, I have to be off.'

'God go with you, Julie,' he called after her.

She cycled away and within moments had reached the end of what she assumed had once been her street. It was unrecognisable, disorientating and confusing, for there was no pub or factory, no corner shop – nothing to mark where her home had been. It was a wasteland of still-smouldering destruction.

She climbed off the bicycle and wheeled it over and around the broken roof slates, the shattered window frames and crumbled bricks. Part of a wall rose out of the debris, and Julie recognised the curtain that flapped through what remained of the window. It was Ma Foster's house, and she could see the mangle that Ivy had hit her head on, standing where the scullery should have been.

Turning, she regarded what remained of her own home. The step her mother had scrubbed so assiduously every morning was buried beneath bricks, mortar and twisted lead pipes, but the black range had survived to stand ponderously in the middle of the carnage, her father's favourite chair perched on top of it. She laid her bicycle down and carefully made her way through the wreckage of broken glass and splintered wood.

She cleared a space and heaved the chair from the range. It was filthy, but still in one piece, so she wrapped her coat around her and sat down. She could almost hear her father laughing at the absurdity of what she was doing, and it made her smile as she regarded the damage through her blinding tears.

The old clock was in a million pieces, the precious wireless crushed beneath a heavy beam, the sink ripped from its moorings to be flung into the middle of the backyard. Her mum's collection of framed photographs had been scattered amongst the debris, the glass gone, the photographs ruined by water, the frames strangely intact.

Julie carefully gathered them, taking the photographs one by one, even the most damaged, and putting them safely in her handbag. She stood in the centre of the devastation, unable to accept that this had once been the very heart of her home. She was about to leave when a gust of wind made something flutter. On closer inspection she saw it was a piece of sodden, dirt-stained cloth, and her heart ached as she recognised it – for it was her mother's best dress.

Julie sniffed back her tears and scrambled over the mess to reach it. The dress had been caught on a nail in a fallen rafter, and she worked at it painstakingly to release it. Finally she stood in the ruins, the dress clutched tightly in her fist. Apart from her father's chair, and the water-damaged photographs, it seemed to be the only tangible reminder of her parents and the home they'd so lovingly made for their children.

'Thank you,' she whispered to them in the silence. 'Know that I'll always love you.'

It was almost three o'clock by the time Julie left Stepney, for after she'd said her goodbyes to her home, she'd gone to the undertaker and made the arrangements for the funerals. Franny would be buried with her parents in the local cemetery. Finding a little corner café that had escaped the carnage, she had bought a restoring cup of tea, then had gone back to the church hall to try and find out what had happened to poor little Ivy.

A small army of women had been helping the two young priests scrub and clean the mess from the hall, and they assured her that Father O'Neil had arranged for Ivy to go and live with her aunt's sister-in-law, who lived out Rainham way. Glad that Ivy had found a home, Julie had thanked them and headed for Poplar, where Stan had lodgings.

The damage was almost as bad here, the skeletons of blasted buildings rising above vast craters filled with rubble. The enemy raid at the end of January had seen whole streets go up in flames, and the houses that had withstood that and the subsequent bombings were blackened from the smoke of hundreds of fires. Most windows were boarded over, and the roofs had been made weatherproof with tarpaulins and sheets of corrugated iron.

The door to Stan's lodgings was to the side of a tobacconist's shop. The narrow street ended in a low wall that kept the Thames at bay, and, as Julie leaned her bike against a handy lamp post, she could see a huge merchant ship slowly making its way towards the East India Docks. The pungent smell of the muddy river was strong, the gulls wheeling and screeching overhead as they squabbled over the rubbish in the gutters. The ship gave an ear-splitting blast from its funnel, which was answered by several more. Julie was glad she didn't have to live here.

Her sharp rap of the knocker was finally answered by the sound of a sash window being drawn up overhead. 'Bugger off! I'm trying to bloody sleep.'

Julie stepped back into the road and looked up into his furious face. 'It's me, Stan,' she called back. 'I need to talk to you.'

He didn't look too happy about it as he slammed the window shut, and she wondered fearfully if he was just going to leave her there on the doorstep. A few minutes passed, and she was about to leave when she heard him thudding down the stairs. Her heart was pounding and her mouth was dry. Perhaps this had been a mistake?

The door was wrenched open and he stood there barefooted, in a pair of trousers hastily pulled over his pyjamas, and an unbuttoned shirt which revealed a muscular, hairy chest. He was tousle-haired, unshaven and clearly not in the best of moods.

'I've been on shift all night and only just managed to get to sleep,' he said gruffly. 'I 'ope it's important, Julie.'

She'd never seen him this unkempt and rough-looking before and she hesitated before answering, trying to quell her nervousness. 'It is rather,' she replied breathlessly as she took a step back. 'But I can see you're exhausted, so I'll leave it until later.'

He opened the door wider and jerked his head

towards the stairs. 'Well, you're 'ere now,' he said ungraciously, 'and I'm awake. You'd better come in.'

It was hardly the welcome she'd expected and, after a momentary hesitation, she stepped into the narrow hall. It smelled of damp and dirt, a thousand greasy meals, and something sharp and cloying which seemed to lodge in her throat.

As he closed the door they were plunged into darkness. 'The gas is off,' he explained sourly. 'Mind your step.'

Feeling more uncertain by the minute, she followed him up the bare stairs to a landing which had four doors leading off it. The strange smell was even worse up here and impossible to ignore. 'What *is* that pong?' she asked, wrinkling her nose.

'A couple of Indian seamen moved in the other day – it's their curry,' he muttered, running his fingers through his hair. 'It tastes all right, but give me jellied eels any day.' He paused as he reached for the door-handle. 'Look, Julie,' he said awkwardly, 'you'll 'ave to ignore the mess. I wasn't expecting visitors.'

'I've probably seen far worse on my rounds,' she replied with a lightness she didn't feel. 'Can we go in and open a window? That smell is turning me stomach.'

He opened the door and hurried towards the window as she followed him. She took in the rumpled, grubby bed, the pile of discarded dirty clothes in the corner, the plates of half-eaten meals and empty beer bottles that littered every flat surface. It was a small, musty room with a single bed, a wardrobe and a chest of drawers, but every inch of the uncarpeted floor was covered in discarded newspapers and what looked suspiciously like pornographic magazines.

She looked away quickly, but Stan must have noticed, because he hastily gathered them up and shoved them in a drawer. He also realised his shirt was flapping open and buttoned it quickly before pulling the unwashed bedclothes straight. 'Sorry there ain't nowhere else to sit,' he muttered, 'but there ain't room to swing a cat in here.'

Julie was shocked by the state of the room and the slovenly way Stan seemed to be living. No wonder he'd never invited her in for a cuppa – not that she'd have come, she wasn't that kind of girl. She perched on the very edge of the insanitary bed, her knees and ankles tightly together, the gas-mask box held determinedly on her lap like a barrier between them.

Stan seemed to have recovered from his initial embarrassment, for he eyed her with his familiar cheeky smile as he rolled a cigarette. 'You look right prim and proper sitting there, gel. What's the matter? Frightened I'll try and 'ave me wicked way?' He chuckled as he stuck the cigarette in his mouth and reached for a box of matches. 'Don't worry, gel. I'm too tired for all that.'

Julie could feel her heart hammering against her ribs. This wasn't the Stan she knew at all. She shouldn't have come – should have waited until Wednesday evening as they'd planned.

He shivered and closed the window, disregarding her obvious discomfort. He rested his behind on the sill and smoked his cigarette, his dark gaze pinned on her through the drift of smoke. 'So what's so urgent it couldn't wait until I'd caught up on me kip?'

Julie licked her dry lips. The doubts were growing by the minute, but she'd come for a purpose and couldn't fail now. She tightened her grip on the gas-mask box and kept her gaze fixed to the tiny chip of diamond in her engagement ring as she told him about the events of the past twenty-four hours.

'I'm sorry to 'ear about that, love,' he said softly. 'They was lovely people. Made me feel right at home, they did.' He finished his cigarette and dropped the butt in an empty beer bottle as another ship gave a deafening blast, which reverberated right through the house. He didn't seem to even notice as he carried on talking. 'I only met Franny a coupl'a times, but she seemed like a nice, quiet little thing. Shame about 'er and the baby.'

'The baby – William – is alive and being looked after at the hospital,' she said quickly. 'He's a little premature, so he'll stay there for a few weeks until he's gained some weight.' She hesitated, then plunged on and told him about her promise to Fanny and the difficulties she would have trying to care for the child on her own.

He narrowed his eyes and watched her with all the concentration of a feral cat stalking a bird. 'Well, you can't, can you? It wouldn't be proper.'

'But I must,' she said urgently. 'I promised.'

Stan's gaze remained steady through the narrowed lids. 'She won't know if you break your promise,' he said flatly. 'And with yer parents gone, it will be impossible. You should foster the kid out, and if its dad don't turn up, then 'e can be adopted.'

Julie stared at him. He hadn't listened to a word she'd said – had absolutely no idea of how much that promise to her dead sister meant to her. 'I'm not breaking that promise, Stan,' she said, her voice edgy with emotion.

'Don't be bloody silly,' he snapped. 'You ain't got nothing but your job and a place at that 'ostel.' He began to pace back and forth in front of the grimy window, animated by his impatience with her. 'If you take this kid on you'll be out on yer ear and no chance to earn, not even somewhere to live. Then what you gunna do? Take in bleedin' washing?'

'I thought I might work part-time and pay someone to look after him.'

He gave a harsh cough of humourless laughter. 'And what sort of work would that be, Julie?' he asked as he turned back to her. 'Single girls with a kid in tow ain't respectable, and you won't be allowed to nurse once word gets out.'

Julie bit her lip, the ready tears blinding her as she watched him resume his pacing. This was far

harder than she could ever have imagined. 'I was
. . . I thought . . . That's to say I hoped . . .' Her
voice faded as her courage deserted her.

His gaze was intense as he came to a sudden
standstill. 'What? Come on, Julie, spit it out.'

'I thought that as we're engaged, we could get
married a bit earlier than we planned,' she said
softly, not daring to look at him. 'Perhaps find somewhere cheap to live and look after William until Bill
gets back.' She glanced up at him but couldn't see
his expression as his back was to the light. 'As a
married woman I could still work,' she rushed on,
'and it can often be cheaper for two to share food
and bills, and once you pass your sergeant's exam
we could . . .'

The words stuck in her throat as Stan took a step
towards her, his face ashen, his eyes glittering
dangerously. 'You've got it all worked out, 'aven't
you?' he growled.

She was incapable of replying, hypnotised by
those eyes which seemed to bore right through her
and pin her to the bed.

She flinched as he leaned forward and rested his
hands either side of her on the bed. 'Well, I ain't
marrying you, Julie – not until you get rid of that
kid.'

'But . . .'

He leaned closer, his sour breath stirring her hair.
'No buts, no ifs, no maybe. I ain't raising another
man's bastard, and that's an end to it.'

Julie gripped the gas-mask box and tried to stand.

He casually pushed her back onto the bed. 'Get rid of the kid and we'll set a date,' he said, his voice low and flat. 'Keep the kid and it's over, Julie.'

She stared at him, terrified now of what he might do. The spell in which he'd held her broke, and she scrambled off the bed. 'I'll think about it,' she babbled, edging towards the door.

He returned to his perch on the windowsill and began to roll another cigarette. 'You do that, gel,' he murmured. 'And when you've seen sense, come back here and I'll show you what you would'a been missing.' He gave her a lascivious smile and winked. 'As you said the other night, gel, it'll be worth the waiting.'

Julie wrenched open the door and fled down the dark stairs. She slammed through the front door and stumbled into the street, gasping for fresh air and from the overwhelming need to get as far away from him as quickly as possible. Retrieving her bicycle, she pedalled furiously down the street, away from that awful room, the squabbling seagulls and the raucous noise of the docks. She didn't stop until she'd reached the hostel.

She was shaking so badly she almost fell off the bicycle as she came to a halt, and she had to stand for a moment to regain her equilibrium. It was rather galling to realise he hadn't chased after her, or even called to her from his window. But there were no tears or regrets for having that awful encounter, for it was obvious she'd had a merciful escape.

Stan was not the man she'd thought he was – and certainly not the man who'd charmed her family with his nice manners and respectable prospects – but someone whose veneer of kindness and urbanity had finally slipped to reveal his true character. She couldn't believe how stupid she'd been to think she loved him when, really, she hadn't known him at all. Looking down at the little engagement ring she'd once treasured, she decided to post it to him first thing in the morning.

She wheeled her bike through the gates and parked it alongside the others under the lean-to, her thoughts whirling. With the engagement over and Stan out of her life, she was now truly alone. She faced that fact, and began to make plans. She had always dealt with the family's correspondence and had the family address book in her bedside drawer. Tonight, she would write to Bill and his family, explaining the situation in the faint hope his parents would take William in. Then she'd write to Eileen and her brothers, and tell them all what had happened.

She watched Horace filling a bucket with anthracite to feed the range, spilling most of it on the path as he carried it into the hostel. Yet her thoughts were elsewhere.

She didn't really expect a reply from Bill's family, but if Eileen wrote back, then at least she'd know she still lived in Cliffehaven and could begin to make plans to go down there. Apart from her brothers, who were fighting in North Africa, Eileen was all the family she had now. Although there was a gap of twelve years between them, they were still family, and that counted for a great deal to all East Enders. Eileen was duty-bound to take her in.

Still rather shaken from that scene with Stan, she nevertheless began to feel more positive about things as she went in through the back door of the hostel and headed for the bedroom. She felt grubby after sitting on that revolting bed, tainted by the sleaziness of Stan and his horrid little room – and the way she'd cheapened herself by begging him to marry her. Apart from that, she could swear the stench of curry still clung to her coat and hair.

Julie grabbed fresh towels and locked herself in the bathroom. A good scrub with soap and hot water would put her to rights. Then she could settle down to writing her letters, and start making plans to take William out of the chaos of London to what she hoped would be the safety of Cliffehaven.

Chapter Six

Peggy Reilly was taking a few well-earned minutes to herself, having been on her feet for most of the morning at the Town Hall where she worked as a volunteer, sorting clothes for those poor unfortunate people who'd lost everything in the raids.

Her sister, Doris, had called in and thrown her weight about, which, as usual, had wound Peggy up to the point where she'd simply turned her back on her and walked away. Doris would make her pay for that moment of exasperation, she had no doubt of it, but for the moment Peggy was just relieved to be out in the fresh air.

She battled against the wind which buffeted her slight frame and brought her bicycle to a halt by one of the stone benches that were dotted along the promenade. She sat down, glad for this quiet moment after the chaos and noise of too many women squabbling over everything from frying pans to pyjamas while their babies screamed and their toddlers ran about under everyone's feet. Beach View Boarding House could manage without her for a while.

It was early afternoon, with streaks of sunlight

piercing the clouds to lie in golden pools on the grey water of the Channel. The horizon was darkening with the promise of rain, but it would be a while yet before Cliffehaven got a soaking, and Peggy decided to risk it. She knotted her headscarf under her chin and pulled up her coat collar. The wind was bitter as it came off the sea, and the bay didn't look its best with huge coils of barbed wire barring the way to the mined beach, but Peggy was warm in the new coat her husband Jim had given her for her forty-fourth birthday, and happy to have this moment of solitude as she drank in the view and let her thoughts drift.

Cliffehaven had been a popular seaside resort before the war, its hotels and guest houses full of visitors, with music and dancing on the pier and hundreds strolling along the promenade. Peggy had lived here all her life, taking over the running of Beach View when her parents retired some years ago. She had seen many changes over that time, but these long months of war had brought the greatest, and she wondered if the town could ever return to how it had once been.

The grand old hotels still graced the seafront, even though they bore the scars of enemy bullets and the general carelessness of the soldiers and Allied servicemen billeted there. The smaller boarding houses and Victorian villas still perched on the hills that sloped right down to the promenade, but there were gaps between them now. The High Street had fared no better, for shops and offices had been turned to rubble, the railway station was reduced to a shell, and the slum housing behind it had been obliterated during that terrible night at the end of December.

Peggy didn't want to dwell on the horrors, and she turned her attention back to the view. The shingled bay curved between tall chalk cliffs to the east and rolling hills to the west, the town nestling amid those hills and spreading out with new factories and hastily built emergency accommodation for those who'd been bombed out. Beyond the town and hidden from view amid the hills was a Canadian army camp, and an all-but-abandoned First World War American airbase. This base was home to a handful of American pilots and engineers who could often be seen about the town, using their heavy machinery to help shore up toppling houses or clear the debris following a raid – but everyone knew they would have preferred to be flying alongside the RAF boys, and their frustration at not being a part of things often led to trouble at closing time.

To the far north lay the extended runways, Nissen huts and hangars of Cliffe airbase, which had become strategically more important as the war went on, and therefore a prime enemy target. This airbase was where Peggy's son-in-law, Martin, flew his Spitfire, and where her youngest daughter, Cissy, now worked as a secretary. They'd both sustained injuries in a particularly vicious raid before Christmas, but thankfully had fully recovered.

Peggy gave a deep sigh as she regarded the beach where she'd played as a child, and where she'd taken her own children to paddle in the sea and hunt for treasures in the rock pools. It didn't look at all inviting now. Concrete shipping traps were dotted across the bay, and ugly gun emplacements were positioned all along the promenade. The entrance to the pier had been blown up so it stood marooned in the water, and noxious dark clumps of oil and tar came in with every tide to cling to the iron footings and lie amid the pebbles. Thousands of tons of shipping had been sunk in the Channel over the past year, and the tar was a tragic reminder of how many had lost their lives.

She shook off these dark thoughts, determined not to spoil these precious few minutes by dwelling on the awfulness of war, and turned her attention to the white cliffs which loomed over the sadly depleted fishing fleet anchored on the shingle. Her father-in-law, Ron, had come from a long line of fishermen, and had run several boats and crews down on that beach before he retired and came to live in the basement of Beach View Boarding House. His eldest son, Frank, had continued the family tradition with his own three sons until the outbreak of war. Now that the boys had enlisted into the Royal Naval Reserve as minesweeper captains, Frank was the only Reilly who still fished off these shores.

Peggy's thoughts drifted from Ron and Frank to her husband, Jim, Ron's youngest son. She gave a wry smile. She'd married Jim during the last war despite her parents' disapproval, and was as much in love with him today as she had been then. Contrary to all the warnings that he was a rogue and a fly-by-night, their marriage was still a happy one – but the depth of that contentment depended largely upon what sort of mischief Jim had been up to.

There had been moments when she could have killed him – when she'd thought his flirtatious ways had led him to being unfaithful – and moments when she'd adored him, and could forgive him almost anything. She'd had to accept that Jim Reilly would always have an eye for an attractive woman and a dodgy deal, and it had taken all her determination and love to keep him on the straight and narrow. Somehow, they had survived, and would soon celebrate their twenty-fifth wedding anniversary, and be further blessed with the birth of their first grandchild.

Peggy snuggled into her coat, warmed by the excitement of this new arrival. Anne and Martin lived in a tiny hamlet to the north of Cliffehaven, but she would be coming home to Beach View Boarding House the following day to be nearer to the doctor's surgery and spend the last two weeks of her pregnancy with her family. Everything was prepared for this momentous occasion, right down to the refurbishment of the old pram which had stood at the back of the shed ever since Peggy's two boys, Bob and Charlie, had grown out of it.

She blinked away the tears that always came when she thought about her two youngest. They were down in Somerset, and although she'd managed to go and see them over Christmas and found them sprouting up like weeds and clearly relishing life on a farm, she'd found it the hardest thing ever to leave them behind and still missed them horribly.

This damned war had a lot to answer to, for not only were her boys happily growing up without her, but Anne had to watch and wait and worry over Martin, who was in charge of a Spitfire squadron; Cissy risked life and limb working on that same airbase, and Jim and Ron had discovered the far-too-tempting opportunities of the black market. And, as if she didn't have enough to worry about, there was also the elderly Mrs Finch, the two young nurses and Rita to take care of.

Peggy watched the seagulls dip and swoop and hover, their haunting cries carried on the wind. She smiled with soft affection as she thought about her 'chicks'. Fran and Suzy had come to live at Beach View shortly after the outbreak of war. Fran was from Ireland, and the livelier of the two, but Suzy happily accompanied her friend on their few hours away from the hospital, and they both lived life to the full, taking advantage of the numerous parties and dances laid on to entertain the sudden influx of servicemen.

Rita was a few years younger and just as lively, for if she wasn't driving fire engines about, she was charging around on her motorbike, organising impromptu races on the abandoned dirt-track circuit at the back of the new factories. These races had become so popular among the servicemen that she'd had to limit the number of entries, but all the money she made through this enterprise was handed over to charity.

Rita was a local girl whose mother had died some years ago, and whose father had enlisted as an engineer on an airbase somewhere up north. She was one of Cissy's friends who'd been a frequent visitor before the war, so when she'd been bombed out, it seemed only right she should make her home at Beach View.

Peggy's oldest 'chick' was Mrs Finch. No one knew quite how old Cordelia was, but although she was frail and birdlike, and twittered on like a demented sparrow, she'd proved to be as stalwart and strong as the best of them. Nothing much seemed to get her down, but being as deaf as a post was a saving grace during air raids, for she could switch off her rather useless old hearing aid and snore through the whole thing to her heart's content.

Mrs Finch was a widow and had moved into Beach View several years ago. Her sons had migrated to Canada after the First War and seemed to have forgotten her, but she'd found her niche with Peggy's family and had become an intrinsic part of it. With the war on and a house full of young people, she'd found new purpose in life. This sustaining discovery gave her the vim and vigour of a much younger woman, and she'd taken on some of the household chores with relish.

She adored Ron and Jim, and would often get as flustered as a young girl when they tried their Irish charm on her. But she knew blarney when she heard it, and had soon got their measure, often being one step ahead of them, her salient advice rescuing them from several close calls with the law. The girls all thought of her as a grandmother, telling her their woes as they helped unravel her knitting, treated her to a new hairdo, or took her to see the latest Hollywood musical at the cinema.

'Yes,' muttered Peggy, 'we've all been blessed by Cordelia's presence.'

She shivered as the chill finally got to her, and decided she'd sat here long enough. There were things to do at home if everyone was going to eat tonight. Having retrieved her bicycle, she pedalled along the seafront, the wind buffeting her and tearing at her headscarf.

The basket Ron had fixed to the handlebars shuddered as the wheels ran over the uneven surface, making her handbag and gas-mask box dance about. She eyed her handbag fretfully, hoping the surprise she'd hidden in there would survive the journey. It had been quite a feat to get it, had cost rather more than she'd expected and would probably not be well received – but she hoped everyone would come to appreciate its benefits.

It was a steep climb from the seafront as Peggy headed towards Beach View Terrace, and she was huffing and puffing like an old steam train by the time she'd gone three blocks and reached Camden Road, which stretched off to her left.

Camden Road ran parallel to the seafront and was the flatter route home from the High Street, but now and again Peggy needed to see the sea and let the salty wind blow away the cobwebs. However, it was tougher going when the wind blew this hard, and she had to stop a minute and get her breath back.

Her gaze travelled over the few shops where she'd registered for her rations and past Ron's favourite pub, the Anchor, to the distant bulk of the clothing factory, the fire station, and the grey stone walls of the sprawling hospital. There had once been a primary school in Camden Road where Anne had taught, but it had been flattened during a bombing raid early on in the war. Mercifully it had been at night and no one had been killed, but it had been the deciding factor when it had come to the safety of Bob and Charlie, which was why they were now living in Somerset.

Peggy took a deep breath and pushed the bicycle across the road and into Beach View Terrace. A gas explosion had destroyed the two houses at the far end and she still found the gap they'd left quite disturbing, but the rest of the terrace of Victorian villas had survived with only a few scars to mark the enemy's passing.

Beach View Boarding House rose three storeys above the pavement, with concrete steps shadowing the basement window as they led to a pillared portico and rather battered front door. There had once been ornate lamps at the bottom of the steps and stained-glass windows on either side of the door, but they'd been blown to smithereens during a raid. The front door was second-hand, and the only thing that had survived the blast was the brass lion's-head knocker which she polished every morning.

Many of the windows had been reglazed and heavily taped to protect them from further blasts, but one or two of the panes had had to be boarded over. There was only so much money to spend, and it would cost a fortune to keep buying new windows when the Luftwaffe would only wreck them again.

Peggy hoisted the bike up the stairs and opened the front door. She was greeted by a delicious smell of cooking, which made her mouth water in anticipation, but as she wheeled the bike into the kitchen, it was to find it strangely deserted.

A glance out of the window told her the reason why. Ron and Mrs Finch were in the vegetable plot having an argument. Or at least, Ron was doing all the arguing, for Mrs Finch had clearly switched off her hearing aid and was ignoring him as his face went puce and his bushy eyebrows waggled in frustration. While this was going on, Ron's dog, Harvey, was rummaging through the compost heap to find the best and smelliest place to have an ecstatic and leisurely roll.

Peggy gave a sigh of despair that was tinged with loving acceptance. Ron and his dog were alike in many ways and rarely seen apart. Harvey was a lurcher, a shaggy-haired Bedlington–greyhound cross with a mind of his own and a prodigious talent for hunting and sniffing out anything that was buried. Ron was a disreputable, shaggy old rogue who liked nothing better than to go poaching on Lord Cliffe's vast estate. They both seemed to relish getting as dirty as possible and couldn't seem to understand that Peggy didn't appreciate them tramping their muck into her house.

And yet Harvey and Ron had earned themselves quite a reputation during the past year, for not only had they rescued an injured pilot and brought him safely down from the hills during an air raid, but they had also managed to find and rescue scores of people trapped beneath their ruined homes and businesses.

Peggy chuckled as she carried the bike down into the basement where Ron and Harvey shared a bedroom next to the scullery. Harvey would probably come tearing into her nice clean kitchen stinking of old cabbage and rotten potato peel, and Ron would follow with muddy boots, his long poaching coat stuffed with ill-gotten gains and still reeking of the two ferrets he'd once carried in one of the many inside pockets. They were both a pain in the neck, and tried her patience to the limit, but she couldn't imagine this house without them.

She glanced into Ron's room, saw the unmade bed, the dirty clothes piled on the floor, the guns and fishing rods leaning against the wall and the line of boots. She gave up any thought of clearing the mess today and closed the door on it all. It was bad enough the old man shared his bed with his dog, but at least he no longer had his smelly old ferrets tucked away in cages beneath her scullery sink.

After a fleeting glance into the room her two young sons had once shared, she closed the door on that too. It had merely become a hidey-hole for the rest of Ron's clutter, and the sight of those abandoned bunk beds made her heartsick. Climbing back up the basement steps into the kitchen, she took off her coat, gloves and scarf, placed the small package on the table, and reached for her wrap-round pinafore.

Ron must have gone down to the fishing station earlier, for Mrs Finch had made one of her delicious fish pies, and the potato topping was browning nicely in the oven. Peggy put the kettle on top of the range and sat down, feeling rather out of sorts.

Perhaps the chill wind had got to her; perhaps it was the spam sandwich she'd had for lunch – or more likely, she was just overtired and feeling her age.

She lit a cigarette and, with a sigh of pleasure, took in her surroundings. She loved this room, for although it was shabby, it was the heart of her home and she wouldn't have changed a thing. The lino was as faded and worn as the oilcloth that covered the big wooden table, and the furniture had been here since she was a child. The window was set above the stone sink and wooden draining board, and looked over the back garden to the lines of terraced villas that climbed the hill behind them.

Below the sink, a faded gingham curtain hid the bucket, dustpan, packets of soap powder and all the other paraphernalia that was needed to keep a house clean. A line of shelves held mismatched crockery; cooking pots hung over the black Kitchener range which stood in the chimney breast; and ration books, photographs, lists and general clutter filled the narrow mantelpiece below the framed photograph of the King and Queen which had been carefully cut from a magazine. The wireless stood on the chest of drawers where she kept her best linen, and two armchairs stood on either side of the range offering comfort and warmth on cold, dark winter nights.

The back door burst open and before Peggy could

shout a warning, Harvey was bounding into the room, tongue lolling, ears flapping, tail going like a windmill as he placed his great muddy paws on her knees and tried to climb onto her lap.

'It's nice to see you too, Harvey,' she said as she wrinkled her nose and tried to push him off. 'But you're filthy and far too big to sit on my lap.'

'Get down, you eejit dog,' rumbled Ron as he plodded into the kitchen in his muddy wellingtons. 'Is it stupid you are? You'll flatten Peggy, so you will.'

Harvey took no notice and continued to clamber, his tongue lapping at Peggy's face and hands as she tried desperately to get rid of him.

'Harvey!' shouted Ron. 'Will ye listen? Down. Now.'

Harvey's ears went back and he tucked his tail between his legs as he reluctantly headed for the range and plonked down in front of it with a much put-upon sigh. Resting his nose on his dirty paws, he eyed them both as if he'd been whipped.

Nobody took a blind bit of notice, for this was a well-worn act and they weren't fooled for a minute.

'Never mind that dog. I need a hand up these steps.'

Ron turned back to Mrs Finch and carefully steadied her as she reached the top step, swaying rather alarmingly and threatening to fall backwards. 'To be sure you're swaying well,' he said. 'Are you sure you've not been hitting the hard stuff while me back's been turned?'

Mrs Finch tugged at her hat and fiddled with her hearing aid. 'I'm paying the going rate,' she said stiffly, 'and I don't need you to tell me it's hard enough even if your back is burned. Though how you did that, I have no idea.' She gave him a look that would have stopped a rampaging bull in its tracks.

That look had absolutely no effect on Ron. He grinned, his eyes twinkling beneath the shaggy brows. 'To be sure, ye're a caution, Mrs Finch.'

'And you're a rogue and a scoundrel,' she retorted, her own grey eyes gleaming with humour as she pulled off her hat and coat. 'Now get out of my way and let me sit down. Arguing half the afternoon with you has quite exhausted me.'

She plumped into a chair and smiled sweetly at Peggy. 'I've been gardening,' she said, 'but Ron seems to think he knows it all and won't take any advice from me.' She shot him an impish glance. 'Silly old fool,' she added quietly.

'I heard that,' muttered Ron. 'And don't call me old – I'm at least ten years younger than you, and know more about onions than you ever will.'

Mrs Finch spread her hands and shrugged. 'See what I mean?' she said to Peggy. 'That's so typical of a man. Won't listen to anything I have to say and changes the subject to his bunions.'

Ron muttered something under his breath as he stripped off his heavy coat and kicked off his boots.

'What's that? Do speak up, Ron.' She fiddled with her hearing aid and made it whine horribly.

'To be sure, there's little point in wasting me breath,' he said, the twinkle still evident in his eyes. 'You don't hear half of what I say – and ignore the rest.'

Peggy stubbed out her cigarette and made a pot of tea. This sparring could go on for hours. As she placed the cup in front of Mrs Finch, she also pushed the package towards her. 'I bought you a little something,' she said.

Mrs Finch brightened considerably. 'Oh, how lovely. I do like presents. What is it?' She plucked at the brown paper to reveal a small box.

'It's a practical thing and not very pretty,' Peggy warned quickly, not wanting her to be disappointed. 'But I think you'll find it's just what you need.'

Mrs Finch frowned. 'Practical and gritty and going to seed? It doesn't sound very nice at all.' She eyed the plain brown box suspiciously, and then lifted the lid. There was a long moment of silence before she closed the box and pushed it back over the table. 'I don't need that,' she said firmly.

'It will help you to hear better,' said Peggy, pushing it back.

'It came with a letter?' Mrs Finch looked round the table. 'Where is it? I can't see it.'

Peggy took the new hearing aid out of the box and held it in the palm of her hand. 'Why don't you just try it?' she coaxed loudly. 'Then if you really don't want it, I'll take it back.'

Mrs Finch looked daggers at Peggy, but curiosity won her over and she removed her old hearing aid reluctantly and placed it on the table. Eyeing the new one, she sniffed. 'It doesn't look up to much,' she muttered. 'Newfangled nonsense.' She looked back at Peggy and gave a deep sigh. 'Go on then, but hurry up. My tea's getting cold.'

Peggy quickly fitted it the way the doctor had taught her, carefully adjusting the sound to one of the lower levels.

'I can't hear a blessed thing,' Mrs Finch complained. 'Damned contraption's useless.'

'How about that?' Peggy slowly and carefully turned up the volume as she continued speaking. 'Tell me when you can hear what I'm saying, Mrs Finch, because I don't want to damage your eardrums by turning it up too—'

'Good heavens, dear, there's no need to shout,' protested Mrs Finch.

Peggy hadn't been shouting at all, which meant the thing was working very well indeed. She turned down the volume just a couple of notches. 'Is that better?' she asked.

'Well, of course it is,' Mrs Finch grumbled. 'I'm not that deaf, you know.'

'Not now you've got a nice new hearing aid that works properly,' murmured Peggy with a gentle smile.

Mrs Finch drank down her tea and clattered the cup in the saucer. She regarded the china for a moment and then her eyes widened and she looked around the room. 'Good heavens,' she breathed. 'I can hear the clock ticking and a robin singing outside – and I can hear Harvey snoring and Ron sniggering.'

She turned and glared at Ron, who was trying to look innocent as he sipped his tea. 'Don't slurp your tea like that,' she scolded. 'It's most impolite.'

'You have no idea what you've done, Peggy,' muttered Ron. 'There'll be no escaping her now, to be sure.'

'There certainly will not,' said Mrs Finch with a beaming smile. 'Now, if you've quite finished complaining, I'd like another cup of tea.'

The last six weeks had been fraught with grief and anxiety, and if it hadn't been for Matron, Julie would simply have crawled under the bed-covers and shut out the world. Matron Starkey had been sympathetic and kind, helping to arrange a post for her in Cliffehaven even though she didn't approve of Julie taking on William. But she'd known that Julie needed to be fully occupied while she waited for William to become strong enough to travel, and had set out a hectic schedule which gave her little time to think, let alone dwell on her loss. Julie had willingly plunged into the work, grateful for Matron's wisdom, and the chance to make amends for her forthcoming departure.

Julie had arranged the funeral so that Franny could be buried with their parents. Somehow she had managed to attend the service, drink tea and talk to the many surviving neighbours who'd turned up, while all she could think of was the sight of those coffins being lowered into the ground. She'd returned to work that same evening, unable to bear the thought of sitting still.

There had been no sign of Stan since that awful scene, and no acknowledgement that he'd received the engagement ring in the post. She was a little piqued that he hadn't even tried to mend fences, but at the same time rather relieved he hadn't come round to the hostel making a nuisance of himself. There could never be any going back, not now she realised what a lucky escape she'd had.

Her letters to Bill's family remained unanswered and she knew now that they would never accept William. The continued silence from Bill himself was unsettling, and she wondered if her letter had got through, or if, like his family, he'd decided to abandon the baby. And yet she couldn't believe that of him. She wanted to keep faith that his silence was only the result of the erratic postal system, and that he'd write as soon as he could – perhaps even be granted compassionate leave.

Her three brothers had written back, devastated by all that had happened and promising to visit her the minute they got leave. Each letter had contained a money order to help pay for the funeral and a decent wake, but all three of them advised her to have William fostered until more suitable arrangements could be made.

It seemed no one understood how important William had become to her, and how impossible it would be to break her promise and give him over to strangers. He was an enchanting child, with his mother's sweet smile and fair hair, and his father's wide-spaced eyes. She'd visited him every day, feeding him, changing him, growing more in love with him as he gained weight and gurgled happily in her arms. She could no more give him up now than fly to the moon.

Julie lay in bed on that last morning in London and waited for the others to wake. They'd had a bit of a farewell party the night before, sharing a couple of bottles of sherry and a midnight feast of spam sandwiches and tinned fruit, and she suspected there would be one or two thick heads this morning. She rested peacefully, listening to the sound of the other girls muttering and snoring. She would miss their friendship and company, the daily round and the evenings spent shedding the cares of that day and feeling young and carefree again.

As the doubts crowded in and the sheer magnitude of what she was about to embark upon set her nerves jangling, Julie threw back the covers. Her bags were already packed and waiting beneath the bed. One was full of baby clothes, nappies and spare feeding bottles, the other held her own few clothes, her mother's knitted blanket, and the few treasured bits and pieces she'd taken from Franny's room.

Her gaze fell on the navy blue dress which she'd carefully placed over the back of the bedside chair. It was her mother's dress which she'd rescued from the ruins, and after it had been washed, ironed and mended, it had come up almost as good as when Flo had last worn it. Julie had decided not to pack it away, for not only was it a symbol of all she'd lost, it was an intrinsic part of her old life and she felt it was important to wear it today as she stepped into the new.

She carefully gathered it up and tiptoed to the bathroom. The bell would go soon and all would be chaos and noise, and she needed these few moments alone to prepare for the emotional goodbyes, and the long journey ahead.

Breakfast was over and everyone was preparing to get on with their day. Julie was already beginning to feel distanced from them as they chattered and bustled and wished her good luck before they hurried off on their rounds, and she was torn between wanting to stay, and knowing it would be impossible.

'Ne'er you mind, me luvver,' soothed Alison in her West Country burr. 'You'm be better down there with them southerners. Mind how you'm be goin' and if you'm don't tek to 'em, you be back 'ere dreckly.'

Julie returned her hug, the tears welling. 'I'll write, I promise,' she murmured.

'Dreckly then,' Alison replied, waving goodbye as she crashed out of the back door.

'I'm going to miss all of you so much,' choked Julie through the lump in her throat.

'And we're going to miss you and all,' said Doris and Ida in unison.

'Mind 'ow you go down there, gel,' added Doris, giving her a hug. 'And if you get the chance, send us a stick of rock. I ain't never been to the seaside.'

Julie swallowed the lump in her throat. 'I doubt they do sticks of rock in wartime,' she managed.

Ida blew her nose. 'It don't matter, really,' she said, her voice thick with unshed tears. 'Just send us a postcard now and again to let us know yer all right.'

Julie gave each of them another hug and they hurried away. She turned to Lily, who was trying her best not to cry. 'I'll come back as soon as I can,' she promised.

Lily forced a wobbly smile. 'I know yer will, but it ain't gunna be the same round 'ere without yer, Jules. I wish I were coming too.'

'There's nothing to stop you,' she replied as they hugged, 'but you'd hate leaving London – you know you would.'

Lily nodded. She'd never ventured far from the Thames, and had no real desire to go further. 'I can 'ear Matron coming down the stairs,' she said urgently, her gaze flitting towards the door. 'Good luck, Jules.' She flung her arms round Julie and they held each other tightly before Lily tore herself away and raced off.

Matron Starkey strode into the room, her gimlet gaze following the flutter of Lily's skirt as she disappeared into the sluice. 'Are you sure I can't change your mind, Sister Harris?' As Julie shook her head she gave a sigh of weary acceptance. 'Your work here has been exemplary,' she said, 'and I'm sure I speak for all of us when I say you will be sorely missed.'

Julie dipped her chin, worried that Matron would see her tears as a sign that her resolve was weakening.

'I have your rail pass here and a letter of introduction to give to Dr Sayers, who is the senior partner in the medical practice.' Matron handed over two envelopes. 'I have not mentioned the child,' she added. 'That is for you to do.'

'Thank you so much for arranging it all, Matron,' said Julie. 'I won't let you down, I promise.'

Matron's expression softened. 'I know you won't, my dear.' She drew a sharp breath. 'Oh, I almost forgot. This came for you earlier.'

Julie took the garishly coloured postcard which showed a pre-war Cliffehaven promenade and crowded pier. Eileen's message was short, to the point, and lacked even a shred of emotion.

Dear Julie,

I regret I could not attend the funeral, but my important work here prevents me from leaving Cliffehaven.

Regards, Eileen.

Julie slipped it into her coat pocket. It might have been cold-blooded and terse, but at least it proved Eileen hadn't left Cliffehaven. She said goodbye to Matron, picked up her cases, gas-mask box and handbag, and left the hostel for the last time.

Chapter Seven

Peggy finished the washing-up and put away the breakfast dishes while Mrs Finch and Anne read the morning newspapers, which miraculously were still delivered come rain, shine, bomb blast or air raid. It was the same with the milk, and the sound of the milkman's horse clip-clopping down the street in the early mornings was comforting – a reminder of calmer, more peaceful days.

Rita, Fran and Suzy had left for work, Jim was having a bit of a lie-in after doing a long stint of fire-watching with the Home Guard, and Ron had taken Harvey up into the hills to see what he could find for the pot. No doubt Lord Cliffe would be minus a few of his game birds before evening, and Peggy just hoped Ron wouldn't get caught.

She sipped her cup of tea and stood gazing out of the kitchen window. The back garden was long and narrow with a flint wall at the end which had been knocked about a bit during the many air raids. The gate led to a narrow alleyway that ran between the backs of the houses and petered out into a muddy track which meandered up the hills to the brow of the cliffs and beyond. Near the house,

Peggy's washing line was strung between the neighbouring fences, while further down, Ron's vegetable plot was just beginning to show some new green shoots beyond the row of leeks. Huddled at the bottom of the garden was the Anderson shelter, its roof covered in turfs, the corrugated iron already showing signs of rust.

There was a path leading from the basement door past the coal bunker, shed and outside lav, through the vegetable plot and on to the back gate. Ron and Jim had fixed up a chicken run beside the shed to accommodate the few hens they'd been given by some grateful Australians. Those hens had proved to be good layers and didn't seem to mind the air raids any more at all. Peggy smiled. It seemed chickens were as good at adapting to things as humans.

'What are you grinning about, Mum?'

Peggy turned and put her arm round Anne's thickened waist. 'I was just thinking how lucky we are to have fresh eggs for breakfast – and what fun it was to have those Australians come to tea.'

Anne smiled back, her lovely face rosy with health, her dark hair shining. 'It was quite a party, wasn't it? Though I seem to remember Joe Buchanan caused a fearful row between Cissy and June. What happened to June, by the way? Is she still nursing at the hospital with Fran and Suzy?'

Peggy hadn't told anyone but Jim about finding June in their bed with a young soldier. She'd thrown her out, bag and baggage. 'She went to live in the nurses' home for a bit,' she said flatly, 'but Fran told me she'd decided to get a nursing post in Leicester to be nearer her family.' And good riddance to bad rubbish, she added silently.

Anne regarded her thoughtfully. 'I get the feeling there was more to it than that,' she said, 'but she's gone now, so I don't suppose it matters. Does Joe still write to Cissy?'

Peggy finished her tea. 'Now and again,' she said, 'but I think they both realise it was just a heat of the moment thing. They'd known each other less than twenty-four hours when he was posted abroad, hardly long enough for it to be a grand romance.'

Anne tucked her glossy black hair behind her ears. 'Poor Cissy, she's such a romantic. It must have felt as if she was in some sweeping drama – the handsome soldier off to war, the girl left behind to pine for him.'

'I expect she did see it that way. You know Cissy, always theatrical. At least she's not prancing about on some draughty stage any more, and actually doing something sensible for a change.'

'Martin says she works jolly hard,' said Anne, easing her back. 'She's quite surprised him.'

Peggy rinsed her cup and set it on the draining board. 'It's probably all for the best,' she said, returning to the subject of Joe Buchanan. 'Joe was a nice boy, but after the war he'll be going back to the cattle farm in Australia, and I can't see Cissy riding the range and branding steers like they do in the westerns – can you?'

Anne laughed. 'Not for a minute. She might chip her nail varnish, and she couldn't cope with that.' She ran her hands over her prodigious bump. 'I think I'll have a bath now the house is quiet. Is there enough hot water, do you think?'

Peggy cupped her daughter's cheek in the palm of her hand. 'Have my share,' she said softly. 'And enjoy a good long soak while you can.'

Anne gave her a gentle hug. 'It's rather nice not having the house so full – it gives us time to be a family again.'

'I was thinking the same thing earlier. But I do feel rather mean not letting out those two spare rooms. There are so many poor souls camped out at the Town Hall.'

'Bless you, Mum,' sighed Anne. 'If it bothers you that much, then telephone Kath at the billeting office. I can always move into the smaller double room and—'

'You're not moving anywhere,' Peggy interrupted. 'That front bedroom is the nicest in the house and I've spent ages making it just right for you and the baby.' She took her daughter's hands. 'I've decided I won't take anyone else in until you're back on your feet and ready to go home to that lovely little cottage of yours.'

Anne giggled. 'If you say so, Mum. But I know

you – one waif or stray, one sob story, and you'll cave in as you always do.'

Peggy shook her head. 'Not this time, Anne,' she said firmly. 'I want to enjoy my grandchild and to look after you both while I have the chance. Those rooms will stay empty.'

Julie hadn't realised how crowded the station would be on a Saturday morning, or how difficult it was to manage two cases, handbag, gas-mask box and a squalling baby. She had considered buying a perambulator, but she'd seen how many had had to be abandoned by the East End women as they'd hurried to get their little ones out of London to the relative safety of the countryside. These prams were coach built, sturdy carriages that took up too much room, and although they were useful for carrying children and baggage, they simply couldn't be accommodated on the packed trains.

Having made a sort of sling to carry William so her hands were free, she managed to find a kindly porter who'd helped load her cases into the guard's van and then found her a window seat.

As the train pulled out of the station, William began to squirm and whimper, his little fists waving furiously as his cries grew ever louder and more demanding.

But gas-mask boxes had their uses, and Julie had filled a thermos with warmed formula milk and packed a spare bottle alongside it. As the train rattled and jolted towards Cliffehaven she carefully poured some formula into the bottle, and began to feed him. Blessed silence fell, and there was a grateful sigh from the other passengers in her carriage.

'Lively little one, isn't he?' said the rather sturdy woman in the unflattering brown tweed suit who was sitting opposite her.

'His routine's been disturbed,' said Julie, giving her a smile. 'He'll go to sleep once he's finished his bottle.' She softly ran her fingers over William's downy head as his eyelids fluttered.

The woman's gaze drifted to Julie's hand, settling momentarily on the absence of any wedding ring. 'Are you taking him to his mother?' she asked. 'Does she live in Cliffehaven?'

There was something rather unpleasant in the woman's eyes and Julie didn't appreciate being given the third degree. 'His mother's dead,' she said flatly.

The woman reddened. 'Oh, I see,' she murmured. 'How very tragic.'

Julie didn't bother to ease her embarrassment; she was a nosy old biddy and didn't deserve it. She looked down at William, saw he was almost asleep, and tucked the empty feeding bottle back into the gas-mask box. With a clean piece of muslin to protect her coat, she hitched William up to her shoulder and gently rubbed his back to get rid of any wind.

William obliged with a rip-roaring burp that elicited smiles from one or two of the other female passengers, and Julie kissed his head. He was fast asleep, lulled by warm milk and the rocking of the train.

The woman in the ugly tweed suit was now rather pointedly reading her Agatha Christie paperback, and Julie turned to look out of the window.

They had left the suburbs of London some time ago, and now they were trundling through small country towns and neat little villages which seemed to be slumbering beneath the clear blue sky. She could see rolling green hills in the distance, grazing cattle, ploughed fields, farmhouses and barns. She caught glimpses of rabbits and the bright plumage of exotic-looking birds as they rose squawking from the dark woods, their long tail-feathers trailing. She leaned forward and watched some land girls guiding a plodding carthorse across a grassy field, the dray loaded with tree trunks. They stopped for a moment and waved to the train before returning to their labours.

Julie smiled as she waved back. The scene reminded her of her childhood when the family used to go hop picking. They'd slept in barns, eaten delicious meals that had been cooked on braziers outside, and had played until the sun went down. She'd turned as brown as a berry by the end of those two weeks, and could still remember how she'd snuggled up to Franny under the blanket, their mattress of straw prickling their skin as they listened to the grown-ups singing and chattering. Her father had loved a good sing-song.

She blinked away the tears and shifted William to her other arm. It was lovely to have such precious memories, but the pain of loss was still too raw, and it often caught her unawares.

The train whistle blew and the smoke from the funnel drifted past the window as they chugged past rivers and streams and huge tracts of wild, deserted marshland where startled birds of all kinds rose from the reed beds and long grass to wheel and flutter before settling again.

Julie took the postcard out of her pocket and read Eileen's brief message. It had been sent a week ago, long after her own letter must have arrived, and far too late for her to write back and tell Eileen she was coming to Cliffehaven with William. What sort of woman was she to be untouched by such a tragedy – and how would she react when Julie turned up on her doorstep? It was a worry, and, as the train puffed closer to Cliffehaven, that worry was growing.

Julie put the postcard back in her pocket and hitched William onto her shoulder. He didn't weigh very much, but after a while he felt quite heavy. He grumbled a bit and squirmed, so she softly stroked his head and back until he settled again.

Her thoughts turned back to Eileen, remembering her as a rather pretty girl, with light brown hair and brown eyes, who jealously guarded her few bits of make-up and her best clothes and shoes from her much younger sisters. Eileen had been old enough to go out with boys, and Julie and Franny had been rather in awe of her, and would watch wide-eyed as she left the house with yet another admirer, swaying down the street in her high heels and best frock. They would have loved to have tried on her clothes and experimented with her powder and lipstick, but after an unfortunate incident involving a pair of high-heeled shoes, they hadn't dared.

Julie smiled at the memory, even though she hadn't thought it very funny at the time. She'd been about five or six, and had sneaked the shoes out of the cupboard. They were lovely shoes, with high heels and a pretty blue bow on the toes, but of course they'd been far too big and she'd clattered and scraped her way out into the backyard and promptly got the heel caught in a grating.

She'd tugged and tugged and the heel broke just at the moment Eileen had come home from the tool factory where she'd worked as a typist. Eileen had clipped her round the ear before going inside to complain loudly to their mother, who'd given her another clip and sent her to bed without tea.

Eileen had left not long after that, and Julie had wondered at the time if it had been her fault. Flo had convinced her it wasn't, but Julie had remained puzzled to this day. She leaned her head back against the white antimacassar and pondered on what she might find at the end of this journey. Was Eileen married, or living alone? Did she really have no regrets that her parents and sister had died without her seeing them since that day? And what did she look like now – would she even recognise her after all these years?

She tried not to let these thoughts niggle at her and was actually dozing off when she felt the almost imperceptible slowing of the train. Opening her eyes, she saw they were travelling through a cutting with high grassy banks on either side. The skeletons of ruined buildings rose from piles of rubble, and a brick wall that had once run along the top of the embankment had a gaping hole in it. Cliffehaven was clearly not as safe as she'd once thought, and she began to have serious doubts about whether she should ever have come.

There was a flurry of activity as the other passengers in her carriage closed books and newspapers and began to haul their suitcases down from the overhead racks. Julie remained seated as the others pulled on coats and gloves and headed for the corridor. As this was the end of the line, there was no point in getting caught in the crush, but it was her reluctance to face her sister that really held her back.

The carriage cleared quickly, and she tamped down on the doubts. Gathering up her handbag and gas-mask box, she settled the sleeping William comfortably in his sling and stepped down from the train. It was far too late to change her mind; she had to see this through and make the best of whatever awaited her.

The guard's van was right at the back, but a dear

old porter offered to collect her two large bags, and once they were safely loaded onto his trolley, he slowly led the way across the concourse and out to the street.

'There's no taxis,' he said, 'but the trolleybus stop is just down there.' He pointed down the hill where the long High Street seemed to run right to the seafront.

'I'm going to Camden Road,' she said. 'Is it far?'

He tipped back his peaked hat to reveal a shock of white hair and regarded her thoughtfully. 'Down past the Town Hall and cinema, then left after that big bomb crater,' he murmured. 'It's a fair way to carry that lot, what with the baby and all. You'd be best off leaving the bags here until you're settled. They'll be quite safe in left luggage.'

Julie realised it was good advice and, after unpacking a few necessities for William and stuffing them into her large handbag, she watched the old man stow her cases. 'Thanks ever so,' she said, giving him a penny tip.

He tugged his cap, slipping the coin into his trouser pocket, his gaze openly curious. 'Visiting from London, are you?'

She smiled at him. 'I'm a midwife, and start work on Monday for Doctor Sayers.' She saw him glance at William and realised this conversation could go on at length if she didn't get a move on. 'Thanks again,' she said brightly, and turned away, heading down the steep hill towards the sea.

So, this is Cliffehaven, she thought as she passed the long queues outside the butcher's and grocer's and carefully navigated the broken paving slabs and huge walls of sandbags that protected the Town Hall entrance. The air was clean after the smog and dust of London, with a tang of salt on the chill breeze. Seagulls screeched and soared against the cloudless blue sky, and the glimpse of sea at the bottom of the hill was tantalising.

Julie eased the sling round her neck, hitched the straps of her handbag and gas-mask box over her shoulder and resisted the temptation to explore the seafront. William would wake soon and need feeding and changing, and despite the bright sun, it was too cold to hang about.

Cliffehaven had obviously suffered in the bombing, for there were large piles of rubble between the shops, and the skeletons of once grand buildings stood open to the elements. Julie walked past the early matinee queue that stretched along the pavement outside the Odeon cinema. Fred Astaire was obviously as popular here as he was in London, and she felt a pang of homesickness as she remembered the old Galaxy where she and Lily would go when time allowed.

Determined not to think about her life in London, or to dwell too long on the rising doubts, Julie hurried on until she reached the vast bomb crater on the corner of what must be the High Street and Camden Road. Running parallel to the seafront,

Camden Road stretched before her, and she began to regret wearing her high-heeled shoes, for they really weren't meant for walking such long distances. All she could hope for was that Eileen's flat wasn't at the far end.

She passed the fire station, where the bright red engines were being enthusiastically hosed down and polished to the accompaniment of dance music coming from a wireless. She reached Solomon and Goldman's factory just as the workers poured out on their lunch break, and had to wait for an ambulance to turn into the hospital entrance. It looked like a big hospital, and would surely have a maternity ward, and she wondered fleetingly why Matron hadn't applied for her to work there.

The Anchor pub was doing a roaring trade, the hubbub of voices almost drowning the efforts of the pianist, who seemed to have rather more enthusiasm than skill. Julie felt a deeper pang of homesickness this time, for although the Anchor bore little resemblance to the Toolmakers', the atmosphere and memories it evoked were all too painful. She took a deep breath, blinked back the tears and took note of the house numbers. There was a row of shops on either side of the road now, with doorways leading to the flats above.

She slowed and came to a halt outside a door sandwiched between the bakery and hardware shop. It looked as if it had been freshly painted, the brass fittings were polished to a gleam, and the single step was freshly scrubbed. Eileen might have left the East End far behind her, but she hadn't quite lost their mother's pride in keeping her home looking nice and neat.

Julie's mouth was dry and her pulse was racing as she reached for the door-knocker. Eileen might not be in – and even if she was, would she welcome her, or slam the door in her face? That postcard hadn't been at all encouraging, and she'd yet to tell Eileen about William. She banished the doubts and gave the knocker two determined raps. Having come this far, she couldn't fail now.

She stepped back as she heard footsteps coming down the stairs. William was, thankfully, still asleep, and looked very sweet wrapped in his sling. She just had to hope that Eileen thought the same.

The door opened to reveal a small, slender, dark-haired woman in her thirties, whose welcoming smile faltered as she regarded Julie. 'Yes?'

Julie's breath caught as she took in the flawless make-up and freshly set hairdo, the neat blouse and skirt, the high-heeled shoes and delicate stockings. There was little doubt this was Eileen, for she looked just like their mother. 'Hello, Eileen,' she said. 'It's me, Julie.'

'Good grief,' Eileen muttered, her gaze flitting towards the far end of the street before returning rather coolly to her sister. 'I wouldn't have recognised you from Adam. What on earth are you doing here?'

Julie swallowed. 'I start as district nurse and midwife at Cliffe surgery on Monday,' she replied, her hand protectively cupping William's bottom.

Eileen's brown eyes settled on William, and her expression hardened. 'Whose is that?' she asked almost accusingly.

'This is William,' Julie replied firmly. 'He's Franny's baby, and I'm looking after him until his father can get home.' She eased back the blanket and sling from his little face. 'Isn't he just beautiful?' she breathed.

'Very nice,' said Eileen.

Stung by her lack of admiration, Julie replaced the blanket over William's little head. This was going to be harder than she'd thought, but she ploughed on anyway, determined to break through her sister's frostiness. 'Do you think I could come in?' she asked pleasantly. 'Only I've just arrived from London and had to walk from the station. Me feet are killing me in these silly shoes.'

Eileen eyed the shoes. 'Nothing's changed there, then,' she muttered. She shot a glance at the bundle in Julie's arms and then grudgingly stepped aside. 'I'm going out later,' she warned, 'but I've got time to make a cup of tea, I suppose.'

She closed the door and led the way up a short flight of carpeted stairs to a square landing. Opening another door, she walked into a pleasant sitting room and pointed to an armchair. 'Sit down while I see if I have enough tea,' she ordered.

Julie sat down on the edge of the chair and held William to her heart. This had been a terrible mistake. She should never have come without thinking it through properly. Eileen was a cold fish, and although she might look like their mother, there was nothing of Flo's warmth and compassion in her.

Julie carefully slipped off her overcoat and looked round the neat, almost impersonal room. A table and two chairs were placed beneath the window, which had been taped against bomb-blast. The plain beige velvet curtains had been lined with blackout material and matched the armchair and couch which stood in front of a gas fire. There were no ornaments or photographs about the place, just a plain clock in a polished mahogany casing which sat squarely on the mantelpiece. A wireless stood in the corner, a mirror hung above the fire, and the niches on either side of the chimney breast had been lined with crammed bookshelves. The only luxury seemed to be the lovely Indian carpet that covered the polished floorboards almost to the walls.

William stirred in her arms, his little fists emerging from the blanket in search of his mouth, and Julie hoped there was enough milk left in the flask to satisfy him until she could collect her bags from the station and retrieve the tins of formula she'd been given by the hospital. She crooned softly to him and kissed the tiny fists, praying he wouldn't start yelling. Eileen clearly didn't possess a single maternal bone in her body, and it wouldn't do to antagonise her further.

Eileen came back into the room, carrying a tray loaded with china. 'I hope you're not expecting more than a biscuit,' she said. 'I've already had my lunch, and as I'm being taken out to supper tonight there isn't anything in the larder.'

Julie's stomach rumbled at the thought of food. 'A sandwich would be nice if you could spare it,' she said, 'but if it's too much trouble . . .'

'It is rather,' Eileen replied flatly. She poured the tea, put a digestive biscuit on the saucer and handed the cup to Julie. 'I'm a busy woman with little time to queue for bread, and I wasn't expecting visitors.'

Julie held onto her temper as she gratefully gulped down the tea and ate the biscuit. 'I'm hardly any old visitor,' she said mildly, 'and as your sister, I would have expected a warmer welcome.'

'You should have written and told me you were coming. That way, you'd have saved yourself a journey.' Eileen crossed her slender legs and tugged at the hem of her skirt as she eyed Julie and William with little emotion. 'You can't stay here,' she said. 'I only have one bedroom and I certainly don't want the inconvenience of a squalling baby to contend with.'

Shocked by her rudeness and lack of compassion, Julie stared at her. 'Why are you being like this,

Eileen? What's made you so . . . so cold? This is little Franny's precious baby, and now that Mum and Dad are gone, I thought . . .'

Eileen stared through the tape on the window at the rooftops opposite. 'I was sorry to hear about Mum and Dad – Franny, too. But it's been a long time, and too much water has passed under the bridge for me to get emotional over them.' She turned back to Julie, her expression unreadable. 'I suppose Mum told you why I had to leave?'

'Nobody said anything,' Julie replied. 'Whatever happened between you that day went with them to their graves.'

'Best it stays there then,' said Eileen. She finished her tea and glanced at her wristwatch. 'You said you're starting at the surgery on Monday, so I'm assuming you have made some sort of plan regarding your accommodation?'

'I was rather hoping we could stay with you and look after William together,' Julie replied, 'but obviously I was mistaken to think you might help.'

Eileen patted her neat hair, the red varnish flashing on her long nails. 'I have an important job with the local council, which means I'm often kept very late in the office, coupled with a very pleasant social life. There is certainly no time for me to nursemaid a baby. I suggest you go to the authorities and have him fostered as soon as possible.'

'I promised Franny I'd never do that,' said Julie.

'Then you're a fool,' snapped Eileen. 'You can't possibly look after a child and hold down a demanding job at the same time.'

'I'll find someone to look after him while I'm working,' Julie retorted. 'I'm willing to pay the right person.'

Eileen regarded William, who was becoming restless in Julie's arms. 'Was Franny actually married to the father?' Julie shook her head. 'In which case it would be better off adopted. You can't risk people thinking it's yours, and I've worked too long and too hard to get where I am to have my reputation sullied by my connection with you.'

'Don't worry, Eileen,' snapped Julie, 'I won't tell anyone you're my sister. The shame of closing your door to the only member of your family who needs you is bad enough, and I'm sure you won't want that item of news getting about to smear your pristine reputation.'

'There's no need to be like that,' said Eileen, her brown eyes narrowing.

'I think there's every need,' retorted Julie. 'In fact, after meeting you again after so many years, I'm almost ashamed to acknowledge you as a member of our family. You might think you're grand and important, but we both come from the East End, where hospitality and family loyalty are of the utmost importance. Leaving Stepney has done you no favours at all.'

Eileen held her glare for a long moment of silence

and then she gave a deep sigh. 'You can stay for tonight,' she said with clear reluctance, 'but you'll have to go to the billeting people this afternoon and find somewhere for tomorrow. I can't have my life disrupted like this.'

Julie didn't want to stay with Eileen at all, but she had little choice. 'Thank you,' she said tightly. 'I'll just feed and change William first, then get out of your hair.' She eyed her older sister thoughtfully. 'I don't suppose you know where I could pick up a second-hand pram, do you?'

'The WVS centre at the Town Hall will probably have one.' Eileen gathered the cups and saucers and placed them carefully on the tray. 'As long as he's fed and changed and asleep before you go out, I'll keep an eye on him.'

Julie was startled by her sister's change of heart. 'Really?' she breathed. 'That would be such a help, because I have to go back to the station to collect me bags and—'

'I'm due to go out at seven this evening,' said Eileen, 'and if you're one minute late back, then I'm going anyway – and the baby will be left to fend for itself.'

'I'll be back, I promise. Thanks, Eileen.'

Eileen made no reply as she carried the tea tray out of the room and quietly closed the door behind her – but her young sister would have been shocked to see her lean heavily against that door, her cold reserve crumbling as she desperately fought back a tide of anguish which threatened to overwhelm her.

Julie had left William fed, clean and asleep in a nest of pillows on Eileen's couch. She hadn't liked leaving him at all, for she doubted if Eileen could cope if he became tearful. But without him, Julie could dash to the billeting office before it closed, and then hurry back to the station to collect her bags, and perhaps buy something to eat for her supper.

She remembered passing the billeting office on her way down the High Street, but when she pushed through the door, she saw the crush and realised she had a long wait ahead of her. She settled on one of the uncomfortable chairs, fretting as the hands on the big wall-clock slowly ticked away the minutes. The shops would soon be closing and she needed to buy food for tonight – and then there was the possibility that the old porter might go off duty and close the left luggage.

Her impatience grew as the time dragged by, and it was almost an hour before she was finally called to one of the three desks.

A small wooden plaque on the desk informed Julie that she was dealing with Katherine Carter. Katherine was a pretty, fair-haired girl who couldn't have been much older than Julie, but she was clearly harassed by the sheer number of people needing her help, and didn't look up as Julie sat down.

Katherine shuffled the paperwork before her and

tried to bring some order to her fair hair, which seemed determined to escape her hairpins. Drawing a sheaf of papers towards her, she began to fire questions at Julie as she filled in a form. 'Name, age, marital status, address, occupation? How many needing accommodation? Do you have small children or elderly dependants?'

Julie answered them all, and then Katherine finally looked up. 'I thought you said you weren't married?'

'I'm not,' she replied. 'William is me sister's child. She died six weeks ago.'

'Oh, I am sorry.' The blue eyes were sympathetic, the smile warm despite her obvious weariness. 'And here you are, all the way from London with nowhere to go.' She frowned. 'I'm surprised Dr Sayers didn't organise something for you. He knows how difficult it is to place very small children, especially when so many of our local residents have been bombed out. Our policy is to encourage mothers with young ones to evacuate to Wales or Somerset.' She looked back at Julie hopefully.

'I have to stay here,' Julie said quietly. 'I can't let Dr Sayers down.'

'Of course,' Katherine murmured. 'In that case, I can only offer you a bed at the Town Hall. It's our emergency holding centre and overcrowded, but I'm sure we could squeeze you both in somehow.' She gave Julie an apologetic smile as she again fiddled with the hairpins. 'Don't you have *any* friends or relatives in Cliffehaven who might take you in for a while?'

Julie thought of Eileen and shook her head. 'I've left William with someone for the afternoon, but she doesn't have any room to spare after tonight. Aren't there any families who would be willing to take me and the baby in? I'd pay extra for babysitting, and do all me own laundry and cooking.'

Katherine sat back in her chair with a sigh and let the drifts of fair hair settle round her pretty face. 'The only person who might take you in is Mrs Reilly at Beach View Boarding House. But I seem to remember she's taken her name off our books for a while.'

Julie sat forward eagerly. 'Is this Mrs Reilly likely to change her mind? Is there any way of getting hold of her to see if she has a spare room?'

Katherine pushed back from the desk, opened an enormous filing cabinet and riffled through the endless buff folders until she found the right one. 'She's asked to be temporarily off the books, but I know for a fact she has two spare rooms – so she might change her mind once she knows the situation,' she said thoughtfully.

Julie's hopes rose. 'Is there any way of contacting her today?'

'She's on the telephone, but I'll have to make the call in our back office.' Katherine's smile was encouraging. 'Hold on there a tick, and I'll see what I can do.'

Julie sat in front of the desk and tried to appear calm, but her insides were churning. A billet in a boarding house sounded far more appealing than camping out at the Town Hall, and she just prayed her luck would finally change and she wouldn't have to spend the night in Eileen's unwelcoming company.

What a fool she'd been to think her sister would take her in without a murmur – and how stupid not to arrange alternative accommodation before she arrived. She really should learn not to jump into things so quickly, letting her heart rule her head without a thought for the consequences. It seemed the years of discipline and forethought as a nurse had taught her nothing when it came to her chaotic private life.

Katherine returned and sat down. 'I'm sorry, Miss Harris, but I was unable to reach Mrs Reilly and could only leave a message with one of her young lodgers. But the girl did say Mrs Reilly wasn't planning to take in any more evacuees until after her daughter has had her baby.' She looked crestfallen. 'I'm ever so sorry.'

'It's not your fault,' Julie assured her. 'But what if I was to go and see this Mrs Reilly? Do you think I might be able to persuade her to change her mind?'

Katherine leaned back in her chair and looked thoughtful. 'It's not our usual policy, but these are difficult times and you're obviously in a terrible bind.' She opened the file and copied down the address.

'Peggy Reilly's an absolute treasure,' she confided, 'and if anyone can help you, she's your best bet. Just don't let on about this, or I'll get shot.' She grinned as she handed over the piece of paper. 'I'll book you in to the Town Hall, though, just in case. You can let them know if you don't need it.'

Julie slipped the piece of paper into her coat pocket. 'Thanks, you're a diamond,' she breathed.

'Better to leave it until teatime just to make sure she's in.' Katherine glanced at the clock and pushed back from the desk. 'That's me done for the day,' she said cheerfully. 'The name's Kath, by the way. Want me to show you where Beach View is?'

Julie smiled at her friendliness. 'Please, call me Julie, and it would be very helpful so long as it doesn't take you too far out of your way.'

'It's not that far, and to be honest, I could do with a bit of fresh air and exercise after sitting in here all day.' Katherine giggled as she slipped on her overcoat and tied the belt round her waist. 'I swear I can feel every spam sandwich and digestive biscuit going straight to my hips.'

Julie returned her grin, recognising a kindred spirit, and the first spark of a new and interesting friendship. Perhaps it wouldn't be too bad in Cliffehaven after all.

Chapter Eight

Julie and Kath left the billeting office and hurried up the hill to the station to fetch Julie's cases. Changing into her sturdier shoes, she sighed with relief as their familiar comfort cushioned her sore feet. It was almost four in the afternoon, and being Saturday, the shops were on the point of closing, but she managed to buy a small tin of spam and half a loaf of bread before they headed towards Camden Road again.

Kath came to a halt at a corner opposite a large Catholic church. 'That's Havelock Gardens beyond the church,' she explained. 'It's the posh end of Cliffehaven, with big houses and gardens that look over the beach. If you go through the little park and turn right into Cliffe Avenue, you'll find the surgery halfway down. Dr Sayers and his son converted the ground floor of their family home some years ago.'

'What's he like?' asked Julie.

'Dr Sayers senior's a bit old-fashioned, and looks like Father Christmas. He can be a bit grumpy at times, but he's ever so nice really. He's a widower and came out of retirement to help his son, Michael, run the practice after war was declared. Michael suffers from asthma, which is why he couldn't enlist.'

'Poor man,' murmured Julie. 'Asthma can be an awful affliction.'

'It doesn't hold him back, though.' Kath took one of Julie's cases and they began to walk down Camden Road. 'He always comes out when he's called, even in the middle of the night, and he runs free clinics at the Town Hall and hospital, as well as his own twice-daily surgeries.' She sighed. 'He's really nice, but far too thin. My mum reckons he needs a wife to fatten him up.'

Julie shot her a glance of curious amusement. 'Do I detect an attraction to the thin but caring young doctor?' she teased.

Kath chuckled. 'I fancied him when I was in primary school, but that's as far as it went. My chap is on a minesweeper somewhere in the Atlantic.'

Julie saw the wistfulness in her face. 'Is he a local too?'

Kath nodded. 'He and his brothers worked on their dad's fishing boats before they enlisted into the RNR. His name's Patrick.' She sighed. 'I do miss him.' She looked back at Julie. 'So, what's your story, Julie? Have you got a chap, and is it as bad in London as it says in the papers?'

Julie gave her a potted history of the war in London and how it had devastated so many lives. She kept it concise and almost impersonal, aware of how easily the tears would start flowing if she let her emotions come into it. 'As for men, I've given up on them,' she finished. 'The last one was a disaster.' She drew to a halt outside Eileen's door and smiled. 'I'll tell you all about him next time – if you want to meet up again, of course.'

Kath grinned. 'Absolutely,' she said, 'and I'll introduce you to some of my other friends and show you round.'

'Well,' said Julie, 'this is me. How far is it to Beach View from here?'

Kath looked up at the window above the bakery. 'Is this where you've left William?' At Julie's nod she grimaced. 'I'm surprised Eileen Harris offered to mind him,' she said. 'She's not exactly the warm, cuddly type, and I've had many a run-in with her over council policies regarding evacuees. Anyone would think she was running the town council, not just a secretary.' Her blue eyes widened as realisation dawned. 'Oh, goodness,' she breathed. 'Is she a relative? Have I put my foot in it?'

Julie smiled. 'Not at all,' she assured her. 'My sister and I have very little in common, which is why I'm looking for somewhere to stay.' She remembered Eileen's dire warnings not to talk about their relationship and quickly added, 'Keep that to yourself, though, Kath.'

'My lips are sealed.' Kath glanced at her watch. 'I'd better get back home. Mum will need help getting the tea. Beach View is down there,' she said, pointing to the end of Camden Road. 'Cross over at the junction into Beach View Terrace and it's the third house on the left.'

'I'd ask you in, but . . .'

Kath grinned. 'It's all right, Julie. I understand. How about we meet for a cup of tea or something tomorrow afternoon? There's a nice little café just opposite the hospital.'

'I'd like that,' said Julie, returning the grin. 'About three?'

'You're on, and good luck with Mrs Reilly. TTFN,' Kath added cheerfully, and hurried back along Camden Road.

Julie knocked on Eileen's door, then, after several anxious minutes, had to knock again. What on earth was she doing? Had she gone out and left William alone? She was about to knock for the third time when, with a sigh of relief, she heard footsteps coming down the stairs.

Eileen silently opened the door then headed back upstairs. 'You'd better have a key,' she said as she gained the landing. 'I can't keep running up and down these stairs all day.'

'I've just popped in with me cases and to check on William before I try to secure our lodgings,' said Julie, as she lugged the cases upstairs. 'How has he been?'

'He's been asleep, thankfully, so I was able to catch up on some of my important paperwork.'

Julie crossed the sitting room and looked down

at the sleeping baby. Resisting the urge to cuddle and kiss him, she turned back to Eileen. 'What is it you do exactly?' she asked.

'I work as personal assistant to the head of the town council. It is a demanding and important post, which keeps me at the heart of all local policy-making and in direct touch with government legislation. That is all I am permitted to tell you.'

'It seems you've come a long way from working as a typist at the tool factory,' said Julie. 'Well done.'

Eileen made no comment as she sat down at the table by the window and gathered the papers strewn across it. 'Have you found accommodation? You've been gone a long time.'

Julie told her about the offer of a bed at the Town Hall, and her hopes of being taken in by Peggy Reilly. 'There are still a couple of hours before you have to go out, so I thought I'd go to the surgery next. I want to introduce meself to the doctors and pick up my duty schedule as well as some sort of map of Cliffehaven. The town's bigger and more spread out than I thought, so I hope they'll provide me with a bicycle.'

Eileen placed the papers in a sturdy briefcase which she locked with a snap. 'I have a perfectly good map you may borrow,' she said, 'but I expect it back as soon as you've made yourself familiar with the area.' She reached across to the crammed bookshelf, found the map and handed it over.

'Thank you.' Julie tucked the map into her coat

pocket. 'So, is it all right if I leave William here a bit longer?'

'I suppose so.'

Julie remembered the flask of formula she'd stowed in her gas-mask box and pulled it out. 'If he wakes, just pour three ounces of this into a clean bottle.' She rummaged in her case and found one, setting it beside the flask on the couch. Hesitating momentarily, she added a clean napkin. 'He might need changing . . .'

'I might not like babies, but I do know my way around one,' Eileen said impatiently. 'Being the eldest sister, I used to help with you and Fran.'

Julie looked into those cold eyes and thought she saw something flicker there, but it was too fleeting to identify. 'Thanks, Eileen,' she said softly. 'I'll be back as soon as I can.'

'See that you are.' Eileen took the key from the table and held it out. 'I want that back first thing tomorrow.'

Julie pocketed the key and checked on William, then hurried down the stairs. She was aching with hunger now, but it would have to wait until she was certain she had somewhere to sleep the following night.

Peggy wearily stepped out of her elderly friends' house where she'd been cooking and cleaning for most of the afternoon, and took a deep, welcoming breath of fresh air. The house had been damaged in a tip-and-run raid the day before, and Jim and Ron had done as much as they could to cover the gaping hole in their roof, make the chimney safe and bring most of their furniture downstairs. The poor old dears were very confused, and simply couldn't cope with all the dust and debris that littered the two habitable rooms, so Peggy had stayed long after Jim had gone off to his work as a projectionist at the Odeon cinema, and helped to scrub the place clean and make sure they at least had a hot meal.

She wrapped her coat about her as she hurried through the gathering gloom towards home. Bert and Mabel were a lovely old couple in their eighties and had lived in Cliffehaven all their lives. They'd been married for over sixty years and refused to be evacuated to their daughter's in Scotland, but Peggy was worried that they weren't eating properly or looking after themselves, especially now that the district nurse had left to join the medical corps.

She closed her front door behind her and leaned against it for a moment to catch her breath. Dragging off her filthy headscarf, she hung her coat on the rack in the hall and kicked off her shoes. She felt grubby from head to foot and just hoped there was enough hot water for a bath.

Anne and Mrs Finch were preparing a supper of fried mince, onions, potatoes and leeks, and Peggy blessed their kindness. 'I left them both with a nice hot meal,' she said, sinking into the armchair by the range, 'but I worry about them, I really do.'

'You look all in, Mum,' said Anne, turning from the range where she was frying the mince. 'Here, have a cup of tea and forget about everyone else for a bit.'

'Thanks, darling,' she said gratefully as she took the cup and cradled it in her dirty hands. 'I'll drink this and then have a bath.'

'There's plenty of water,' chirped Mrs Finch. 'The girls haven't come in yet.'

Anne tipped the mince mixture into a large pie dish and began to cover it in mashed potato. 'It's a bit early to put this in the oven, so I think I'll go for a bit of a walk,' she murmured. 'The baby's been restless today and I need to stretch my legs and get some fresh air.'

Peggy regarded her anxiously. 'It's getting quite dark out there, Anne. Don't go too far, will you?'

'I'm not planning a route march, Mum,' Anne teased, 'just a gentle stroll down to the seafront to ease the aches and pains.'

'Pains?' Peggy said sharply.

'Just the same little niggles and aches that I've had for weeks,' Anne soothed. 'Enjoy your bath and I'll be back before you know it.'

Peggy caught Mrs Finch's eye as Anne left the room. 'I suppose it won't do any harm,' she sighed, 'but I don't like the sound of those aches and pains.'

'You worry too much,' said Mrs Finch. 'Anne's a bright girl, she knows what's best.'

Peggy gave a deep sigh and then finished her tea. 'Where's Ron?'

'Out with Harvey and his old man's army,' said Mrs Finch, with an impish smile. 'All spruced up in his uniform so he can go and court that Rosie Braithwaite at the Anchor when he's finished his silly manoeuvres.'

Peggy smiled. Rosie Braithwaite was the landlady of the Anchor, a delightful, glamorous woman of indeterminate age whom Ron had lusted after for years, and who seemed to enjoy the chase. She dragged herself out of the comfortable chair. 'I'm glad he's got Rosie to spar with,' she murmured. 'At least she keeps a spring in his step and a twinkle in his eye – and that's got to count for something in these dark times.'

She walked barefooted into the hall and went into her bedroom where she gathered clean clothes together before traipsing up the stairs to the first-floor bathroom. Locking the door behind her, she pulled the blackout curtain, turned on the light and lit the boiler, which always threatened to singe the lashes and brows of the uninitiated.

She sat on the edge of the bath and turned the taps, once again thanking her lucky stars for the luxury of an indoor bath. It was worth every hard-earned penny, but she did wish the government restrictions allowed more than just a couple of inches of water to soak in.

She sighed as she stripped off her filthy clothes and left them in a pile on the linoleum. 'At least I no longer have to sit in a tin tub in front of the kitchen range,' she muttered, 'and that's a blessing if ever there was one.'

The cold little room filled with steam and she daringly let the water rise to four inches before turning off the taps with a silent promise to make up for her selfishness by using the water to soak Ron's vegetable patch.

Sinking into the enveloping warmth, she slid down until the water lapped at her ears, and then closed her eyes. Peace, perfect peace – at last.

Julie had decided the doctors didn't need to know about William just yet. There was little point in rocking the boat before she'd managed to sort out accommodation and a babysitter, but time was running out, and she was all too aware of how very difficult things would get if she had to move into the Town Hall.

As it was Saturday afternoon, there was no surgery, and the elderly Dr Sayers had welcomed her warmly and shown her into his consulting room. They had struck up an instant rapport, and Julie was pleased at how well this initial interview was going.

She sat patiently and waited for him to finish reading Matron's letter of introduction. Kath's description suited him admirably, for he was a natty, wholesome-looking man in his seventies, with impeccably groomed white hair and beard, the moustache twirled and waxed, his eyebrows brushed into sweeping wings above friendly grey eyes. He wore a tweed suit and matching waistcoat, with a gold watch-chain looped across his flat midriff, and the hands that held the letter were square and capable, the nails clean and short. He exuded confidence and kindness, and she had no doubt that he was beloved by his patients.

'That all seems in order,' he said in a deep baritone. 'I must say, your application arrived at the most opportune moment, Sister Harris. Our district nurse left almost a month ago, and it's been almost impossible to find her replacement.' He gave her a friendly smile. 'You'll find things a bit quieter here than in London, but I can promise you'll be kept busy.'

'I like being busy,' she assured him. 'Are there other nurses linked to the practice, or will I be on me own?'

'There are two young volunteers, and Sister Beecham is my practice nurse. She is in overall charge of the nursing side of things, so you'll refer to her regarding your schedule and so on. We will of course provide you with a uniform and bicycle.' He grinned. 'Cliffehaven is quite spread out, and very hilly, so I hope you've got strong legs.'

Julie chuckled. 'I've cycled most of London, so I think I can manage.'

He pushed back from his leather chair, picked up the briar pipe that lay in a nearby ashtray and stuffed it into his jacket pocket. 'Welcome aboard, Sister Harris. We'll see you bright and early Monday morning.'

His handshake was dry and firm and Julie left the house feeling rather lucky to have such a pleasant doctor in charge. She had yet to meet his son, or the practice sister, but she was sure she'd get along with them too, for the whole place had a happy, homely atmosphere.

As she stepped out of the front door and headed for the gate, she looked at the luminous dial on her watch. It was almost six o'clock and the only light was from the moon. Mrs Reilly was bound to be at home by now. She hurried into the little park which had been turned into one huge allotment, then jumped as the wail of a nearby siren started up. Her thoughts raced. She was too far from William to get to him, and she had no idea where the nearest public shelter was, or where Eileen might take him. If she ran fast enough, perhaps she could intercept her?

Her heart was pounding as she ran through the darkness and emerged from the park, disorientated and unsure in the blackout of how to get back to the flat. This wasn't the same road she'd come in from – where was the church, the High Street? She scrabbled in her pocket for Eileen's map, but it was too dark to read it.

She dithered, the panic rising as more sirens began to wail throughout the town. And then she heard the shout of a warden, and was caught up in the hurrying mass of people who seemed to be heading towards what looked like a playing field. She tried to battle against the tide, her fear for William growing, her need to get to him paramount. But the warden had grabbed her arm and was propelling her along, yelling at her to get a move on. There was no way to escape this surging mass of humanity.

Searchlights were spluttering into life, their phosphorescent fingers criss-crossing the clear, starlit sky. Eileen must have left with William by now, she reasoned as she was swept along. All she could do was pray she'd keep him safe.

The field lay to the north of the little park, the shelter dug deep beneath the ground and surrounded by walls of sandbags. Julie's breath came in sharp gasps as the jostling crowd carried her inexorably down the steep concrete steps and into its depths as the first ack-ack guns shot tracers of red into the sky.

The underground shelter was poorly lit and smelled damp, but there were benches and chairs, and the floor had been concreted. Burlap screens had been set around buckets to provide makeshift lavatories, the stink of the chemicals inside them pervading the vast cavern. Julie found a space by the door and desperately searched for sight of Eileen and William, but in the gloom and the crush, it was impossible to see anything clearly.

She shivered as the warden slammed the door shut and turned the locking wheel that would effectively seal them in. She hated that sound, hated the claustrophobia of so many people crammed in together – hated the thought of how far underground they were, and how swiftly they could all be crushed. But most of all she feared for William – the noise and the strange surroundings would terrify him, and Eileen wouldn't know how to soothe him. She might even lose her patience and . . .

She closed her eyes and willed the raid to be over quickly, but even as she prayed, she could hear the sound of enemy aircraft overhead, the rat-a-tat-tat of the local guns and the booms of the Bofors she'd glimpsed on the seafront and along the cliffs. Was Cliffehaven the target tonight, or poor old London? Either way, William was in as much danger here as anywhere, and she had to trust that her sister would protect him.

When Peggy heard the siren, she grabbed their coats and the box she kept ready with supplies, and quickly helped Mrs Finch down the cellar steps and into the garden. Rita and the other two girls would stay on duty until the raid was over; Jim was at the cinema and Ron was probably at the Anchor. 'I'll get you settled,' she shouted above the noise of the guns, 'and then go and find Anne.'

Mrs Finch's grip was surprisingly strong as she grabbed her wrist. 'You mustn't go out in this,' she shouted back. 'Anne said she was going to the seafront, so she'll be quite safe in the shelter under the Grand Hotel.'

'I can't be sure of that,' said Peggy as she bundled the elderly woman into the Anderson shelter and helped her into her deckchair, then frantically stuffed cushions around her to keep her from slipping out. 'She's been gone for nearly an hour. If she's caught in this she won't be able to run very fast. I have to find her.'

Mrs Finch looked up at her, her pale eyes bright with tears. 'Please don't go, Peggy. It's too dangerous.'

'I have to.' Peggy lit the kerosene lamp and tucked a blanket round the little woman. 'Stay here,' she ordered, handing her a packet of biscuits from the box, 'and if you get at all frightened, turn off that hearing aid so you can go to sleep. I'll be back as soon as I can. I promise.'

Mrs Finch grabbed her sleeve. 'God go with you, Peggy,' she said, the tears streaming down her lined face.

Peggy swiftly kissed her cheek then hurried out of the shelter. Once she'd made sure the door was fastened properly, she raced out of the back gate and down the alleyway to the main road that led straight to the seafront. She could hear a warden shouting in the distance and knew that if she was caught without her gas-mask box she'd be heavily fined – but that wasn't important. Her daughter was out there, and Peggy just knew she was in trouble.

The sirens were all going now, right through the town, the searchlights weaving back and forth as the first phalanx of enemy planes advanced over the Channel and the RAF raced to intercept them. The guns on the cliffs were booming, the tracer bullets zipping through the black skies as the bright yellow pom-poms burst to light up the enemy planes and give those guns a good target.

The continuous bursting of shells lit her way as she ran down the hill towards the seafront. She stumbled as her bedroom slippers caught in the rough pavement, and she kicked them off. Running in her bare feet, she called out to Anne in the hope she could hear above the awful racket of the numerous dogfights overhead.

The seafront was deserted but for the soldiers manning the guns, and there was no answer to her desperate calls. She continued running along the pavement, past the boarded-up private hotels, until she reached the Grand. It was in total darkness and, as she tried the front door, she found it was locked.

She stood there panting and in terror. Perhaps Anne was in the shelter beneath the Grand – in which case she should go back home. But something told Peggy that wasn't the case. She might have changed her mind and not even come this way. But where could she have gone? The main communal shelter was on the far side of town. Surely she wouldn't have walked that far?

Peggy dithered, and then the thought came that Anne might have gone to see her father at the cinema. She often called in to share a cuppa with him in the projection room. In a fever of anxiety, she ran along the seafront, hardly noticing the heavy booms of the nearby guns, or the roar of the planes overhead. Nor did she realise that her feet were cut and bleeding, or that she had a sharp pain in her side as she began to run up the steep hill towards the Odeon. All she could feel was a growing dread that her daughter needed her. 'Anne!' she screamed. 'Anne, where are you?'

A low-flying enemy plane roared above her, bullets spewing from its underbelly to crack and thud all around her. Peggy threw herself into a nearby doorway and curled into a ball, her head buried in her arms as the bullets ricocheted off brick and thudded into the road.

The Gerry plane roared away and Peggy lifted her head, ready to make a run for it. But as she warily emerged from her makeshift shelter she saw it turn sharply and come in low and fast – heading straight towards her, guns blazing. The bastard was coming back for a second go.

Peggy dived back into the doorway, her terror too great even to cry out as the bullets rattled and thudded and whined within inches of her. And then she was almost lifted off the step by the heavy blast from a nearby explosion.

Her ears were ringing as she cringed and trembled, and the house shook and debris rained down on her to scatter and tumble across the road and down the hill. 'Anne, oh, Anne,' she moaned. 'Please, please, God, don't let her be out in this.'

The presbytery had been standing next to the Catholic church for decades, but the nearby bomb-blast had finally signed its death warrant and, as

Peggy huddled on the step, the walls began to crumble. Guttering screeched as it buckled and tore from its moorings, slates slid with a crash to the ground and the old house groaned as, bit by bit, it began to topple.

Peggy darted out just as a huge lump of concrete thudded onto the step. She stared at it, frozen in horror by how close death had come. Now the walls were beginning to bow, the window frames threatening to snap under the pressure. A slate came winging from the roof like a discus and she leaped out of the way as it thudded into the ground where she'd been standing.

Spurred into action, Peggy stumbled away, clambering over the debris, oblivious to the fact that the enemy was heading back over the Channel, the RAF boys in swift pursuit.

'Anne! Anne!' she called, her throat rough and dry, the smoke and dust making her cough and her eyes burn. The back of the church was on fire, and several buildings had collapsed following that terrible blast, and she could barely see anything. 'Anne,' she called again, more in hope than expectation.

'Mum?' The voice was faint, but unmistakable. 'Mum, help me.'

Peggy looked wildly round. 'Where are you?' she yelled. 'I can't see you.'

'The post office,' came the hysterical response. 'Under the post office.'

Peggy clambered and clawed her way over the

rubble which lay strewn across the road, her heart pounding as she took in the devastation. 'I'm here,' she called. 'Keep talking, Anne. You have to help me find you.'

'Be careful, Mum,' Anne sobbed. 'The whole place is about to collapse and I'm trapped down here.'

'Keep calm, love. I know what I'm doing.' Peggy eyed the layer upon layer of bricks, beams, windows, doors and shattered concrete in despair. Ceiling laths were scattered like matchsticks; electricity wires threaded through the rubble, hissing like snakes as they came into contact with a leaking water pipe. She hadn't a clue how she would get to Anne, but she'd damned well find a way, even if it was the last thing she ever did.

'Keep talking,' she said grimly, picking her way over the ruins with catlike caution.

'I'm frightened, Mum,' Anne said tremulously. 'I think the baby's coming.'

'Dear God,' breathed Peggy as she homed in on her daughter's voice and carefully began to clear a way through. 'Don't cry, darling,' she soothed, 'just keep breathing deeply and evenly and everything will be all right. I'm almost there.'

She tossed aside a pile of lath and plaster and a block of bricks, hauled a shattered door out of her way and threw lead piping across the spitting tail of an electricity cable. There was a bit of a hole now, but all she could see down there was profound darkness. 'Can you wave something so I can see where you are?' she called down.

A flutter of something pale moved far below. 'Can you see my scarf, Mum?'

'Yes,' said Peggy, 'and I'll be with you in a minute.' They were brave words meant to shore up Anne's courage as well as her own, but as Peggy worked furiously to make the hole bigger, she knew that one false move could bury them both. The whole pile of rubble was unstable, sliding and slipping beneath her bare feet, threatening to collapse at any moment.

'I'm having another contraction,' moaned Anne. 'The baby's definitely on its way.'

'Work with it,' said Peggy breathlessly as she smeared the sweat from her face and tried to find purchase on the jagged, slippery pile with her toes as she continued to work at making the hole bigger. 'Breathe deeply, Anne, keep calm. Have your waters broken yet?'

'I don't know,' she sobbed. 'But I think I've just wet myself.'

'That's nothing to be ashamed of.' Peggy heaved bricks, slates and window frames out of the way.

'I'm frightened, Mum,' sobbed Anne.

'I know, but you must try and be brave, darling. I'm almost there.' She knelt by the narrow opening she'd made and gauged it was big enough to slip through. She took off her overcoat, her sweat chilled by the bite of the cold night air. 'I'm going to throw you my coat,' she called. 'Put it over you while I climb down.'

'I . . . I can just about . . . I've got it.' Anne's voice was thick with tears. 'Please be careful, Mum.'

Peggy didn't need telling, but now was not the time to hesitate or falter. She gingerly spread her weight close to the edge of the hole. The rubble beneath her shifted and dust sifted down. Peggy froze. 'Put the coat over your face,' she ordered, 'and use whatever you can to shield you.'

'I'm ready when you are,' shouted Anne, her voice now muffled by the coat.

Peggy looked about her, searching for something to help her get down the hole without taking the rubble with her. She caught sight of a sturdy length of wood, which looked as if it might once have been a door frame, and slowly and carefully drew it towards her until it lay across the opening. Grasping it with both hands, she inched her body onto it, thankful she didn't weigh much, and praying it would hold her.

As she tentatively lowered her legs into the void, Peggy heard the enemy planes returning. But this was not a moment to panic, or to think about anything but Anne. She shifted her hips until the wood cut into her waist, then shifted again, her fingers clawing for purchase as she swung like a pendulum. The debris was shifting, sliding, threatening to give way.

'Can you see my legs?' she yelled above the roar of planes.

'Yes,' shouted back Anne. 'You're about two feet to my right, with a drop of another two.'

'Right,' Peggy grunted. And let go.

She plunged into the darkness and hit the bottom with a jarring thud. Her bare feet slid off something smooth and she felt a sharp pain in her ankle as she fell in a heap, but all she could focus on was the pale shape of her daughter, who seemed to be trapped beneath a heavy rafter.

'Are you all right?' called Anne.

'Yes,' she breathed, wincing at the pain in her ankle and the sharp cut of something beneath her bare toes. Her eyes adjusted quickly to the darkness and she scrambled through shattered glass and broken bricks, then reached for Anne's hand, gripping it tightly and holding it to her lips. 'It's all right, darling,' she said brokenly as Anne clung to her. 'I'm here now.'

'Oh, Mum,' sobbed Anne. 'You're so brave.'

'There's nothing brave about falling down a hole,' said Peggy as she did a quick assessment of their situation. The beam was lying across one of Anne's legs and, apart from being far too heavy to lift, shifting it would bring the whole pile of rubble down on top of them. The space was about eight feet square and, she judged, about seven feet down from the gap she'd made in the rubble. There was very little room, and it was impossible to stand up except beneath the hole. Anne had been saved because of the enormous counter which had landed on its side next to her. Thankfully there was no smell of gas, or sign of fire.

'Let me make you more comfortable,' she soothed. Taking her overcoat, she folded it and pillowed Anne's head, using her handkerchief to clear some of the dust and grime from her face. 'How quickly are the pains coming, do you think?'

'I don't know,' Anne replied with a soft moan. 'I lost track of time in the darkness, but . . .'

'Don't worry,' said Peggy as a fighter plane screamed overhead. 'If all else fails then I'll help deliver my grandchild.'

'I don't know how you came to find me, Mum,' said Anne, her voice high with rising hysteria, 'but I'm so glad you're here. It was awful being buried and alone in the dark. I thought I was going to die.'

'That's quite enough of that sort of talk,' said Peggy firmly. 'Do pull yourself together, Anne, or you'll upset that baby, and I think it has enough to contend with at the moment, don't you?'

'Sorry, Mum,' Anne whispered.

'That's all right.' Peggy kissed her fingers, thinking that it hadn't been much fun either, getting caught out in the middle of the raid and having Gerry chase after her, but she said nothing. They had found one another – that was all that mattered now – and whatever was in store for them would be seen through together.

Peggy sat in the darkness, gripping her daughter's

hand, her thoughts in a whirl of rising panic and dread. She'd promised Anne she'd help if the baby came before they could be rescued, but she had no medical knowledge past bandaging scraped knees. Having four children of her own didn't count, for she'd followed the midwife's instructions in a haze of pain, not really taking much notice of what the nurse was doing at the other end of the bed. If Anne's labour progressed and something went wrong, then she'd never forgive herself.

As Anne breathed deeply through yet another contraction, Peggy looked up at the narrow patch of night sky through the opening, yearning to hear the 'all-clear' and the welcome arrival of the rescuers. But the only sounds were the ominous shifting of the pile of rubble that surrounded them, and the soft whisper of falling dust.

The all-clear sounded and Julie was on her feet and waiting first in line to get out of the shelter. As the warden slowly turned the wheel and the door creaked open, she squeezed through and ran up the steps, gulping in the cold air.

As the others emerged from the shelter and made their way across the field, Julie followed them in the hope that she'd find her way back to the High Street and, ultimately, Camden Road. It was clear that Cliffehaven had been badly hit by the enemy bombers, for the lovely old church was on fire, the presbytery now just a jumble of broken masonry.

The sight of such devastation did nothing to ease her fretfulness over William and Eileen and, as she reached what appeared to be the lower end of the High Street, her fears increased. Several buildings had been reduced to rubble and there was a vast crater where the High Street met the promenade. She began to run.

The streets radiating off the High Street all looked the same, and as the signs had been removed, she couldn't tell which was Camden Road. Then she remembered there had been a bombed out building on the corner, and a fire station a short way down from it. She ran harder up the steep hill, her breath coming in painful gasps, her gaze fixed to what appeared to be her goal.

As she reached the bomb site, she realised her mistake, for this was a recent collapse and there was a knot of men frantically trying to clear the rubble while a large shaggy dog stood barking into what looked like a hole. She was about to hurry past when a powerful light was shone right in her eyes.

'Oy,' said the gruff voice. 'You there. You're a nurse, aren't you?'

She shielded her eyes and tried to see who was behind the torch. 'Yes, but how . . .?'

The old porter shifted the torch so she could see him. 'We met earlier at the station,' he said, his face as begrimed as his warden's uniform. 'We need you to get down that there hole and help the lady what's down there.'

Julie looked at the dog which was still barking furiously, his shaggy head submerged in that ominous hole. She shivered with dread. 'I can't,' she stammered. 'I have to find William.'

'You can, and you will,' he said firmly, grasping her arm. 'You're a nurse, and about the right size. See, none of us is small enough to get through, and the lady down there's about to have a baby, Gawd help her.'

Julie looked frantically round for help. She couldn't go down that hole, she just couldn't. It was too reminiscent of the one in Stepney. And then there was William. She had to know that he and Eileen had survived the bombing, and that he was safe. 'I can't,' she said again, beginning to back away. 'Have you called for an ambulance?'

'It's on its way, but it's you what's here now, and you what's going down that hole,' he said, grabbing her coat. 'Get that off and we'll lower you in.'

Julie realised she had a duty to the poor woman down that hole and this was not the time to let her morbid fears of being buried alive get the better of her. 'I'll need me medical bag,' she said as she took off her coat. 'It's at thirty-seven A Camden Road, the flat above the bakery.'

'I'll send someone to fetch it.' He turned and spoke to one of the other wardens, who hurried off into the darkness. 'Right, love,' he said more gently. 'Let's get you safely down. The girl's mother has already managed to get herself down there, and the lads have shored it up as best they can until the heavy lifting crew can get here.'

'I'll need hot clean water, soap and towels,' she said urgently. 'I can't deliver a baby with dirty hands.'

'We'll get them, don't fret.' He turned and yelled up to the man who seemed to be in charge of the barking dog. 'Get Harvey out of there, Ron. He'll have the whole blooming thing down in a minute.'

The man grabbed the dog's collar and swung him, struggling, into his sturdy arms before carrying him down the mound. 'To be sure, 'tis a grand dog ye are, but give it a rest. You've done your bit.' He regarded Julie from beneath his brows as the dog lay panting in his arms. 'I know you'll do your best for 'em, girly,' he said. 'Good luck.'

Julie took a deep breath for courage and tentatively stepped onto the pile of rubble. She slipped and slid her perilous way to where two beefy men lay on their stomachs either side of the hole. She looked down into the profound darkness and shivered, the old fears of dark, enclosed spaces returning a hundredfold.

'To be sure, 'tis all right, me wee girl, we won't be dropping you,' said one of the men in a soft Irish lilt. 'That's me wife and daughter down there, and I need you to look after them for me.'

Julie swallowed the lump of fear. 'What do you want me to do?'

'Put this torch in your mouth, then give us your

hands,' he replied. 'Once you feel secure, swing your feet over the edge and we'll lower you down.'

She bit hard into the sour-tasting rubber then reached forward and felt her hands and forearms being clasped in vice-like grips which almost lifted her from her feet. With the sob of fear trapped in her throat, she closed her eyes, bit harder onto the torch and lifted her legs. Then she was being lowered, her arms almost torn from their sockets as she hung in the void.

Hands grasped her ankles then slid up to her knees and a woman's voice echoed in the tense silence. 'It's all right. I've got you. Lean towards me and let go.'

Julie did as she was told and grabbed the other woman's shoulders as she slid to the rubble-strewn floor. She switched on the torch, dispelling the surrounding blackness. 'Thank you,' she breathed, shocked at how small and slight her helper was. 'I'm surprised you found the strength to break my fall.'

The woman shrugged. 'I'm tougher than I look.' She led Julie towards the young woman who lay a few feet away. 'This is my daughter Anne,' she said, stroking back the damp hair from the girl's forehead. 'Her contractions are coming every two minutes by my reckoning. Her waters broke just before you were lowered down.' She looked back at Julie. 'I heard the warden say you were a nurse – is that right?'

Julie nodded. 'Nurse and midwife,' she replied as she flashed the torchlight over Anne, noting the heavy beam that pinned one of her legs to the floor. Her mother had obviously done her best by removing her underwear and placing her coat beneath her bottom, but it was going to be a tricky delivery and certainly couldn't be performed with the girl flat on her back.

Julie ignored the darkness surrounding them, and the looming ceiling of rubble that hung suspended only inches above her, focussing only on the beam of torchlight. 'I need me bag and the hot water and soap you promised,' she called up to the men.

'They're here,' shouted the Irishman. 'We're just lowering them down now.'

Julie felt a small surge of relief: the arrival of her bag meant that Eileen must be safe at home. She watched as her precious bag was lowered down, swiftly followed by a large tin bowl in a string bag in which lay soap, a flask, and several towels.

'Thank you.' She swiftly untied everything and washed her hands and arms. The water was tepid, but it was better than nothing. She opened her bag and knelt by the girl, who was moaning in pain. 'Hello, Anne,' she said softly. 'My name's Julie, and I'm going to help you deliver your baby. Have you been injured anywhere else other than your leg?'

Anne shook her head. 'I want to push,' she panted.

'All right, I'll wait until the contraction ends, then I need to examine you.'

'She will be all right, won't she?' asked Anne's mother anxiously.

Julie kept her voice calm and soothing as the contraction ended. 'Could you hold the torch steady for me? I need both hands free.' She ducked between the beam and the overturned desk into the tight space above Anne, and did a quick examination. The second stage of labour was well advanced, but the leg injury was another matter, and would have to be dealt with later.

She pulled the girl's dress down over her knees and edged up until she was squatting by her side. 'The head is almost crowned, and your labour is progressing normally,' she said quietly. 'Now, I'm going to help you roll over onto your side, and I want you to put your free leg up towards your chest. Can you do that, Anne?'

She nodded as another contraction made her groan.

'Try not to push too hard this time,' Julie said calmly. 'Keep panting and let your body do the work. When this contraction is finished, I'll roll you over. All right?'

Anne had the look of utter concentration on her face that was common to all women about to give birth, and Julie waited for the contraction to ebb, then gently but firmly rolled her onto her side towards the beam.

'It's hurting my leg,' Anne moaned as the torch-light jiggled in her mother's nervous hands.

'I'm sorry,' said Julie, steadying the other woman's hand on the torch. 'But there's no other way of getting your baby out.' She quickly took the rubber sheet out of her bag and placed it beneath the girl before checking again on the baby's progress. 'The head is crowned, so on the next contraction, I want you to push as hard as you can.'

Anne groaned and grunted as Julie gently eased the head from the birth canal and cupped it in her hands. 'Good girl,' she soothed. 'Now push when you're ready and your baby will be born.'

Anne gathered her strength and pushed long and hard. Julie eased the tiny shoulders out and waited. Anne gave one last determined push and the baby slithered into Julie's hands. 'That's it, well done,' she breathed. 'You have a lovely baby girl.'

'Let me see.'

'In a minute, I just need to check that all's well.'

'She's lovely, Anne,' breathed her mother. 'Little Rose Margaret is quite, quite perfect.'

'Is it a girl, you say?' shouted the excited Irishman.

'It certainly is,' shouted his wife.

'Please hold the torch steady,' said Julie urgently. 'I need to see what I'm doing.' She cleared the tiny mouth and nose and held the baby up by her feet to free any excess mucus before swiftly wrapping her in the clean towel and giving her chest a rub. She was breathing, but not easily, and there was a tinge of blue round her mouth which made Julie suspect her heart wasn't coping very well.

'What's the matter?' said Anne sharply. 'Why isn't she crying? I thought all newborns cried.'

'She's having some trouble getting her breath,' Julie replied calmly as she dealt with the umbilical cord. 'You can cuddle her for a minute, Anne, but she really needs to be taken to hospital where she can be treated away from all this dust.'

'She's not going to die, is she?' Tears sparked in the torchlight and ran down Anne's face as she took the tiny bundle into her arms.

'Not if we get her help quickly,' Julie said.

'But how can we get her out of here?' Anne's mother asked tremulously.

'I've had an idea.' Julie grabbed the tin bowl, threw out the water and lined it with the rest of the clean towels. Picking up the string bag which was still tied to the rope dangling from the hole, she opened it out and wedged the bowl back inside.

Taking the torch from Anne's mother, she shone it on the Irishman who was leaning precariously above the hole. 'The baby needs to go to hospital,' she called up to him, 'so I'm going to put her in this bowl, and when I tell you, I need you to pull slowly and gently on the rope until you have her safely in your hands.'

'Bejesus,' he muttered. 'By all the saints . . .' He crossed himself and closed his eyes as he nodded.

Julie gave the torch back to the other woman and turned to the sobbing Anne. 'You'll see her later,' she said softly as she took the baby from her arms and placed her in the cocoon of towels. She looked so tiny and vulnerable in that big tin bowl. Julie didn't dare think what might happen if the knots slipped, but it was the only way to get her out of here and into an oxygen tent.

'Pull slowly and don't jerk the rope,' she called up to the very anxious grandfather.

Julie and Anne's mother stood with their hands outstretched beneath the precious, swaying cargo, ready to catch her if she fell. Slowly and precariously, the bag was drawn towards the hole. Their relief was immense as the Irishman grasped the bowl and disappeared from view.

'Thank God for my Jim's safe hands,' breathed Anne's mother as she collapsed onto the rubble-strewn floor. 'And thank you, Julie, for everything you've done tonight. I never could have managed alone, and that's a fact.'

Julie smiled and took her trembling hand. 'I get the feeling you could have managed,' she said softly. 'After all, you got yourself down here without any help, didn't you?'

The little woman gave her a shaky smile. 'The name's Peggy, by the way. Peggy Reilly, and if there's anything I can ever do for you, Julie, then you only have to ask.'

Julie stared at her in amazement and wondered if she really meant it, but even if she did, now was not the time to mention her need for accommodation. The baby might not make it, and Anne's leg looked a mess. The Reilly family had enough to contend with.

Chapter Nine

'It's all right, darling,' crooned Peggy. 'You'll see your baby soon enough, and she's in the best possible place – really she is.'

'But I should be with her,' sobbed Anne.

Peggy understood all too well how frightened Anne must be, for she too was in a turmoil of dread for that tiny wee scrap. She murmured soothing nothings as she held her distraught daughter's hand and Julie helped deliver the afterbirth. Then Peggy watched silently as the young nurse checked on the injury to Anne's leg. It looked nasty, and Peggy suspected the crushing blow of the falling beam must have broken the bones badly.

'At least she's not bleeding,' she said as Julie crawled back to her side.

'It's probably because the beam is acting as a tourniquet,' Julie replied quietly, her gaze fixed determinedly on the torchlight. 'The rescue crew will have to be very careful when they lift it away.'

Peggy could just imagine what might happen and shivered. 'We're all in a bit of a mess, aren't we?' she said with forced cheerfulness. The situation was bad enough without being gloomy about it.

Julie looked beyond the torchlight into the darkness that surrounded them and shivered. 'You could say that, Peggy,' she muttered. 'How long do you think the rescue crew will be?'

Peggy realised the girl must be suffering from claustrophobia and took her hand. 'They won't be long – not with Jim and Ron badgering them.' She squeezed Julie's fingers. 'Try to keep focussed on the light, dear,' she said, 'and keep talking. It will help.'

'I know,' Julie replied shakily, 'but it's so dark, and this space is so small and—'

'Rose Margaret will be all right, won't she?' Peggy interrupted, in an effort to get the girl's attention away from their surroundings.

'I hope so, Peggy. She's a good size, and Anne is obviously healthy. It was quite a quick birth, and I expect the dusty atmosphere was making it difficult for her to breathe.' Julie moved to Anne, who had fallen into an exhausted but restless sleep. Having checked her pulse and her temperature, she covered her with the coat. 'She's fine,' she reassured Peggy. 'Sleep's the best thing for her at the moment.'

Peggy nodded and shifted her legs, which were getting cramped.

Julie gasped as the torchlight beam fell over Peggy's feet. 'Peggy, where are your shoes? Your feet have been cut to ribbons!'

'They do hurt a bit,' she admitted with a grimace, 'but what with Anne and everything, I hadn't noticed until now.'

Julie opened her bag and cleaned the deep cuts and angry abrasions with cotton wool soaked in Dettol, and then swiftly began to bandage both feet. 'I used to be amazed at how far a mother would go when her child was in danger,' she murmured, 'but since I've had William, I know just how strong that urge to protect can be.'

Peggy glanced at the capable hands which were winding the bandage round her sore feet. There was no sign of a wedding ring, but that meant nothing. 'Why don't you tell me about William,' she said softly.

As Julie hesitantly told her about her young sister and the loss of her parents, Peggy's heart went out to her. It was clear she still had nightmares about the way in which her parents had died, and it must be agony for her to be trapped down here, but throughout her sad tale, there was the ray of light that was William.

'But why bring him to Cliffehaven? Surely you realised we're right in bomb alley here?'

Julie hesitated and twisted her fingers in her lap. 'I came to live with my sister, Eileen. She's the only relative we have now until our brothers come home.' She paused again, clearly reluctant to continue. 'But there isn't really any room in her flat and she's got a very important job at the council offices which means she . . .'

Peggy frowned. 'Is your sister Eileen Harris?'

Julie nodded. 'Do you know her?'

Peggy certainly did, but she wasn't about to voice her opinion of the woman to Julie. 'We've met a few times,' she said instead. 'So, Julie, have you managed to find somewhere else to live?'

'Kath Carter's got me a temporary place at the Town Hall,' she replied quickly. 'We'll be fine there.'

'I'm not having you and William living there,' said Peggy firmly. 'You'll come to me where you can both be looked after properly. I don't know what Kath was thinking about. She knows I'd never turn anyone down who really needed a place.'

Anne stirred from her fretful doze and gave a weak smile. 'I knew you'd change your mind, Mum. Didn't I tell you?'

'That's as maybe,' said Peggy. 'But Julie's a special case. I couldn't possibly leave her at the Town Hall after all she's done for us.'

'But you have so many other things to worry about,' said Julie. 'Are you sure?'

'I wouldn't have offered if I wasn't,' Peggy replied stoutly. 'And you're not to worry about young William. There are enough of us at Beach View to help look after him while you're at work.'

Julie grasped her hand, the unshed tears gleaming in the torchlight. 'Thank you,' she breathed. 'Thank you ever so much, Peggy. You can have absolutely no idea how much this means to me.'

Peggy looked into that sweet, dirty little face and thought she knew all too well how much it had meant. Of course there had been room for her and the baby in Eileen's flat. But Eileen Harris had always been a cold-hearted cow, and after what she'd done to poor Rosie Braithwaite, there had been little sympathy for her amongst those in the know. The whole thing had been hushed up, of course, and it had been expected that Eileen would leave Cliffehaven out of shame. Yet she'd brazened it out and carried on as if nothing had happened at all – and now she'd got her hooks into poor, deluded George Unwin, who was head of the Town Council and old enough to know better.

Peggy took a grim satisfaction in the knowledge that Eileen would not be at all happy to learn that Julie would be living at Beach View from now on.

'The heavy lifting crew is here,' shouted Jim a while later. 'We're sending down blankets and tin hats, so cover yourselves as best you can.'

Julie and Peggy covered Anne and huddled close to her beneath the blankets as the sound of men's voices and whining machinery carried down to them. 'It's all right,' soothed Peggy. 'Jim and Ron will get us out soon.'

Julie kept her grip tight on her precious medical bag and closed her eyes as she battled with the rising panic. She could hear the timbers creak and the concrete and bricks slide and rattle above her – could taste the dust and soot that sifted down, could feel the chill of this tiny cavern seep into her bones. She flung back the blanket and switched the torch on, desperate to banish that encroaching, stifling blackness, but the air was full of choking dust and she hastily drew the blanket back over her head and reached for Peggy's hand.

The three of them waited for what felt like a lifetime as the men worked above them to make the hole bigger and the pile of rubble safe. They could hear the dog barking as the men shouted to one another above the roar of machinery, and Ron and Jim called down with progress reports. Then wonderful light filled their prison and they blinked against it as they dared peek over the blankets. Spotlights had been set up, and a ladder was slowly being lowered.

Julie scrambled over and made sure it was fixed onto a firm piece of floor, and then was almost knocked down by the dog which hurtled down the rungs and flung itself at Peggy and Anne.

Julie and Peggy made a grab for the animal and managed to hold it by the collar. 'Someone get Harvey,' shouted Peggy. 'He's about to bring the whole shooting match down on our heads and we can't hold him for long.'

The sturdy figure of Ron descended the ladder and grabbed the dog's collar. 'Sit and stay,' he ordered in a tone that brooked no argument. The dog whined and slumped down, nose on paws, ears and eyebrows twitching with concern.

Ron crawled across the narrow space and squatted beside them. 'To be sure, there's not enough room for the men to work easily down here,' he muttered to Peggy. 'You and young Julie must go up the ladder now with me.'

'I'm not leaving Anne,' said Peggy, gripping her daughter's hand.

'We don't have time to argue,' said Ron. 'You will do as I say for once, Peggy Reilly – you too, girl,' he added to Julie.

'Anne's my patient and I have to stay with her,' said Julie.

'You've done enough,' said Ron. 'Young Dr Sayers can manage from now on.' He patted Anne's hand and wrestled Peggy away. 'Get up that ladder, woman,' he growled. 'Jim's waiting for you.'

Julie remained at Anne's side while Ron chivvied a protesting Peggy up the ladder, the squirming dog held firmly beneath his meaty arm. Willing hands reached to help them the last few steps, and then they were gone.

'Julie, get up here now,' ordered Ron moments later.

'You'd better go, Julie,' said Anne. 'I'll be all right, really.'

Julie shook her head. She would have liked nothing better than to be in the fresh air again, but now that light was flooding into their prison her fears had been vanquished. 'We'll both be all right,' she murmured, taking Anne's hand and feeling the thready pulse as two men began to climb down. 'The men will soon have us free.'

A tall, thin man in a heavy tweed coat reached the bottom of the ladder, surveyed his surroundings, adjusted his tin hat and the big black bag he held, then began to crawl towards them. 'Good morning, ladies,' he said cheerfully. 'Quite a cosy place you have here.' He squatted beside them and held out his hand to Julie. 'Michael Sayers,' he said with a broad smile.

His handshake was as warm and firm as his father's had been and it imbued her with courage and determination. 'Julie Harris,' she replied and smiled back. 'Nice to meet you.'

Michael Sayers examined Anne's leg as the other two men began to shore up the walls and ceiling of their prison. He asked Anne how she was feeling and listened attentively as Julie gave a quick résumé of the birth.

'Your baby is doing very well,' he reassured Anne. 'She's in the special baby unit for now, but I expect her to make a full recovery. Now, I'm going to give you an injection so that these nice men can move that horrid old beam off your leg without it hurting too much.'

He swiftly filled a syringe and injected Anne's thigh. Once he was satisfied that the local anaesthetic had taken effect, he turned back to Julie. 'I'll need you to be quick off the mark once they move that beam,' he said quietly, his dark eyes regarding her solemnly. 'We'll need to tourniquet that leg, or she'll bleed to death.'

Julie nodded as he wound a length of rubber round Anne's thigh and left it loose. The beam had come down across Anne's lower leg and, in the bright lights, Julie could see the gleam of shattered bone beneath it. Her own pulse began to race as she realised Anne would be lucky to survive this without losing her leg, but she made sure none of her thoughts showed in her expression.

The men had finished shoring up the walls and ceiling now and had crawled to Anne's side. 'We daren't cut the beam,' said one of them. 'So we'll have to lift it. Be ready to pull her out the minute we give the shout.'

Julie and Michael exchanged worried glances. 'We'll need more help,' she muttered. 'I can't tighten the tourniquet and lift her out at the same time.'

'Ron,' shouted Michael. 'We need you down here.'

Ron came sliding down the ladder like an old sea dog and scrambled towards them, his face lined and ashen with worry. 'I'll take her top half, you do the other end,' he muttered once Michael had explained the situation.

The three of them tensed, poised to play their part as the two burly rescuers grasped the beam. As their straining began to shift it there was an ominous creaking overhead and smaller pieces of debris began to rain down. Everyone froze.

'It's the only way,' rasped the man in charge. 'On

my count of three, lift and then it's every man for himself.'

Julie reached for the rubber tubing, her hand slick with sweat as the man counted.

'One, two, three.' With a mighty groan they lifted the beam.

Blood shot from Anne's injury like a fountain and Julie tightened the tourniquet then scrambled back as Ron and Michael lifted her away. The two men slowly and carefully replaced the beam, aware that the roof was creaking and groaning and threatening to bury them all.

There was an ominous rumble overhead and the walls of the small cavern began to shift.

Michael had just finished tightly bandaging Anne's shattered leg when the rumble became more ominous and the walls of the cavern began to slide inwards.

Ron grabbed her, almost threw her over his shoulder and raced up the ladder, Julie and the others following swiftly.

Hands reached out to them, dragging them into the dawn and virtually carrying them down the steep side of the trembling mound. More willing hands took Anne, and within moments she and Peggy were being whisked away in an ambulance for the hospital.

Julie let Michael guide her to safety, but her legs were trembling so badly she almost fell into his arms. He led her towards a slab of concrete on the other side of the road and she slumped onto it, her head buried in her hands as the tears of relief and pent-up fear streamed down her face.

The rumble behind her deepened and, with a clatter of wood and concrete and glass, the mound caved in and settled amid a cloud of dust.

'Whew, that was a close call,' muttered Michael. 'Are you all right, Julie?'

She nodded and hastily blew her nose and dried her eyes. 'I'm fine,' she said rather unsteadily.

'I prescribe a cup of hot sweet tea, a bath and a good long sleep,' he said, reaching for his medical bag. 'Well done,' he added softly, his dark brown eyes regarding her with kindness. 'I'll see you tomorrow.'

Julie watched as the tall, slender figure in the dusty overcoat pushed through the crowd of rescuers and bystanders and strode away. Michael Sayers had proved to be dependable and strong, assured in his skills and his sense of duty, and Julie wondered if she could have been quite so brave those last few moments if he hadn't been down that hole with her.

'John Baker, *Cliffehaven News*. You're Sister Harris, aren't you? What was it like down there?'

Julie looked up at the elderly reporter and frowned in confusion. 'I have to get home to William,' she murmured as she grabbed her medical bag and got unsteadily to her feet.

'Is William your husband?' he persisted. 'You're not local, are you?'

She tried to push past him, but the crowd was too tightly packed and he was determined. 'You're quite the heroine,' he said. 'Come on, love, it's a great story. Give me something for tomorrow's paper.'

'Leave the wee girl alone,' rumbled Ron as he put his arm round Julie. 'Let's get you out of here before this hack really starts to irritate me.'

She let him elbow their way through the crowd, but once they were clear she shot him a smile of thanks and freed herself from his grip. 'I have to find William,' she gasped, and before he could reply, she'd broken into a run.

It was much easier to find her way now it was light and it took only minutes to get to Eileen's. But the dread returned when she saw that the door bore the scars of having had the lock broken – which could only mean that the men had had to break in to retrieve her medical bag. Julie's mouth was dry, her fears all-consuming as she raced up the stairs towards the sound of William's angry wails. Had Eileen left him alone as she'd threatened?

Stumbling into the room, she found Eileen pacing the floor, William in her arms, her expression stony. 'And about time too,' she snapped, dumping the screaming baby into Julie's arms. 'Where the hell have you been all damn night?'

Julie held William close and tried to soothe him but he continued to wail, squirming in her arms, his cries going right through her head. 'I was caught in the raid,' she said wearily, and went on to explain all that had happened during the night. 'I'm sorry about your door, Eileen. I'll get someone to fix it.'

'Yes, you will, and you'll pay for it.'

'But the raid was over. Where were you?'

'The bakery has an Anderson shelter and I stayed on for a cup of tea and some toast.' Eileen looked woefully at her once pristine blouse and dabbed at a stain with her handkerchief. 'He puked all over me,' she muttered. 'I need to get changed.'

There was a sharp rap on the front door. 'Miss Harris? Miss Harris, I would really like to speak to you – perhaps get a photograph for the piece?'

'Who the hell is that?' hissed Eileen furiously.

'It's the reporter from the *Cliffehaven News*. Just ignore him.' Julie laid William on the couch and began to change his sodden nappy. 'When was the last time you fed and changed him, Eileen?'

'A couple of hours ago,' she replied distractedly as the reporter continued banging on her open front door. 'You're going to have to leave. I can't have reporters on my doorstep.' She eyed Julie coldly. 'I hope you didn't tell him anything.'

'I've said nothing, but there were enough people at the bomb site to see what happened, and I've no doubt someone's talked to him.' She made William comfortable and carried him into the kitchen to warm a fresh bottle of formula.

Eileen picked up the telephone receiver as the reporter continued to shout from the doorstep. 'I'm calling the police,' she said grimly, 'and once he's gone, you can leave.'

Julie was exhausted to the point of sleeping on her feet as she waited for the kettle to boil on the two-ring hotplate. 'I'm feeding William first,' she retorted, 'then I'll be out of your hair.' She eyed her sister with little affection. 'I won't bother you again – you can be sure of that.'

The police arrived and escorted the reporter away, and within a few minutes there was a man repairing the front door lock. Eileen stood over him, making sure he did the job properly, and when he'd finished she slammed the door and stumped upstairs to her bedroom to get changed.

Julie finished feeding William, her eyelids drooping with weariness, her whole body aching for the comfort of a soft bed. Once he was settled and asleep, she made a spam sandwich which she stuffed down with a cup of scalding tea as she packed away William's things. 'I'll have to leave the two cases here and pick them up later,' she said as Eileen came back into the room.

'I'll get someone to deliver them to the Town Hall before tonight.'

'Don't bother,' Julie said flatly. 'I'm not going to the Town Hall.'

Eileen frowned. 'Where then?'

'Beach View Boarding House.'

Eileen went quite pale beneath her heavy make-up. 'You can't go there,' she rasped.

Julie wondered fleetingly why Eileen was so against her going to Peggy's, but she was long past caring what her sister thought about anything. 'I can go wherever I want,' she replied as she wrapped William into his blanket. 'At least Peggy Reilly will give us a warm welcome, which is more than can be said for you.'

She picked up her medical bag, slung the straps of her gas-mask box and handbag over her shoulder and cradled William. Without another word, or a backwards glance, she hurried down the stairs and out into the fresh, breezy morning.

Eileen heard the slam of the front door and felt the silence close in on her as she stood frozen to the spot. The little world she'd so carefully constructed around her was beginning to crumble, and there was absolutely nothing she could do about it.

She wrapped her arms round her waist and tried to quell the rising tide of emotions that threatened to overwhelm her. She had to stay strong and detached, had to continue as she had done all those years ago, brave it out, keep going until the gossip died down. But it would be harder this time, much harder, and she didn't know if she had the strength to do battle again.

Eileen's sigh was tremulous as she blinked back the tears. The old wounds had been opened up, the old sorrow and shame returning – and once again she was alone to bear their burden. 'I shouldn't have spoken so harshly,' she whispered into the silence. 'I should have welcomed her, given her a home here instead of pushing her straight into Peggy Reilly's arms. But how could I have known that's where she'd go?'

She sank onto the couch, the tears now streaming down her face as she plucked William's forgotten mitten from beneath the cushion. 'Oh, God,' she sobbed. 'What a mess I've made of everything.'

Chapter Ten

Anne had been taken straight into theatre and as a distraught and anxious Peggy waited for news, she let the doctor examine her feet and stitch the deeper cuts. She hadn't noticed how painful they were, being too taken up with Anne and the baby, but now, despite a painkilling injection, they were throbbing and made walking difficult.

Jim arrived while this was being done, his face drawn with concern and weariness, his clothes grey with dust and ash. He held her hand and kissed her brow. 'To be sure, me darlin' girl, that's a terrible mess you've made of your feet.'

'They'll get better,' she said, wincing as the doctor finished bandaging them. 'Have you managed to get hold of Martin yet?'

'I used the cinema telephone to contact the airbase. Martin isn't available at the moment, but his commanding officer has promised to let him know what's happened as soon as he's returned. He'll get a few days' compassionate leave, as well, which will help Anne no end, I shouldn't wonder.'

'The good thing is that Rose Margaret is doing well,' she reassured him as he helped her hobble to the waiting room. 'Dr Sayers has been up to talk to the paediatrician, and he expects her to be well enough to come home in about ten days.'

Jim kept his arm round Peggy, his cheek resting in her dusty curls as they settled on the hard chairs. 'What about our Anne? That leg looked pretty smashed up.'

Peggy's voice quavered with the tears she'd been holding back for so long. 'I don't know, Jim. The surgeon rushed off with her before I could speak to him, and Dr Sayers won't commit himself. But it doesn't look good.' She leaned against him, the weariness and pain and worry weighing heavily on her heart. 'Oh, Jim. What if she loses her leg? What if she . . .?'

'There, there, me darlin' girl,' he soothed. 'She'll come through, you'll see. Anne's a Reilly, and a fighter, and I'll not have you thinking such terrible things.'

Peggy kept her doubts to herself, praying that Jim was right and that her darkest fears wouldn't be realised. But the memory remained of the filthy beam that had crashed down on Anne's leg, and of all that dirt and dust, and she simply couldn't dismiss the thought of all those germs and what harm they might have done to shattered skin and bone.

She looked up expectantly as the door to the waiting room opened. 'Oh, Ron,' she sighed with a mixture of disappointment and relief. 'I thought you might be the doctor.'

He looked older and infinitely weary as he stood

there in his filthy, ragged Home Guard uniform and asked for news. As Peggy told him the little she knew, he nodded and stepped back into the corridor. 'I've left Harvey tied to the hospital gatepost, so I need to get him home. I'll come back as soon as I can.'

'Could you check on Mrs Finch? Only I left her all on her own last night, and she must be frantic by now.'

'Aye, I'll do that, Peg. And what about the wee girl, Julie? I overheard you talking last night. D'you want me to sort out a room for her and the wain?'

'Top front room,' said Peggy, glad to have something else to think about for a moment. 'Rita and the other girls can help get it ready. Use our cot for now. I'll get another from the Town Hall if they have one. If not, someone's bound to be selling one.'

He let the door clatter behind him and Peggy heard his footsteps slowly fade into silence. She leaned back into Jim, desperately trying to keep her eyes open, but Jim's arm was round her, his shoulder solid and infinitely comforting. Her eyelids fluttered and sleep finally claimed her.

Ron untied the sturdy rope that had tethered Harvey to the hospital gatepost and, having let him free to run before him, set off at a steady pace for home. He was weary beyond belief, but the knowledge that Harvey had heard Peggy's calls and led him to her and Anne, and that everyone had been rescued from that hole which could have become their tomb, kept him going. He didn't dwell on the terrible possibility that Anne might not pull through, for thinking like that did no good to his already depleted spirits.

He trudged through the back gate, along the path and into the basement, Harvey close to his heels. He was getting too old for all these shenanigans, and having miraculously survived the first war, he hadn't expected to have to worry himself silly through another. But his family relied on him, and now there was a great-granddaughter to look after, it gave his role of patriarch an extra special importance. At least he was useful, he thought grumpily – not like some of the old codgers in the Home Guard who had nothing more to think about than ill-fitting false teeth and their next meal.

Rather cheered by this thought, he tramped up the concrete steps to the kitchen and was greeted by four very anxious females who'd clearly learned enough of the night's events to badger him with endless questions.

He answered them as best he could, told them about Julie and William, and made sure Mrs Finch had come through her solitary night unscathed. She seemed a little more dithery than usual, but he put that down to the fact they were all on edge after their grim night.

Once he considered he'd fulfilled his duty, he dragged off his coat and plumped into the easy chair by the range. 'I'll have a cup of tea with a drop of rum to liven it,' he said through a vast yawn, 'and a saucer of the same for Harvey. He's earned that much tonight.' He looked fondly at the dog which was now sitting at his feet.

Fran rushed to pour the tea and find the rum as Suzy fussed over Harvey and Rita carried Ron's filthy coat and boots back down the cellar steps. 'Ah,' he said with deep satisfaction as he slurped the scalding alcoholic tea. 'Now that's what I call a lifesaver, eh, Harvey?'

The lurcher was too busy lapping to bark his agreement, but his tail was windmilling very happily as he chased the saucer over the floor.

'Ron,' said Mrs Finch hesitantly. 'I have a confession to make.'

He eyed her affectionately and grinned. 'What terrible sin is it you want to confess? To be sure, you've not sold the family silver while our backs have been turned?'

'Well, it is a terrible mess,' she said fretfully, 'and although it was cold, and made me shiver, I didn't like to burn the oil heater for too long. And then the lamp went out and I tried to light it, and that's when it happened.'

He put down his cup and took her hand, immediately concerned that he'd not noticed she was very upset over something other than the family. 'What is it, Mrs Finch? What happened last night?'

She reached trembling fingers into her wrap-round apron pocket. 'I took out the lovely new hearing aid so I could go to sleep,' she said, 'and then woke up in the dark and forgot it was in my lap. I got up to light the lamp and . . .' She drew the remains of the hearing aid out of her apron pocket and held them out to him. 'I must have stepped on it,' she finished shakily.

He smiled at her, relieved that her fretfulness had been over something so minor. 'Never mind,' he said, taking it from her. 'Worse things happen at sea, and it'll be quite like old times without you earwigging on every word I say.'

She frowned back at him, clearly not understanding what he'd said. 'What's that about wigs?' she demanded. 'I do not wear such a thing. How dare you insinuate—'

'I never said you wore a wig,' he yelled so she could hear. 'I said I'll see what I can do to fix this.' But as he dangled it before her, he didn't hold out much hope. Her dainty size four feet had smashed the blessed thing to smithereens.

Julie discovered that Beach View Boarding House was one of a terrace of Victorian villas in a side street that seemed to end in a bomb site. She dithered outside as she checked her watch and wondered what to do. It was still quite early, and the family were probably at the hospital. Perhaps she should have waited until later to descend on them – but she had nowhere else to go, and if she didn't eat properly and rest soon, she would simply collapse right here on the pavement.

She hitched William to a more comfortable position in her arms and rapped the lion's-head knocker, not at all sure about her welcome. Would they even be expecting her?

'There y'are,' said Ron as he flung the door open. 'Come in, come in. Your room is almost ready, and I've taken the cot up for young William, so he'll be as snug as a bug in a rug.' He poked a rather grubby finger into William's blanket and tickled his chin. 'To be sure, he's a fine fellow, so he is.'

Julie smiled at the praise and stepped into the pleasant hall as he closed the door behind her. His welcome had banished her fears and at last she felt she could relax. 'Thank you, Mr Reilly,' she said shyly. 'I wasn't sure if you'd be expecting me. How's Anne and the baby?'

'Call me Ron,' he said, and smiled. 'Everyone else does in this house,' he added with feigned grumpiness, 'regardless of the fact I'm an old man who suffers from me shrapnel wounds something terrible, and should be treated with respect.'

'Oh.' Julie didn't quite know how to take his sudden change in humour.

Ron wriggled his eyebrows, his blue eyes twinkling again. 'Take no notice of me, girly. I like a good grumble now and then.' His expression sobered. 'Anne's in theatre and Peggy and Jim are waiting at the hospital for news. The baby is well by all accounts, and expected to be home within the fortnight.'

'That's very good news,' replied Julie, distracted by the sound of footsteps pounding along an upstairs landing.

'That sounds like Rita. She'll find you something to eat and show you your room,' said Ron. 'I have to get washed and changed and back to the hospital. Nice to have you with us,' he added over his shoulder as he headed out of the hall.

Julie smiled at the young girl who'd come running down the stairs. Small and slight with a halo of dark curls, she looked a real tomboy in trousers, boots and an old flying jacket. 'Hello, Rita. I'm Julie, and this is William.'

'Oh, what a darling,' she cooed as she peeked into the folds of the blanket. 'It's nice to meet you, Julie, and I'm sure you'll be as happy as we all are here. But I've heard all about what happened last night,' she said breathlessly, 'so I expect you're that tired you just want to climb into bed and sleep for hours instead of standing here talking to me.'

'Actually,' said Julie, 'I could do with some food. I haven't eaten more than a spam sandwich since yesterday morning.'

Rita's big brown eyes widened. 'Goodness, you must be starving. Come on into the kitchen while I make you something.'

Julie followed her into the homely kitchen and sank into one of the comfortable armchairs that had been set beside the small black range in the chimney breast. She eased the blanket open so William wouldn't get too warm and looked about her. It was obviously the heart of the home, with shabby furniture, worn lino-leum and peeling paint, but it was so like the kitchen back in Stepney that it made her heart ache.

Rita was chattering away as she made a doorstep sandwich with thick bread, home-made chutney and a slab of corned beef. 'The others are about some-where,' she explained, 'but it's been a long, worrying night for everyone, so I expect they're catching up on their sleep.' She shot Julie a grin as she handed her the sandwich and a cup of tea. 'Want me to hold William while you eat?'

Julie smiled back and tenderly passed him over before she ravenously attacked the delicious sand-wich and restoring tea. 'How many people live here?' she asked once her initial hunger had been satisfied and she could think straight.

Rita carefully settled back in the other chair, William snug in her arms. 'There's Peggy and Jim, of course, and Jim's dad, Ron. Mrs Finch is a permanent lodger, but we all think of her as our grandmother.' She grinned wickedly. 'She's as deaf as a post, but don't let that fool you. Smart as a whip, that one, and not afraid to speak her mind.'

She fell silent for a moment, mesmerised by William who was squirming and pulling faces in his sleep. 'Fran and Suzy are nurses at the hospital, and Cissy's a secretary with the WAAF. She's Peg and Jim's youngest daughter, and we went to school together,' she explained. 'There are two younger boys, but they've been evacuated to Somerset. Then there's me.'

Julie smiled back at her, delighted with her friendliness. 'Are you a Reilly too?'

Rita smiled broadly. 'No, but I've known the Reillys all my life, so when I got bombed out, Peggy insisted I move in. She's a diamond, is Aunt Peg,' she ended with an affectionate smile. 'You won't find a better home than this, Julie. I promise.'

Julie thought fleetingly of the little house in Stepney that had once been the centre of her world, then determinedly pushed the memory away before it summoned tears. The sandwich and the tea had left her feeling sleepier than ever, and if she sat here for much longer, she'd nod right off. 'Thanks for that,' she said, wearily getting to her feet and placing the china on the wooden draining board.

'You look all in,' said Rita, still carrying William. 'Which is hardly surprising after what you've been through. Come on, I'll show you your room before you fall in a heap.'

Julie gathered up her bag, gas-mask box and handbag and followed Rita back into the hall and up the stairs.

'You're at the top of the house in the front,' Rita chattered happily. 'Suzy and Fran are next to you, and Cissy Reilly's along at the end of the landing. I'm in the middle one on the first floor, next to where Anne and Rose Margaret will sleep until Anne's ready to go home to her own place.'

She finally took a breath before rushing on. 'Mrs Finch is next to the bathroom. And watch out for the boiler – it goes off with a terrible bang and can singe your eyebrows if you aren't careful. Peggy and Jim sleep on the ground floor off the hall, and Ron's in the basement with Harvey,' she added breathlessly as they reached the top-floor landing.

Julie tried to take it all in, but with so many names to remember, her weary brain just couldn't cope. She trudged after the lively, chatty girl and followed her into a delightful, sunny room that smelled faintly of beeswax furniture polish.

It was under the eaves, with a window over-looking the nearby roofs and beyond to a glimpse of the sea. A single bed had been made up with fresh linen and a sprigged eiderdown to match the curtains, which had been lined in blackout material. The cot stood beside it, cosy with miniature sheets and blankets. There was a gas fire, a wardrobe, chest of drawers and bedside table, and in the window alcove was a small dressing table. The sun streamed through the window from a cloudless February sky and shone on the polished furniture and wooden floor, making it cheerful and welcoming.

'It's lovely,' Julie breathed. 'Thanks ever so much, Rita.'

'It was no bother, really,' she replied, sweeping back her dark curls. 'I'm just glad to help after all you've done for Peggy and Anne.' She frowned as Julie dumped her bags and gas-mask box on the floor. 'Haven't you got any other luggage?' she asked. 'Only Ron said you'd come down from London.'

'It's at me sister's,' Julie replied through a vast yawn. 'I've got clean bottles, nappies and formula for William. I'll collect the rest of it after I've had some shut-eye.'

'Right you are,' Rita said cheerfully as she handed William over. 'You get your head down for a bit, and if William wakes, don't worry. One of us will look after him for you.' She closed the door and hurried back down the stairs.

Julie gently lowered William into the cot and, without waking him, changed his nappy and covered him with the lovely soft blanket and sheet. Dragging off her coat and kicking off her shoes, she realised she stank of dust and ash and dirt and damp, and she could really have done with a good bath. But she was too tired to worry about that now, a quick scrub with a flannel would have to be enough.

Having found the bathroom, she didn't feel up to lighting the rather daunting-looking boiler, so she washed quickly in cold water then traipsed back to her room. The comfortable bed was calling her, and she pulled off her skirt and jumper and clambered in between the sheets in her underwear. Sinking her weary head into the soft pillow, she was asleep before she'd even drawn the blankets to her chin.

Peggy woke as the door to the waiting room opened. She was surprised to see Ron sitting on the other side of the room with his tatty old slippers on his lap, and a quick glance at the clock on the wall showed that almost four hours had passed since Anne had been rushed into theatre. But the arrival of the doctor swept away all these minor observations, and she pushed back her filthy hair from her face and looked at him fearfully, trying to gauge the seriousness of his news from his expression. She felt her heart thud against her ribs and a surge of hope as he smiled.

'Your daughter is a very lucky young woman,' he said, taking his briar pipe out of his pocket. 'She has several oblique fractures to her tibia and fibula, but they were clean breaks, easily reset. These will knit in time as long as we can contain any infection. The quick thinking of Dr Sayers and his nurse meant there was very little blood loss and I was able to repair the damage to the artery.'

He paused for a moment to light his pipe, and the tense atmosphere in the waiting room heightened.

'But she is very weak,' he continued solemnly through the cloud of smoke. 'The trauma of her accident and the onset of labour and delivery have depleted her resources, so I've ordered an intra-venous drip to help restore her and to fight any infection.'

'But she will recover?' Peggy sat forward anxiously.

'In time,' he said with a smile. 'But she must remain in hospital until we are absolutely sure there is no septicaemia.'

'And if there is?'

He eyed her thoughtfully. 'Let us not speculate on the negative, Mrs Reilly. Your daughter is a healthy young woman who has so far come through this ordeal with great fortitude. I have every confidence she will recover.'

'Can we see her?' asked Jim.

'Not yet. She's still heavily sedated and needs constant observation by my nurses. I suggest you go home, have a rest and something to eat, and then return this evening.' He gave them an encouraging smile before turning to leave.

'Do you think we could visit Rose Margaret?' asked Peggy, gripping Jim's hand and struggling to feel positive.

'I'll let the nurses know you're on your way,' he said, 'but make it a short visit, the special baby ward is a busy place.'

Peggy collapsed back into Jim's embrace as the doctor left the room. 'Oh, Jim,' she sobbed. 'I thought we'd lost her. I really did.'

'I told you she was tough,' he murmured as he stroked her hair. 'Just like her mam. Come on, acushla, dry your tears, put on Da's old slippers, and we'll go and see our granddaughter.'

Peggy blew her nose, eased her painful, bandaged feet into the unsavoury slippers, and tottered, weary to the point of collapse. But she managed to put one foot in front of the other as she shuffled arm in arm with Jim and Ron down the endless corridors to the nursery.

Rose Margaret was asleep, her sweet rosebud mouth working as if at the breast, her coxcomb of hair dark against the snow white sheet. Cocooned tightly in a soft blanket, she looked like a tiny chrysalis beneath the oxygen tent that had been placed over the special cot.

Peggy marvelled at the long dark eyelashes that drifted so softly on the peachy cheeks, and felt the tears prick as those tiny lips pursed and little fingers flexed against them. 'She's perfect,' she breathed.

'Aye, that she is,' murmured Jim, his eyes suspiciously bright. 'Reminds me of Anne when she was that size. You forget how wee they were, don't you?'

Peggy looked up at him, saw the unshed tears and cupped his stubbly cheek. 'I do love you, Jim Reilly,' she murmured, her heart full.

Ron cleared his throat and shuffled his feet, not quite able to disguise the pride that shone in his eyes as he looked down at the baby. 'Aye,' he muttered. 'She's a Reilly, so she is.' He glanced back at Peggy and Jim. 'Now, if you two have quite finished billing and cooing, I'm in need of me tea.'

Peggy's smile was radiant as she linked arms with the two men she loved most in the world and headed for the warmth and comfort of home.

Chapter Eleven

Julie snapped out of the nightmare in which she was being buried in a bomb crater, and woke to utter darkness. Disorientated and terrified, she thought for a moment that it had been no dream, but a living horror. But as her senses returned and she breathed in the scent of beeswax and clean linen, she remembered where she was, and shakily reached for the bedside light.

Almost blinded by the sudden brilliance, she realised someone had drawn the blackout curtains and taken the bag with the nappies, bottles and formula. Her gaze flew to the cot. William wasn't there.

Throwing back the bedclothes, she was about to reach for her dirty clothes when she saw her two suitcases standing by the wardrobe. With a sigh of thankfulness, she unpacked her warm dressing gown and, realising it must be the middle of the night, tiptoed hurriedly down the two flights of stairs.

As she reached the bottom she couldn't help but see the beautiful cream and navy coach-built pram standing in the hall. It was deep and luxurious, with shining wheels and mudguards, a parcel shelf beneath the sturdy body, and a neat navy rainproof cover. She ran her fingers over it jealously, wondering how much such a magnificent pram might cost, and if she could afford one for William.

With a sigh of acceptance that such a thing was way beyond her means, she quietly moved towards the flickering light that came from the kitchen, and the murmur of a gentle lullaby being softly hummed.

Standing in the doorway, Julie felt the tears prick. How perfect this little scene would have been if only it was her mother sitting there, holding the grandson she'd waited for so eagerly. Julie stifled the longing and sniffed back her tears.

Harvey was lying protectively by Peggy's heavily bandaged feet as she finished feeding William in the glow from the range fire and continued to sing him to sleep. The dog lifted his head momentarily, decided Julie posed no threat, and returned to his vigil. Peggy looked exhausted, but there was a gentleness to her sweet expression that told Julie she was contented and at peace.

As Peggy looked up, their eyes met, and they exchanged an affectionate, understanding smile. 'He's almost asleep,' Peggy murmured. 'I hope we didn't disturb you.'

The dog seemed to know Julie needed something to distract her and give her time to compose herself, for, as she sat down, he rested his chin on her lap, demanding to be stroked. 'I didn't hear a thing,' she admitted as she ruffled Harvey's ears. 'I was out like a light the minute my head hit the pillow.'

She glanced up at the clock on the mantelpiece and gasped in horror. It was two in the morning. 'Go to bed, Peggy, you must be exhausted.'

'I couldn't sleep,' Peggy replied, 'and when I heard him stirring, I brought him down to keep me company.' She smiled back at Julie. 'This is far more restful than listening to Jim snoring, and I thought I should get some practice in before Rose comes home. I'm a bit rusty at coping with such young ones.'

'You certainly look very comfortable,' said Julie, 'and so does William. Thank you, Peggy – for everything.'

Peggy shrugged away her thanks and continued to rock William. 'You had a visitor this afternoon,' she said softly. 'Kath Carter came round with that lovely pram and said she'd love to have that cup of tea with you once you were settled.'

'Kath brought that pram for me?' Julie gasped. 'But I thought it must be Anne's.'

Peggy shook her head and smiled. 'Our old pram's up in Anne's room.'

Mortified that she'd forgotten all about their arrangements to have tea this afternoon, and knowing she'd be hard pressed to find the money to pay for such a generous gift, Julie bit her lip. 'I must pay her back,' she said, 'but it might be a while before—'

'You don't have to fret about that,' interrupted Peggy. 'She said to tell you it had been left at the Town Hall by a young mother who was being evacuated to Wales. It cost her nothing, but if you want

238

to give a donation to the rehoming charity, then that's up to you. She just thought you deserved a "welcome to Cliffehaven" present, saw the pram and knew it was the perfect gift.'

Julie was overwhelmed by Kath's thoughtfulness on such a short acquaintance. 'How kind of her to make such a lovely gesture,' she managed through a constricted throat.

Peggy chuckled softly. 'Kath's a sweet girl; wears her heart on her sleeve a bit too obviously at times, but she'll be a true friend, and I'm glad you've got to know one another.'

'So am I. We seemed to hit it off straight away and were supposed to meet up this afternoon. But with everything that's happened, it slipped me mind. I'll pop in and see her tomorrow while I'm on me rounds.'

'That reminds me,' said Peggy, 'Michael Sayers telephoned. You don't have to be in tomorrow until midday. He says you've earned a lie-in,' she added with a smile.

Julie smiled back. 'That's very kind of him, but it wouldn't be diplomatic to be late on my first day – there's nothing more guaranteed to put people's backs up than if they think the new girl's taking liberties.'

'You could be right there,' Peggy murmured. 'Eunice Beecham certainly won't stand for any signs of favouritism. But under all that bustle and starch she's got a good heart,' she added quickly.

Julie felt a twinge of foreboding but decided to form her own judgement of this Eunice. 'Is she the practice nurse?'

Peggy nodded. 'She's been with the doctors for about five years and knows how much they depend upon her now the district nurse has left.' She sighed. 'Poor Eunice is in love with Michael, of course, but I suspect it's unrequited, because over a year has passed since he was jilted and he's shown no sign of interest in Eunice.'

'Jilted? How awful, poor man.'

Peggy looked down at the sleeping baby and gently ran her fingers through his golden hair. 'She left him for a Canadian pilot two days before the wedding. Michael was devastated – they'd been childhood sweethearts, you see.'

'Life is complicated, isn't it,' sighed Julie.

Peggy handed William over. 'The war just makes it more so – especially for the little ones.' She became businesslike, gathering up the dirty nappy and empty bottle. 'I've put a bucket and bleach under the sink for the nappies. The copper boiler's in the basement, so use it whenever you need. I know how many of these things a baby can get through.'

'Don't worry, Peggy. I'll do our washing and help as much as I can, but are you sure you can cope with William while I'm working?'

Peggy looked rather startled by her question. 'Of course I can. Goodness me, haven't I already said so?'

'But when Rose comes home—'

'I'll have two of the little darlings to coo over and look after.' Peggy grinned with delight. 'It'll be quite like old times, and I'm looking forward to it, really I am.'

Julie wasn't at all sure Peggy knew what she was letting herself in for but decided that tonight wasn't the time to cast doubts on the situation. She would help as much as she could, and if it proved too hard for Peggy, then she would work part-time to ease the load.

'I've left your supper in the larder,' said Peggy. 'It just needs warming through. Help yourself to tea or cocoa; there's enough milk until the milkman comes at five.'

'I could do with a cuppa, and that's a fact.'

'This is your home for as long as you want it, and you must treat it as such.' Peggy's smile was soft and understanding. 'I realise this can never replace what you've lost, but if you ever need to talk, or feel a bit down or lonely, you can always come to me, Julie.'

Julie felt the onset of tears again and hastily sniffed them back as Peggy gave her a quick hug.

As they drew apart, Peggy smiled and eyed Julie's dressing gown. 'I see you found your cases,' she murmured. 'Jim fetched them after we'd been to the hospital.'

'How is Anne?'

'Not really awake yet, but she's got a good colour and the nurses are looking after her beautifully.'

Peggy gave a deep, tremulous sigh. 'Her leg's in plaster from her hip to her toes, poor little love, with it stuck up in the air by a series of pulleys. But she's been pumped so full of painkillers that she's hardly aware of anything yet.'

'They'll monitor her pain relief so she stays comfortable,' Julie said reassuringly. 'Now, go to bed, Peggy, and try not to worry.'

Peggy gave her a weary smile. 'Easier said than done,' she replied, 'but I'll do my best. Goodnight, Julie, love.'

Julie stayed in the warm firelit kitchen long after Peggy had left, her thoughts drifting over the past two days in which so much had happened. It was strange to feel so at home here after such a short while, but she'd met so many lovely people and been made to feel so welcome, it was almost like being back in the East End again.

Julie had bathed and dressed after snatching another two hours of sleep before William woke demanding his breakfast. Afraid he would disturb everyone, she fed and washed him in the kitchen and then placed him tenderly in the lovely pram. The springs bounced silently and he was soon rocked gently to sleep in his cocoon of blankets.

It was still only six in the morning, so she moved quietly as she made her bed, unpacked her cases and tidied the room. Gathering up the dirty clothes from the floor, she eyed her mother's dress with a wry smile. It seemed determined one way or another to get involved with bombing raids.

Down in the basement there was no sign of Ron or Harvey, who must be very early risers. She quickly worked out how to use the boiler and soon had a line of clean clothes and towelling nappies flapping in the breeze. It promised to be a lovely day after the heavy rain during the night, and she just hoped the Luftwaffe wouldn't come along to spoil it.

Returning to the kitchen, she scrubbed her medical instruments clean and buffed up her leather bag. Once this was done to her satisfaction, she put the kettle on the range and crossed the hall to explore what looked like a formal dining room.

The windows had been boarded up, so it was gloomy, but she could see soot stains on the coving and in the ceiling rose, and patches where the wallpaper had begun to peel away, and the paint was chipped. Chairs had been stacked in one corner, the small tables pushed back against the wall, along with a rolled up carpet which had probably once covered the varnished floorboards. The room didn't look as if it was used much.

Julie went back to the kitchen and began to set the table with cutlery and china. It would be a bit of a squash with seven sitting round the table, but that was how they'd managed back in Stepney before they'd all grown up and left home, and she had an idea that Peggy liked it that way too.

She made a pot of tea, pulled on a cardigan, and wandered out into the garden with her cup to enjoy the fresh, brisk air and early sunshine. The birds were singing and she could smell the saltiness of the sea as she stood there and regarded the large vegetable patch and the ugly Anderson shelter at the far end. It reminded her strongly of the back garden of the nurses' hostel, except for the henhouse and birdsong. She gave a wry smile. The London birds were usually coughing like seasoned smokers at this time of the morning, their songs stifled by the heavy smog from thousands of chimneys.

Returning to the kitchen, she was greeted sleepily by two young women who were slumped over cups of tea. 'Good morning,' said the one with fiery red hair which seemed to have a life of its own beneath the nurse's cap. 'I'm Fran, and this old sleepyhead is Suzy. You must be Julie.'

Julie smiled with pleasure. 'Hello. Nice to meet you at last. I hope William didn't wake you in the night.'

'Not at all,' said Suzy through a vast yawn. 'I just hate early shifts.'

'William's a darling wain, so he is,' said Fran in her lilting Irish brogue. 'To be sure, we've drawn up a rota to mind him, and it'll be quite like home. Mammy had a baby every year, regular as clockwork, so she did, so I've plenty of practice.'

'Everyone's been ever so kind,' Julie murmured.

Suzy looked at Julie over the rim of her teacup.

'We're just glad to help,' she said, her vowels rounded and very English. 'What with the war and everything, it's only right to do what we can for each other.'

Fran hurried into the hall as the letter box clattered and returned with the newspaper. 'Well,' she breathed as she unrolled it, 'would you look at that, Julie? You've made the front page of the local rag.'

Julie felt a frisson of horror as Fran held out the paper so they could both see the grainy black-and-white picture of her coming out of Eileen's doorway with William in her arms. 'Bloody hell,' she breathed, reaching for it. 'That's going to put the cat among the pigeons and no mistake.'

'I don't see why,' murmured Suzy. 'It's not a bad picture, considering you obviously didn't know it was being taken.'

'That's not the point. My sister will blow a flaming gasket when she sees this.' Her gaze swept over the screaming headline which almost filled the top third of the page:

Heroine Nurse Delivers Baby While Trapped Below Ground

Julie raced through the short paragraph below and turned the page to discover more photographs taken at the bomb site. The reporter had obviously been skulking outside Eileen's flat after the police had released him, and had certainly done his homework on her relationship to Eileen and her posting at Cliffe surgery. But the most harmful thing of all was his

245

speculation over William's identity. The piece might have been carefully worded, but it was all too clear he was insinuating that William was her illegitimate baby, and that Eileen had probably – and quite rightly – refused to take her in.

She closed the newspaper and slid it across the table. 'I just hope the doctors don't see that,' she said crossly. 'Because if they do, then I'll probably be out on me ear before I've even started.'

'Everyone will see it,' said Suzy with a sigh. 'It's the local paper and the main source of cinema and theatre times, as well as advertising dances and such. But why should they sack you? You saved Anne and her baby, and were terribly brave going down into that hole.' She shivered. 'I know I couldn't have done it, not for all the tea in China.'

'I didn't tell them about William when I applied for the job – or when I went for me interview the other day,' Julie explained.

'There's no shame in raising your sister's wain,' said Fran stoutly. 'Tell them the truth and be damned, is what I say. They need you more than you need them, and there'll always be a job for a good nurse.'

'Fran's talking a lot of sense, for once.' Peggy had bustled into the room, seen the headline, and quickly scanned the article. 'Take her advice, Julie, and I'll have a word with the editor about his scabrous reporter,' she said furiously.

'Scabrous?' Fran giggled. 'To be sure, that's a hell of a word for this time of the morning, Peggy.'

Peggy grinned back as they all chuckled. 'It is rather, isn't it,' she said proudly, 'and although I'm not at all sure what it means, it felt just right.' The dark mood having been broken, she pulled on her flowered apron, wrapped it round her slender frame and tied it firmly at the waist. 'Right,' she said. 'Who wants a boiled egg for breakfast?'

Julie checked that William was clean, fed and comfortable and that Peggy had everything she might need until she returned home. Peggy had had to shoo her out of the door as she'd dithered, but now she was finally on her way to the doctor's surgery she felt ready to get stuck in and do battle if necessary.

Morning surgery had yet to begin, and when Julie arrived at the front door she was greeted by the sight of a large woman on her knees, her vast backside swaying like jelly beneath her floral wrap-round apron as she scrubbed the hall floor.

'Hello, ducks,' she said, sitting back on her heels and adjusting the scarf she'd tied over her curlers. 'Maud's the name, pleased to meet you.' She gave a broad smile which revealed ill-fitting dentures. 'I do for the doctors every morning, but I never expected to meet a real-life heroine,' she said with a chuckle. 'Quite made me day, it has.'

'That's quite enough chatter, Maud – and you've missed a bit.' A tall, rather imposing young woman dressed in a starched and pristine nurse's uniform stood on the other side of the hall and pointed to an almost indiscernible spot on the black-and-white tiled floor.

'Right you are, Miss Beecham.' Maud slowly got to her feet to wipe over the offending spot, muttering about them's what give orders should have her arthritis and see how they liked it.

Julie bit back on a smile and, having heard something about this woman from Peggy and Kath, took the opportunity to give the posh-sounding Eunice Beecham the once-over. She was at least four inches taller than Julie, and attractive in a healthy, rather robust way, with fair hair, a trim figure, and a good complexion that needed little make-up. Eunice was probably in her early thirties, and sounded as if she was the product of a private girls' school somewhere in the Home Counties. She was clearly proud of her position here at the surgery, but Julie suspected she would feel equally at home in a stable yard or on a hockey pitch.

Eunice must have become aware of her scrutiny, for she turned her very blue eyes on Julie and regarded her coolly.

If her imperious gaze was supposed to daunt Julie, she was mistaken, for having dealt with some of the most withering and terrifying matrons in London, Julie was quite capable of holding her own. 'I'm Sister Harris,' she said, as she carefully made her way across the still damp floor.

'I know who you are,' Eunice replied, looking down her patrician nose.

'You must be Eunice Beecham,' said Julie, gripping her medical bag.

'*Sister* Beecham,' she corrected. 'You're early,' she added, almost as an accusation.

'I know. I didn't need extra time off as Dr Michael suggested, and Dr Sayers Senior asked me to be here by eight, so I could get me uniform sorted out.' Julie's Cockney accent sounded harsh after the dulcet tones of the other woman. 'He also said you'd have me schedule and casebook, and that there's a bicycle I could use on me rounds.'

The nostrils thinned as if they'd come in contact with a nasty smell. 'What part of London do you actually come from?'

'Stepney,' Julie replied, lifting her chin, almost daring the woman to say more.

Eunice sniffed and turned on her heel. 'As you appear to be splashed all over the newspapers this morning, the doctors will want to see you before we go any further,' she said. 'Wait in there.'

Julie walked into the large waiting room and sat down on one of the hard chairs, her medical bag gripped tightly on her knees. Eunice Beecham was a snooty cow, and no mistake, and it had been hard not to rise to her sneering. But Julie's dad had always advised her to keep her brain in gear and her gob shut when goaded, and she was glad she'd heeded that advice today, for she could have given her a right mouthful – which would have only made things worse than they already were.

She eyed the posters on the wall exhorting women to inoculate their children, and informing them that coughs and sneezes spread diseases. There were others calling for women to join the VAD and the Land Army, and warning that careless talk cost lives. She looked at that one with a heavy heart. The reporter's groundless gossip might have already cost her this job.

'The doctors will see you now.' Eunice led the way to the consulting room Julie had visited the other day, and tapped discreetly on the door before opening it.

Michael and his father both stood as she entered the room, and she was only vaguely aware of Eunice closing the door behind her. 'I suppose you wanted to talk to me about that article in the paper?' she said, forestalling any awkwardness.

'I'm less concerned about that scurrilous piece of nonsense than I am about you lying to me over that child of yours,' said the elderly doctor. 'If you can lie about that, then how can I trust you with anything?'

'I think we should let Sister Harris explain before we start accusing her, Father,' said Michael quietly. He shot her a sweet smile of encouragement.

Bolstered by that smile, Julie told them everything, from her sister's death to her arrival in Cliffehaven. 'I didn't tell you about William because, at the time, I thought me sister would help. Now I have Mrs Reilly and the girls at Beach View to look after him, and I can assure you, me work won't suffer in any way because of him.'

'But what if he's taken ill?' said the older man.

'There are two other nurses in the guest house, and Peggy has enough experience as a mother to know what to do.'

'It sounds as if you've really had your work cut out, but you seem to have made all the necessary arrangements,' Michael murmured. 'I admire your tenacity.'

'Well, it's all very irregular,' said his father, reaching for his pipe. 'In my day young women either had a career or became mothers. All this juggling with both will end in trouble, mark my words.'

Julie looked at him fearfully, her hands knotted tightly on her lap as an uneasy silence filled the room. This was it. This was the moment they'd dismiss her.

'I think we should continue as planned, Father,' said Michael calmly. 'After all, we desperately need a district nurse and midwife, and Julie – Sister Harris – has more than proved her capability.'

Julie silently blessed Michael for his unwavering support and willed the old doctor to agree.

'Hmmph.' He sucked on his pipe, his eyes narrowed beneath the snowy brows as he considered the options. 'All right, but on your head be it, Michael. I will not have this surgery disrupted every time she has to run off to tend to that baby. And if there's any more scandal, then she'll have to go. I can't have the reputation of this surgery sullied.' He glared at them both. 'Be off with you,' he rumbled. 'Surgery starts in half an hour and I haven't had my morning coffee yet.'

Michael caught Julie's eye as they left the consulting room together. Maud was pretending to polish the wood panelling in the hall, and Julie just caught a glimpse of Eunice's starched apron as she flitted into the waiting room. No doubt they'd both been earwigging.

'Father's bark is worse than his bite,' said Michael apologetically. 'He'll soon calm down, you'll see.'

'I'm sure everything will be just fine once he realises I won't let him down,' she assured him, 'but I will need the uniform he promised and somewhere to change.'

'I'll have Sister Beecham fetch it from the linen store. You can change in that cloakroom over there.' He smiled that sweet, gentle smile which wiped away the years and softened the lines of care on his face. 'Welcome to Cliffe surgery, Julie. I hope you'll be happy here.'

She was about to reply when Eunice's voice broke in. 'Dr Michael, could I have a word, please?'

Michael gave Julie a sly wink and followed the bustling and efficient Eunice into the waiting room.

'Never you mind, ducks,' said Maud conspiratorially as she edged closer. 'That one's only jealous, you know. Never 'ad *er* picture in no paper, for a start, and you're way prettier than the last district nurse.'

'Thanks, Maud,' said Julie, biting back a giggle. 'I'd better get on, though, 'cos I've got the feeling I'm about to have a very busy day.'

She hurried into the waiting room and was just in time to see Michael disappearing into his consulting room. 'Do you have me schedule and uniform, Sister Beecham?' she asked, keeping her tone pleasant and her smile warm.

'You are extremely fortunate the doctors are so understanding,' Eunice said coolly. 'But I am in charge here, and if you court further attention from the press, then I shall have no option but to advise them to dismiss you.'

Julie wanted so badly to defend herself, but realised it would only make things worse between them. 'Can I have me uniform, please? I need to get on.'

'It's in the linen room, which is through that door over there.' Eunice handed over the schedule, along with a rather tatty casebook and a dilapidated street map. 'The volunteer nurses have their own lists today,' she said frostily, 'but I'm sure someone of your experience will manage adequately without their help.'

Julie didn't rise to the snub as she placed the map back on the other woman's desk. 'I have me own map,' she said, just as coolly. 'Where's me bicycle?'

'In the shed in the back garden.' Eunice became engrossed in her appointment book and Julie left her to it.

The uniform was a pink-and-white striped cotton

dress with starched collar and cuffs and a rather unflattering storm cap. The previous district nurse had been a large woman, and Julie struggled for a while to tuck all the folds of material neatly into her belt so that it didn't billow round her. She had her own thick black stockings and sturdy shoes and, once she'd pinned her Queen's badge on her cap and given the huge dress another tug here and there, she felt ready for the day.

The bicycle was old, but the chain had been carefully oiled, the tyres were plump and sturdy and the basket on the front firmly fixed. Wheeling it out into the road, Julie took out her map, found the street where her first patient lived and set off, the warm navy cloak billowing behind her. It was good to be back doing what she loved best, and despite Eunice and Eileen, she had a feeling that life in Cliffehaven would suit her very well indeed.

Chapter Twelve

Two fraught weeks had passed since Anne and her baby had been rushed to hospital, and March had begun with bright skies and brisk winds. Unfortunately, the sunny days and frosty, starlit nights had also brought enemy planes, and both Portsmouth and London had taken a hammering. There had been numerous air-raid warnings in Cliffehaven, and it had become almost commonplace to hear the roar of the RAF planes overhead as they continued to bombard Cologne, Hamburg and Berlin, and defend the English coastline.

Following Churchill's impassioned speech to Roosevelt, ending 'Give us the tools, and we will finish the job,' the American president had finally had his Lend-Lease bill passed. Roosevelt's speech the previous night had been a real tonic, not least for the local American servicemen, who were frustrated at not playing any part in the hostilities. With the bill passed, it was generally expected that America must surely now enter the war.

On the home front, the new national call-up included all men between the ages of eighteen and forty-one, and women without dependants between the ages of twenty and thirty and, following the heavy losses of shipping, Bevin was asking for another fifty thousand more workers at the docks. It seemed that Hitler's spring offensive had begun, and the men and women of Great Britain were steeling themselves for the toughest battle of their lives.

Like everyone else in Cliffehaven, Ron had kept abreast of the news and continued to play his part, knowing that even his small effort was needed to win this war. His duties with the Home Guard and the fire-watch team meant he had less time to go into the hills with Harvey, but he still jealously guarded his precious few hours with Rosie each day.

This is the life, he thought as he sat back in the comfortable chair, feet on a stool, cup of tea in his hand and a slab of cake on a plate at his elbow. Rosie's upstairs parlour was cosy and a little too feminine for his taste, but welcoming all the same, and he felt strangely at home among the chintz and the frills.

It had become an afternoon ritual to share a cup of tea with Rosie after he'd changed the barrels and brought the crates of bottles up from the cellar in preparation for the evening session. He watched her now as she sashayed across her sitting room in her high heels, admiring her long, slender legs and narrow hips, and the curve of her breasts beneath the frothy white blouse. No one knew how old Rosie was, but Ron thought she was about fifty – which he considered a ripe, luscious age when a woman was in her prime and at the height of her self-assurance and sensuality.

He might be in his sixties and considered past it, but by jingo, Rosie could stir the dead. He crossed his legs and tried to concentrate on his cup of tea.

Rosie grinned at him as she kicked off her shoes and curled like a contented cat into the corner of the couch opposite him. 'Tea too hot?' she asked innocently, her wide blue eyes gleaming with fun as she patted the neat waves and curls in her platinum hair.

'It's just fine,' he muttered, the hot brew burning his mouth. 'To be sure, Rosie girl, a man could be driven to distraction, so he could.'

She raised a fine eyebrow and smoothed the hem of her skirt over her knees.

He chuckled and reached for the cake. ''Tis your cake I'm praising,' he teased, holding her gaze. 'Very distracting, it is.'

She giggled and lit a cigarette. 'I'm glad you're enjoying it. It's not often I get to do any baking, and I thought you deserved a treat now the butter ration has been increased.'

Ron tucked into the delicious jam sponge as Harvey stretched along the rug in front of the rather miserable fire in the grate. Ron had been after the luscious Rosie for years, and his pursuit had become a bit of a game between them – a game they both enjoyed, but which he'd never dared push beyond mild flirtation and a friendly peck on the cheek. He regarded her surreptitiously as he ate, marvelling that such a woman seemed to enjoy his company.

Mrs Rosie Braithwaite had moved to Cliffehaven many years ago to take over the Anchor. No one knew where she'd come from, or anything about her life before she'd arrived, and although it was most unusual for a young woman to run a pub single-handedly, she'd captained a tight ship and had become a well-respected and much admired landlady. Despite her obvious attractions and her flirtatious ways, she stood little nonsense from her customers, and no hint of scandal had ever been attached to her.

There had been no sign of a Mr Braithwaite, despite the wedding ring she still wore, and his whereabouts remained a topic of speculation amongst the regulars. Ron had dared to ask about him once, and she'd told him rather firmly to mind his own business. He hadn't broached the subject again until Tommy Findlay had put in a surprise appearance just before Christmas.

Ron's thoughts drifted. Tommy had turned up over the years in Cliffehaven like a regular bad penny. Where he came from, and where he disap-peared to, Ron didn't know, and didn't much care. The man was nothing more than a lounge lizard and a spiv, who preyed on vulnerable, silly women dazzled by his flashy clothes and glib tongue. Ron had been astounded when Rosie had admitted she'd known him for years, and trusted him enough to let him behind the bar. What their relationship was, he had no idea, and Rosie had refused to discuss it. Ron had found that most unsettling.

He gave a deep sigh and ate the last of the cake. There had been no further sighting of Findlay since Christmas, and he wasn't going to spoil this precious time with Rosie by speculating about him.

'Whatever's making you frown like that?' she asked.

He forced all thoughts of Tommy Findlay out of his head and shot her a cheeky smile. 'Well, now, Rosie. That would be telling.'

She grinned back. 'You don't fool me, Ronan Reilly,' she retorted. 'Something's on your mind – and it's not the usual,' she added mischievously.

'These past two weeks have been enough to try anyone,' he replied, 'and now I'm a great-grandfather, I feel I'm entitled to frown now and then.' He wiggled his bushy brows. ''Tis a serious business, you know.'

'I'm sure it is,' she murmured, 'but don't worry, Ron – you look very well on it.' Ron puffed out his chest at this praise, and Rosie giggled. 'How is Anne?'

Ron licked the jammy crumbs from his fingers with schoolboy relish and set the plate aside. 'She's brighter now Martin can visit every day, but she's still stuck in that bed with her wee leg strung up in the air.'

'Poor Anne. It can't be much fun. I'll sort out some magazines and books and you can take them with you later.'

'I think she's fretting over the wain – they only bring her down twice a day to see her, and even then she's not allowed to feed her.' He reddened as he always did when talking about such intimate womanly things. 'It's the drugs she's on,' he said gruffly as he stuffed his pipe with tobacco.

'Will the baby be discharged soon? She's been there two weeks already.'

Ron nodded as he tamped down the tobacco and hunted in his pocket for matches. 'Peggy's picking her up tomorrow,' he said. 'Lord knows how she'll cope with two wains in the house.' He sucked on his pipe as the tobacco crackled beneath the flame of the match. 'Mind you,' he added, 'that wee William is a good baby, hardly ever cries.'

She concentrated on stubbing out her cigarette. 'It can't be easy for Peggy, but knowing her, she'll manage somehow,' she said with a sigh. 'All the fuss over that young nurse couldn't have helped, but at least it seems to have died down now.'

'I think her sister probably had something to do with that,' said Ron. 'I heard she'd threatened to sue the editor for libel if it went any further.'

'Really?' Rosie sniffed. 'Can't say I'm surprised,' she said coldly. 'Eileen Harris has always been very careful about her precious reputation, regardless of what it might do to others. But she didn't come out of this latest mess in a very good light, and it serves her right.'

Ron was alerted to the unusual edge to Rosie's

voice and he regarded her with interest. 'You make it sound as if she's been the target of gossip before,' he said mildly.

'She managed to hush that up, too,' said Rosie, swinging her feet to the floor and hunting for her shoes. 'If I'd had my way, I'd've hung the bitch out to dry in the town square.'

Ron stared at her in amazement. He'd never heard her so bitter before and it hurt him to see the gleam of tears in her eyes. 'What the divil did she do to you?' he asked softly.

Rosie shook her head as she pulled on her shoes. 'It was a long time ago, and I don't want to talk about it, Ron,' she said firmly. She picked up the dirty china, loaded it onto the tray and, without another word, carried it through the dividing curtain into the tiny kitchen.

Ron sucked on his pipe, deep in thought as he heard her moving about in the other room. He'd never met Eileen Harris and wouldn't know her from Adam, but she'd clearly upset his Rosie, and he was curious to know what had happened between them. Now the atmosphere of the cosy afternoon had been ruined, and it was time for him to leave. Tipping the dottle from his pipe into the smouldering fire, he stuffed it back in his pocket and ambled to the kitchen door. 'I'll finish bottling up and be off,' he said.

'Thanks, Ron.' Rosie didn't turn from the sink where she was washing up.

Ron frowned and reached out to her. 'What's the matter, Rosie?' he asked softly.

'Nothing,' she rasped.

He firmly turned her to face him and was horrified to see tears streaming down her face. 'Rosie, darlin' girl. What is it? What have I said to upset you so?'

She shook her head, refusing to look at him. 'I'll be all right in a minute,' she said thickly as she scrabbled for a handkerchief in her skirt pocket. 'So silly of me to be like this after all these years.'

'This is to do with Eileen Harris, isn't it?'

She blew her nose and struggled heroically to regain her composure. 'Don't take any notice of me, Ron,' she said with a brittle smile. 'Women my age often cry about nothing.'

He knew that was utter nonsense but didn't press her. Rosie was a woman made for fun and laughter, and his heart ached to see those tears. He wanted to help but didn't know how, so he said the first thing that came into his head. 'Would you like a drop of gin?'

'Oh, Ron,' she sighed. 'You know me too well.' She cupped his grizzled chin in the palm of her hand and kissed his cheek. 'A gin and It would set me up no end,' she murmured, 'but only if you'll stay and have one too.'

He poured the drinks while Rosie went into her bedroom to fix her make-up and prepare for the evening rush, which would start the minute the doors were opened at six. When she returned there was no sign of the tears, but the shadows behind her smile told him that whatever Eileen Harris had done to her still had the power to wound.

Seeing her like this wounded him, too, for Rosie was in his heart, his darling girl – and he silently vowed he would find out what lay behind those tears, and, if it was in his power, put things right for her.

Julie had written letters to Bill and to his parents, informing them of her new address and William's slow but steady progress. She wasn't too concerned that she'd heard nothing from his parents, but Bill's lack of response really worried her. Had he decided just to ignore his son after all, or were his letters simply held up by the erratic mail service? She had to hope it was the latter.

It was a lovely bright Saturday, with a crisp wind coming off the sea as she wheeled the pram along Camden Road. She and Kath had just had tea at their favourite little café opposite the hospital, and they'd spent most of the afternoon gossiping about the play they'd gone to see the night before. *No Time for Comedy* was on a short run in Cliffehaven and had a strong cast, which included Rex Harrison, who they'd both agreed was one of the handsomest men in England. The fact that there were rumours linking him to his co-star Lilli Palmer had guaranteed a full house, and added extra excitement to the evening.

They'd finally said their goodbyes and Kath had hurried home to help her mother get tea for their lodger. Julie continued down the pavement, enjoying her weekend off from her long district round and the continued frostiness of Eunice Beecham. The uniform dress had been altered with Peggy's help, so she didn't look quite such a fright, and she'd certainly been kept busy during the past two weeks. It seemed the volunteer nurses were always needed elsewhere. However, now that she knew her way around the town which sprawled between the hills and the sea, she had come to appreciate the solitary nature of her daily travels.

Her thoughts meandered as she walked, happy with life in general and thanking her lucky stars that she'd found a warm and loving home with the Reilly family. They were such good people, and Peggy was an absolute star – but with Rose Margaret coming home tomorrow, would she be able to cope? It was a worry, but one that could be put off on this lovely sunny day. She would wait and see how things went, and then, if it proved too much for Peggy, she would try and find a nursery place for William while she worked.

She came to a halt outside Eileen's door and hesitated momentarily before pushing the map through the letter box. They hadn't spoken since the morning she'd left, and although Julie would have liked to clear the air, she didn't think her sister would appreciate her turning up unannounced.

She was about to walk away when the door opened and Eileen came out onto the step. 'I was just bringing your map back,' Julie said hurriedly. 'Thanks for the loan.'

'That's all right. How are you settling in?' Eileen asked, her eyes wary, her smile tenuous.

Delighted by this change in her sister, Julie returned her smile. 'Everyone's been marvellous,' she said. 'Peggy and the family have made us feel very much at home.' She hesitated and then plunged on. 'Look, Eileen, I'm sorry about all that fuss in the paper. It was none of my doing, honest.'

Eileen wrapped her skinny arms round her narrow waist. 'I know,' she admitted stiffly, 'and I'm glad you're happy at Beach View.' She hesitated, looking for once a little unsure of herself. 'That's a very smart pram. How is William?'

Julie smiled and pulled back the blankets just enough to show him off. William was awake and giving her a toothless grin. 'He's still a little small for his age, but he's a good baby and now sleeps right through.'

Eileen peered into the pram, her arms still tight about her waist as William gurgled up at her. 'He has Franny's smile,' she murmured as she straightened. 'But I still believe you're very foolish to keep him.'

Julie bristled but kept silent. Eileen was making overtures of friendliness, and although she didn't agree with her, it would be daft to fall out again.

She was about to reply when a passing motorbike backfired, making them both jump.

It was Rita, dressed as usual in her leather jacket and old flying helmet and goggles. Julie returned her cheerful wave and looked back at Eileen, who was regarding William with a deep frown. 'Whatever's the matter?' Julie asked, peering anxiously at the happy baby.

Eileen shook her head. 'Nothing,' she said.

'Something's bothering you,' persisted Julie. 'What is it?'

Eileen shrugged. 'I don't know anything about babies, and it was probably just my imagination.' She regarded Julie thoughtfully. 'Has he had a check-up at the doctors' since you arrived in Cliffehaven?'

Julie felt a chill of foreboding. 'He was given a clean bill of health when we left London,' she replied uneasily. 'Why?'

'I just thought it a bit strange that he didn't react to that backfire.'

'Is that all?' Julie looked down at the happy William. 'He's just used to loud noises. After all, he was born in the middle of an air raid, and we've spent many a night in the Anderson shelter listening to the racket overhead and the bombs going off.'

Eileen folded her arms again. 'That's as maybe,' she said quietly, 'but you should get one of the doctors to check his hearing.'

'There's nothing wrong with him,' Julie retorted. 'He's a perfect baby.'

Eileen's expression softened. 'I hope I'm wrong, Julie,' she said, 'but when that motorbike backfired he didn't react at all, and the noise was sudden enough and loud enough to make both of us flinch.'

Julie looked down at William, who was now gaily batting his mittens against the soft blue teddy she'd strung from a ribbon above him. She didn't want to believe Eileen, couldn't bear to think that William might not be perfect after all. But there had been moments of suspicion that all was not well, and certain little incidents suddenly made awful sense. She looked at her older sister, unable to voice the growing dread.

'You didn't see because you didn't want to,' said Eileen softly. 'You made the mistake of loving him too much, and he's not even yours, you foolish, foolish girl.'

Julie blinked back her tears and grabbed the pram handle. 'I've got to get back,' she managed through the lump in her throat. 'Foolish or not, he's my responsibility – and yes, I do love him, with all my heart, and I'll do everything I can to make sure he comes to no harm.'

Eileen grabbed her arm. 'Just remember that one day you might have to hand him over to his father, Julie,' she said softly. 'Try not to love him too much. It will only break your heart.'

Julie pulled her arm away. 'For someone who's never had a child and seems not to possess a maternal bone in her body, you're very free with your advice, Eileen.' Without another word, she strode off, blinded by tears of anguish.

Eileen watched her hurry away and knew from the set of her shoulders that she was crying. She hadn't meant to hurt her, but the realisation that William might be deaf had made it impossible for her to keep silent. She hoped with all her heart that her suspicions would be proved unfounded, but if it turned out she was right, then Julie would have to come to terms with William's disability. Which could, in turn, become a real burden if the father refused to take him on. Poor Julie, she'd done what she thought was the right thing, but she'd made the fatal mistake of loving William as her own – and now her life would be ruined.

Eileen turned and closed the front door behind her, leaning against it for a long while before she slowly trudged upstairs to her flat. Her advice had come from the heart, and had been given with good intent, but Julie could never know how deeply her parting words had cut.

Julie could barely see where she was going through her tears as she hurried along the narrow lane between the tall terraced houses and through the back gate. How dare Eileen insinuate there was something wrong with her precious William? How dare she spoil what had been a perfect day with her unwanted advice? What did she know about babies?

She refused to acknowledge the niggle of doubt as she wheeled the pram down the path between Ron's vegetables and into the basement. William was absolutely fine, and all new mothers worried about every little thing their babies did or didn't do.

She came to a halt, standing there in the deserted scullery, hearing the lively chatter in the kitchen above her as cold reality washed over her. There *had* been times when she'd wondered about his hearing, for he didn't seem to notice the sirens or the exploding bombs, nor even the terrible shrieking of enemy fighter planes as they streaked overhead. William slept through air raids and the clatter and noise of a busy house. Yet he responded to her voice and touch, returning her smiles and becoming fractious when he needed changing or feeding. Perhaps he was just contented – a naturally sweet-natured baby who was used to loud noises and took no notice of them?

Julie pulled back the covers and lifted him out of the pram. He waved his arms about and grabbed a strand of her hair in his fist, dribbling with delight. She clicked her fingers close to his left ear, and then to his right. He didn't respond – but then perhaps he was concentrating too much on pulling her hair to notice.

She blinked away her tears and held him close. All the excuses in the world couldn't allay the fears that had lain dormant until today. But now they'd been woken, she had no choice in the matter. She would have to ask Dr Michael to check him over.

'But we'll leave all that until Monday,' she whispered to him. 'With Rose coming home tomorrow, we don't want to spoil things for Peggy.' She took a moment to compose herself and then carried him upstairs.

Peggy couldn't bear to see Anne's distress, and she'd left Martin at her bedside, seeking refuge in the almost deserted corridor outside the ward. She could absolutely understand that a surgical ward was no place for a young baby – and yet it was all so unfair. Poor Anne, and poor little Rose Margaret; they needed one another and should be together in these first few very important months, but Anne's leg injury made that impossible.

She peeked through the round window in the swing door and watched as Martin put his arm around Anne, their tiny daughter lying between them. Dear Martin, he was such a good man and he was trying so hard to do the best for his little family. However, he could only snatch a few hours away from the airbase, and even these short respites were often interrupted by enemy raids.

She sighed as she watched them. At least he was no longer flying, which gave Anne some comfort, but airfields weren't the safest place to be these days, and his new role as Air Commodore meant he was often sent to other bases, and he could be away from Cliffehaven for days at a time.

Peggy turned from the window and hobbled back

down the corridor. Her feet still troubled her, and she hated going out in Ron's slippers, but the stitches would be taken out the next day and she hoped that would be an end to it. There were so many things to be done, so many people who needed her, and she was frustrated at being so hampered.

She reached the vast hall and made her way down the steps and into the sunshine. It was a lovely Sunday afternoon, with a brisk breeze coming from the sea, and fluffy white clouds scudding across the blue sky: a perfect day for Rose Margaret's home-coming, if it hadn't been for the regular noisy comings and goings of the RAF planes from the local base.

She eyed the pram she'd left by the steps. All her children had been carried in it, and although it was a bit battered and shabby, it was right that the next generation should use it. With a wry smile she settled comfortably on a low pillar at the bottom of the steps, took the packet of Park Drive out of her pocket and lit a cigarette. It could be a while before Cissy settled down to marriage and babies; she was having far too good a time at Cliffe airbase and hardly ever came home now. And yet Peggy had few qualms over Cissy's undoubtedly hectic social life, for despite her rather dizzy ways, she had a sensible head on her shoulders and wouldn't do anything rash that might jeopardise her reputation or her freedom.

Peggy smoked her cigarette, her thoughts drifting

to Julie, who was living proof of how hard it was to raise a child without the benefit of a husband. The poor girl worked long hours and was often exhausted by the time she came home. Yet she'd proved to be a caring, attentive mother to little William, and was never too tired to look after him, even if he woke in the night.

Peggy was glad Julie had fitted in so well at Beach View and that she and the other girls got on famously. She was even making friends through Kath Carter, and Peggy had been delighted to babysit while they went to the pictures or the theatre. A young woman like that needed friends and the stability of a good, settled home after all she'd been through. There was still sadness in Julie's eyes, and Peggy could only hope that time and distance would eventually chase that sadness away. How the girl would cope if the father turned up and took William from her didn't bear thinking about, for it was clear that she loved William as her own.

'There you are!' Martin's voice broke into her thoughts. He smiled at Peggy as he carefully carried Rose Margaret down the steps. 'I've never felt more nervous,' he admitted as he handed her over. 'All those stairs and slippery corridors to navigate – I was convinced I'd drop her.'

Peggy returned his smile. 'She was in the safest pair of hands I know,' she assured him as she tucked the baby warmly into the old pram. 'How was Anne when you left her?'

Martin smoothed his handlebar moustache and adjusted his heavily decorated uniform cap. 'Tearful, which is hardly surprising,' he said sadly. 'But I've promised she'll see Rose every day without fail, even if I'm not around.'

Peggy began to wheel the pram across the broad turning circle towards the large pillars that had once held ornate iron gates. 'Don't worry,' she murmured, enjoying the feel of pushing a pram again. 'I'll make sure they have as much time together as possible.'

'That is very good of you, Peggy. I wish I could be more help, but . . .'

'You have heavy responsibilities, and it's my pleasure to look after her, so we'll say no more about it,' she said firmly. They walked in silence for a while, enjoying an easy companionship and the lovely day.

'I went to see my parents last weekend,' he said as they reached the line of small shops which were shuttered and abandoned on this Sunday afternoon.

Peggy glanced at him, hearing the bitterness in his tone and knowing how deeply hurt he was that his parents still couldn't accept her Anne as his wife – not even now they had their first grandchild.

'They said all the right things, of course, but with my sister's wedding arrangements in full flood, they found plenty of excuses not to come and visit.' He dug his hands into the pockets of his dark blue uniform jacket, his chin tucked close to his shirt collar. 'I do so wish they'd at least try to accept things.'

Peggy remembered his and Anne's wedding, and

how his snooty family had kept themselves to themselves before leaving the reception early – and how tempted she'd been to give that toffee-nosed mother of his a piece of her mind. She hadn't, of course – it would have spoiled the day for Anne – but Peggy had never forgiven Martin's family for snubbing her daughter, and it was probably best they stayed well away from Cliffehaven, for she might not be able to hold back the next time they met.

'Perhaps, once Rose is a bit bigger, you could take her to see them,' she suggested. 'After all, who can resist such a sweet baby?'

Martin nodded. 'Maybe,' he murmured, 'but I wouldn't count on it. Ma and Pa are very set in their ways, and once they've made their mind up about something, nothing short of an earthquake would shift them.'

Peggy simmered with resentment but said nothing. This was a happy day and Martin's family could go hang for all she cared. She wasn't going to spoil Rose's homecoming by giving them another thought.

Chapter Thirteen

'Hello, ducks.' Maud looked up as she continued to wipe the damp cloth over the black-and-white tiles. 'You're early today,' she said cheerfully.

Julie usually enjoyed Maud's welcome, but she was too on edge this Monday morning to stand about gossiping. 'Is Dr Michael in yet?' she asked.

Maud sat back on her heels, her expression immediately alert. 'You don't want to be bothering him at this time of the morning, dearie,' she said. 'He's been up half the night with poor old Mrs Wells and needs a bit of time to hiself before the rush starts.'

Julie dithered and then decided she simply couldn't wait any longer. Carefully crossing the damp floor, she went into the waiting room. Thankfully there was no sign of Eunice and, emboldened, she tapped lightly on his consulting room door.

'Come in.'

Julie closed the door behind her and shot him a tentative smile as he stood to welcome her. 'Please, don't get up,' she protested. 'You look ever so tired, and I'm sorry to disturb you, but I wanted to ask your advice about something.'

He waved her to the chair in front of his desk

and sat back down, his dark eyes regarding her questioningly. 'What is it, Julie?'

'It's about William,' she said quietly. As she told him all the worries that had plagued her over the weekend, she immediately felt better about things. It had been so hard to bottle it all up, to say nothing amid the excitement of Rose coming home.

'I'm not a specialist in these things, Julie,' he said when she'd finished, 'but I know a man who is, and I think you should take William to see him as soon as possible.'

Julie twisted her hands in her lap. 'So you do think there might be something to worry about?'

He smiled his gentle smile and rose from his chair to come and sit on the corner of the desk. 'I think you've worried yourself enough and now it's time to get an expert opinion. Whatever the outcome, you'll feel much better for it.'

'You're right,' she replied softly. 'I've barely slept all weekend.'

He grinned and returned to his chair. 'I know just how you feel,' he replied, reaching for the telephone. 'But try not to worry. I'll call Sam Watson now and see if he can fit you and William in later today. Why don't you go and make yourself a cup of tea, and I'll come and find you when I have some news.'

'Thank you,' she murmured, 'but could we keep this to ourselves? I don't want your father or Eunice using this as an excuse to dismiss me.'

'Good heavens,' he spluttered. 'You're far too

valuable to dismiss – and William's care is a private thing. Don't you worry, Julie, anything you say to me in here will go no further. Now make that tea and try to relax.'

Julie left his room and headed for the small staff kitchen which was on the other side of the large square hall.

'You look much happier,' said Maud as she carried the bucket to the sink and poured the dirty water down the drain. 'Had a face like a wet weekend, you did earlier.' She grinned up at Julie, her dentures slipping. 'Dr Michael's lovely, isn't he? Ever so kind, and I reckon he's taken quite a liking to you, young Julie.'

Julie had no intention of getting drawn into this and merely returned her smile. 'A cup of tea, Maud?' she asked instead, reaching for the cups and saucers.

'Better not,' Maud replied with a grimace. 'That Eunice will be here in a minute and I haven't finished tidying the waiting room.' The bucket clanged as she stowed it beneath the sink, and then, armed with duster and polish, she waddled off.

Julie made a pot of tea and took a cup to Michael, who acknowledged it with a nod as he carried on talking on the telephone. She left him to it and returned to the kitchen, her nerves in tatters.

Having drunk two cups of tea, she felt slightly better, and, rather than hanging about doing nothing, which would give her too much time to think, she began the Monday morning ritual of checking the contents of her medical bag. She replaced cotton wool and gauze, scrubbed her instruments until they shone, changed the lining in the bag and buffed up the leather. Old habits die hard, and she found some comfort in the familiar weekly task.

She heard Eunice come in and head straight for the waiting room, where it sounded as if poor Maud was getting a tongue lashing for leaving smears on her desk. Then she heard Michael's voice, and his purposeful footsteps approaching across the hall, and suddenly all her nervousness returned.

He came into the kitchen and placed his cup and saucer on the drainer. 'Don't look so worried,' he said kindly. 'I've spoken to Sam Watson, and he'll see you and William at five-thirty in his hospital consulting room.'

'How much will it cost?' she asked fearfully.

'His initial consultation will cost nothing.' He smiled at her look of surprise. 'We were at med school together, and he owes me several fairly hefty favours which I've called in.' His smile became a grin. 'Sam was a bit wild back then, and I could tell a tale or two, but he's turned into a first-class paediatrician who specialises in ears, nose and throat.'

'Thanks ever so,' she murmured.

'Would you like me to come with you? Only I know how daunting these consultations can be, and it's likely you'll be so tense, you won't take in half of what he tells you.'

'Would you really?' she breathed. 'You don't mind? But what about your evening surgery?'

'I've already spoken to Father, and he's agreed to do it.'

Without thinking, Julie grasped his hand. 'Thanks, Michael. I really appreciate everything—'

'Sister Harris.' Eunice appeared in the kitchen doorway, her expression stony as her gaze latched onto the entwined hands, which swiftly flew apart. 'You have a busy day and there is no time for dawdling,' she snapped. 'Dr Michael, your first patient is waiting.' Turning sharply on her heel, she stomped away.

Julie blushed as she caught Michael's twinkling eyes.

'Oops,' he said. 'I think we've upset our estimable Sister Beecham. We'd better get on, or we'll never hear the end of it.'

Julie knew for certain that Eunice would make her pay for that little indiscretion and steeled herself for the awkward moment when she'd have to face her again. 'I'll meet you outside the hospital at five-fifteen,' she replied quietly.

Michael strode off and Julie took a moment to compose herself before picking up her medical bag and following him. The waiting room was already packed, the redoubtable Eunice behind her desk. Julie noted the frosty glare but hoped Eunice was too much of a professional to start an argument in front of the patients.

She took the list from Eunice and quickly scanned through it, noting it was even longer than usual. 'I will need to finish me round by four o'clock this afternoon,' she said firmly. 'These six patients can either be dealt with by the volunteers or wait until tomorrow.'

Eunice's cold blue eyes regarded her for a long, silent moment. 'Why do you need to leave early?'

'I have something important to do and can't be late.'

'Nothing is more important than your patients, Sister Harris.'

'Maybe not, but in this instance, it's vital I finish early.'

'Why?'

'That,' said Julie quietly, 'is none of your business.'

The gaze was steely. 'I do not approve of your conduct,' Eunice said, quietly, obviously aware they could be overheard, 'and if I see you behaving in that way with Dr Michael again, I will have you dismissed.'

Julie didn't flinch beneath that glare. 'Please rearrange me schedule, Sister Beecham,' she said flatly, 'or I will be forced to do it meself.'

Eunice's mouth thinned as she snatched the list and turned her attention to adjusting all three schedules. She handed it back with little grace and Julie hurried out of the waiting room as Dr Sayers Senior buzzed for his next patient.

Both babies were yelling fit to bust, and as Harvey sought refuge in the cellar from the noise, Peggy and Mrs Finch hurried to change their nappies as the formula warmed. Blessed silence fell as Rose and William greedily latched onto their feeding bottles and both women sighed with relief.

'There are times,' said Mrs Finch, 'that I'm glad I don't have that new hearing aid. I'd forgotten how a baby's cry can go right through one's head.' She softly ran her finger over William's fair hair and smiled tenderly. 'But it is rather lovely having these young ones in the house. Reminds me of when mine were little.'

Peggy smiled and nodded as she hugged Rose, but she could see the wistfulness in the older woman's eyes and knew she still yearned for her own sons and their families. It must have been very hard for her when they'd left for Canada – harder still now there were grandchildren she would never see. Families could break your heart, she thought sadly.

Harvey had obviously deemed it safe to return and was now slumped by Peggy's feet, his watchful gaze flitting between the two women.

She looked down at him fondly, knowing he'd taken on the role of guardian to the babies, and that he spent a good deal of his time lying by the pram as they slept. 'Good boy, Harvey,' she murmured. 'I'll give you a treat when I've finished here.'

He waggled his eyebrows and thumped his tail on the floor in anticipation.

Peggy looked back at Mrs Finch. She'd been worried that it all might be too much for the old lady, but she'd rolled up her sleeves and willingly joined in the endless round of feeding, changing and washing, and now seemed very contented as she fed William. 'I tried to get the new hearing aid mended,' she said. 'But it's beyond repair.'

'I'm so sorry, Peggy. It was terribly clumsy of me, and I know how expensive it must have been, but my pension comes through next week, so I can pay you back.'

Peggy knew how meagre that pension was. 'No you won't,' she said quickly. 'It was a gift, and I'll not take a penny for it.'

Mrs Finch eyed her over her half-moon glasses rather sternly, and then broke into a warm smile. 'Then I'll just have to find another way of paying you back.' She looked down at William, who'd fallen asleep, and took the half-empty bottle away. 'He doesn't eat enough,' she fretted, lifting him to her shoulder and patting his back. 'No wonder he's so small.'

Peggy watched as Mrs Finch rubbed the tiny back and elicited a burp from William. He was small, but he seemed healthy and contented enough. 'Julie's not very big either, and from what she's told me, William's mother was very tiny.'

'You don't think . . . That's to say . . . He's not really Julie's, is he?'

Peggy shook her head as she took the empty bottle from a drowsy Rose. 'Julie made a point of showing me his birth certificate.'

Mrs Finch sighed as she carefully wrapped the

soft blue blanket round William. 'He's a dear little thing, but Julie will be heartbroken if his father turns up and carts him off. There's nothing worse than losing a child once you've loved it.'

Peggy frowned as she set Rose over her shoulder and tried to wind her. 'You said that as if you've experienced such a terrible thing.'

'I had a little girl,' Mrs Finch replied softly, her gaze settled on the sleeping baby in her arms. 'She died shortly after she was born, but I'll never forget her – never.' She blinked rapidly and took off her glasses. 'You'll have to take William and put him in the pram,' she said rather briskly. 'I can't get out of this damned chair without both hands free.'

Peggy cocooned Rose in her own pink blanket and placed her gently in the old family pram before gathering up William and putting him beside her. Drawing a soft sheet over the pair of them, she wheeled the pram into the hall. They looked so sweet lying there – one so fair, the other so dark.

Harvey sauntered into the hall and made himself comfortable by the pram. He would stay there now until Ron took him out for their usual walk across the hills.

Peggy reached into the pocket of her apron and gave him two dog biscuits, which he began to chew with alacrity. She returned to the kitchen just as Ron came up the cellar steps and dumped an armful of firewood onto the floor. 'Ron,' she protested. 'I've just cleaned the lino.'

He began to stack the small logs in the basket by the range. 'Time we had new lino in here anyway,' he muttered. 'I'll see what I can find.'

Peggy doubted very much that there was any lino to be had in Cliffehaven – but then Ron and Jim were always surprising her with the things they managed to find. 'That would be nice,' she sighed, 'but I don't want it if it isn't come by honestly.'

He looked up at her as he knelt by the range, his blue eyes twinkling. 'Now, Peg,' he said, 'as if I'd do anything like that.'

She giggled as she sat down and lit a cigarette. 'You already have,' she retorted, 'but there's obviously little point in me trying to keep you on the straight and narrow.'

'Marrow?' said Mrs Finch. 'I thought we were having brisket tonight?'

Peggy assured her they were, and watched as the old woman gathered up her vast knitting bag. Mrs Finch loved knitting, but her arthritic hands made it difficult, and she kept dropping stitches and making a right mess of it all. The matinee jacket she'd started six months ago had never been finished and now she was trying to follow a complicated pattern for a jumper, which she planned to give Ron on his birthday. By the look of things, that wouldn't be finished either.

Ron finished stacking the wood and swept up the bits from the worn lino before making a pot of tea.

He sat down with a grateful sigh, waiting for the tea to steep, and then poured them all a cup.

Peggy watched this unusual display of domesticity and wondered what he was after. She carried on smoking her cigarette, knowing she'd find out sooner rather than later.

Ron sipped his tea and fiddled about with his pipe and tobacco. 'Peggy,' he said eventually, 'there's something I wanted to ask you.'

She smiled. 'I thought there might be. What is it, Ron?'

'What do you know about Eileen Harris?' he asked flatly.

His question startled her, and she was immediately wary. 'Not much. Why?'

'Did she and Rosie fall out over something? Was there a scandal some time ago which involved the pair of them?' He left his tea to cool as he regarded her steadily through the pipe smoke.

This was dangerous ground, for she'd thought that old scandal long dead and buried. 'Has Rosie said something about it, Ron?' she asked carefully.

'Not in so many words, but enough to make me curious, and I'll not be having my Rosie upset for anything.'

'Oh, Ron, I'm sorry, but it's not me you should be asking. Rosie and Eileen did fall out, but it was some years ago, and picking away at old sorrows does little good. I'd advise you to let it rest. There's nothing you can do about it – not now.'

'So you do know what happened?' he persisted.

Peggy nodded. 'But I made a promise to Rosie, and I'm not going to break it, Ron. If she decides to tell you, then that's up to her. But I doubt she will – she's too wise to pick over old bones.'

He was about to reply when there was a loud rapping at the door. Harvey began to bark, Rose Margaret began to wail and Mrs Finch dropped her knitting.

'I'll see to Rose, you get the door,' said Peggy, rushing into the hall.

Ron stumped moodily after her and flung the door open, ready to give whoever it was a piece of his mind for interrupting such an important conversation.

One look at his eldest son told him this was no social call, and he went cold with dread. 'What is it, Frank?' he rasped.

'It's . . . It's . . . ,' he stuttered, the tears welling, his handsome face lined with grief as he stepped into the hall and silently handed his father the telegram.

Ron's hands shook as he drew the single sheet of paper from the brown envelope. The words, so terse and cruel, struck at his heart.

DEEPLY REGRET TO REPORT DEATH OF YOUR SONS SEAMUS AND JOSEPH REILLY ON WAR SERVICE * LETTER FOLLOWS * COMMODORE RNR BARRACKS CHATHAM

'My boys,' sobbed Frank as he stood like a crumbling monolith in the hall, his great calloused hands clenching and unclenching at his sides. 'My beautiful, precious boys are gone, Da. And Brendon's still out there on the Atlantic and . . .'

Ron could barely see him through his own tears and his heart was squeezed with a terrible pain as he gently guided his son into the kitchen and pressed him into a chair. Frank had always been strong, both in mind and in body, and here he was, a shell of a man, withered and shrunken by his overwhelming and bewildering loss.

Frank didn't even look up as Peggy placed a glass of brandy in his hand, just sat there deep in his grief, as his father perched on the arm of the chair and held him close. 'Pauline's on her way back from visiting her mother in Dorset,' he finally managed after a restorative sip of the brandy. 'I don't know how I'm going to tell her.' His voice cracked. 'She loved those boys more than life itself – and it will break her heart.'

'When is she due home, Frank?' asked Peggy softly. 'Do you want me to tell her?'

Frank shook his great head, his dark hair falling over his red-rimmed eyes. 'Thanks, Peg, but I'll . . . I'll do it.'

Ron's own sorrow weighed heavy, his memories of those boys intense and heart-breaking, yet he had no words of comfort for his son. What could he say that would ease this awful pain; what meaningless clichés could possibly cut through the crippling grief that beset them both? He kept his arm round the broad shoulder and held on tight as his rugged, virile son shrank into him and wept like a small boy.

Julie had managed to get through the day by not stopping for her usual gossip or cup of tea with her elderly and rather lonely patients. Her thoughts were continually returning to William and the appointment at the hospital, her hopes and fears battling one another as she tried to concentrate on the job in hand.

Despite her troubled thoughts and the need to be at the hospital on time, she knew the minute she walked into the house that something terrible had happened, for she could hear the sound of sobbing in the kitchen.

Peggy was red-eyed, her voice tremulous as she told Julie about Frank's two boys, and Julie's soft heart went out to her. She knew what it was to lose those closest to her, understood the awful, mind-numbing anguish Frank must be going through, but was all too aware that there were no words to soothe. Grief was such a personal thing – it set a person apart from the world, and it was only through time that the healing process could begin.

As Peggy poured out her heart, the thought of her own three brothers who were in the middle of the fighting somewhere in Africa made Julie go cold.

She couldn't lose any more of her family – she simply couldn't. And yet, the longer this war went on, the more likely it was that she too would get one of those awful telegrams. She shivered, battling to overcome the gnawing fear that gripped her.

'They've gone to the station to meet Pauline's train,' Peggy said through her tears. 'Poor Pauline, she'll know the minute she sees them together that it's bad news. You see, Jim and Frank fell out years ago and they've hardly spoken since.' She sniffed back her tears and determinedly dried her eyes. 'It was probably over some silly thing, but this – this is something that must bring them together. Surely?'

'Let's hope so,' murmured Julie, her mind still on her brothers. 'Family is so important, especially now.'

'We're hoping Brendon will get compassionate leave,' sighed Peggy as she attended to a wailing Rose Margaret. 'But it would be even better if he could be taken off those Atlantic convoys and brought home to a safe desk job – or better still, back to Frank's fishing boats. It would be too cruel if Frank and Pauline were to lose all their sons.'

Julie kept her own dark fears at bay and comforted Peggy as best she could. But time was moving too swiftly and, if she wasn't careful, she'd be late for her appointment. She fed and changed William and, after checking that Peggy was occupied with Rose, hurried upstairs to change out of her uniform.

Peggy seemed calmer by the time she returned to

the kitchen, but Julie didn't really want to leave her. 'I'm sorry, Peggy, but I have to go out with William,' she said hesitantly. 'Will you be all right on your own?'

Peggy frowned at this change in Julie's routine but didn't question it. 'Mrs Finch is having a bit of a lie down, but Cissy is on her way, and the other girls are due back any minute.' She shot Julie a watery smile. 'I'll be fine, really.'

Julie gave her a hug and hurriedly left the house, almost breaking into a run as she pushed the pram along Camden Road. Beach View's happy atmosphere had been shattered, and she wanted very much to help Peggy in any way she could. At least she had her family around her, and that had to count for something, Julie thought sadly, for there was nothing worse than having to bear such a burden alone.

She determinedly shook off the gloomy thoughts and decided Dr Michael didn't need to know what had happened at Beach View this afternoon – not yet, anyway. No doubt the news was already spreading through gossip-riven Cliffehaven, but now it was time to concentrate on William and the appointment.

She arrived at the hospital with five minutes to spare, to find Dr Michael waiting anxiously on the forecourt. 'I didn't think I'd make it,' she panted as he helped her lug the pram up the steps and into the large reception hall.

'I saw your list for the day and didn't think you would either,' he said dryly. He smiled down at William, who was blowing raspberries and batting his hands against the blankets. 'Seems a lively young chap,' he said warmly before he set off down the long corridor.

Julie almost had to run to keep up with him as they headed to the back of the hospital, and when they'd reached the plush annexe which housed the consultants' rooms, she was more out of breath than ever. 'Hang on a minute,' she gasped. 'I need to get me breath back.'

'Sorry,' he said ruefully. 'I forget sometimes that not everyone has such long legs.'

Julie adjusted her beret and scarf, tugged off her gloves and tried to restore some sense of calm. 'Right,' she said, her pulse still racing as she lifted William from the pram. 'I'm as ready as I'll ever be.'

Julie's first impression of Sam Watson was of a well-dressed, handsome man who looked less care-worn than Michael, and rather too young to be an expert in anything. But the name plaque on his door and the certificates on his wall confirmed that he was, and Julie felt a little more reassured.

He clapped Michael on the back and shook Julie's hand, his manner easy, his smile warm and friendly as he exchanged pleasantries with Michael and waved them towards the comfortable armchairs that had been set beside a low table.

'I try to keep things informal,' he said cheerfully.

'Mothers are nervous enough when they come and see me, no point in frightening them further.'

Julie eyed the room as she sat down with William in her lap. It had been painted a pale yellow to match the pretty nursery curtains at the window and the lino on the floor. A box of toys stood in a corner next to an old rocking horse, the chairs were covered in chintz, and there was a pile of comics and rag books on the low table in front of her. It was certainly a pleasant room, but she found it hard to relax when so much was riding on this consultation.

'So, Sister Harris, I understand you have some concerns over William's hearing?' He rested his elbows on the arm of his chair, his fingers steepled against his chin. 'As I don't have any medical notes to rely upon, perhaps you could start by telling me about his mother's medical history, her labour and delivery.'

As Julie began to tell him about Franny's childhood attack of rheumatic fever, he pulled a pad towards him and unscrewed the cap of a fountain pen. He wrote copious notes as she continued through Franny's pregnancy and delivery, her voice breaking as she relived the last few terrible moments of her life.

He stopped writing and looked at her with compassion. 'Is there any history of deafness in the family?' he asked softly.

Julie shook her head. 'Not in mine, but I don't know anything about the father's.'

'Then tell me about William,' he coaxed. 'I assume he was given a clean bill of health by the hospital before you brought him down here.'

She nodded. 'He was kept in for a few weeks because he was a little premature and rather small. And although he's still a bit underweight for his age, he's feeding well and seems very contented.'

'Has he suffered any chest infections or colds recently?' As Julie shook her head, he rose from his chair and reached out his arms for William. 'May I?'

Julie handed him over and William kicked his legs enthusiastically as the doctor smiled at him and jiggled him about.

'Hello, little chap,' he murmured, testing the strength of those kicks with his hand, bending and flexing the waving arms. 'This is a good game, isn't it?' he continued, his capable fingers gently probing his neck and feeling his head.

Julie watched anxiously as he carried William to the far side of the room and placed him on a small examination couch. With deft fingers he undressed the baby and carried on talking while he continued to test and probe. Then he put a stethoscope on William's tiny chest and listened for what seemed like ages before he turned his attention to William's ears, peering through his otoscope.

Julie had shifted to the very edge of her chair as the examination went on, her gaze fixed on the doctor's every movement and the slightest change in his expression. But she could tell nothing from that pleasant face. She glanced at Michael, who was also watching, but he wasn't giving anything away either.

Sam Watson covered William with the blanket and turned back to Julie with a smile. 'That will do for now,' he said. 'You can dress him again while I make some notes.'

Julie dressed him swiftly and carried him back to her chair. There was a heavy silence as the consultant scribbled on his pad, and she was beginning to get very frightened for William.

He finally put down his pen and sat back. 'I think I can safely say that his deafness is caused by otitis media, or what we in the trade call glue ear,' he said with a warm, encouraging smile. 'It's a common condition in small children and nothing to be too alarmed about.'

Julie felt an immense surge of relief. 'So, William isn't deaf?'

'His hearing is certainly impaired in both ears for the moment, but I have every hope that will change very soon. Thankfully there doesn't seem to be any infection in the middle ear, but there is some inflammation and a build-up of fluid.' He smiled. 'I'm sure I don't need to tell you, Sister Harris, that the three tiny bones in the middle ear carry sound vibrations from the eardrum to the inner ear. When fluid is present, the vibrations aren't transmitted efficiently and sound energy is lost. This means everything is muffled or inaudible to William.'

'I should have realised what was wrong,' she said fretfully.

'Not at all,' he replied firmly. 'As there is no infection, he didn't show any outward signs of fever or pain, and he wouldn't have been bothered by it at all.'

'But you can do something about it?'

'This type of hearing loss is almost always temporary,' he said. 'His eardrum looks dull and pulled inwards, and bubbles and fluid are visible behind the eardrum – all classic signs of glue ear. It is highly likely to be the cause of his hearing loss.'

Julie's medical training had included lectures just like this, but she was so grateful that William could be cured, that most of it went over her head.

'So,' he said as he set the model aside. 'What do we do next?' He smiled. 'It's really a case of wait and see.'

'But doesn't he need antibiotics, or something to clear that fluid?' asked Julie.

'This type of otitis media usually clears up on its own within a month or two and, as there is no infection, I don't recommend antibiotics or surgical intervention such as grommets. As William gets older the Eustachian tubes will widen and lie at a sharper angle, which will help them drain much more easily.'

'But how will I know if the inflammation has gone down? And how do we get rid of that fluid?'

'Studies have shown that the fluid will drain naturally if you raise the head of the cot, put a pillow under the pram mattress and feed him in a more upright position. I don't recommend the use of a dummy – all that sucking will merely put pressure on the inner ear. Wipe any fluid away and keep the outer ears clean. You must also do your best to avoid people with coughs and colds. We don't want him getting a chest infection, which could exacerbate the situation.'

'Thank you so much,' she breathed, holding William up to her shoulder. 'You have no idea what a relief it is to know he'll get over this.'

'Michael can keep an eye on him from now on with regular monthly check-ups.' Sam rose from the chair and shook her hand. 'Don't worry, Sister Harris, he's a healthy, happy little boy, and he's very lucky to have you.'

'Thanks, you're very kind,' she murmured.

'Not at all. Now, if you wouldn't mind, I'd like to have a quiet word with Michael.' He must have noted her immediate anxiety and hastened to reassure her. 'It's nothing for you to worry about,' he said. 'Mike and I are in charge of organising a charity rugby match, and we need to go through the list of players and sponsors.'

Julie eyed them both, not fully convinced. She knew what doctors were like, and the patient was usually the last person to be told anything. 'It's not about William?' she persisted.

'Not at all,' he said with a jovial smile as he opened the door. 'We won't be long, I assure you.'

Julie stepped into the corridor and heard the door click shut behind her. She was tempted to put her ear to it, but concentrated instead on tucking a small blanket under the mattress so that William wasn't lying flat. She pushed the pram back and forth, rocking it gently so he went to sleep. She could hear nothing through that thick door and there were too many people about to give in to the temptation of listening at the keyhole.

Michael appeared a few minutes later, his expression calm and friendly. 'There,' he said, giving her a warm smile. 'That wasn't too frightening, was it?'

'Have you got a full team for the rugby?' she asked, testing him.

'Absolutely,' he replied. 'Even managed to get old Dr Whittaker to come and referee, though I doubt he'll last more than ten minutes – he *is* over seventy.'

'So you weren't having a private talk about William?'

'William is fine,' he said firmly and turned to head down the corridor. 'You heard what Sam said. We're not hiding anything from you, I promise.'

'Sorry,' she muttered, catching up with him, 'but I can't help worrying when two doctors get their heads together.'

'Cynic,' he teased.

She grinned back at him. 'It's what comes of dealing with you lot day in and day out. You can't blame me.'

They reached the entrance hall and he helped

carry the pram down the steps. 'What if I give you a free ticket to the rugby match? Will that convince you?'

'It might,' she said and giggled. 'But I prefer going to the football. Now there's a game I understand.'

'My dear girl, your education is sorely lacking. I shall make it my personal charge to bring you up to standard before I can allow you to set foot on the sidelines.'

She laughed. 'My dad supported West Ham all his life, and if it was good enough for him, it's good enough for me. Rugby's for toffs.'

'I might have known you'd think like that.' He sighed dramatically as they crossed the forecourt and reached the pavement. 'Just give it a chance, Julie. You might find it's far more exciting than any silly football game.'

She smiled up at him. 'Seeing as how kind you've been to me and William, I can't really refuse, can I?' As he shook his head and grinned down at her, she reached for his hand. 'Thanks ever so, Michael. I really appreciate what you've done today.'

He squeezed her fingers. 'Glad to be of service. And if there's anything else I can do, you only have to ask.'

They stood outside the hospital, their hands still linked. 'Oh, I think teaching me the rules of rugby will be enough for now,' she murmured, warmed by his friendship and the easy way they could talk to one another.

'Rugby has laws, not rules,' he replied, his smile teasing. 'There you are, your education has begun already.'

Neither of them saw Eunice Beecham come out of the newsagent's further down the street. She stood on the pavement, her expression venomous as her narrowed gaze fell on the linked hands and the intimate way they were looking at one another.

She watched them until she couldn't bear it any longer, then turned and fled back to her flat at the bottom of the High Street. Her heartache and bitter disappointment were nothing compared to the urgent, driving need for vengeance. She had loved Michael for five years. After he had been betrayed by his childhood sweetheart, she had bided her time in the hope he would finally notice her and realise they were meant to be together.

Michael belonged to her, and only her. One way or another, she would have to get rid of Julie Harris.

Chapter Fourteen

Ron had no idea how Frank had managed to drive his delivery truck to Beach View without killing himself. He'd certainly been in no fit state to get it to the station to pick up Pauline and take her home to their fisherman's cottage in Tamarisk Bay, and had put up little resistance when Jim had insisted upon getting behind the wheel.

It was a tight squeeze with the four of them packed in the small driver's cab, made even more uncomfortable by the sound of Pauline's heart-rending sobs and the pall of grief that hung over all of them. The winding, steep track between Cliffehaven and Tamarisk Bay was pitted and rutted by the army lorries that went back and forth between the gun emplacements and lookouts, and it was clear that Jim was finding it hard to concentrate, for the wheels seemed to find every lump and pothole.

Ron stared out of the window at the sparkling sea beyond the tank traps and rolls of barbed wire that stretched across most of the bay, his thoughts continually returning to his two grandsons whose loss was like a terrible weight round his heart. They'd been bonny wee lads, growing tall and strong like their father as they'd learned the vagaries of the wind and tides in the family fleet of fishing boats. The sea had become their life, and now it had claimed them, taking them away from those who loved them, and from the shores of home, where they would never sail again. He could only pray that Brendon would make it back, and made a silent covenant with God that if He spared the boy, he would attend mass again, repent all his many sins, and try to be a good Catholic.

They arrived at the row of pretty little cottages which overlooked the small bay, and Frank carried Pauline indoors, taking her straight into their bedroom. Ron and Jim silently made tea and sat in heavy contemplation, staring out at the row of fishing boats that lay at anchor on the short stretch of cleared shingle as the bedroom door remained shut and the sound of sobbing continued. Eventually, feeling useless and intrusive in such tragic circumstances, they decided it would be best to leave the couple to their private grief and come back tomorrow. Now they faced the long trek over the hills to get back home.

Ron felt the weight of his years and had to will himself to put one foot in front of the other, as the chill wind bit into his bones and his muscles ached with weariness. But the vengeance in his heart kept him going. He glowered at the evening sky, which was ominously clear, the sickle moon floating over the water. The bombers would be back, shattering the tranquillity of the hills with their deadly thunder, but he would be waiting for them from now on. He would demand a post in one of the gun emplacements, so he could shoot them down and make them pay for all those lost young lives.

He was startled from his dark, angry thoughts by Jim's voice. 'Sorry,' he muttered. 'What was that?'

'I said, I can't begin to imagine what Frank must be going through.' Jim was panting as they tramped up the final hill and reached the top. He came to a halt and tried to get his breath back. 'The poor wee man was broken, so he was.'

'Losing those two boys is enough to break the strongest man. All we can do now is support him and Pauline and pray to God that Brendon will be sent home. Frank needs his family round him more than ever now.'

'Aye, he does that,' murmured Jim, staring out at the moon's silver glow on the rippling sea.

Ron eyed his youngest son thoughtfully. 'It's time to forget whatever set you apart, Jim, and be his brother again.'

Jim nodded and sighed. 'But it won't be easy, Da. We've exchanged hard words over the years, and the cut of them went deep – perhaps too deep for either of us to ever forget or forgive.'

'There's enough trouble in this world without brother fighting brother,' Ron muttered as they began to walk again. 'I think you'll find Frank is willing to let bygones be bygones in the light of what's happened.'

'I don't know that he will, Da. The trust between us was broken a long time ago – and once that's gone . . .'

Ron pulled his pipe out of his coat pocket and spent a while tamping in the tobacco and getting it going satisfactorily. 'What was it you fell out about, anyway?' he asked, his voice deceptively casual.

Jim dug his chin into his coat collar, his hands rammed deep in his overcoat pocket, as they continued along the headland, the silence stretching between them. 'Something happened in France at the end of the last war,' he said finally. 'And every time I see Frank, it brings it all back.'

Ron frowned, but said nothing. This was the first time either of his sons had shed even a glimmer of light on the feud that had lasted over twenty years, and now it seemed that Jim was ready to talk. Perhaps he needed to talk, as a balm to his conscience, or as an atonement to his brother, whose family had been ripped apart by something none of them could change.

They reached a copse of trees which had once been part of an ancient orchard on the edge of Lord Cliffe's estate, and Jim drew to a halt, slowly sinking to the grass, his back resting against the rough bark of a gnarled apple tree. He lit a cigarette and then hugged his knees, his gaze fixed to the horizon, his expression unreadable.

Ron sat beside him and smoked his pipe, willing to wait for as long as it took for Jim to speak.

'We were in the middle of nowhere, making our way north,' Jim said softly. 'It was towards the end of the war, though we didn't really believe it then – there were always rumours, as you know.'

Ron grimaced. They'd been told that damned war would be over by the first Christmas, but it had lasted four soul-destroying years – and here they were, fighting another one.

Jim smoked his cigarette, his gaze still fixed to the horizon. 'A group of us had been detailed to go on ahead of the rest to flush out any remaining pockets of the enemy and clear the mines or booby traps they'd left behind. We came to this village,' his voice faltered, and he took a moment to steady himself. 'The Huns had rounded up the women, children and the elderly and were lining them up against the church wall. As we watched, they opened fire and killed every last one – even the babies in their mothers' arms.'

Ron looked sorrowfully at his son as he fell silent. Jim's eyes held the haunting shadows of atrocious memories. Ron understood, for he too had witnessed the craven depths to which men fell when blood-lust and violence ruled.

'The bastards never saw us come out of the surrounding woods. They'd turned from their killing and had raided the nearby bar, drinking and laughing as those poor defenceless people lay dead in the shadow of their little church.' Jim fell silent again and ran his fingers through his hair in agitation, then went on. 'I'd never believed in seeing red until that day, but as I watched those brutes and saw those bodies, it was as if my eyes and my head were full of blood. I'd never known such rage.'

He took a deep breath. 'I learned afterwards that everyone felt the same – even Frank. We marched into the village square as one and opened up our guns, killing the lot of them, firing over and over again, even after we'd run out of bullets.'

Ron could imagine the scene, for he'd known such rage himself, though his training with the special ops unit had taught him to rein it in and use it only when there was no other option. His sons had only done what any other man would have done in the circumstances.

'You did what you had to,' he murmured. 'There's no shame in that.'

Jim scrubbed his face with his hands and tucked his chin back in his coat collar. 'I feel no shame for it,' he admitted. 'They were the enemy, and they'd committed a heinous crime against women and children. It was what happened afterwards that is shameful.'

Ron felt a flutter of unease. He'd wanted to know the reason behind his sons' feud for years, but now he wondered if he really wanted to hear what had happened. His imagination took flight and he had to struggle to keep the images at bay. 'You don't have to tell me if you don't want to,' he said quietly.

Jim's dark, steady gaze settled on his father. 'It's time, Da. Frank and I have kept it between us for too long.'

Ron bit down on the stem of his pipe, his heart pounding in dread.

'That red mist was like opium, and the adrenalin was pumping as we tried desperately to find any survivors amongst the villagers. But there was no one alive, so we found picks and shovels and dug a mass grave behind the church, which we marked with a rough wooden cross. Young Sapper Jones always carried a Bible, so he said a few words over them, and then we ransacked the bar for brandy and wine and set about getting drunk.'

'Aye, it would seem the thing to do,' Ron murmured.

'I had a terrible thirst, Da, and wanted to blot out the horrors by drinking myself into oblivion. But no matter how much I poured down my throat, I stayed sober. Frank and most of the others soon passed out, and I was sitting among them staring at the bullet marks on that church wall when I caught sight of Phil Todd emerging furtively from the ruins of a nearby house.'

Jim grimaced. 'Todd was a weasel-faced, light-fingered Cockney who had an aversion to soap and water, and thought nothing of stealing from kitbags while his mates were asleep. The abandoned houses and the sight of all those bulging pockets on the dead Germans had obviously proved too tempting.'

Ron eyed his son and shivered with apprehension. Jim had always been drawn to crooked deals – and he himself often walked the fine line of the law – but had his son stooped so low as to rob the dead? It was unthinkable – but then the unthinkable often happened in war, as proven by Jim's terrible story.

'I went and told him to put the stuff back. Looting was forbidden, and if he was caught, he'd probably be shot. Not that I cared a jot if he had been shot, but the honour of our group was at stake.' Jim's lip curled in disgust. 'He just grinned back at me and showed me what he'd taken from the houses as well as the dead Germans' pockets. He even offered to share it with me if I kept my mouth shut. I told him in no uncertain terms where he could stick his loot and then punched him.' He grimaced. 'There was a certain satisfaction in feeling his nose crunch under me fist, and seeing his blood spill.'

Ron experienced a wave of enormous relief that was tinged with shame for ever thinking his son might be complicit in stealing from the dead – even if they were Huns. He knew in his heart that Jim was a better man than that.

Jim's expression was grim as he stared out over the cliffs to the sea. 'I left him lying in the dirt and went back to my place beside Frank and started working on a fresh bottle of brandy. I needed to get the taste of death out of my mouth.'

Ron remained silent, for he couldn't figure out

why this short, very nasty little episode should have caused such a rift between his sons.

Jim smoked his cigarette in silence for a while, his gaze on some horizon far more distant than the one before him. 'The brandy finally kicked in and I fell asleep, only to be woken some time later by the familiar sound of British tanks approaching. Todd was sprawled in a heap next to me, so I checked my pockets to see if I still had my wallet.'

He ground the cigarette butt under his heel as if it was Todd's head he was crushing. 'It was there, but so were two wedding rings and a roll of German banknotes. I stuffed them back in Todd's pocket, checked he hadn't left any other nasty, incriminating surprises and then turned to Frank, who was just coming to. Major Brown was now entering the village with the rest of the men. He took one look at the state of us and ordered everyone to stand to attention.'

Jim gave a harsh bark of humourless laughter. 'We were in a terrible shambles and most of us couldn't stand, let alone form a straight line. But having found Todd's loot in my pockets, I'd sobered enough to think straight. I grabbed Frank, who was still stupid with the drink, and virtually had to hold him up to stop him from falling flat on his face. The Major listened grimly to our Sergeant's slurred report on what had happened, then gave us a bollocking like none we'd heard before or since. After regarding the bullet marks on the church, he went to look at the mass grave we'd dug, and then spent a long time inspecting the dead Germans. When he came back, his face was like thunder, and he gave the order for every man in the detail to be searched.'

Jim ran his fingers through his hair. 'Todd was standing further down the line, but he made a point of smirking at me, his ratty little eyes gleaming with malevolence as I was searched. I almost laughed out loud when I saw the look on his face as he realised his efforts to pay me back for bloodying his nose had failed and that there was a very real possibility that I'd given the stuff back to him. He reached for his pockets, but it was too late. The Sergeant was already in front of him, and within seconds he'd found that roll of German money and the two rings, which fell out with it into the dirt.

'Todd started shouting that he was innocent and he'd been set up, pointing the finger at me and several others as the Sergeant and one of the other men did a more thorough search. They discovered bits of jewellery, two gold lighters and several packs of German cigarettes. The Major ordered Todd to be arrested and he was dragged kicking and yelling to the Major's staff car, where he was held at gunpoint until the Major decided what to do with him.

'There was a general feeling that Todd had at last got what he deserved and good riddance. He'd been a thorn in everyone's side, and no one liked a man who tried to shift the blame onto others. The Major told us to clean up and get sober. We'd be leaving within the next two hours and would march through the night.'

Bewildered, Ron looked at his son. 'I'm glad Todd was caught, but I still don't understand how any of this reflects on your feud with Frank.'

Jim smiled for the first time in many hours, but it was a mere drawing back of his lips and didn't touch his eyes. 'Frank was starting to sober up, but he could still barely stand, and certainly wouldn't have got far once we'd started to move off. So I took him away from the rest and stuck his head in a water trough. I kept dunking him until I thought he'd had enough.'

Jim heaved a deep, wavering sigh that betrayed his inner turmoil. 'He stood there dripping wet, swaying like a giant candle in a breeze, his expression so fierce I thought he was about to knock me flat for soaking him. I braced meself, ready to dodge his mighty fist – but it was what he said that flattened me.'

Ron watched the differing emotions flit across his son's face and ached for the pain he was going through.

'He said he'd seen me and Todd going through the Germans' pockets, and had watched as I'd hidden my share of the loot on Todd so he'd get the blame. He'd never liked Todd, but now he was disgusted with me. I was a thief who stood back and let another man take the blame. I was no longer his brother.'

'Holy Mother of God,' breathed Ron.

'Aye.' Jim closed his eyes and lifted his face to the starlit sky, his jaw working as he battled with his tears. 'I loved the bones of him, Da. He was my big brother, my hero – but he thought so little of me that he believed I could do such a thing.'

'But surely, when you explained . . .'

Jim shook his head. 'He refused to listen when I tried to explain that he'd been drunk and had misinterpreted what he'd seen. He got angry, and so did I. No man, not even my brother, calls me a liar and gets away with it. I hit him and he hit me back, and suddenly we were wrestling and punching and rolling about in the dirt until we were dragged apart and put on charge.'

He dipped his chin, his voice muffled by his scarf. 'At least he refused to say what had caused it, but he said afterwards that he'd stayed silent because the shame of what I'd done would have damaged all of us and he never wanted our mother to know what a contemptible man I really was.' His voice broke. 'Frank believes to this day that I'm a liar and a thief, and nothing I can say will change that.'

Ron heard the bitterness in his son's voice and could now understand it. ''Tis an awful mess, so it is,' he murmured, his own guilt at doubting his son making him feel sick with shame.

'Aye, Da, that it is.' Jim lit another cigarette as a squadron of RAF bombers roared above them on their way to the other side of the Channel. 'But it

311

has gone on long enough,' he said in the ensuing silence. 'Regardless of what Frank thinks of me – and I admit I'm no saint – we're brothers, and it's time to put away the auld troubles.'

Ron relit his pipe and sucked on it for a moment as the distant booms carried across the water and the dark horizon blossomed with the glow of fire. He felt sad for both his sons, but there was little he could do except hope things would turn out all right in the end. 'You're right, Jim, it's time to close the door on it and make peace with Frank – and with yourself. 'Tis a terrible burden you've been carrying, son, but I suspect Frank is weary of it too.'

Another squadron of bombers droned overhead, followed swiftly by Hawker Hurricanes and Spitfires. The sirens were beginning to wail all through the town, and the searchlights from the hill emplacements began to stutter into life.

Ron got to his feet and held out his hand. 'Come on, son. Let's get out of here before the fireworks start.'

Jim grasped his hand and got to his feet. 'You do believe me, Da, don't you?' he asked, his handsome face shadowed by sudden doubt.

Ron gathered him into his strong arms and held him close as the wailing sirens rent the air. 'I've always believed in you,' he murmured. 'You're a good man, so y'are – and so is Frank.' He drew back, unashamed of the tears in his eyes. 'I love the bones of you both, and it's breaking me auld heart, so it is, to see the pair of you at such odds.'

'I'll do me best to put things right, Da, but—'

'I know you will.' Ron clamped his hand on Jim's shoulder. 'Let's be going home,' he said gruffly. 'Our loved ones are waiting, and we should be with them now. None of us knows what this night might bring, and it's time to hold them near.'

Chapter Fifteen

Julie and the other girls took over the running of Beach View Boarding House as well as caring for the two babies. It was no easy task, for they all worked different hours, and the long days and nights were often disturbed by raids or the noise from the planes taking off at Cliffe airfield. But Beach View was a house in mourning and they were determined to lift some of the responsibilities from Peggy's shoulders so that she could spend time with Pauline and Frank, as well as visiting Anne in hospital.

Three weeks had gone by since Frank had received that awful telegram, and they knew now that there would be no funeral, no grave in the local churchyard to mark the brothers' passing, for Seamus and Joseph had been buried at sea along with the rest of the two minesweepers' crews who had perished with them. However, there would be a memorial service at St Mary the Virgin the following day, and it was hoped that Brendon would be home in time.

It was now early April and, like many other Cliffehaven residents, Julie and Kath were taking advantage of the lighter evenings by strolling along the seafront. The two babies were warmly tucked up inside the pram, fast asleep, their little heads close together on the raised mattress. They stopped by one of the stone benches to sit down, and Julie checked that William's mittens and bootees hadn't come adrift, for his little hands and feet always seemed to be cold.

'Are you still going to the service tomorrow?' she asked.

Kath nodded, her fair hair flying loose from the pins as usual and blowing about her face in the early spring breeze. 'The fishing families are a close-knit community, and with my father now working the tugs down in Portsmouth, and Patrick still at sea, Mum and I need to be there to offer our support.' She gave a tremulous sigh. 'But it won't be easy. I've known Frank and his sons all my life, and Joseph was my Patrick's best friend.'

Julie took her gloved hand and gave it a squeeze. It wouldn't be easy for anyone, and the memory of Peggy's ashen face this morning as she'd brushed down Jim and Ron's best suit jackets and pressed the trousers still haunted her. Julie didn't really know what to say to Kath, for everyone dreaded the arrival of that awful telegram, and with the continued raids during the days as well as the nights, it seemed they were all living on the edge of disaster.

They sat looking out past the gun emplacement to the ruined pier, the shipping traps and the thick coils of barbed wire that closed off the mined beach. It was hardly the most attractive view, but Julie loved being so close to the sea. She was invigorated by the clean, salty air, which was so refreshing after the smog of London, and although she still had moments of terrible homesickness, she enjoyed the sound of the waves crashing on the shingle and the sharp, mournful cries of the gulls as they swooped and hovered on the wind.

'What about you?' Kath asked finally. 'Will you be going with the Reillys?'

Julie shook her head. 'Mrs Finch and I are babysitting, because Fran and Suzy are on duty from midday and Rita's shift at the fire station starts at two.' She gave a sigh. 'I'm worried about Mrs Finch, though. She's taken the news of those boys very badly, even though she admits not having really known them. But she adores Frank.' She gave a deep sigh. 'I came across her crying again this morning, just sitting there in the kitchen with her knitting forgotten in her lap, the tears streaming down her face.'

'Oh, no, how awful,' sighed Kath. 'She's usually such a sweet, chirpy old lady.'

'That's what worries all of us. She seems to have lost her spirit, and when we try and console her, she just shakes her head and mutters that life's unfair, and that it's she who should be dead, not all those young ones.'

'That sounds serious.' Kath's blue eyes regarded her solemnly.

'I've talked to Michael about it, and he's prescribed a tonic, but I don't think it will do much good. She needs to know she's much loved and depended upon, and that we couldn't manage without her. I use Rose and William shamelessly,' Julie admitted, 'because when she's caring for them, she seems much brighter.'

'This damned war is getting all of us down.' Kath took a deep breath and made a tremendous effort to pull herself out of the doldrums. 'Come on, let's walk. I don't know about you, but I'm getting cold sitting here.'

They strolled along towards the far end of the seafront in the hope that the little beach café would be open so they could buy a cup of tea. The breeze was certainly brisker now, and Julie wrapped her scarf a little more closely to her neck. She was enjoying the walk. She loved the way the green hills dipped so gently towards the water at this end of the promenade, and how the white cliffs towered over the fishing boats at the other. Cliffehaven had proved to be the perfect place to start again, despite the fact that so much had happened since her arrival.

These last three weeks had been particularly fraught, and the only really good thing to have happened was the fact that William's hearing was back. He heard the slightest noise now and, like Harvey, wailed at the sound of the sirens – but strangely enough managed to sleep through most air raids quite happily.

'Have you seen much of your sister?' asked Kath

as they walked past the big houses overlooking the beach from Havelock Gardens.

'I went round and told her the good news about William's hearing. She seemed pleased enough, and even offered me a cup of tea, but she isn't really interested in anyone but herself and her pursuit of councillor what's-his-name.'

'Unwin,' said Kath, and grinned. 'She's welcome to him, if you ask me. He's a fat fool with too much money and a high opinion of himself.'

The café was closed, so they turned back and headed towards the playing fields which had been dug up to provide the biggest shelter in Cliffehaven. Kath and her mother lived in one of the little houses that overlooked the field, and which backed onto the steep incline where the old asylum had once been. The remains of the asylum could still be seen amid the surrounding trees, and Julie had heard from Rita all about the night it had taken a direct hit.

Kath's mother was on night shift at Solomon and Goldman's factory, where they now made parachutes as well as uniforms. 'I won't stay long,' said Julie as she parked the pram in the hall, checked the babies and followed Kath into the kitchen. 'I want to make sure Mrs Finch gets to bed safely. She's very unsteady on her pins, and the last thing we need now is for her to take a tumble.'

Kath made the tea, raided the biscuit tin and raked the fire in the range to a glow. 'How is dear Eunice?' she asked wryly, her blue eyes sparkling.

'She's still a cow,' said Julie, and giggled. 'She times me when I write up me notes and have a cuppa, makes me count every blasted packet of dressing and bit of cotton wool every day, and makes a note of what I've used. I dropped a syringe the other morning, and blimey, you'd have thought I'd broken the Crown jewels.'

Kath laughed. 'She obviously thinks you're after her man.'

Julie had come to the same conclusion, and it worried her, for the happy atmosphere at Cliffe surgery had changed. 'Michael and I get along, and he's a sweet, kind man. But we're just friends, Kath.'

'Are you sure?'

Julie met her steady gaze. 'Positive.'

'If you say so,' murmured Kath.

Peggy was very grateful to Alf the butcher for taking her in his delivery van to Tamarisk Bay every other day. He would take her there at lunchtime, then pick her up after he'd shut his shop and drop her at the hospital so she could visit Anne. Before the war, Tamarisk Bay could be reached at low tide along the beach, but with barbed wire, shipping traps and mines, it was now impossible, and she simply didn't have the strength or energy to cycle all the way over the hills.

She took off her headscarf and pushed back her hair from her sweaty forehead, then pulled off her apron. It was hot and stuffy in the little kitchen with the range blazing away, but Pauline liked to have all the windows closed once the shadows closed in.

The wooden cottage was at the end of a row of five, nestling at the foot of the hill amongst the pale pink fronds of wild tamarisks, which grew in abundance amid the tussocks of long, windswept grass and knots of gorse and stunted trees. The kitchen led into a sitting room with French windows leading out onto a veranda, and had an uninterrupted view of the tiny bay. There were three bedrooms upstairs, and Frank had rigged up a copper boiler and an enormous enamel bath in a lean-to at the side of the house. Lobster pots, nets, fishing rods, old anchors, grappling hooks and discarded bits of machinery littered the space beneath the veranda, and Pauline had long given up trying to get Frank to sort it out and clear it away.

Peggy checked the pot of fish stew and took it off the hotplate. She didn't want it to spoil, though she doubted if Pauline or Frank would feel like eating very much tonight. The kitchen was neat, with the pile of logs that Jim had cut this morning stacked tidily by the range, and the shoes Ron had polished earlier were lined up on newspaper by the door. Satisfied all was in order, she walked into the shabby sitting room.

Pauline was chain-smoking as she sat on the sagging couch facing the French windows and watched Frank messing about on his fishing boat in the twilight. He'd been out there most of the day, his face set, talking to no one, and clearly reluctant to return to the house where the atmosphere was heavy with mourning and the memories of his boys.

Both women understood that he needed time to himself, especially this evening, for the next day they would have to get through the ordeal of the memorial service. To make matters worse, there was still no sign of Brendon, despite the authorities assuring them he'd been given compassionate leave and was on his way home.

Peggy placed a gentle hand on Pauline's shoulder. 'Alf will be here soon,' she said quietly. 'Is there anything else you need me to do before I leave?'

Pauline was a fair-haired little woman who was only a few years older than Peggy, but her prettiness and vivacity had been wiped away by tragedy. She sat thin and ashen-faced, staring out of the window, probably not seeing Frank, or anything much, lost as she was in her stupor of grief. 'You've done so much, Peg,' she said brokenly. 'I don't know how I'd have coped without you.'

Peggy knew that Pauline would have liked her mother to be there, but the old lady was far too frail to travel such a long distance, and probably wouldn't have been much help anyway. Peggy sat down next to her and took her hand. 'We're family, Pauline, of course we want to do everything we can to help.' She stroked the thin, cold hand. 'I've ironed your black dress and Frank's shirt, and brushed down his best suit,' she said quietly. 'They're hanging up in your bedroom.'

The narrow shoulders shuddered, but Pauline remained dry-eyed. 'Brendon's not coming, is he?' she managed.

'There's still time,' murmured Peggy, 'but you know how upside down everything is, and how far he has to come. I'm sure he's doing his very best to get here.'

Pauline nodded, her gaze still fixed on the view from the window. 'He knows how much we need him here,' she muttered. 'Frank won't settle until he knows for sure that he's safe.'

Peggy heard the whine of an engine approaching. 'That'll be Alf,' she said. 'I'd better not keep him waiting.' Pauline struggled to get out of the couch, but Peggy pressed her back. 'Stay there, love,' she said softly. 'I'll see you tomorrow.'

Pauline just nodded as she stubbed out the half-smoked cigarette, lit a fresh one and returned to her vigil at the window.

Peggy went back into the tiny kitchen where she slipped on her coat and gathered up her string bag and gas-mask box. She could see Alf's truck making its ponderous way down the steep, rutted slope. He's such a kind man, she thought as she opened the front door and stepped outside. She and Jim must find a way of repaying him.

She waved as he pulled up by the gate and was about to shut the front door behind her when the passenger door opened and a handsome, dark-haired young man in the uniform of the Royal Naval Reserve stepped down.

'Brendon,' she breathed as he strode towards her and wordlessly gathered her into his arms. 'Oh, Brendon,' she sighed against his broad chest. 'It's so wonderful to see you. We didn't think you'd make it in time.'

'How's Mammy and Da?' he asked, his dark blue eyes shadowed with worry as he released her.

Peggy blinked away her tears, her heart full of thankfulness. 'They'll be better for seeing you,' she murmured, patting his cheek and giving him a kiss. 'Your mother's indoors and Frank's on the beach. I'll leave you to it.'

She stood on the step just long enough to hear Pauline's joyous cry of welcome, and then closed the door. They didn't need her any more tonight.

Breakfast had been a solemn, almost silent meal which hardly anyone had touched. Ron and Jim had left soon after with Harvey to walk the hills, and everyone else saw to the housework and the babies, glad to be kept busy before they could escape the bleak atmosphere.

Julie was due to help Michael at the free Saturday morning clinic he'd set up for mothers with young babies at the Town Hall and, as Rose and William were due for their check-ups, she'd donned her uniform and taken them both with her.

Feeling rather guilty at how good it was to escape that house of mourning, Julie wheeled the pram up the High Street, her starched apron crackling beneath the warm cloak. It was a dull sort of day, but there were patches of blue amid the scudding clouds which promised a better afternoon, and the salty wind revived and refreshed her.

She reached the Town Hall and willing hands helped her up the steps with the pram. Smiling and chatting as she headed for the big room that was set aside once a week for the clinic, she realised she'd become a familiar face in Cliffehaven and was now considered an intrinsic part of the community. This knowledge warmed her, and she was smiling as she parked the pram in a corner and took off her cloak.

'Hello, Julie.' Fay and Jess, the two young volunteer aides, came and peeked into the pram. 'Oh,' Fay cooed, 'aren't they just adorable?'

'So sweet,' murmured Jess, gently pulling back the blanket. 'You are lucky they're so good.'

Julie chuckled. 'You should hear them at five in the morning,' she said. 'But yes, they are perfect, aren't they?'

'What do you mean by bringing those babies in here?'

All three girls turned to find Eunice glaring at them. 'Dr Michael gave me permission,' said Julie. 'William and Rose are due for their monthly checkup, and because of the memorial service no one else is free to bring them.'

Eunice's jaw was working, and her eyes were like flint. 'See to it they don't disrupt your duties,' she snapped before turning on her heel and bustling away.

'It's time someone taught that one some manners,' said Fay darkly. 'And why does she always pick on you, Julie? Anyone would think you were her worst enemy the way she goes on.'

Jess grinned as she took off her coat and adjusted her neat starched cap and apron. 'Well, it's obvious, isn't it?' she said. 'She's waited for ages for Michael to notice her and along comes Julie, who's prettier and far nicer – and who Michael notices immediately.'

'If that's the case,' said Fay, 'then I'd watch it, Julie. Eunice is not someone I'd like to upset, and that's a fact.'

'Thanks,' Julie murmured as they began to lay out the weighing scales, the blankets and examination tables. 'But don't worry about me. I can handle Eunice.'

Yet, as they continued to set out all the paraphernalia for the clinic, Julie wasn't quite so sure that she *could* handle Eunice. The woman had made her dislike clear from the offset, and now this perceived relationship Julie was supposed to have with Michael was making things worse.

As the doors opened and Michael came striding in, Julie noted how his gaze went straight to her – and that Eunice had noticed it too. Julie could feel her animosity from across the room as she shot him a distracted smile and hurriedly turned away to sort through her patients' notes. She would have to talk to Eunice and clear the air, but also make Michael aware of what was happening. Was he really so blind that he couldn't see the adoration in Eunice's eyes every time she looked at him; did he not notice that she made little biscuits to go with his morning coffee, tidied his surgery and sewed the loose buttons on his jackets? Julie gave a deep sigh. Men could be so dim at times.

The clinic was as busy and chaotic as every Saturday morning, with Jess and Fay trying to keep the toddlers amused with the big box of toys while mothers gossiped and babies wailed. Eunice, Michael and Julie worked throughout the morning, weighing the babies, checking that all was well, filling in charts and notes and giving advice on breastfeeding and the hundred and one other concerns that new mothers fretted about.

Julie realised the same apocryphal stories were going round as the ones in London, the same vying to prove their baby was more advanced than any other – and the same sniggering and whispering as they exchanged the latest bit of scandal. Julie felt right at home, and if it hadn't been for Eunice glaring at her every five minutes, she would have thoroughly enjoyed the morning.

'Right,' said Michael as his last patient joined the rest of the women who were going in search of a cup of tea and a further natter. 'That's it for the morning. I'll see to Rose and William now if you'd like to bring them over, Julie.'

'*Sister* Harris still has Mrs Owen to see before she helps to clear things away,' said Eunice rather forcibly. 'I'll get the babies for you.'

Michael frowned. 'No, that's all right, Sister Beecham. You see to Mrs Owen. I need Julie here while I examine both babies.'

Eunice's lips formed a thin angry line as she shot Julie a venomous glare and rather brusquely ordered Mrs Owen to hurry up and bring her squalling baby to her examination table.

'Whatever's the matter with Sister Beecham this morning?' asked Michael as Julie brought Rose to him. 'It's not like her to be so sharp with everyone.'

If only you knew the half of it, she thought. 'I expect she's just feeling a bit out of sorts after the raids last night,' she said as she undressed the gurgling Rose and settled her in the scales.

He eyed her thoughtfully and then shook his head, turning his attention to little Rose, who was waving her sturdy arms and legs about. 'She's putting on weight nicely,' he murmured, lifting her out of the scales and placing her on the examination table. He checked her ears, mouth and throat, listened to her heartbeat and ran his fingers over her skull and down her spine, before testing her joints and reflexes. 'All is well,' he said with a beaming smile. 'You and Peggy are to be congratulated.'

Julie chuckled as she dressed Rose and put her

back in the pram. 'It's a joint effort from every woman at Beach View,' she said. 'With so many "mothers" to call on when they need something, the pair of them are in danger of becoming spoilt.' She plucked William from the pram and nuzzled the sweet spot in his neck which always made him gurgle.

'I understand Anne will be discharged within the next two weeks, so that should lift some of the responsibility from your shoulders.'

Julie wasn't so sure, for although it would mean Peggy didn't have to go to the hospital every day, Anne's leg would still be in plaster and she'd be unable to do very much at all. 'It will certainly give Anne more time with Rose,' she murmured as she gently placed William on the scales. Sliding the weights back and forth until they balanced, she let out a sigh. 'He's hardly put on any weight at all.'

Michael lifted him out and began to examine him. 'His ears have cleared up nicely.' He reached for his stethoscope. 'But he's certainly still underweight for his age. I presume he's taking more solids now to supplement his milk?'

Julie nodded and watched anxiously as Michael listened to William's chest. William was still far too small and, in fact, looked undernourished after the plump little Rose. Was there something wrong with him, or had he simply inherited his mother's slenderness?

Michael hung the stethoscope back round his

neck, his expression thoughtful as he felt William's hands and feet.

'I can never seem to keep them warm,' said Julie, 'even with two pairs of bootees and mittens and a hot-water bottle at night.'

He nodded, his expression still solemn. 'You can get him dressed again,' he said, reaching for the grey folder that was on the table beside him.

Julie read William's name on the front of that unfamiliar folder, and her hands trembled as she struggled to dress a squirming William. She didn't like the way Michael was frowning over what could only be William's medical notes. 'What is it?' she asked fearfully.

He closed the folder. 'These were sent down a couple of weeks ago from London with a covering letter from Mr Philips, the surgeon who delivered him.' He looked bashful. 'It seems they got mislaid in the mess in my office, because I only found them this morning. I can't think how they ended up at the bottom of my desk drawer – but then I've been so busy, it's hardly surprising I've become a little absent-minded.'

Eunice dealt with the post every morning and, as Julie didn't want to even consider that she'd stoop so low as to hide the notes, she dismissed the suspicion. 'Is there something in there that I should know about?' she asked with dread.

Michael looked at William, snug in Julie's arms, and nodded with clear reluctance.

'What is it?' she breathed, her pulse racing.

'Perhaps it would be better if we discussed this back at the surgery.'

Julie shook her head. 'No,' she said firmly. 'If there's something wrong then I want to know now.'

Michael regarded her solemnly and then gave a sigh. 'Mr Philips detected a slight heart murmur,' he said softly, 'but put it down to the trauma of his birth and the fact that he was a little premature.'

'Murmur?' Julie held William closer.

'It's only a slight murmur,' he said hurriedly, 'and I'm hoping that as William grows, it will settle down.'

'But it hasn't yet, has it?' she said, her fear making her sharp with him. 'You can still hear it.'

He nodded. 'I'm sorry, Julie, but Sam Watson heard it too, and that's why I got Mr Philips to send down the notes.'

'So you weren't really discussing rugby that afternoon, were you?' she said accusingly.

He shamefacedly shook his head.

'I might have known,' she snapped. 'And what about Mr Philips? He gave William a clean bill of health and mentioned nothing about any heart murmur.' Her voice was rising as the fear and anger took hold. 'Didn't any of you think I should know? When were you actually planning to tell me – when he got sick, when . . .?'

She clutched William and fought back the tears. 'Oh, God,' she breathed, 'he's not got heart disease, has he? He's not going to suffer all his life like poor little Franny?'

'Of course he isn't,' Michael said hastily. He rushed round the examination table and put his arm round her, unaware of Eunice's glower, Mrs Owen's avid curiosity or Jess and Fay's exchange of knowing looks. 'The murmur just means that there's probably a tiny hole in his heart which will heal as he grows.'

She looked at him in horror. 'A hole? In his heart?'

'It's not as serious as it sounds,' he said firmly. 'It's a very small heart, and therefore will be a very tiny hole, and it is absolutely possible that it may close of its own accord. At the moment it is causing William some problems, like his failing to thrive and his cold extremities, but he seems to be holding up well.'

Julie felt chilled to her very core. 'What happens if the hole doesn't heal naturally?'

'After reading through the notes, I spoke to Sam before I came here this morning, and it is possible he will need an operation – but,' he added quickly, 'no surgeon would dream of doing that while he's still so small. It's not crucial, Julie, so I don't want you thinking otherwise. Babies are incredibly resilient, and although he's small, he's tougher than you think, and in no immediate danger.'

Julie stared at him, unable to voice the terror that had her in its grip.

Michael held her firmly by the shoulders and looked straight into her eyes. 'I know you're frightened, Julie, but I promise Sam Watson and I will give him the very best of care, and you are to promise me that you'll come to me any hour of the day or night if the slightest thing is worrying you.'

She looked through her tears into his kindly eyes and knew she had to trust him. 'Is there anything we can do to help him get better?'

Michael became businesslike and reached for his prescription pad. 'Sam has suggested I put him on diuretics so he doesn't retain fluid, and give him something to strengthen his heart and make it more efficient, which will improve his circulation. This combination of medication will make him more comfortable, which will, in turn, probably improve his appetite.'

'Is that it?'

'I will need to see him every month, but if he gets a cold, a chest infection or anything similar, you're to call me at once. That's very important, Julie, because I will need to get Sam to check him over.'

Julie could see herself rushing to Michael every time William sneezed or frowned, and wasn't at all sure if she could cope with this devastating turn of events, let alone trust the others to be as watchful. 'Perhaps I should think about cutting down me hours,' she murmured. 'I can't expect Peggy and the others to take on that kind of responsibility.'

Michael's smile was understanding and kind as he handed her the prescription. 'I know you'll panic over the slightest thing,' he said softly, 'but it's only natural and doesn't matter a jot.' He squeezed her arm encouragingly. 'As for cutting down your hours, I won't hear of it. The important thing is for you and William to carry on as normal. He won't benefit from being fussed over, and if he gets a cold, I can deal with it. Let him be with other children, enjoy him and don't feel you all have to treat him like cut crystal. He needs to continue to be a part of the rough and tumble of the family at Beach View, just as you need to continue doing the job you love. As long as you're both contented he has a better chance of thriving.'

Julie nodded, realising that his advice made a lot of sense. Yet she couldn't dismiss the thought that she would never forgive herself if anything were to happen to William while she was at work. On the other hand, if she gave up her job, she'd have no money to pay for William's prescriptions and all his other needs. They didn't come cheap – and neither did Sam Watson.

'I'll see how things go,' she said reluctantly.

'You aren't alone in this, Julie,' he said softly. 'We'll look after him together.'

She looked up at him and suddenly wanted him to hold her, to be her rock and provide the strength she would need to get through this. She swayed towards him as they looked into one another's eyes.

'Dr Michael, I need to talk to you about one of my patients.'

The sound of Eunice's voice snapped Julie from

the trance that had enveloped them both and almost sent her into Michael's arms. She masked her embarrassment by turning away to settle William in the pram and used the moment to regain her poise. She would have to be very careful from now on, she realised suddenly, for despite all her protests to the contrary, she was as drawn to Michael as he was to her.

Eunice had bitterly watched that little scene between Michael and Julie, and had noted the sly glances exchanged by Jess and Fay. It seemed she wasn't the only one who'd noticed the growing attraction, and it was time to put an end to it.

She kept her thoughts to herself as Michael waved a cheerful goodbye and hurried off. Ignoring Julie and the other two girls, she finished with Mrs Owen, tidied up her corner and swept out of the hall without a word to anyone. It wasn't a long walk back to the surgery, but she didn't hurry, for she needed time to think clearly.

She'd seen the suspicion in Julie's eyes, and had felt ashamed that she could think she was capable of hiding medical files. She was a professional, and despite her animosity towards Julie, she would never have put a patient at risk like that. But William's heart problems actually played right into her hands. She had a real weapon now, and as long as she used it wisely, it would reflect on her rather well – and perhaps get rid of Julie once and for all.

The surgery was closed, Michael was at the rugby club where he spent most Saturday afternoons, and Dr Sayers would be in his garden tending his roses. The timing was perfect.

She found the elderly doctor sitting on a bench in the sunshine, a gardening manual on his lap as he inspected the black spots on the leaves of his favourite climbing rose. 'Dr Sayers,' she said warmly. 'I'm so sorry to disturb you, but I wonder if I could ask your advice on something?'

He smiled back at her, saw her anxious expression, and reached for her hand. 'My dear, of course you can.' He patted the bench. 'Sit down, Eunice, and tell me all about it.'

Chapter Sixteen

Julie had returned to Beach View in a daze of confusion and worry. That short interlude with Michael had been a moment of madness, she decided. Of course she didn't love him. She'd merely fallen into the same trap as a thousand nurses and patients before her and had seen him as some sort of saviour – a kind man who really cared, a knight in a white coat who had the answer to everything.

She wheeled the pram through the back garden and into the basement. Both babies were awake and beginning to complain that they needed feeding. She picked up Rose and carried her up into the kitchen where she found a rather sad-faced Mrs Finch staring out of the window above the sink.

'They've all left for the service,' she said with a sigh. 'I do hope it's not too awful – but then that kind of service is never easy to get through.' She seemed to make an effort to shrug off her gloom by fetching cups and saucers from the wooden draining board and warming the teapot. 'The kettle's almost boiled. I expect you could do with a cuppa.'

'Could you take Rose while I fetch William?'

Mrs Finch's little face brightened considerably and she sat down in the fireside chair and held out her arms. 'I never mind holding them,' she said softly. 'Such sweet babies.' She placed a soft finger on Rose's cheek and started clucking at her.

Julie fetched William and quickly changed his nappy. 'Could we do a swap? I need to change Rose and then get their food prepared.'

'We can't go down to the shop at the moment, dear,' said Mrs Finch, 'and anyway, my clothes don't need changing. They're perfectly adequate.'

Julie gave her a wan smile and exchanged William for Rose, saw to the sodden nappy and put her in the playpen that Ron had managed to squeeze in a corner. William and Mrs Finch looked very happy with each other, so she left him in her care and hurried to make the formula for Rose and mix up a small dish of vegetables for William.

She fed Rose while Mrs Finch managed to persuade William to eat some of the mashed vegetables whilst getting most of it down his front and all over his face. It took quite a while and Rose was already drowsy by the time Mrs Finch gave up. Carefully putting Rose back in the playpen and covering her with a blanket, Julie made up the formula for William and added the correct dosage of the medicines she'd brought back from the chemist. She gave the bottle a shake to make sure it mixed well, tested its heat, and handed it to Mrs Finch.

Mrs Finch eyed Julie and the bottle with suspicion

as she did her best to clean William's face and bib. 'What's that you put in there?'

'William needs to have some medicine,' Julie said loudly and clearly so there would be no misunderstanding. 'The doctor says he has a heart problem and that medicine will make it stronger.'

'Oh, poor little mite,' Mrs Finch quavered as she held William closer and gave him the bottle. 'His heart, you say? What's the matter with it?'

Julie explained it simply, and reassured her that William was in no immediate danger. 'But please don't say anything to Peggy or the others just yet. They've got enough to cope with at the moment.'

'You can rely on me, dear. I'm the soul of discretion.'

Julie suspected she couldn't keep a secret for more than five minutes, but let it pass. 'In the meantime, I'll need you to help me keep an eye on him, Mrs Finch,' she said. 'He will need lots of cuddles and love, but he musn't catch a cold or get sick, so we'll have to be extra especially careful – and I'm going to have to rely on you to keep watch over him while I'm at work.'

Mrs Finch's gaze was steady as she looked back at Julie. 'Of course I'll love him and look after him, and take the greatest care of him as I do Rose. But I'm not a fool, Julie. I know why you've asked me to do this.'

Julie kept her expression non-committal as she returned that gaze. 'I asked you because you're reliable and wise, and obviously dote on both babies.'

Mrs Finch chuckled. 'You're a sweet girl,' she said, 'but you'd make a terrible poker player.' She gave a sigh and stroked William's peachy cheek. 'I know I've been a bit down in the dumps lately, but I can see now that I was being rather selfish and silly. We have one life, and should live it to the full, not wish it away – and there's nothing like caring for others to take your mind off things.' She looked back at Julie, her eyes twinkling. 'It's all right, Julie,' she murmured. 'I'm not ready to throw in the towel just yet.'

Julie smiled. Her strategy had worked, and at last Mrs Finch seemed to be regaining her spirits.

Monday morning was one of those lovely, crisp days when the world seemed all fresh and new, with blossoms from the trees floating like pink and white confetti in the brisk breeze, and green shoots poking up between the bluebells and crocuses. Julie still hadn't said anything to the others about William, but she knew that Mrs Finch would keep a close eye on him and ask for help if she needed it, so she felt reasonably happy about leaving him.

Feeling tired and rather anxious after being out half the night attending to a delivery in a remote cottage north of the town, she arrived at the surgery to find that there was no sign of Eunice or Michael. But the elderly Dr Sayers was in the waiting room going through patients' notes while Maud crashed the noisy Hoover against the chair legs. His expression didn't bode well. He was obviously having one of his famous grumpy days.

He looked up and glowered at Maud. 'Turn that thing off and find something else to do that doesn't make so much noise,' he barked.

Maud's look was sour as she took the Hoover out. Seconds later they heard the clatter of buckets in the kitchen, each bang and crash a forceful condemnation of his rudeness.

'Damned woman can't seem to do anything without making a racket,' he grumbled. He finally looked at Julie. 'Sister Harris,' he said solemnly, 'you and I need to have a talk.'

Julie felt a quiver of unease as she followed him into his consulting room and closed the door behind her. She sat on the edge of the chair, her starched apron carefully smoothed over her knees.

He sat behind his large desk, his hands folded over his midriff. He didn't look at all jolly this morning, and as her gaze fell on William's medical folder, which lay between them, she felt a pang of fear.

'I was very sorry to learn of William's problems,' he said, coming straight to the point as he always did. 'It must be difficult for you.'

'Michael and Mr Watson have promised to keep a close eye on him,' said Julie nervously. 'It's a big worry, of course, but the family at Beach View are very understanding, and I know I can rely on them to look after him while I'm working.'

'Have you considered that your place is with William rather than here? I would understand completely if you wished to hand in your notice.'

Alarmed, she caught her breath. 'I need to work to pay for his medication and everyday expenses,' she said quickly. 'As long as William is able to cope with this disability, I intend to carry on.'

'I see,' he said quietly. His gaze was steady beneath the curling white brows. 'That is all very well, Sister Harris, but if things do take a turn for the worse, I cannot be expected to find your replacement at the drop of a hat. I did warn you that I will not tolerate any interruption to the smooth running of this surgery.'

Julie's pulse was racing and her mouth was so dry she could barely speak. 'Are you asking me to resign?'

'I'm asking you to guarantee your reliability,' he said gruffly.

She twisted her hands in her lap. 'There are no guarantees, Dr Sayers, especially when it involves a sick child.'

'Then I think you should seriously consider your position here,' he said flatly. 'It is important to maintain a continuous service to our patients in this town, and unless you can assure me that your tenure here will be uninterrupted, then I must start looking for another midwife.'

Julie closed her eyes and tried to remain calm, but her thoughts and emotions were in turmoil. 'You can't sack me,' she replied bravely. 'Not over this. I work hard and efficiently, I'm never late, and although me round seems to get longer and longer, none of my patients suffer because of it. Ask Michael. He'll tell you.'

'Ah, yes. My son.' His lips thinned between the waxed moustache and white beard. 'I have become aware that there have been moments of inappropriate behaviour between you, and it will not do at all, Sister Harris.'

He silenced her interjection with a dismissive wave of his hand. 'I realise you rely on him to look after William, and that you probably admire him for his skill and kindness. But anything more is unseemly, and I will not tolerate it. Do you understand?'

Julie suddenly realised that William's condition was not the main reason for this conversation – it was really about her supposed relationship with Michael. She knew then that Eunice had stirred up the trouble, and she experienced a wave of cold fury.

'I understand exactly what you mean, Dr Sayers,' she replied icily, 'and I can assure you there is nothing unprofessional about my dealings with your son.'

'I'm glad to hear it,' he retorted. 'Just see that it stays that way.'

Julie waited as he reached for his pipe and tobacco and took the time to try and calm herself. Eunice Beecham was a bitch, and it was clear she'd poured poison into the old man's ear – but she was damned if she was going to let her ruin everything she'd worked so hard for. There was no way she would simply hand in her notice and walk away without a murmur.

'So, Sister Harris,' he said once he had the pipe going to his satisfaction, 'what conclusion have you reached as to your position here?'

'I will continue working as usual,' she said firmly. 'If you wish to employ another midwife, then I would suggest we share the workload, and both work part-time. That way you can be assured of the smooth running of the district duties, and I can continue to earn enough to pay for William's medical care.'

He eyed her thoughtfully through the pipe smoke in the long silence that followed this brave little speech, and then nodded. 'That sounds very practical in the circumstances,' he said gruffly. 'I'll place an advertisement in next week's medical journals.'

Julie's emotions were mixed as she pushed back her chair and prepared to leave. She'd just talked herself out of getting the sack, but working fewer hours a week would leave her very short of money, and she hadn't a clue as to how she would manage.

He stood to escort her to the door. 'You're an

excellent midwife and nurse, Sister Harris, and although I don't approve of this infatuation you seem to have for my son, I can't really afford to lose you.'

She eyed him with a cool detachment that belied her inner turmoil. 'I'm a professional woman with heavy responsibilities, and far too mature to have infatuations about anybody,' she retorted. 'Your son is quite safe with me, Dr Sayers.'

He grinned for the first time that morning as he opened the door for her. 'I'm glad to hear it, Sister. Now cut along, and ask Maud to bring in my morning coffee, will you?'

Julie stood in the hallway for a moment to catch her breath, and then determinedly walked into the waiting room where Eunice was overseeing Maud's polishing. Maud bustled off to get the doctor's coffee and Julie turned to Eunice.

'It was very kind of you to be so concerned for William, but Dr Sayers is such an understanding man, isn't he?' Her gaze was even and appraising, the smile barely touching her lips.

'I'm sure I don't know what you mean,' Eunice murmured, her gaze fixed on the day's list of patients.

'Oh, I think you do, Eunice,' Julie replied softly, 'but you don't get rid of me that easily.'

Eunice cleared her throat and shuffled the papers on her desk. 'I have absolutely no idea what you're talking about,' she said stiffly.

'Then let me enlighten you,' Julie replied, leaning towards her, her voice low and flat with dislike. 'Despite your best efforts to get me the sack, I will continue working here with Dr Sayers' approval until I'm ready to leave. Any more backbiting, and I'll make sure Dr Michael knows exactly what sort of bitch you really are.'

Eunice went ashen and her hand trembled as she placed Julie's casebook on the desk between them. 'The list is rather long this morning,' she said unsteadily. 'So I've teamed you up with Fay.'

Julie took the book and tucked it under her arm as Fay and Jess came hurrying in, faces glowing from the brisk wind. She turned her back on Eunice and returned the girls' happy smiles. 'Don't bother taking your coat off, Fay,' she said with enforced cheerfulness. 'We've got a long day ahead of us and need to get on.'

Jim had bided his time since that talk with his father, but now a week had passed since the memorial service, Frank had made no effort to respond to his help or his offers of sympathy and brotherhood, and he'd waited long enough. He tramped purposefully over the hills, his hands dug deep in his pockets, his thoughts keeping him company.

He'd left the house early, telling Peggy only that he needed to be somewhere and didn't know when he'd be back. Peggy knew him too well to question him, for he came and went as he pleased most of the time, and she didn't really want to know the things he got up to unless she suspected they would upset the harmony of the family. She had merely kissed him goodbye and asked him to at least be back in time to visit Anne.

He always felt guilty, for Peggy was trusting and loyal, and he didn't deserve her. There had been moments when he'd been tempted to stray, moments when his pride and vanity had been roused and he'd forgotten momentarily that he was a family man approaching his forty-fourth birthday. But his love for Peggy had never faltered and he'd remained true despite the temptations.

He knew he was a flirt. What was more, he could never resist a dodgy deal or a bit of black market-eering if there was a profit in it. Lord only knew his father had taught him well over the years when they'd taken the fishing boat over to France and come back with tobacco, brandy, and a host of other things the excisemen would have copped them for. But he'd never done anything to hurt anyone – had never been tempted to rob a bank or get into serious trouble. It could get very tedious sitting in that projection room for hours on end, and he needed the deals and the flirting to add spice to his life.

Jim wasn't used to so much exercise, and he was out of breath as he reached the top of the track that led down to Tamarisk Bay. He could see over the cottage roofs to the beach where the boats had been winched up above the high-water mark, and he stood for a moment to watch Frank. He was alone, just sitting in his boat, smoking a cigarette and staring out to sea. There was no sign of the motorbike and sidecar Brendon had bought soon after his arrival home, and Jim rather hoped he'd taken Pauline out for a spin on this blustery but bright Saturday morning.

He pulled up his coat collar and made his way down the steep, rutted slope to the cottage. Without announcing his arrival, he walked past the front door and took the side path which led straight down to the beach. His heavy boots crunched the shingle as he made his way determinedly towards the man sitting in the boat.

'What do *you* want?' said Frank, not taking his gaze from the sea.

'I've come to talk to you,' said Jim, 'and I'll not be taking no for an answer.' He climbed into the boat and sat beside his brother.

'Oh, aye? And what do you have to say that I'd want to listen to?'

Jim knew this was going to be the hardest thing he'd ever done, but he was determined to see it through. It was time to be honest and straightforward, to say what was in his heart. 'I love you, Frank,' he said firmly. 'I admire you and look up to you, and I've missed not having you around.'

Frank's expression didn't change as he stared out to sea and continued to smoke his cigarette.

Jim licked his lips. 'I know you think I'm a thief and a liar, and I admit I've always walked a fine line when it comes to the law, and told a few little fibs to get me out of trouble with Peggy. But I'm *not* guilty of robbing the dead, and *certainly* not guilty of setting Todd up to wriggle out of things. He took that stuff and planted it on me – I was merely returning it to him.'

Frank threw his cigarette over the side and left it to burn to nothing in the shingle. After watching it for a moment, he turned his great head and regarded his younger brother with dark eyes as cold and blue as the Arctic. 'Go away,' he said with ominous calm. 'Leave me in peace to mourn my sons instead of dragging up these things that don't matter any more.'

'They matter to me,' said Jim fiercely. 'They're still raw, even after all these years, and it's time we settled this once and for all.'

Frank stood up, making the boat rock as he towered over Jim. 'What do you want from me?' he roared, his weather-beaten face suffused with rage as his huge fists curled at his sides.

Jim felt very vulnerable sitting there, but he had known it might come to this and had prepared for it. He swallowed his fear and stood to face Frank. 'I want you to admit you were wrong,' he replied. 'I want you to stop and think, to go back over what you thought you saw and try to see how it really was.'

Frank glowered, his hands flexing. He brushed past Jim, clambered out of the boat and began striding along the undulating banks of shingle.

Jim scrambled after him, grabbing his arm and pulling him off balance. 'Don't turn your back on me,' he shouted. 'I've had twenty-three years of this, and I've had enough.'

Frank let out a mighty roar and swung his meaty fist.

Jim ducked.

Frank was unbalanced, but he swung again.

Jim dodged the blow, crouched low and, with the full weight of his body behind it, rammed his head into Frank's midriff.

Frank stumbled on the shingle and fell, winded, to his knees. 'You'd better sling yer hook, because if I catch you, I'll kill you,' he panted.

Jim stood his ground, his fear overridden by the raging need to make his brother see that he couldn't just shrug him off, couldn't threaten or ignore him any longer. 'I'll leave when you accept I'm an innocent man,' he said fiercely.

Frank staggered to his feet and although Jim was prepared to be punched, he hadn't expected Frank to give him a shove in the chest which sent him flying and left him flat on his back. 'Get out of here,' Frank roared above him. 'Go home, Jim, before I really do you some damage.'

Jim staggered to his feet. 'Why do you hate me so?' he yelled back. 'Would hitting me make you

349

feel any better?' He stood tall and straight. 'Go on then,' he shouted, jabbing Frank in the chest. 'Hit me and see if it takes away your pain.' He jabbed him again. 'Come on, Frank,' he goaded. 'Let's finish what we started back in that village and let it be an end to it. What are you waiting for?'

The weathered lines in Frank's face were carved as if in stone as his fist came from nowhere and thudded into Jim's jaw.

Jim saw red for the second time in his life, and with a howl of pent-up frustration and anger unleashed a mighty right hook which almost knocked Frank off his feet. Within seconds they were silently and fiercely exchanging blows, wrestling for dominance on the shingle that slipped and slid beneath their trampling feet.

Jim knew he was no match for Frank, but he didn't care, and as his punch found its mark and Frank stumbled and fell, he clung onto him until they were both rolling on the shingle and in danger of getting caught in the barbed wire.

And then Frank suddenly went limp beneath him.

Jim looked down at him fearfully, sure that he'd done him serious harm.

Frank's craggy face seemed to change as he lay there, the lines softened and there was terrible pain in his blue eyes as he looked up at Jim. And then his great body began to shudder, and those eyes filled with tears as the huge arms wrapped round Jim in a bear hug. 'I don't want to fight you,' he rasped. 'I want to fight the world – this war – the bastards that killed my sons.'

Jim held tightly to his big strong brother, his heart hammering with love and hope as Frank clung to him and wept bitter, heart-rending tears. Jim wept too, not only for the loss of his two nephews, but for the years that he and Frank would never have back again.

And yet he knew, absolutely, that this was a new beginning. It wouldn't be easy for either of them, and they had a great deal to talk over before things could get back to how they'd once been. But it was a start, and his whole being rejoiced in it.

Peggy was furious with Jim, for he'd been gone all day, had missed visiting Anne, and now it was almost midnight. She'd worked herself up to give him a very big piece of her mind, but when he finally came into the kitchen and she saw the blackened eyes, the split lip and bruised chin, her anger turned to horror.

'What on earth happened?' she gasped.

He stood before her with a stupid grin on that battered face, and answered her by picking her up and swinging her round. 'I've made peace with Frank,' he said joyfully as he finally set her back on her feet. 'We had a terrible fight, so we did, but it cleared the air, and we've spent hours just talking.' His eyes gleamed with unshed tears. 'I've got me brother back, Peg,' he said hoarsely.

Peggy held him to her heart, so glad the feud was over and that her Jim was safe home and very nearly all in one piece. She bathed his face, cleaned up the blood and put a cold compress over his eyes as he excitedly told her what had happened.

'But there's even more good news, Peg. Brendon's commanding officer has given him a Blighty posting.'

'Frank will be very relieved to have him back on that boat,' she replied happily. 'I know how difficult he's found it with only old Pat and Tom . . .'

'No, me darlin' girl, he'll not be living down here.' He drew Peggy onto his lap and held her close. 'He's to be a tug pilot on the Thames estuary, and although it's not the safest place to be, it's better than having to sweep up mines in the middle of the Atlantic.'

'I suppose so,' said Peggy doubtfully.

'He's got that motorbike now, and has promised to come home whenever he can. You've no idea how relieved Frank and Pauline are.' He nuzzled her neck and gave her a squeeze. 'I love you, Peggy Reilly, and now I've made me peace with Frank, I'm the most contented man in England.'

Peggy snuggled against him, feeling complete and safe in his arms, loving him more than ever.

A week had passed since that night, and this morning he was trying her patience to the very limit.

'I asked you to clear all this out,' she said, flinging open his side of the wardrobe to reveal a collection of old suits and jackets hanging above a jumble of shoes, sweaters and dubious underwear which had been stuffed on the bottom shelf. 'You don't wear half of it, and the WVS could do with it down at the Town Hall.'

Jim was perched on the end of the bed, fiddling with an old fishing reel he'd found behind the chest of drawers. 'I'll sort it all in a minute,' he muttered.

Peggy had reached breaking point. She snatched the reel out of his hand and threw it out of the bedroom door and into the hall, where it hit the floor with a clatter and rolled out of sight.

He looked at her, his eyes wide with surprise. 'What did you go and do that for?'

She put her hands on her hips and glared at him. 'Because I need you to concentrate, Jim Reilly,' she said crossly. 'Anne will be here tomorrow and I have to get this room straight. Will you *please* sort through this lot and take what you want to keep up to the front bedroom so I can get on?'

Jim eyed her warily as he got up from the bed. 'I'll be taking it all then,' he said.

'Oh, no, you won't,' she muttered. She reached into the wardrobe and started throwing out sweaters, cardigans, crumpled shirts, old shoes, slippers and vests. She noted that he kept retrieving things from the growing pile but said nothing.

When she'd finished clearing the wardrobe, she turned her attention to the large stack of things Jim had placed on the bed. 'You don't want to keep these,' she said, grabbing several shirts. 'The collars and cuffs have been turned so many times, they're falling to bits.' Despite his protests, she threw them back onto the reject pile, along with the slippers that were falling apart and the shoe which seemed to have no mate.

'These trousers no longer fit – that jacket makes you look like a bookie's runner, and I've always hated it – the vests are fit only for cleaning rags, and this sweater has got more holes in it than my colander.'

'Not the sweater,' he said, hastily retrieving it. 'It's me favourite.'

She looked at him, eyes sparking with fury. 'I'll not have you seen in that,' she stormed. 'It's fit only to be unravelled and made into something useful.'

He shoved the sweater behind his back and edged towards the door. 'I think I can hear Da calling me,' he muttered, and then fled.

'And don't forget I want that cot and chair down here, Jim Reilly,' she shouted after him. 'I'll not ask again.'

There was no reply and Peggy sank onto the bed with a groan of frustration. Why did men have to be so damned useless – and why cling to a bit of old clothing they hadn't seen in years, let alone worn? On top of all that, they took their blasted time to do anything she asked them to do, and if she dared ask more than once she was accused of nagging.

Feeling rather better after this silent rant, she took a deep breath and set aside the few pieces that were worth keeping before gathering up nearly everything else he'd left on the bed and adding it to the pile on the floor. Some of it, like the sweaters, could be used again. The rest would either be donated to the WVS, committed to Ron's bonfire, or kept as cleaning rags.

Peggy finally sorted through everything and, with a neat parcel made up for the WVS, and a bag of rags to go under the sink in the basement, she gathered up the sweaters and put them next to Mrs Finch's knitting bag for her to unravel at her leisure. Returning to her bedroom, she took the last of their things upstairs and then set to work getting the room ready for Anne and Rose.

It would be lovely to have Anne home again but, because her leg would still be in plaster, it was more practical to have her and Rose downstairs. Peggy was quite looking forward to sleeping in the big front room upstairs. It would be like moving house in a way, but she knew it would feel strange after so many years of living downstairs and having her own bed.

Peggy was humming to herself as she polished and dusted and put fresh linen on the big bed she and Jim had slept in all their married life. She was still humming as she went upstairs to collect the last of Anne's bits and pieces, and then saw that the cot was still there, along with the nursing chair she'd managed to find in a second-hand shop. Stomping back down the stairs she went fuming into the kitchen.

Jim and Ron had left dirty pans in the sink, and plates, cups and bowls were strewn across the table. Harvey was licking the plates while the two men were poking about in her larder – no doubt looking for something else to eat. Peggy's patience ran out and she snapped for the second time that day.

'I want the cot and the chair downstairs within the next five minutes,' she ordered briskly. 'When you've done that, you can clean up this mess, chop more wood for the range and make a start on the vegetables for tea.'

'Now, darlin' girl, there's no need to get all—'

'Don't you darlin' girl me, Jim Reilly,' she said furiously. 'Just do as I ask for once. The pair of you are driving me round the bend.'

Jim and Ron stared at her in amazement and Peggy would have left it at that if she hadn't noticed the corners of Ron's lips twitch. 'It's not funny, Ron, and if you laugh, I won't be responsible for my actions.'

Before he could reply, she'd turned away and headed for the sanctuary of her bedroom, rather shaken by the fury she'd unleashed – but feeling quite justified, and somehow better for it. She sank onto the freshly made bed and listened as the men tramped upstairs. At least her jag of bad temper had achieved something this morning.

A short while later she had everything done to her satisfaction, and felt in a much happier mood. The room looked lovely and welcoming, with pretty curtains hiding the blackouts, Anne's brushes and scent bottles beside the photograph of Martin on the dressing table, and the cot and chair placed just so. She added a cushion to the chair, straightened the rug and closed the door. All she had to do now was make the bed upstairs and tidy everything away.

She stepped into the sunlit room to find Julie had already made a start on the bed. 'You don't have to do that,' she said, hurrying across the room.

'I want to help,' Julie replied, smoothing the sheet over the mattress. 'You've been working hard all day, and by the sound of it you're getting tired.'

Peggy reddened as she helped tuck in the sheet. 'Oh, that,' she blustered. 'Don't mind me, Julie. Jim and Ron need to be reminded now and again that I'm neither a doormat nor a workhorse, and that my patience has limits – otherwise I'd never get anything done around here.'

'Me mum was the same,' said Julie. 'She was the sweetest person, but Dad and me brothers could wind her up something rotten, and when she let loose, they could probably hear her all the way from Stepney to Watford.' She smiled fondly. 'She was only a skinny little thing, but she scared the living daylights out of all of us when she really got going.'

They worked in companionable silence for a

moment as a pigeon cooed from the windowsill and two gulls squabbled on a nearby lamp post. 'William seems to be coming along nicely,' said Peggy as she quickly hung the clothes in the wardrobe and filled the drawers with underwear and sweaters. 'What does Dr Michael say?'

Julie smiled as she drew the eiderdown over the blankets. 'He's very pleased with him. William's heart is beating more steadily, and I've noticed he's eating better as well.'

'His little feet and hands certainly feel warmer now,' said Peggy as she laid out the glass dressing-table set, which consisted of a bowl for powder, a tray, a perfume bottle, a dish for hairpins, and two candlesticks. 'All in all, you wouldn't know there was anything wrong with him, would you?'

Julie shook her head and finished plumping up the pillows. 'Michael warned me that once he starts crawling he might get a bit breathless, but I'm not to fuss, because William will rest quite naturally when he gets too tired.'

'Easy for him to tell you not to fuss,' Peggy replied. 'I find I'm looking at him every five minutes to make sure he's all right – it must be even worse for you.'

'It's hard to go to work and leave him,' Julie admitted, 'but at least I know he's safe with you and Mrs Finch.'

Peggy caught something in Julie's expression that she'd noticed a few times over the past couple of weeks. It had worried her then, and it concerned her now. 'Everything going smoothly at the surgery?' she asked casually.

Julie let her short brown hair swing over her face as she smoothed the already neat eiderdown. 'I'm out on me rounds most of the time,' she replied. 'So what happens at the surgery doesn't really involve me.'

Peggy moved across the room and touched her arm. 'But something's bothering you,' she said quietly. 'What is it, Julie?'

'Nothing much, not really,' Julie said hesitantly. She chewed her lip, then her words came out in a rush. 'I might be working fewer hours soon, and I'm worried I won't be able to earn enough to look after William properly.'

Peggy sank onto the bed and pulled Julie down beside her. 'I think you'd better tell me what's been going on,' she said solemnly. As Julie told her about Eunice's meddling, the old doctor's ultimatum, and her own agreement to share the load with another district nurse, Peggy realised the poor girl was between the devil and the deep. 'How are things between you and Michael?'

Julie shook her head. 'There's never been anything between us – not in the way Eunice and his father seem to think, anyway. But in the last couple of weeks he's become a bit cool and distant, keeping things very much on a professional basis. He doesn't come and have morning tea with me any more, or try to teach me the laws of rugby – in fact he seems to be avoiding me altogether.'

'Oh, dear,' sighed Peggy. 'It doesn't sound a very happy ship.'

'Better an unhappy ship than no ship at all,' said Julie firmly. 'I could get a job at the hospital, but I love being a district nurse and don't want to let me patients down. Besides, I have to think of William. Michael is his doctor and deeply involved in his care. I can't risk alienating him any further by taking umbrage and leaving.'

'It sounds to me as though you and Michael need to clear the air,' said Peggy. 'Someone's obviously been saying things to him to make him the way he is.'

Julie shook her head. 'If he can be swayed so easily, then his friendship doesn't amount to much,' she said flatly. 'I don't feel I have to justify meself, and as long as he's caring for William, I'm prepared to leave things as they are.'

Peggy could tell that, despite her brave words, Julie had been hurt by Michael's sudden coolness. 'These things often have a way of working themselves out,' she murmured.

'Yeah, I know.' Julie got to her feet. 'It's a storm in a teacup, as me dad used to say, and his advice was to keep me head down, get on with things and wait for it to blow itself out.' She shot Peggy a brave grin. 'And that's exactly what I'm going to do.'

'Good for you.' Peggy returned her smile as they

smoothed the bedcovers, but her thoughts were in a whirl. Poor Julie had enough to contend with without trouble at work, and if Michael was that weak, then he wasn't the man she'd thought. But Eunice was clever and manipulative, and she'd clearly done her best to be rid of Julie by going to the old man with her tale-telling. It struck Peggy that Eunice and Michael deserved one another, but it made her very angry to think that Julie had been made a scapegoat and might have to pay a high price in this war of attrition.

Chapter Seventeen

There had been heavy raids throughout April, with London, Merseyside, Belfast and Portsmouth being the main targets. In early May, Cliffehaven had had its own fair share of excitement when an enemy bomber had collided with one of its fighters, and they'd crashed into the remains of the old asylum.

The fires had spread rapidly into the surrounding trees and threatened the rows of houses which lined the bottom of the hill, and Kath and her mother had spent a very worrying night on camp beds in Peggy's dining room, wondering if they would have a home to go back to.

Rita and her colleagues had eventually put it out and the houses had been saved, but it was not to be the last fire they attended, for a series of tip-and-run raids had caused a fair bit of damage on the industrial estate to the north of the town, and a gas explosion had ripped through a line of cottages only two streets down from Beach View Terrace.

Nonetheless Ron was a very contented man as he strode across the hills with Harvey racing before him. Lord Cliffe was away on his twice yearly visit to the House of Lords and would no doubt still be sleeping off an expensive dinner at his London club. Ron had spent the best part of the night out here, and the deep inside pockets of his poacher's coat were heavy with three fat ducks, a brace of quail, and a cock pheasant which had virtually walked into his trap as he'd lain in wait in the long grass. There was a certain satisfaction in knowing the old man wouldn't even notice they'd gone, and with no gamekeeper looking after the estate now, it was just begging to be raided.

Ron's contentment went deeper than pulling one over on Lord Cliffe, for his sons were making their peace, sadly accepting that they couldn't regain those lost years, but wise enough to realise this new beginning could be far more enriching. Brendon was away in London on the tugs, and came down to see everyone when time allowed, and Pauline and Frank were slowly and painfully coming to terms with their terrible loss. Anne was at home, and making much better progress now she could be with little Rose, and Martin had even managed to stay for a few days before he'd been sent off to take charge in the setting up of another airfield further west.

The only fly in Ron's ointment was the fact that he'd been refused a posting to the gun emplacements on the seafront, or even here on the cliffs. It seemed he was regarded as too old by the military, and although he'd wanted initially to vent his rage on the enemy for the death and destruction they'd caused, not only to his town, but to his beloved family, time and common sense had cooled his thirst for revenge.

The other niggle was Rosie Braithwaite, who still kept him at arm's length and refused to discuss whatever it was that had happened between her and Eileen Harris. Peggy hadn't been forthcoming either, and it was frustrating. He'd considered going to see this Eileen woman, but had changed his mind when he realised it would probably only stir things up for Rosie, who, no doubt, wouldn't appreciate his meddling. But long-kept secrets had a habit of rising to the surface when things were stirred up, and although it might take a long time to get to the truth, he didn't doubt for a minute that it would all come clear sooner or later.

He shrugged off these minor inconveniences and hitched his gas-mask box over his shoulder, the long poacher's coat flapping round his ankles as the wind blew in from the sea. Harvey was on the scent of something, his nose to the ground, tail windmilling as he raced back and forth, and Ron left him to it. Harvey had spent far too many hours in the house watching over those wains lately and needed the exercise.

It was very early morning, with the sun just breaching the horizon, pearling the sky and the tendrils of mist that still clung to the trees and veiled the far hills. It promised to be a lovely May day, and Ron breathed deeply of the clean air which held the tang of salt and the almost sensuous smell of damp earth, lush grasses and the ripening of spring. The abandoned orchard was a beautiful sight now that the trees were covered in blossom and the blue-bells and crocuses formed a carpet beneath them, and he knew that later in the year he'd be picking the sour little apples for cider and the elderberries for wine.

He tramped homeward, at peace with the beauty and tranquillity of these hills, glad that he could come here and be at one with them, for they soothed away the cares of this troubled world and made him feel whole again.

Julie was a keen letter-writer and looked forward to the replies from Lily and the other girls back in London, although they did make her homesick for the happy days they'd all spent working and living together, and the familiar sights, scents and sounds of the city she loved. Yet it was fun to catch up on the gossip, to read all about Lily's latest boyfriend and Alison's continued rebelliousness, which still got her into scrapes with Matron. They seemed to be coping cheerfully with the continued raids, even though most of the hostel's windows were boarded up now, and there was a crater where the neigh-bouring house used to be.

She folded the letter she'd received from her oldest brother and put it away in the box she kept in her wardrobe. All three brothers wrote regularly, even though there was often a delay in their letters getting to her, but despite her having written several times to Bill, there had still been no reply.

She sat in the early sunlight streaming through her bedroom window, and lovingly watched William as he lay on a blanket on the floor and floundered in his attempts to get his arms and legs co-ordinated enough for him to crawl. Bill's lack of response had worried her before, but now she'd come to think it might be for the best. William was, to all intents and purposes, her baby now and she loved him deeply. He was still less energetic than Rose and slept a great deal, but he was beginning to thrive, and although the day might come when he'd have to have an operation, he was safe and well and contented with her – and she couldn't imagine life without him.

Her starched apron crackled as she bent to lift him from the blanket. Holding him close, she kissed his soft cheek and ran her fingers softly through the golden curls that glinted in the sun. She hated leaving him, but she had no choice.

'Mummy's got to go to work,' she murmured as he gurgled at her and made a grab for her flowing cap. She kissed him again and carried him down-stairs, aware that she was in danger of being late at the surgery.

Anne was in the kitchen, her plastered leg resting on a footstool, her crutches leaning against her chair as she fed Rose. She looked up at Julie and smiled. 'This will be the last morning I'll be tied to the house,' she said cheerfully, 'and I can't wait to get this plaster off. It itches like mad.'

Julie chuckled as she put William in the playpen and handed him his favourite soft toy. 'That's where Mrs Finch's knitting needles come in handy.' She quickly poured a cup of tea from the pot on the table and sat down. The kitchen was unusually deserted. 'Where is everyone?'

'Mrs Finch is getting dressed, Grandpa's been out all night with Harvey and isn't home yet, and Dad's gone fishing with Frank. The girls are all on early shift, so they left ages ago.' Anne looked down at Rose, who had almost finished her bottle. 'Mum was up with the lark as usual, but she's looking really tired, so I ordered her to go back to bed.' She grinned at Julie. 'She won't stay there for long, of course, and is probably worrying about a thousand and one things and not resting at all.'

Julie had noticed Peggy had been unusually out of sorts lately and had put it down to the trauma of the past few weeks. However, it was very unlike her to go back to bed, and that was worrying. 'I hope she's not going down with something,' she murmured as she watched William playing with his soft blue and white rabbit.

'Don't worry,' said Anne as she finished winding Rose. 'She's just exhausted after everything that's happened, and as long as we all help around the house, she'll soon bounce back.'

Anne handed Rose to Julie so she could put her

in the playpen next to William. The two babies started gurgling and waving their arms and legs about. 'They seem very happy with each other,' Anne said fondly. 'It'll be a shame to separate them when I have to leave.'

'But it won't be for a while yet, will it?'

Anne dipped her chin, the colour rising in her face. 'I haven't told Mum yet, but Martin and I have decided that once I'm able to get about, it would be best for me to take Rose to Somerset until things quieten down. I'll probably go next month.'

'Oh, Anne, I can see that makes a lot of sense, but it'll break Peggy's heart to lose you both.'

Anne took a deep, shuddering breath. 'I know, but I have to think of Rose now, and Martin agrees with me that we're just too vulnerable here so close to the Channel.' She looked back at Julie, her lovely face shadowed with sadness. 'I'll be staying on the farm where my little brothers are living, so at least I won't be entirely without my family. You will keep an eye on Mum while I'm gone, won't you?'

'Of course I will,' said Julie. 'But you'd better tell her soon, Anne. She needs time to get used to the idea of you leaving.'

Anne chewed her lip. 'I know,' she admitted softly, 'and I'm dreading it.'

Peggy's bare feet made no noise as she tiptoed back upstairs to her bedroom and closed the door. She hadn't meant to eavesdrop on the conversation, but now she knew Anne's plans, at least she could prepare herself and try not to make it difficult for the girl to leave.

She sank back onto the unmade bed, her thoughts in a terrible jumble as she tried to come to terms with losing yet more of her family. It would be lovely for Bob and Charlie to have their sister and niece living with them, and Violet would take the same loving care of them as she did with the boys. But it seemed to Peggy that Violet was getting the best deal out of this blasted war, for she'd been handed a ready-made family to love and cherish – which left Peggy adrift and wanting.

She felt her throat thicken and the rise of a desperate need to cry, but she refused to let her emotions get the better of her. There had been enough sadness these past weeks, and she was determined to remain strong. Impatient with her inability to do anything much these days without either flying off the handle or bursting into tears, Peggy clambered off the bed and began to tug furiously at the sheets and blankets. This bloody, *bloody* war was turning her into someone she hardly recognised any more. She couldn't be selfish, not when their safety was at risk, but she would miss Rose Margaret, for that little girl had stolen her heart.

'Pull yourself together, woman,' she muttered as she pummelled the pillows with unnecessary force and blinked back the ready tears. 'If you carry on like this you'll be fit for nothing – and then where would we all be?'

Julie set out on that warm May morning, her bicycle tyres humming nicely on the road as she headed for Cliffe surgery. She enjoyed these few minutes of solitude first thing: they set her up for the day, and when the sun was shining and the sea glittered so prettily, she felt as if she was on holiday.

Walking in through the back door she encountered Michael in the kitchen. 'Good morning,' she said with determined cheerfulness.

'Good morning, Sister Harris,' he replied, his dark eyes sweeping over her almost with indifference before he turned his attention back to the teapot. 'There's tea if you want it.'

Julie didn't want tea – she wanted him to talk to her like he used to. 'Dr Sayers, about the rugby match,' she began. 'I won't be able to go, so you'd better give me ticket to someone else.'

'I see,' he murmured, still not looking at her. 'Probably for the best, in the circumstances.'

She wasn't going to give him the satisfaction of knowing how his casual words had stung. 'Yeah, I'm being kept very busy at the moment and two of me expectant mothers are due that day.' She left him standing in the kitchen and had to go to the cloakroom to steady herself. She was angry and hurt, and it wouldn't do to let Eunice see how badly her hands were shaking. When she'd mastered her emotions enough to face Eunice, she went to fetch her casebook and daily list of patients.

Eunice was looking very pleased with herself, her make-up flawless, her freshly washed hair neatly curled back from her face in what the fashion magazines called 'Victory Rolls'. It was clear she was pulling out all the stops in her quest to get Michael's attention, and Julie suspected she'd been angling for that ticket to the rugby.

'You'll have Jessica with you this morning,' Eunice said as she handed over the list. 'She needs to learn how to take out stitches and dress ulcers, and I want you to supervise her.'

'I see there's a new patient on me list,' murmured Julie. 'Do you have his notes?'

Eunice handed them over. 'Mr Hopkins is diabetic and has leg ulcers. He telephoned and asked if you could call in and change the dressings.' Her blue eyes regarded Julie with an unspoken challenge – and perhaps a little glint of victory. 'I will need a full written assessment of Jessica's work by tomorrow morning,' she added coolly.

Jess came bustling into the hall, fair curls bouncing under her cap, face alive with youthful exuberance as she greeted Julie. 'Has Sister Beecham told you about me applying to train as a proper nurse?' she asked breathlessly as they headed for the bicycle shed.

'I guessed when she asked me to do a full assessment at the end of the day,' Julie replied with a smile. 'Well done you. I'm sure you'll make a first-class nurse.' She liked Jess, for she was young, keen and bright, and had so far proved to be an excellent nursing aide. 'Come on, we've got a long list today. Mr Hopkins is first on our list – he lives in Havelock Gardens and I'm looking forward to seeing the inside of his house.'

'They're ever so smart, aren't they?' said Jess as they cycled down the tree-lined street where the houses stood back from the road behind high brick walls.

They certainly were, and Julie was reminded of the leafy upper-class suburbs of London as they rode through the imposing gateway and along the sweeping gravel drive to the front door, where the porch was sagging beneath the heavy branches of an ancient wisteria.

'Mr Hopkins is obviously not a gardener,' muttered Julie as she leaned her bike against one of the wooden pillars holding up the porch and noted the weeds pushing through the gravel and the over-grown flowerbeds. 'But then he is in his fifties, and the diabetes will have slowed him down.'

'He's certainly let the place go,' said Jess disap-pointedly as she eyed the peeling paintwork and rotting window frames. 'No wonder he keeps all his curtains closed. I dread to think what it's like indoors.'

Julie's rap on the knocker was answered by a man's voice coming from the depths of the house. 'Who is it?'

'It's the district nurse, Mr Hopkins.' She and Jess

exchanged amused glances as they heard him turn a key and draw back two bolts.

The door opened just enough for them to see a man in baggy trousers, scruffy cardigan and tartan slippers standing in the shadows of his hallway. He'd yet to shave, his greying hair was untidy, and his hazel eyes regarded them suspiciously.

'Hello, Mr Hopkins,' said Julie with a smile. 'I'm Sister Harris, and this is Jess Miller, my assistant. May we come in?'

He stood back and quickly closed the door behind them. 'They're a nosy lot round here,' he muttered as he led the way down the dim hallway. 'I expect they've already seen you arrive and will no doubt make something out of it.'

Julie and Jess made no comment as they followed him. The wallpaper was peeling where patches of damp had seeped through, and there was a thick layer of dust coating the hall table and mirror. The rug was almost threadbare, and it had been a long time since the floor had been swept and polished. It was all very dreary and most disappointing.

Then he opened a door, and the hallway was flooded in sunlight. Stepping into the book-lined room, Julie's breath caught as her gaze went immediately to the wide bay windows which looked directly out to sea. She could imagine she was on the bridge of a ship.

'What a lovely view,' breathed Jess. 'You are lucky, Mr Hopkins.'

'You get used to it,' he muttered. 'I hardly notice it any more.'

Julie saw he was looking decidedly uneasy, and thought he was probably dreading the dressings coming off. 'There's nothing to worry about,' she soothed. 'I know it's unpleasant and painful having your dressings changed, but Miss Miller will be very gentle.'

His gaze went from Julie to Jess and back again. 'I don't actually need the dressings changed,' he admitted, his hands twisting nervously in the pockets of his sagging cardigan. 'I've got you here for something else.'

Julie frowned. 'What do you mean?'

His face was etched with lines of some terrible worry as he looked back at her. 'It's my daughter who needs you, not me.'

'Your daughter should have made the appointment then,' she replied. 'This is all very irregular, Mr Hopkins.'

'Melanie only came home yesterday, and isn't registered at the surgery yet. But I need you to look at her with some urgency, Sister. She's not right, but she's refusing to go to the hospital, and I'm really very worried.'

With rising alarm, Julie looked back at him. 'How old is your daughter, Mr Hopkins?'

'She's sixteen, and has been living with her mother in Guildford. Look, Sister,' he said, his concern making his voice rise, 'I know this isn't how you usually work, but I would be very grateful if you could give her the once-over.'

Julie pulled her casebook out of her bag. 'I'm going to need her details, Mr Hopkins, so she can be registered as one of our patients, and I'm not only going to have to report on this visit to the doctors, but charge you for it too.'

He regarded her intently as he shuffled impatiently from one foot to the other. 'I'd rather you didn't tell anyone,' he said nervously. 'Is it really necessary? I don't mind paying, but . . .'

Julie suddenly didn't like the feel of this at all. 'What happens here will go no further than Dr Sayers unless it's illegal,' she said rather sharply. 'Where is your daughter?'

'Upstairs in the front room.' He opened the door into the hall. 'Turn left at the top, it's the second door,' he muttered. He ran his fingers through his hair as he edged towards the bottom of the stairs. 'I'll . . . I'll leave you to it then.'

All of Julie's instincts told her that something was very wrong here and, as she and Jess reached the bedroom door, she could see the other girl was just as uneasy. 'Just follow my lead, Jess. This could be tricky.'

The room was in darkness, and she could barely make out anything. 'Draw the blackouts, Jess,' she said quietly.

'Who's that?' The voice was young and high with fear.

As light flooded the room, Julie saw the huddled outline of a figure beneath a pile of blankets. 'I'm Sister Harris, the district nurse,' she said quietly as she approached the bed. 'Your father tells me you aren't feeling very well, Melanie. What seems to be the matter?'

The girl gave a deep groan and shifted beneath the mound of covers. 'You've got to help me,' she whimpered. She groaned again, giving a sharp cry of pain. 'Make it stop, please make it stop,' she whimpered.

Julie swiftly drew back the covers and caught her breath as she saw the blood-soaked sheets and what lay between Melanie's thighs. She understood everything now.

She glanced at Jess, who was standing wide-eyed by her side. 'There's a telephone on the hall table,' she said quietly. 'Call an ambulance, and then ring the surgery. There's a protocol for situations like this, and the police will have to be informed.'

As Jess raced back downstairs, Julie stacked books from a nearby shelf under the end of the bed in the faint hope it might help stop the bleeding. She then shrugged off her cloak, opened her medical bag, and pulled on thin rubber gloves. 'Melanie,' she said softly. 'I need you to try and stay calm while I examine you.'

'I'm frightened,' the girl moaned.

Julie did a swift internal examination, which revealed that Melanie was right to be frightened. Whoever had performed this piece of butchery had seen to it that the girl not only lost this baby, but probably any hope of having another.

She dealt with things as best she could in the circumstances, and then reached for the hypodermic and the small phial of analgesic she always carried in her bag. 'You'll feel a bit of a scratch on your leg, and then in a few minutes the pain will start to fade.'

Jess came back with towels and a jug of hot water. 'Dr Michael's on his way and so is the ambulance,' she said. 'What do you want me to do?'

'Help me strip the bed and clean her up,' Julie replied. 'There's nothing much else we can do but try to keep her warm and comfortable until the doctor gets here.'

It had been a long, distressing day for both of them, and Julie and Jess returned very late from their round to find Dr Michael waiting for them in the kitchen. 'You're both to be commended for your handling of the situation with dignity and calm this morning,' he said solemnly.

'Did Melanie pull through?' asked Julie.

He shook his head. 'It has been a sad day all round, and unfortunately this won't be the end of it. There's bound to be a police inquiry, and you will both be expected to give a clear and concise account of the events of today.' He took a deep breath and let it out on a sigh. 'But, with Melanie dead and her father denying all knowledge of the abortion, it thankfully won't go to court. I've had a word with the coroner, and he's promised to hold his inquiry in camera. The last thing we need is for our practice to be linked to such things.'

Julie felt a stab of fury. God forbid his precious practice should be tainted by a girl desperate to risk her life and that of her baby to go to some old crone in a back street. If fewer people kept silent, that particular trade would disappear altogether. But she knew better than to say anything. She was tired and saddened by the day and just wanted to write up her notes and get home to William and the comfort of Peggy's kitchen.

Julie let herself in and headed straight for the pram where both babies were sleeping. She wanted to pick William up and hold him for the comforting feeling of his warm little body after her awful day, but she knew that if she did it would disturb them both, so she resisted and went into the kitchen.

It was a haven of peace, with Mrs Finch sitting beside the fire with her tangle of knitting, Harvey snoring on the rug and Anne reading a book. The plaster was off her leg, leaving it looking pale and wasted against the other.

'How does it feel to have two legs again?' Julie grabbed the oven glove and reached into the warming compartment of the range for her supper plate.

'A bit strange, to be honest – and I'm much more nervous about putting any weight on it than I thought I would be.'

'That's quite normal. You'll soon be dashing about as usual.' Julie placed the hot plate on the table and lifted the metal cover to discover not only a sausage, but thick gravy and mashed potato. 'My goodness,' she breathed as her mouth watered. 'This is quite a treat.'

Anne laughed. 'Mum managed to get the sausages this afternoon and came back with them as if she'd found the hidden treasures of El Dorado. Dad was so pleased, he's taken her out to the Anchor for a drink.'

'Have you managed to tell Peg about you leaving?'

Anne nodded. 'She was very good about it, really, but we both ended up in tears.' She gave a weary sigh. 'I hate what this war's doing to our family.'

'Oh, dear,' muttered Mrs Finch. 'I can't seem to get this sleeve right, and I so wanted to have it finished for Ron's birthday.'

Anne reached for the knitting as if glad to have the distraction. She eyed it doubtfully. 'It looks a bit too big, Mrs Finch,' she said. 'Grandpa would need to be eight foot tall for arms this long.'

'Well, it's obvious I've got it wrong,' the old lady replied rather crossly. 'That's why you need to sort it out for me.'

Anne smiled at her with affection and began to unpick the sleeve. 'By the way, Julie,' she murmured, 'there's a letter for you. It's up on the mantelpiece.'

Julie glanced up at it as she finished the delicious meal. She felt drained of energy and ached for her bed, but a letter from London would cheer her up no end. Having washed up, she dried her hands and reached for it. But the postmark wasn't London – it was Yorkshire.

'I'll read it upstairs,' she said with a calmness that belied the awful turmoil in her heart. She left the kitchen, gently plucked William from the pram and carried him upstairs. Once he was settled in the old cot she'd found at the Town Hall, she sank onto the bed and turned the letter over and over in her hands, dreading opening it, but knowing she must.

There was only a single page of neat writing, signed at the bottom by Edith Wigglesworth – Bill's mother. With a sense of foreboding, Julie began to read.

Dear Miss Harris,

Firstly, I apologise for not replying to your letters. It was very kind of you to keep us informed of William's whereabouts, and we are extremely grateful that you are taking care of him. I would have written before, but I was advised to wait until Bill returned home on leave, so he could decide what to do for the best.

It is with great sadness that I have to tell you now that our son has been listed as 'Missing in Action and presumed dead'. The telegram arrived a month ago, and I haven't had the heart to write until now. Bill was our only child, and it is as if a light has gone out in our lives. But a part of our precious boy lives on in young William, and we feel

it is only right to acknowledge him and raise him
as our own. I realise it will be hard for you to let
him go, but you are young and free and will have
babies of your own one day. It is too late for us, and
I beg you to give us the precious gift of our son's
child. We promise to love and cherish him as much
as we did Bill.

As my husband and I are unable to leave the farm
to make the long journey south, my sister, Charity
Farnsworth, will be arriving in Cliffehaven within the
month to collect William and bring him home to us.

I look forward to hearing from you very soon,
Edith Wigglesworth

Julie's tears smudged the ink and she set the letter
aside, her heart aching with the terrible burden of
this coming loss. She'd begun to hope that this day
would never come, had ignored the warnings and
started to believe that William would always be with
her. Now this had happened.

She gently lifted William from his cot and held
him to her heart, breathing in his sweetness and
warmth as the tears streamed down her face. She
felt bound to him as only a mother could – and yet
he was not hers to keep. How cruelly Fate played
her games – and how empty her arms would feel
when he was taken from her.

'Oh, William,' she breathed, 'my precious, precious
boy.'

Chapter Eighteen

Almost three weeks had passed since Julie had received the letter, and now Charity Farnsworth was due to arrive on the late afternoon train. Julie's emotions were in turmoil as she pushed the pram down the High Street in the warm June sunshine and turned into Camden Road. These would be her last few precious hours with William, and she couldn't begin to imagine how the pain of losing him could grow any harder to bear than it was already.

She paused and reached into the pram, where William was sitting up batting at the rattle she'd tied to the hood. Her fingers caressed his soft cheek, earning her a beaming smile which revealed four tiny teeth. At six months old, William was still rather small, but he'd filled out and his little face was glowing with happiness beneath the cotton bonnet that shielded him from the sun. How on earth could she hand him over – how could she find the strength and courage to let him go now he'd become such an intrinsic part of her life?

She took a deep breath and was about to continue her stroll when she heard someone calling her. Turning, she saw Eileen hurrying towards her, and felt rather ashamed of the swift stab of resentment she felt at her intrusion on this intimate moment. 'I was just on my way home to give William his lunch,' Julie said coolly.

Eileen was looking very smart in a pair of tailored slacks and crisp white shirt, her hair freshly washed and set, her make-up immaculate as always. She regarded Julie thoughtfully. 'You can spare me a minute, surely?' she replied. 'After all, we are sisters.'

The stab of resentment came again and Julie tightened her grip on the pram handle. 'Not that you'd know it,' she muttered. 'You made it quite plain when I arrived that you wanted nothing to do with me or William.'

Eileen had the grace to look uneasy at this truth, and swiftly turned her attention to William. 'He's looking very well, considering his heart condition,' she said, her expression softening as she tickled him under the chin and made him gurgle.

'The doctors are very pleased with him,' Julie replied, unable to stifle the quaver in her voice as the pent-up emotions threatened to overwhelm her.

Eileen looked at her sharply. 'What's the matter, Julie?'

'Nothing for you to worry about,' she replied, blinking back the tears and struggling to maintain a cool façade.

'You don't strike me as being someone who cries over nothing,' Eileen said tightly. 'Even as a kid you put a brave face on things, as I remember.' She put her cool hand on Julie's arm. 'Why don't we go to my place and have a cuppa?'

Julie had found some solace in pouring her heart out to Peggy, but despite her kindness and wisdom, Peggy wasn't family. Perhaps it was time to take the olive branch being offered by her sister? 'That would be nice,' she murmured, the tears blinding her. 'But I can't be too long. I have to get back . . . back in time . . .'

'Come on, we can't have you crying in the street.' Eileen steered the pram and Julie down the road and parked the pram outside her door. 'Bring William, and I'll put the kettle on,' she said as she opened the door and hurried upstairs.

Julie's breath hitched as she undid the baby-harness and lifted William out of the pram. She held him close, her tears dampening his sun bonnet as she followed Eileen and went into the sunlit sitting room. Loath to let him go for even a moment, she sat down and settled him on her lap as Eileen clattered about in her tiny kitchen. Now she was here, she didn't really know what to say to her sister. They were hardly close, and Eileen couldn't possibly understand what she was going through – let alone offer advice on how to cope with this piercing agony.

Eileen returned with a tray and set it on the table beneath the window. Quietly and efficiently, she poured the tea and handed William a biscuit finger, which he proceeded to gnaw with gusto and a great deal of dribbling. 'Why don't you take that blanket off the back of the couch and let him sit on the floor? Then you can drink your tea in peace.'

'He's absolutely fine where he is,' she managed through the lump in her throat. Setting the cup and saucer on the floor, she held William close, not caring that the soggy biscuit crumbs were sticking to her skirt and blouse.

'What is it, Julie?' Eileen's voice was soft, her expression concerned.

'She's coming to take William away,' she blurted out on a sob, 'and I don't know if I can bear it.'

Eileen shifted from her chair by the table and came to perch beside Julie on the couch. She reached for Julie's hand. 'Who's coming, Julie?'

Julie could no longer hold back the tide of anguish and pain that had been building ever since she'd woken that morning, and the words came pouring out of her as if a dam had been broken. 'She'll be here this afternoon,' she finished, 'and she'll stay the night before she takes William back to Yorkshire. I can't let him go, Eileen. I just can't.'

Eileen took William from Julie's arms and set him on the floor with his biscuit, then held her sister as the storm of tears slowly ebbed. When Julie finally had her emotions under control, she gave her a clean handkerchief. 'You were upsetting William,' Eileen explained as Julie looked down at him, 'so I put him there until you'd pulled yourself together.'

Julie could see that William's little face was

screwed up in concern and realised Eileen had been right. She quickly blew her nose and did her best to appear calm. The last thing she wanted was for him to be in tears too. 'How can I let him go?' she whispered as he returned to gumming the biscuit. 'I love him so much, Eileen.'

'I know you do,' she sympathised, 'but sometimes we have to forget what we want and do the right thing. William was never yours to keep, Julie – and deep down you always knew that. He has a family – his father's family – and now it's time to let him go.'

'But how can I? I've loved him from the minute I saw him, and he's part of Franny – a part of our family too.'

Eileen looked down at their entwined hands. 'I do understand, Julie,' she murmured. 'I know how hard this is for you, but William needs to be raised in a proper family, where he'll get the love and guidance from two parents who will have time for him. He'll be given a name and respectability, and the opportunity to understand who he is and where he belongs in the world. I'm sure they won't let him forget you, or his little mother.'

Her candid and sensible advice gave Julie little comfort. 'Wise words, Eileen, but you can't possibly understand what I'm going through,' she muttered. 'How could you, when you've never had a child?'

Eileen took a deep, shuddering breath and released Julie's hands. She stood and walked towards the open window, reaching for the pack of Players cigarettes that sat on the sill. The click of her lighter was the only sound in the room. 'The pain is like a knife to the heart,' she said softly through the cigarette smoke. 'It comes in great waves that sweep over you and take your breath away. It fills your dreams and your days until you think you can bear it no longer.'

Julie's heart was drumming as she watched the different expressions flit across Eileen's face. 'That's it exactly, but how . . .?'

Eileen continued as if Julie hadn't spoken, her gaze fixed to some distant horizon far beyond the window. 'It eases eventually, like the pain of bereavement, but it's always there – tucked away, waiting to catch you out when something reminds you of what you've lost.'

Julie stared at Eileen as realisation hit. 'Oh, Eileen,' she gasped. 'I didn't know.'

Eileen turned from the window and stubbed out her cigarette in the glass ashtray. 'Nobody knew,' she said flatly. She folded her arms round her narrow waist as she gazed down at William, who was happily mashing the soggy biscuit into the rug. 'That's why it was such a shock when you turned up here with him. It brought it all back, you see – and I didn't know how to cope with it.'

Julie grasped her sister's arm and gently tugged her down to sit beside her. 'I'm sorry,' she murmured, 'but I had no one else to turn to.' She put her arm round Eileen's thin shoulders. 'Was that why you left home so suddenly?'

Eileen shook her head. 'I didn't realise I was pregnant then,' she admitted quietly. 'I simply wanted to be with the man I loved.' Her lips twitched with distaste. 'I was young and stupid, dazzled by his charm and what I thought was sophistication, all too willing to believe his lies. Dad warned me he was a waster, and that no good would come of it, but I wouldn't listen. I wish I had now, then perhaps things would have turned out very differently.'

Julie clasped her hands, her own sorrow edged aside for a moment in the light of her sister's obvious torment. 'What happened, Eileen?'

Eileen lifted her chin and took a deep breath. 'I packed my bags and caught the first train down here. I think you could say he was surprised to see me,' she said bitterly. 'It turned out he had a wife and kids already, but as they were living further along the coast, he saw nothing devious in finding me this place so we could be together when his work and family commitments allowed.' She sighed. 'I'd burned my boats with Mum and Dad, and didn't have the courage to go back home and admit they'd been right all along. And I was still dazzled by him, so I went along with it even though I knew it was wrong.'

Julie didn't know what to say, but her heart went out to Eileen, who was clearly struggling with this confession and the memories it evoked.

'He promised he'd get a divorce,' she continued flatly, 'and like a fool, I believed him. It was only when I found out I was expecting that he showed his true colours.' She blinked and sniffed back her tears. 'He accused me of being unfaithful, denying the baby could be his – and then when he realised he couldn't get away with that, he said he'd pay to get rid of it.' She took a shuddering breath. 'I couldn't do that, Julie, I really couldn't.'

Julie had an awful, fleeting memory of poor, desperate little Melanie Hopkins, and quickly shut it away. 'Why didn't you come home? Mum and Dad would have come round to it eventually, just as they did with Franny.'

'I couldn't,' said Eileen, shaking her head. 'I'd shamed them enough by running off in the first place, and I was too proud to admit how wrong I'd been.' She rose from the couch and lit another cigarette, dragging the smoke deeply into her lungs as she stood stiffly by the open window.

'But you stayed here,' said Julie. 'It couldn't have been easy with him on your doorstep.'

'He did a moonlight, and I didn't see him again for almost eighteen months.' She grimaced. 'By the time he came back, I'd dealt with the gossips, had the baby adopted and was working in the council offices. He had the gall to come round here expecting things to go back to the way they'd been before, but I wasn't having none of it, and sent him off with a right flea in his ear.'

Julie noted how brave her words sounded, but they belied the anguish in her eyes and the tremble of her lips. 'Was the gossip very bad?' she asked softly.

'Bad enough, but I handled it. Giving my baby away was the hardest part,' Eileen said hoarsely. 'You see, I had to stay in the maternity home with her for two weeks before I had to hand her over to the adoption people. And in that time I got to love her.' She took a shuddering breath. 'The agony of that moment when I gave her away is still there, buried deeply – but it comes back to haunt me when I least expect it.'

She stubbed out her cigarette, her features contorted with pain. 'I called her Flora,' she whispered.

'Oh, Eileen.' Julie rushed to her side and they clung to one another. As their tears flowed and mingled they became sisters again, giving and receiving strength and courage for what lay in the past – and for what was to come.

Peggy was in a daze as she walked towards home, her thoughts and emotions plummeting and soaring in turn as if she was riding the old roller coaster that used to stand on the end of the pier. And yet she knew she must keep this maelstrom under control and maintain her usual outward calm, for change was coming to Beach View, and she would need courage and fortitude to see them through as well as guide Anne and Julie during the coming storm.

She stiffened her spine and lifted her chin determinedly as she reached Beach View Terrace and ran up the steps. Charity Farnsworth was due to arrive at teatime, and she needed to make sure her room was prepared and someone had made a start on the evening meal. It was most inconvenient for her to turn up on Ron's birthday, for it was bound to put a damper on things, and she just prayed the woman was as charitable as her name. Poor little Julie would be devastated at having to let William go – just as she herself would be when Anne took Rose Margaret down to Somerset at the end of the following week.

With these thoughts came the cold reality of what she was facing. She stepped into the hall, closing the front door behind her with the knowledge that the changes at Beach View had already begun, and were out of her control. As she hung up her hat and scarf and slipped her feet into her slippers, she heard a gale of laughter coming from the kitchen and, glad of the distraction, went to see what was going on in there.

Jim, Anne and Rita were still laughing as Peggy walked in, and now she could understand why. Ron's face was a picture of confusion and helplessness as he stood there in the sweater Mrs Finch had knitted him for his birthday. The wool had been unravelled from old sweaters and cardigans, and the stripes of colour clashed quite alarmingly. The dubious garment billowed to his knees, one sleeve dangling over his hand, the other reaching just past his elbow. He looked like a striped lollipop.

'To be sure and 'tis a lovely sweater, Mrs Finch,' he spluttered as he rolled up the extra-long sleeve and tugged at the short one. He grinned and wriggled his bushy brows at her. 'But did you not think to measure it a wee bit?'

'It was indeed a pleasure,' she twittered back, 'and I'm delighted you like it.'

'To be sure, ye look a right eejit, Da,' muttered Jim with a twinkle in his eyes. 'Perhaps we should plant you outside as a garden gnome.'

'I'll give you gnome,' he rumbled, glaring at his son from beneath his brows as he tried to tuck the swathes of wool into his trousers.

Peggy stifled a giggle as she tied the strings of her wrap-round apron at her waist. 'It's all right, Ron,' she murmured. 'I'll sort it out for you on the quiet.'

'To be sure, it needs something doing to it,' he muttered as he eyed the dangling sleeve that kept falling over his hand. 'She must think I'm Quasimodo.'

Peggy was still smiling as she looked down at Rose Margaret, who, regardless of the noise going on around her, was fast asleep in the playpen. 'That baby's so good,' she crooned, resisting the impulse to pick her up and give her a cuddle. 'You are lucky, Anne.' She blinked away the ready tears. 'Right,' she said purposefully, 'it's time to get on before Mrs

Farnsworth arrives. Has anyone started on the tea yet?'

Anne grinned back at her. 'We've all been hard at work while you've been gadding about round the shops. There's a rabbit stew in the oven, and the potatoes are peeled, ready to boil. Dad managed to get hold of some extra flour, sugar and butter, and Mrs Finch has made us an apple sponge for pudding to celebrate Grandpa's birthday.' She shot her a grin. 'So, did you buy anything? You were gone long enough.'

Peggy had forgotten she was supposed to have been on a shopping spree, and she said the first thing that came into her head. 'I didn't see anything worth the trouble,' she replied, turning away so her daughter couldn't see her discomfort at lying. 'Best not to waste those precious clothing coupons when I've got better stuff in my wardrobe upstairs.'

As Anne and Rita started chattering about the fire-station fund-raising dance which was to be held the following night, Ron stomped downstairs muttering something about getting ready for his evening celebration with Rosie, and Mrs Finch began to lay the table. Rita had very few dresses, but Anne was happy to lend her one for the occasion, and as they fell into deep discussion about the shoes to go with it, they were joined by Fran and Suzy, who'd just come off shift at the hospital.

Peggy listened to their happy talk as she fetched a duster from under the sink, but she was all too aware of Jim's towering presence beside her and his unusual silence. 'I'm just going to check the room's ready for Mrs Farnsworth,' she muttered, not daring to look at him.

'Aye, you do that,' he said quietly. 'And when you've got a minute, you can tell me what you were *really* doing all afternoon.'

Peggy scuttled out of the room and scampered up the stairs. She might have known Jim wouldn't be fooled by her fibs. He knew her too well. But the truth would be far harder to tell, and she dreaded the moment when she would have to reveal it.

Julie had stayed with Eileen for the rest of the day, and they'd talked together as young women who shared not only similar experiences, but memories of home and family. It had brought them together in understanding and friendship – a friendship they both knew would sustain them for the rest of their lives.

Eileen had offered to come back with her to Beach View, but Julie had gently dissuaded her. She understood now how hard it would be for Eileen to go through the trauma of seeing another baby handed over, and she didn't want her to suffer any more than she already had. And yet, as she made that last, lonely journey with William down Camden Road, Julie wasn't at all sure if she had the strength or courage to see through the next few hours without her.

Julie had slipped back into the house while everyone was occupied elsewhere, and now she was lying on her bed, William beside her, his little arms and legs waving about as she tickled his tummy and nuzzled him under the ear. Charity Farnsworth was due to arrive within the hour, and she desperately craved a few still moments with him.

'Oh, William,' she sighed. 'What a mess our family has made of things. If only it could all have been different.' She curled her body round him, the tears pricking as she ran her fingers through the golden curls that were beginning to darken. 'But they're not, are they? And I have to be brave and let you go, no matter how hard it is. But I promise I'll keep in touch so we don't forget one another, and if you should ever need me . . .'

She closed her eyes and held him gently. She was only torturing herself, and it would do neither of them any good in the end. William would be loved and cherished by Bill's parents and she couldn't deny him that, but her freedom to carry on with her life and career was costing a heavy price, and she didn't know if she truly had the heart to pay it.

Impatient with her inability to keep the doubts and fears at bay, she climbed off the bed and gathered a set of clean clothes for William. A small case had already been packed to go with him, and it stood by the door – a constant reminder of what the morning would bring.

She took her time changing his nappy and

dressing him before reluctantly carrying him down-stairs and into the kitchen for his evening feed. The room was warm and the atmosphere happy as Suzy and Fran used cold tea and an Oxo cube to stain Rita's legs so they looked as if they were sheathed in nylons.

'Will you be holding still, there, Rita?' laughed Fran as she carefully drew a pencil-line up the back of her leg.

'It tickles,' she protested.

'It'll be worth it,' murmured Suzy as she worked on Rita's other leg.

'I don't know what the world's coming to,' muttered Mrs Finch as she peered at the shenanigans over the top of her glasses. She sighed happily and shot Julie a grin. 'I wish I was young again,' she said, 'but these old legs won't pass muster any more.' She stuck them out and eyed their bony and rather knobbly length distastefully. 'I used to have good legs. Old age is a devil, and no mistake.'

Julie's spirits were so low that she was untouched by the warmth and harmony in that kitchen, but she dredged up an answering smile and skirted round the other girls so she could prepare William's food. There was mashed potato and vegetables, and a tiny bit of rabbit from the stew along with some gravy. William enjoyed his food now, and as Julie sat him in the high chair, he started banging his hands on the tray with anticipation.

She had just tied the bib over his clean matinee

jacket when there was a sharp rap on the door knocker. 'Could you make a start here, Anne?' she asked, handing over the spoon. 'That's probably Mrs Farnsworth.'

'Good luck,' Anne murmured, taking the spoon.

Julie's heart was pounding as she crossed the square hall, and she took a deep breath before she opened the door, praying that she could get through this without making a complete fool of herself and upsetting William.

Despite the balmy summer evening, the large woman on the doorstep wore a heavy gabardine mackintosh that was tightly belted beneath a pendulous bosom. Sturdy brogues shod big feet, the columns of her legs were sheathed in wrinkled lisle stockings, and the hand that clasped the small suitcase and gas-mask box looked as strong and capable as a man's. A felt hat completed the outfit, squashed over a severe bun of iron-grey hair, the brim shadowing a pair of humourless grey eyes and a downturned mouth.

Julie stared at her as icy fingers of dread ran down her spine. 'Mrs Farnsworth?' she managed through a tight throat.

'*Miss* Farnsworth, aye,' she replied grimly, 'and I'll not be left standing on this doorstep a minute more.' She stepped into the hall without further ado and eyed her surroundings with little pleasure as she put down her case. 'I tek it you be lass what's looking after our William,' she said, looking Julie up and down.

She resisted licking her lips, but her mouth was dry with dread. 'I'm Julie Harris, yes.'

Charity sniffed with what looked like disdain. 'Yon train were late,' she said, taking off her hat, 'and there's nowt more I could do with right now than a strong brew of good Yorkshire tea.' She turned that piercing gaze on Julie again. 'I tek it they know how to brew proper tea down 'ere?'

Julie hadn't quite lost her power of speech, but she found she was unusually daunted by Charity Farnsworth, and didn't like it one bit. 'It might not be as strong as you'd like,' she managed, 'but it'll be wet and warm.'

'Happen it'll do if there's nowt else,' Charity muttered. She unbelted her navy blue mackintosh to reveal a brown tweed skirt and hand-knitted sweater that strained over the headland of bosom and thick waist. She hung her coat on the rack and picked up her case. 'Lead on,' she ordered. 'I've not come all this way to stand mithering in t'all.'

'My landlady, Mrs Reilly, has set out the dining room so we can talk in private,' stammered Julie.

'By 'eck, you southerners tek strange ideas,' Charity muttered. 'There's nowt to be said between thee and me that's private.' With that she strode across the hall and stomped into the kitchen.

Julie hurried after her, her heart pounding, the fear rising with every beat. She couldn't let this awful woman take William – she just couldn't.

'How do?' she barked at the room in general as

she plumped down in the armchair opposite Mrs Finch. She didn't seem to notice the stunned silence that greeted her. 'Which one's our William then?' Her stern gaze went from Rose in the playpen to William, whose face was smeared with gravy and mash.

The babies immediately started to wail and Anne and Julie rushed to pick them up and soothe them.

'Good heavens,' muttered Mrs Finch, her hands covering her ears as she glared at Charity Farnsworth. 'Does everyone north of the Thames shout as if they're in the middle of a field?'

'Happen I don't tek kindly to folk looking down their noses to us oop north,' Charity retorted with a glower.

'And I don't take kindly to people who come into my home and start throwing their weight about,' snapped Mrs Finch.

Julie quickly stepped between them. 'This is William,' she said, trying to get his face clean and soothe his tears. But William was clinging to her neck as if the sight of Charity frightened the life out of him. Which was hardly surprising, she thought grimly. That woman would frighten anyone.

The grey eyes regarded the sobbing baby with little pleasure. 'Happen it's best we do the introductions when he's stopped that racket,' she said dourly. 'Where's that brew you promised?'

Julie exchanged a worried glance with Anne and hurried to pour a cup of tea. She was a horrible woman, and the thought of her going anywhere near William was making her feel sick.

Charity Farnsworth eyed the cup of very weak tea in disgust. 'Call that a brew? Looks more like dishwater, if you ask me.'

'Well, it's the best we have,' said Peggy as she strode into the room and introduced herself. 'There is a war on, you know.'

Charity eyed Peggy with a gleam of caution in her eyes. 'Happen it'll do,' she muttered, and took an experimental sip.

'Right, now that's settled, I think it's time to finish feeding those babies and get them ready for bed so we can sit down to our tea in peace.' Peggy turned to Julie. 'I did remember to get that prescription for William while I was out. The bottle's in the larder.'

'What's wrong with babby that he needs prescriptions?' asked Charity sharply.

Julie carefully explained about his heart condition, and the very real need for him to continue his medication. 'But the doctors are very pleased with his progress,' she finished, 'and they think there's a real chance that the hole will heal itself.'

'You never said owt about this in yon letters,' Charity rasped. 'And medicines cost money. My sister can't afford to tek on a sick babby.' She eyed Julie with fierce intent from beneath wayward greying brows. 'There's no history of heart disease in our family,' she said stoutly. 'Strong as oxen we are – have to be, living in Dales.'

'Then perhaps it would be best if you left William here,' suggested Julie with quiet desperation.

'Aye. Happen it would.' Charity sipped her tea and grimaced. 'I warned 'em agin teking him on. Knew it were mistake right from start.' She took another sip of tea, unaware of the almost tangible silence that filled the room. 'I'll think on it overnight,' she murmured almost to herself. 'Aye, that would be best.'

Julie's heart was pounding as she held William close. 'If you have to think about it, then you don't deserve him,' she said flatly. 'I love William and want the best for him. It don't matter to me if his medicines cost money. They're making him strong and well, so he can grow up like every other baby.'

'Think on, lass,' Charity warned. 'Babby's not yours. Probably not Bill's neither, if truth be known.'

'How dare you?' breathed Julie.

'I think this has gone far enough,' said Peggy with unusual sharpness. 'Mrs Farnsworth, let me show you to your room so you can freshen up before supper. Julie, see to William, and the rest of you get on with something useful.'

'It's *Miss* Farnsworth,' snapped Charity as she heaved herself out of the chair. 'Never had need of a man. Most of them not worth trouble.' With barely a glance at William or Julie, she stomped off after Peggy.

Julie's legs threatened to give way and she sat down with a bump on the kitchen chair. 'I won't give him up to her,' she breathed into William's hair. 'If Bill's parents are anything like her, then William will . . .'

'Never you fear, Julie,' said Mrs Finch. 'A few minutes with Peggy Reilly and that woman will be going back to Yorkshire empty-handed.'

Julie didn't have the heart to argue. She knew only that this would be the longest night of her life. Charity Farnsworth and her family were entitled to take William and raise him as their own. The birth certificate proved it.

Ron hated scenes, but he hated fat, loud women even more, and after two minutes of listening to Charity Farnsworth, he'd had enough. Sneaking out of the kitchen while everyone's attention was taken by the spat between Charity and Mrs Finch, he hurried downstairs and fetched his hat and coat. He'd lost his appetite for rabbit stew and apple sponge. What he needed now was a large whisky and Rosie's soft, sweet company.

He ordered a whining Harvey to stay indoors, and tramped through the hazy twilight of the early summer evening, relishing the tranquillity as he breathed in the scent of the sea and the alluring sweetness of the few roses that had survived the raids in a nearby garden.

He stopped by the wall at the end of the street, and with a hasty look to make sure no one was watching, plucked a pink rose from the bush that clambered over it. Its perfume was quite heady; it was the perfect gift for Rosie. Tucking it into the buttonhole of his suit jacket, he dug his hands in his trouser pockets and began to whistle 'The Rose of Tralee', which he considered most fitting for the occasion.

He arrived at the Anchor to find it already busy, with Rosie supervising two middle-aged women behind the bar. Barmaids with pretty faces and youthful figures were as rare as hen's teeth these days, but these two looked capable enough, and at least they weren't sour-faced like that Charity Farnsworth. She was enough to put any man off the drink.

Rosie sashayed delightfully towards him. 'Well, well,' she said admiringly. 'Don't you look smart?'

'I do me best,' he replied with a bit of a swagger.

She gave him a beaming smile and placed a large glass of whisky on the bar in front of him. 'Happy birthday, Ron,' she murmured with a wink.

Ron's heart swelled with pride as she continued to smile at him. He must be the envy of every man in the room. 'To be sure, you're a sight for sore eyes, so y'are, Rosie Braithwaite.' He grinned back at her. 'Are ye ready to be danced off your feet?'

She giggled. 'Give me five minutes, and I'm all yours,' she murmured. 'You're a bit earlier than I expected and you've caught me on the hop.'

'It'll be worth the waiting,' he replied, the silly grin still on his face as he relished the idea of having Rosie all to himself for the evening. 'And while you're at it, perhaps this rose might go well with your dress.'

She took the rose and buried her neat little nose in the velvety petals. 'Heavenly,' she breathed, her lovely eyes warm with pleasure.

Ron's gaze followed her as she left the bar and headed through the door towards the stairs. He'd managed to buy tickets to go to the Grand Hotel on the seafront for one of their big fund-raising dances, and the thought of having Rosie in his arms for the rest of the evening was definitely worth any wait. He eased his collar and tie, unused to the restrictions of dressing carefully, but his chin was smooth, his hair tamed with Brylcreem, and his suit was pressed. All in all, he thought, as he caught his reflection in the mirrors behind the optics, he was looking very dapper.

He'd just finished his whisky and was contemplating asking for another when he saw Rosie peek round the door that led to the stairs. She beckoned him, her slender arm encased in a long black glove, and he hurried over.

Rosie quickly shut the door behind him. 'I didn't want them wasting our time together with their gawping and asking questions,' she whispered. 'Let's go the back way.'

Ron took her hand and stilled her as she was about to turn away from him. His admiring gaze followed the curve of her figure in the black silk dress which clung to her like a second skin, and settled on the pearls at her throat and in her ears. His rose was pinned just below her shoulder, the petals almost caressing the peachy swell of her breast. 'Rosie, you look beautiful,' he managed.

She reached for her white fox fur wrap and then leaned towards him, brushing her soft lips against his cheek. 'You don't look half bad yourself, Ronan Reilly.' Then she was gone with a delightful chuckle, pushing through the door and into the alleyway that ran between the pub and the shop next door.

Ron was in a daze as he hurried after her, his senses filled with the scent of her skin, the promise in her eyes, and the softness of her lips.

She tucked her hand in his arm and draped the fox wrap over one shoulder. 'I get the feeling this is going to be a very special night,' she murmured as they began to walk towards the seafront.

'It already is,' he replied softly.

The atmosphere in the kitchen was tense, making that night's supper the most awkward meal ever endured at Beach View. The only glimmer of relief came from Charity's silence as she greedily tucked into her food, and refused to be drawn into the stiffly polite conversation.

Julie had no appetite, and had spent most of the meal pushing food round her plate. Peggy too seemed distracted, and Julie noticed that she'd hardly eaten either. Ron had disappeared, no doubt down to the Anchor to be with Rosie, and the whole celebratory supper seemed pointless and flat without him.

As the last bowl was scraped clean the tension broke with an audible sigh of relief. No one lingered round the table over cups of tea as they usually did, but made their hurried excuses and fled. Mrs Finch plumped down in her armchair, turned off her hearing aid and picked up a book. Jim muttered something to Peggy which made her frown, and then headed off to do his fire-watch duties, and Anne pleaded a headache and took herself off to her bedroom where Rose Margaret was already asleep in her cot. Which left Julie with Peggy and Charity.

'I'd better go and check on William,' Julie murmured as she pushed back from the table, desperate to escape.

'You'll hear him right enough if he's wanting,' said Charity. 'I'll say this fer 'im, he's got a good pair of lungs for a scraggy bairn.' Her withering gaze held Julie until she sat back down again. 'Tell me about yon sister,' she ordered.

Julie glanced across at Peggy, who was trying to be inconspicuous as she washed the dishes. They caught each other's eye, and Peggy gave her a nod of encouragement. Julie licked her lips and began to talk about Franny.

Charity listened, her expression giving nothing away as she slurped yet another cup of weak tea. She waited until Julie had finished and then folded her arms beneath her bosom. 'None of you sound as if you've a healthy bone between you,' she said, 'and I've been looking at babby – don't take after our William at all.'

Julie had prepared for this, and pulled the precious birth certificate from her pocket. 'I was able to register this because of the letters Bill had sent to Franny,' she explained firmly. 'He acknowledged repeatedly that he was William's father. He had made arrangements for Franny's lodgings during her pregnancy, and they were making plans to marry when he came home on leave.'

'Tha's all very well, lass, but many a man has been fooled by a pair of lying blue eyes.'

'If you're so determined that William isn't Bill's, why did you bother to come at all?' Julie said in exasperation.

'Needed to tek a look for mesen,' she muttered. 'My sister's too soft to know her own mind, and she left it to me to decide.' She took a deep breath and placed her hands on the table. 'She's always relied on me for advice. That husband of hers is good for nowt when it comes to making decisions.'

'So, what have you decided, Miss Farnsworth?' Peggy perched on the chair next to her, her expression tight and anxious.

'Babby's sickly and nothing like our William,' she said firmly. 'I'll not be teking 'im.'

Tears of joy and relief sprang into Julie's eyes and she could have flung her arms round the old trout and given her a kiss on that whiskery chin – but she resisted and quietly rose from her chair and hurried upstairs.

William was asleep in the cot, his thumb plugged into his mouth, and Julie knelt on the floor beside him and just watched him. Her heart was so full of joy she couldn't find the words to express it, so she remained sitting there, drinking in the sight of him, knowing he was now hers to cherish and keep.

Chapter Nineteen

Peggy closed the door quietly on Mrs Finch, who was fast asleep, and listened to the loud snores coming from the room next door. That awful woman was making enough racket to wake the bloody dead, and since her arrival the atmosphere in the house had become poisonous. She'd be glad when she was gone.

She went back down the stairs to her kitchen to tidy up and have a last, peaceful cigarette before going to bed. It was nice to have the kitchen to herself for a change, and after clearing away the last cups and saucers, she sat down with a sigh of pleasure and stroked Harvey's silky head.

Ron and the girls were still out, Jim was on firewatch, and Julie and Anne were tucked up in bed, their babies asleep in their cots. All should have been right with her world, but it wasn't, for she hadn't yet managed to find a quiet moment to talk to Jim, and he'd gone off to his warden duties in a sulk.

'It's all a bit much, isn't it, Harvey?' she murmured. 'All right for him to fib and get up to mischief, but when the boot's on the other foot, he gets all moody and dog in the manger – if you'll pardon the expression.'

Harvey waggled his eyebrows and laid his long nose on her lap, his eyes beseeching.

Peggy found a crumbling dog biscuit in her apron pocket, and he took it in his soft mouth and proceeded to crunch it on the mat. Life was so simple for a dog, she thought wearily. All they needed was kindness and they were loyal to the end – whereas humans were far more complicated.

Her thoughts turned to Charity and she grimaced. The damned woman had rejected darling little William as if he were a bit of scrag end on a butcher's slab – but Julie had been so joyful not to lose him that she hadn't minded.

Peggy smiled as she watched Harvey chase the last few crumbs of biscuit with his nose. The thought of William going to such an appalling family had worried her sick, and it had been a moment of inspiration on her part to tell Charity about William's deafness – not that she'd said anything about how temporary it had been – and there was little doubt in her mind that this piece of information, dropped so casually as she showed the woman to her room, had been the deciding factor in Charity's rejection.

The first hurdle was over, but there were more to come, and she was doing herself no good sitting here worrying about them. She finished her cigarette and threw the butt into the range, which she'd damped down for the night. 'Keep watch, Harvey,' she murmured as she switched off the light and stepped into the hall.

The clamour of the telephone ringing almost stopped her heart, and she raced to pick up the receiver, dreading the bad news – for nothing good came from calls so late at night. 'Yes?'

'I'm sorry to disturb you, Mrs Reilly. This is Dr Michael, and I need to get an urgent message to Sister Harris.'

'She's in bed asleep. I'll take the message to her,' said Peggy, reaching for the nearby pad and pencil. She listened as he gave her the name and address where Julie was needed, and repeated it back to him once she'd written it down. 'I'll tell her at once,' she said, and put down the receiver.

As she was about to climb the stairs she heard the first sinister wail of the sirens and realised the long day wasn't over yet. Knocking on Anne's door, she peeked in and found she was already out of bed, so she ran up the stairs shouting to Julie and Miss Farnsworth to get up.

She reached Charity's door as Julie came hurrying down the stairs with William straddling her hip, her medical bag and gas-mask box gripped in her free hand. The girl obviously hadn't been to bed yet, for she was still fully dressed. 'Get Anne to take the box of things while I rouse the others,' said Peggy as she began to knock frantically on the door of Charity's room.

The snoring persisted as loudly as a herd of hogs from the other side of the door, and Peggy finally lost patience. She went into the room, switched on the light and roughly shook the woman's shoulder. 'Air raid,' she yelled over the screaming sirens. 'Get downstairs and into the Anderson shelter immediately.'

'Wha's tha doin'?' She rose like a monolith in the narrow single bed, her hair straggling round her face as she blinked in the bright light.

'Air raid,' Peggy snapped. 'Get up.' As the wailing grew in strength, Peggy realised that Gerry was on the move in numbers tonight, and she didn't have a moment to waste.

The sound of Hurricanes and Spitfires overhead meant the raid was imminent, and she dashed back along the landing and went into Mrs Finch's room. The lovely old dear was dead to the world, her snores rather more ladylike than Charity's, but deep and contented. Peggy switched on the light and gently drew back the blanket so as not to startle her. It was the only way to wake her when she'd taken out her hearing aid.

'Oh, dear,' sighed Mrs Finch as she let Peggy help her into her slippers and dressing gown. 'I was having such a lovely dream.'

'Never mind,' muttered Peggy as she grabbed the hearing aid and slipped it into her pocket. 'You'll soon get back to it once you're settled again.'

She steadied the old lady as she slowly made her sleepy way down the stairs with her walking stick, and then guided her through the dark kitchen, where she grabbed her gas-mask box, overcoat and handbag. Navigating the stone steps to the basement, they finally reached the garden.

The summer evening sky was cloven with the bright phosphorous fingers of the searchlights and, as the wailing sirens reached their ear-splitting pitch, another squadron of Hurricanes came roaring overhead. The earth shuddered beneath their feet as Peggy helped Mrs Finch along the garden path, the very air trembling with the noise.

Harvey rushed past them and scrambled under one of the sturdy benches Ron had built into the sides of the Anderson shelter. He could put up with all the whizz-bangs but hated the sirens, and he now cowered behind Anne's legs, his eyebrows drooped in misery.

Anne and Julie had already lit the primus stove so they could boil a kettle, and both babies had been placed, with a great deal of protest, in the special gas-mask cots which had been wedged side by side on the floor. The box of essentials Peggy restocked after every raid was tucked away under the other bench, where a pile of blankets had been stacked in readiness should it get too cold.

What with the sirens, the RAF and the screaming babies, it was hard enough to think, let alone hold a conversation. Peggy settled Mrs Finch in her deck-chair and wedged her in with pillows so she wouldn't slip out of it when she fell asleep. There was still no sign of Charity – what was the blasted woman doing?

She was about to rush back to the house when she saw the doughty figure lumber down the garden path, fully dressed in hat and coat, and carrying her suitcase.

'It's a bit of a tight squeeze,' shouted Peggy, 'but hopefully the raid won't last long.'

'Ee, by goom, you 'ave it rough down 'ere in south,' Charity boomed above the racket as she sank onto the bench and made it creak under her weight. She grimaced as she took in her surroundings. 'Happen it smells in here, and I'll not abide spending night with dog, neither,' she added, glaring at Harvey, who eyed her warily from beneath the other bench.

'The dog is one of the family,' retorted Peggy. 'He stays.' She'd had enough of Charity Farnsworth. She turned to Julie and pulled the slip of paper out of her pocket. 'Sorry, love, but Dr Michael just phoned,' she shouted in her ear. 'You're needed at twenty-seven, Hazelwood Avenue. Mrs Morris has gone into labour, and it's advancing rapidly according to her husband, who seems to be in a bit of a lather.'

'Great timing,' said Julie wryly, 'but then it is her first, and her poor husband panics at the slightest thing.' She glanced at Charity, who was sitting like a malevolent Buddha on the opposite bench, her suitcase clasped to her chest as she glared about her. 'Don't let William out of your sight,' she said in Peggy's ear.

414

Peggy smiled and nodded her understanding as she accompanied the girl to the shelter door. 'You take care out there, Julie.'

'I'll do me best,' she shouted back as she clamped the tin hat over her head and pushed her bicycle through the back gate.

Peggy closed her eyes momentarily and prayed she'd be all right before she went back into the cramped Anderson shelter and closed the door. A long, trying day was clearly about to turn into an even longer and more trying night for everyone.

Air raids didn't stop a good night out and, as the first siren began to wail, everyone had taken the party into the basement beneath the Grand Hotel.

The hotel definitely lived up to its name, for the basement proved to be almost as wide and high as the main ballroom, with chandeliers hanging from the ceiling, and a proper dance floor laid over the concrete. There was a bar at one end, and a gramophone at the other – not even the Grand could accommodate a fifteen-piece band in its basement. There were low tables, and comfortable couches and chairs to rest on between dances, and a good air-filter system that stopped it from getting too smoky or hot.

The girls' pretty dresses and the smart uniforms of the many Allied servicemen made it a colourful scene as they whirled on the dance floor, and Ron looked round him in awe. He'd never been down here before, and had seen nothing like it in his life.

'Certainly beats my cellar,' said Rosie as she sipped a gin and Italian and admired the surroundings. 'No room in there to swing a cat, let alone do the foxtrot.' She put down her glass and grabbed his hand. 'Come on, they're playing "Begin the Beguine", and it's my favourite.'

Ron set his whisky glass on the low table and led her onto the floor, which was as smooth and flexible as the one up in the ballroom. No wonder they charged such fancy prices, he thought. This place must cost a fortune to run.

'Stop thinking, Ron, and enjoy the music,' murmured Rosie in his ear.

He held her close, breathing in her womanly fragrance as her lithe body moved in perfect harmony with him across the floor. Rosie was the belle of the ball, and he was a very lucky man. It would be foolish to waste a moment thinking of anything else.

As one lovely tune followed another they became lost in the dance and in each other, the drone of aircraft and the distant, muffled crump of bomb blasts seemingly coming from another world – a world that could no longer touch them in this bubble of happiness.

Julie wasn't having much fun at all, but then neither was poor Mrs Morris, who was cramped up on the narrow bottom bunk of their Anderson shelter. Her husband was pacing the concrete floor, wringing his hands and constantly sweeping his fingers through his tangle of hair with impatience. Mrs Morris was taking her time having this baby, and it felt as if it had been going on for hours.

'You won't make it come any quicker by huffing and puffing, Alf,' said Mrs Morris after the latest contraction had eased. 'Why don't you go back to your fire-watch duties and leave us women to it?'

Alf worked for the electricity board and was a plodding sort of chap, unused to drama and clearly out of his depth. His short-sighted gaze flitted between Julie and his wife as he shifted his feet and pushed his glasses up his nose. 'I dunno what to do for the best,' he said fretfully.

'Your wife's right,' said Julie. 'She could be ages yet, and you have an important job to do out there. Why don't you go back on fire-watch duty and come home when the raid's over?' She really didn't want him hanging about, because he looked like a fainter, and there simply wasn't any room in this shelter for him to be stretched out on the floor at the first sight of blood.

He squeezed his wife's shoulder in a bashful sort of fashion, picked up his tin hat and hessian bag and backed out of the shelter. 'See you later then,' he murmured, and was gone like a scalded cat as his wife began to groan again.

'That's right,' Julie soothed as the bombers thundered overhead and the contraction deepened. 'You can make as much noise as you like now. No one will hear you over that racket.'

She sat with Mrs Morris as the fighters and bombers roared overhead and the hurricane lantern swung and flickered shadows across the tin walls of the shelter. They listened to the distant crumps of explosions and the whine of straining engines as the fighter planes did battle overhead, but their main concern was the baby that seemed reluctant to come out.

'Can't say I blame the poor little bugger,' chuckled Mrs Morris. 'If I were him, I'd stay in there until this lot have finished and all.' Her smile faded suddenly and her eyes widened. 'Oh, Gawd,' she gasped. 'I think this is really it.'

Julie saw the look of concentration on her face and was prepared for what she suspected would be a very swift delivery after all that hanging about.

As Mrs Morris gave an almighty push, her baby was born and began to cry furiously. 'It's a little girl,' Julie said delightedly as she dealt with the umbilical cord. Wrapping the squalling baby in one of the clean towels Mrs Morris had prepared, she handed her over.

'My word,' breathed Mrs Morris, her face soft with love and pride, all the pain and worry vanquished by the sight of her newborn. 'She's got a set of lungs on her, and that's a fact.' She looked up at Julie with sudden concern. 'Alf wanted a boy,' she said, 'do you think he'll mind?'

'She's beautiful,' replied Julie with a soft smile. 'I think your husband will just be so relieved it's over that he won't mind at all.'

Mrs Morris grasped Julie's hand. 'Thanks ever so for coming out on a night like this, Sister – and I'm sorry it took so long.'

'Just rest and enjoy your baby while I clean up and get you comfortable. We could be here a while yet, so would you like me to make you a cup of tea?'

'That would be lovely,' she sighed. 'Me throat's as dry as a parrot cage after all that puffing and blowing.'

Julie finished dealing with Mrs Morris while the kettle boiled, and then handed her a cup of tea and took the baby. Having washed and dressed her in the sweet little knitted suit that Mrs Morris had hand-embroidered, she placed her back into her mother's arms.

Weary from the long, tense day, she longed for her bed and the reassurance that William was safe. But Mrs Morris couldn't be left alone, and it was her duty to remain with her until the all-clear sounded, and her husband returned. She pulled the spare blanket over her shoulders and concentrated on the noise overhead in an effort to stay awake.

It was five in the morning when that welcome sound heralded the end of the enemy raid, and although the party was still in full swing, Rosie and Ron had had enough. 'We must be getting old,' she murmured as they strolled back to the Anchor in the pearly dawn light.

'Never,' he rumbled, patting her hand, which was

neatly tucked into the crook of his arm. 'Why, Rosie, we're just spring chickens compared to some – and being with you makes me feel young again.'

As they reached the side door to the pub, she drew to a halt and looked up at him, her expression unreadable. 'We can't go on like this, Ron,' she said softly. 'You do know that, don't you?'

He swallowed painfully and his heart seemed to be squeezed with dread. 'But we've had a lovely night,' he stammered. 'I thought you . . .'

She placed a soft finger on his lips. 'Shhh, Ron. Don't say another word until I've finished.' She regarded him for a long, tense moment and then closed her eyes and kissed him – not on the cheek, but on the mouth.

Ron thought he'd never tasted anything so sweet. He had never known the power of such a kiss before, or dared to dream this moment would really come. After an instant of hesitation, he gently pulled her to him and tried to convey his depths of feeling in his own kiss.

They eventually drew apart, and Rosie blushed and dipped her chin. 'I'm sorry, Ron. I shouldn't have done that – but I've wanted to for ages,' she confessed softly.

He cupped her lovely face in his hands and looked deeply into her eyes. 'Why didn't you then?'

She looked back at him, a ghost of a smile on her lips. 'It's not a girl's place to make the first move, Ron, you know that.'

'But why tonight?'

'I don't really know,' she murmured. 'I suppose I just got carried away in the moment.' She looked up at him through her lashes. 'Am I very brazen?'

'You can be as brazen as you like,' he murmured as he captured her lips again and held her close. 'You're my Rosie,' he murmured some minutes later, 'and I love the bones of you, girl.'

She gave a deep, sad sigh as she rested her head on his shoulder. 'I know you do,' she murmured, 'and I love you too, but it was wrong of me to give you false hope.' She drew from his embrace, her lovely eyes bright with tears. 'And it is false, Ron,' she said sadly, 'for we can have no future together.'

Ron felt a stab of fear. 'If we love each other, then I can't see . . .'

She silenced him with a sweet brush of her finger over his lips. 'I'm not free, Ron. We could never be together, not properly – not the way we both want.'

Ron's thoughts were in turmoil. There'd been rumours that Rosie was either widowed or divorced, or had merely used the wedding ring as a subterfuge to keep predatory men at bay. His throat tightened. 'You're still married,' he rasped.

She nodded.

The disappointment weighed heavily round his heart as the joy of the last few moments melted away. 'But you've lived here for years and there's been no sight of him, not even a whisper that he existed. That's not a marriage, Rosie.'

'I know,' she replied, reaching into her small handbag for her cigarettes and lighter. She blew smoke into the pale dawn light, her gaze distant. 'But divorce is out of the question.'

Ron took the cigarette from her trembling fingers and threw it in the gutter. Grasping her arms, he gently forced her to look at him. 'Why, Rosie?' he asked softly.

She took a deep, quavering breath and let it out on a sigh. 'Jack's been very ill for a long time. He's being looked after in a secure section of a special sanatorium and will never come home again,' she murmured. 'The law says I can't divorce him, even though he's insane, so I must live in this limbo until he dies.'

Ron gathered her to him and buried his cheek in her hair. 'Oh, Rosie, me darlin' girl. What a terrible burden you've been carrying all these years. Why did you not confide in me?'

'I couldn't,' she said, her breath hitching against his suit jacket. 'Not until I was sure you felt the same way as me.' She finally drew away from him. 'I'm so sorry, Ron. Tonight has been wonderful, and now I've gone and spoiled it.'

He softly kissed away the single tear that dewed her cheek. 'The night has not been spoiled at all,' he murmured. 'I've waited so long to kiss you, and now that I know you love me, my heart is full.'

'Oh, Ron,' she breathed, her face shining with love and hope.

He took her hands and looked deeply into her eyes. 'I will keep on loving you for as long as I've breath in me body. But I'll not be impatient, Rosie, or take things further than you wish. What we share is too precious, and I'm prepared to wait for as long as it takes to make you me own.'

She looked back at him with just a glimmer of the old teasing light in her lovely eyes, and the curve of a smile tugging at the corners of her mouth. 'Is that a proposal, Ronan Reilly?'

Ron grinned and kissed the tip of her nose. 'You can call it a proposal of a proposal,' he said. He gave her a light slap on her delicious bottom. 'Now get indoors and go to bed before I start making a fool of meself.'

She giggled, unlocked the door and stepped inside. 'I do love you, Ron. Sleep well, you old scoundrel, and I'll see you this evening.'

'Less of the old,' he retorted. But he was talking to a closed door.

He shoved his hands into his pockets, knowing he had a silly grin on his face as he went back into Camden Road and headed for home. But he didn't care. Rosie loved him and he was walking on air. His heart sang, the birds were trilling, and it was going to be a beautiful day.

Peggy's nerves were worn to a frazzle after spending those long, fraught hours in the Anderson shelter. Charity had complained about everything, the babies wouldn't be soothed, and Harvey had disgraced himself by letting off a huge fart, the smell of which had lingered sickeningly for what felt like hours.

They had trooped back into the kitchen, glad to find they still had water and electricity, and there didn't appear to be any damage to the house or in the street. Once both babies had been changed and fed and tucked into the pram together, Peggy and Anne set about preparing breakfast. Charity Farnsworth didn't offer to help, merely sat at the kitchen table reading the newspaper while Mrs Finch tried to lay cutlery and china around her.

It was still and silent after the noise of last night, and the dawn sky promised a lovely day. But Peggy knew her troubles were only just beginning when she saw Jim come into the kitchen. He looked at her with questions in his eyes that she couldn't answer – not here, not now, and certainly not in front of the others.

'Was it very bad out there?' she asked him, her tone deliberately casual. 'It sounded pretty alarming from where we were sitting.'

He took off his tin hat and warden's jacket, dumping his gas-mask box on a nearby chair. 'More noise than anything,' he said moodily, easing his braces over his shoulders and leaving them to dangle from the waistband on his trousers. 'A couple of incendiaries came down close to Lord Cliffe's manor, and an enemy bomber ditched in the sea. Rita's still out there dealing with the fire up at the manor, but all in all we got away lightly compared to Portsmouth, which took the brunt of the attack.'

'That's good,' she said, turning her back on him and concentrating on the powdered eggs and milk she was stirring in a saucepan. The chickens had obviously been disturbed by the noise last night, for there were no fresh eggs, and this powdered stuff didn't scramble well at all.

She heard the scrape of a chair against the lino and his muttered greeting to Charity, who immediately started questioning him about why he wasn't in the forces.

'I'm forty-four,' he muttered. 'And I did my bit in the last war – not that it's any of your business,' he added gruffly.

Peggy was alerted to his unusual rudeness. His feathers were well and truly ruffled, and if she didn't do something about it soon, there would be ructions. She continued stirring the scrambled eggs, her thoughts in a whirl. There would be ructions anyway, she concluded, so whatever she did she couldn't win.

The early morning meal was eaten almost in silence, the atmosphere as tense as it had been the evening before. Peggy could see that Anne and Mrs Finch had noticed the way Jim kept glaring at her, and it was making her most uncomfortable. When Ron came home with a silly grin on his face half an hour later, she was glad of the distraction and hurried to fetch his breakfast.

With the arrival of Suzy and Fran, the mood

lightened somewhat, and Peggy felt she could relax a little. 'You look very pleased with yourself, Ron,' she murmured over her teacup. 'Good night, was it?'

'Well now,' he beamed, 'you could say that, Peg. But a gentleman never talks of such things.'

Peggy smiled at the thought of Ron and Rosie finally getting together. Perhaps there might even be a wedding in the family before too long? She finished her tea and started on the washing-up, glad not to have to sit and look at Jim's grumpy face as he pretended to be immersed in the newspaper. But the time was fast approaching when she knew she couldn't avoid the confrontation any longer – and in a way, it would be a relief to get it over and done with.

She heard the sound of someone at the front door, followed by weary footsteps in the hall. A moment later, Julie appeared in the kitchen. The poor girl looked exhausted.

'I'll be off then,' said Charity as she clattered her empty cup into the saucer. 'Yon train's due in an hour and I don't want to miss it. Goodbye, Miss Harris.' She gave a curt nod in Julie's direction, then stomped out into the hall.

Peggy followed her and opened the front door as Charity picked up her case and gas-mask box.

'I can't say it's been a pleasure,' said Charity. 'Always been one to speak me mind.'

'So I noticed,' said Peggy dryly. 'Goodbye, Miss Farnsworth. Safe journey.'

She watched as Charity lumbered down the steps and strode down Beach View Terrace towards Camden Road. 'And good riddance,' she hissed before slamming the door.

'Right, Peggy Reilly. It's time you and me had a talk.'

Peggy turned and found she was staring at Jim's chest. She looked up into his face and realised the moment had come. 'We'll talk upstairs,' she said firmly, and eased round him before running up to their bedroom.

He followed her through the door and shut it behind him. There was no cheeky smile, no wicked twinkle in his eye as he leaned against the door – just a stony glare and a chin that jutted with determination. 'Well?' he demanded.

'Now, Jim, there's no call to get all hot and bothered,' she said, her nerve beginning to fail her. 'I admit I told a fib, but really, there is absolutely nothing sinister behind it.'

'It's not like you to lie at all. What have you been up to, Peggy?'

'I didn't go shopping the other afternoon,' she confessed, twisting her hands nervously in the folds of her apron. 'Because I had an important appointment to keep.'

He folded his arms, his eyes narrowing. 'Who with? And why was it so important you had to lie to me about it?'

'Jim Reilly, shut up a minute and let me talk,' she

hissed. 'I can't think straight with you glaring at me like that.'

She could feel her heart pounding and her mouth was dry, but there was no turning back from this. 'I've been feeling run-down and tired lately, and went to see Dr George at the Hazelwood clinic to ask him for a tonic to buck me up,' she said quickly. 'I thought I might be going through the change, or something. Things haven't been right for a while.'

His suspicion and anger immediately disappeared and he hurried towards her with concern in his eyes. 'There's nothing wrong with you, is there, Peg?' he asked hoarsely.

She shook her head. 'Not *wrong* exactly,' she murmured, not daring to look at him. She took a very deep breath and the words came out in a rush. 'I'm three months pregnant, Jim.'

'What?'

Everyone in the kitchen looked up at Jim's roar. 'It sounds like Mum's told him something he's not too pleased about,' muttered Anne, packing away the duster and polish under the sink. 'I think it might be best if we all make ourselves scarce until it blows over. Those two can go at it hammer and tongs, but when they make up afterwards it gets embarrassing.'

'I'll get out of me finery and take Harvey into the hills,' muttered Ron, who was still wearing a silly grin and his best suit.

'Suzy and I will probably sleep through it all,'

said Fran, 'but if you think that's bad, you should hear my Da and Mammy clearing the air. They can be heard all the way from Dublin to Bantry Bay.'

Julie finished her breakfast and carried her dish to the sink as Jim's loud voice continued to drift down to them, the words indistinct and giving no hint of what the argument was about. It was quite like old times, she thought sadly. Mum and Dad had always enjoyed a good row – but Anne was right. It got embarrassing when they started cooing and making up afterwards.

'It's still a bit early, but I think I'll take William to visit Eileen and then Kath, and share me good news,' she said. 'What about you, Anne?'

'A stroll along the seafront and a cup of tea down at the kiosk will suit me just fine after that long night. Rose Margaret could do with some fresh air, and I'm going to miss the sea when I'm in Somerset.'

Julie's happiness at knowing William would never be taken from her now that Charity had left for Yorkshire made her glow on the inside, and she knew it showed on her face. She smiled as Jim's great shout of laughter rang out upstairs. 'Whatever it was seems to have blown over,' she murmured. 'But I think we should leave them to it anyway.'

Chapter Twenty

What with Ron acting like a lovesick schoolboy, and Jim going about with a great silly grin on his face, the last week had not been easy for Peggy. It was all right for Ron – his romancing of Rosie Braithwaite was common knowledge, and half the town had seen them mooning over one another at the Grand Hotel dance – but Jim was another matter entirely. It had been the devil's own job to stop him from broadcasting their news to all and sundry, and she'd had to resort to dire threats when she suspected he was on the verge of blurting it out. The discovery had shocked her to the core and she'd barely had time to take it in, let alone make it public.

The day had arrived when Anne would be leaving for Somerset, and Jim broached the subject once again as they were getting dressed. 'I don't see why we can't tell Anne and the rest of the family,' he complained. 'After all, 'tis a wondrous thing.'

Peggy finished brushing her hair and watched him in the mirror as he stood behind her and buttoned his shirt. 'If we tell Anne she'll refuse to go to Somerset, and you know it isn't safe for her here, not now she's got Rose Margaret.'

'Well, she'll have to know sooner or later,' he muttered. 'You can't hide something like that for long.'

'I'll write to her when she's good and settled down there, and when I'm ready,' she said firmly.

He put his arms about her waist, his chin resting lightly on her shoulder as he regarded their reflections in the mirror. 'Are you not happy about this baby, Peg? Is that why you're so reluctant to tell anyone?'

She turned within his embrace and leaned her cheek on his chest. 'I really don't know how I feel,' she confessed. 'It's all come as such a shock, and one minute I'm over the moon, the next I'm dreading it.' She looked up at him. 'I'm a grandmother, Jim. I shouldn't be having a baby, not at my age.'

'Ach, you're a wee spring chicken, and grandparents or not, I'm tickled pink.' He puffed out his chest and gave her a broad smile.

'I might be the chicken, but don't go playing the old rooster with me, Jim Reilly. It won't be you giving birth to it, getting up in the middle of the night to feed it, or washing nappies and dealing with croup and—'

He silenced her with a kiss.

She pushed him away finally, and turned to make the bed. That was the sort of behaviour that had got her into this mess, and although she absolutely adored him, she simply couldn't think straight when he kissed her like that. And she needed her wits about her today, for Anne's departure would be hard

431

enough to bear, without worrying over Jim's inability to keep his mouth shut.

'I just hope Cissy and Anne won't take the news too badly,' she murmured as she pummelled the pillows. 'It won't be easy for them to come to terms with their mother having a baby after all these years. As for Doris, well, she'll probably refuse to speak to me ever again.'

Jim snorted. 'As far as that sister of yours is concerned, then it would be a blessing. Doris is a terrible snob, so she is, and you don't see eye to eye at all, so I'm surprised you even care what she might think.'

Peggy giggled as she straightened the eiderdown. 'She winds me up like a clock when she comes round here turning her nose up at everything. I might enjoy telling her, just to see the look on her face. It's bound to be priceless.'

Jim stilled her by taking her hand. 'I don't care about Doris, or how the other wains take it,' he said softly. 'I care about you, and how you feel. 'Tis a miracle, Peggy, and I want you to rejoice in it with me.'

She looked up at him, her emotions in turmoil. 'It's only just sunk in,' she admitted, 'and although it won't be easy what with air raids, rationing and a full house to look after, I've realised I'm thrilled at the thought.'

'Honestly?'

'Honestly,' she murmured and smiled up at him.

'But my emotions are all over the place right now, and with Anne leaving with Rose Margaret, it's going to be hard to adjust to the reality of having none of my children at home. I want to tell everyone, of course I do. But not yet, Jim – not until I'm really ready.'

'You have my promise, Peg.' He drew her close and kissed the top of her head, which just about reached the tips of his shirt collar. 'But I need you to promise that you'll look after yourself and do what the doctor tells you.'

'I'll be fine,' she said briskly. 'Good heavens, Jim. I've had four babies already, and this one will be no different.'

'You were younger then, and there wasn't a war on,' he said solemnly. 'If you meant what you said about really wanting this baby, then you'll rest and eat properly and not put it or yourself at risk.'

'I promise,' she replied, her mind going over all the things she had yet to do before Anne left home.

'Peggy, you're a wee pain in the arse, so you are – but I love you anyway.' He gave her a smacking kiss on the cheek and tugged her hand. 'Come on. Everyone will be waiting for their breakfast, and I could eat a horse, so I could.'

'You'll get dried egg on dry toast and like it,' she retorted happily. 'They've just cut the butter ration again.'

Breakfast was the usual chaos, with babies demanding to be fed, nurses dashing in and out on their way to work, Rita swotting for her mechanic's final exams, and Harvey trying to steal toast and anything else the babies dropped on the floor.

Julie was trying to feed William, who was sitting in the high chair banging his spoon on the tray; Rose Margaret was smearing as much jam as possible into her hair while Mrs Finch dithered about trying to be helpful and Anne struggled to keep the jam off her good skirt. Ron was the only still being in this whirl of noise and activity, sitting there at the end of the table, lost in his own world as he contentedly drank his tea.

Peggy sat in her kitchen as the clock ticked away the minutes and the noise went on around her. She poured the tea, passed the jug of milk or pot of sugar, and let the chatter drift over her as she watched her lovely daughter. Anne had left home when she and Martin had bought their little cottage, so it shouldn't feel so painful to see her preparing to leave again. But it did, for this time she would be taking Rose Margaret with her, and the little girl had become such an intrinsic part of Peggy's life she couldn't imagine the house without her.

They heard the roar and screech of a car pulling up outside and the excited tooting of a horn. 'That'll be Martin,' said Anne, pushing back from the table and hauling a protesting Rose from the high chair. 'He's much earlier than I expected, and Rose needs a bath before I take her anywhere.'

Before Anne could extricate herself from Rose's

sticky fingers, the kitchen door swung open and Cissy breezed in, trailing a rather bemused, but obviously besotted, young airman behind her.

'I couldn't let you leave without saying goodbye,' she said. 'This is James, by the way. He's been such a sweetie to drive me down from the base.'

Peggy smiled at the young flying officer, who'd blushed to the roots of his hair at Cissy's praise, and then went to hug her daughter. Cissy was elegant in her WAAF uniform, her fair hair neatly pinned back beneath the jaunty cap, her slender figure enhanced by the rather severe jacket and straight skirt. She'd always been the lively one, the romantic with a soft heart who fell in and out of love at the drop of a hat, and Peggy rather hoped that this James was not the next victim – he looked rather nice.

Peggy smiled at her daughters, delighted to have them together, however briefly. 'It's so lovely to see you, Cissy,' she breathed as they hugged.

'Well, I couldn't let her go without giving this precious girl a big kiss, could I?' she asked, her big blue eyes full of laughter. She reached for Rose and recoiled. 'Yuk,' she grimaced. 'She's all sticky with jam and bits of egg.'

'To be sure, you were the same at that age, Cissy,' laughed Jim. 'All babies are messy eaters, so they are, and—'

'You'll find out for yourself one day,' interrupted Peggy, shooting him a warning look.

Jim gave a deep sigh and turned his attention to Cissy's young man, sitting him down with a cup of tea and the offer of a cigarette. It was clearly time for the men to form some sort of barrier against the noise of all those chattering females. With all the girls talking at once, it was hard for Mrs Finch to follow what they were saying, but that didn't put her off in the slightest and she joined in with gusto.

Peggy sat back, warmed by the sight of her two beautiful daughters as they hastily bathed Rose Margaret in the kitchen sink and changed her into clean clothes. They weren't alike at all, one dark, the other fair, and as children, had fought like cats. Yet now they were young women, they'd formed a very close bond, especially since Anne had had Rose. She began to daydream about the tiny being that was growing inside her. Would it be dark or fair, a girl or boy? Would it have Jim's eyes, or Anne's smile?

'Mum! Mum, whatever's the matter?'

'What?'

'I've been talking to you and you haven't heard a word I've been saying.' Cissy pouted. 'You looked as if you were miles away.'

Peggy pulled her ragged thoughts together. 'Sorry, darling. I was wool-gathering.'

'Martin's arrived, and he wants to know if it's all right to take the old cot. Only Violet doesn't have one, and he can easily tie it to the roof of the car.'

'Better he leaves it here,' said Jim.

Cissy frowned. 'Whatever for, Dad? William's got his own, and our old thing probably won't be needed again for years.'

Jim opened his mouth to say something but Peggy hastily forestalled him. 'Of course they can take it. Anne can have the old pram as well if she wants.'

'He's driving a small Ford, Mum, not an army truck or Aunt Doris's Bentley.' Cissy put her hands on her hips and gave an exasperated sigh. 'Honestly, Mum, what *is* the matter with you this morning?'

'Nothing,' Peggy said briskly, and hurried into the hall to see if there was anything she could do to help. But Ron had already dismantled the cot and was tying it firmly to the roof of the car, Martin was stacking cases in the boot, and Jim had followed her out and was now standing with young James, their heads buried beneath the bonnet of the little car, deep in contemplation of its working parts.

The car was finally packed, and Anne took a last look round the bedroom to make sure she'd remembered everything. She stood in the hall of Beach View Boarding House with Rose Margaret on her hip, clearly torn between leaving her home and parents for the second time, and the need to take her baby to safety.

Peggy put her arms round them both. 'Take care, darling,' she murmured, kissing her cheek. 'And ring me the minute you get down to Violet's so that I know you've arrived safely.' She kissed Rose's sweet face, breathed in her precious baby smell and stepped back, unable to prolong the agony of this parting.

With her arms folded tightly about her thickened waist, she watched Anne say goodbye to Ron and her father, and then gently kiss Mrs Finch. Cissy of course made a great drama out of the whole thing by bursting into tears and had to be soothed by the ever-helpful James.

As everyone milled about in the hall, Peggy's emotions were all over the place. She wanted this moment to be over, but didn't want them to leave; wanted to tell everyone about the baby she was expecting, but knew this was not the time. So she stood dumbly to one side, waiting.

'I've got ten days' leave,' said Martin as he came to stand beside her. 'So I'll be with her while she settles in. Don't fret, Peggy. They'll both be safer there.'

'I know,' she said, and dredged up a smile.

He squeezed her arm in sympathy and went over to Anne. 'Come on, darling,' he said firmly. 'We have a long drive ahead of us, and nobody likes drawn-out farewells.'

Jim came to stand beside Peggy on the top step as Martin settled Anne and the baby in the passenger seat. She leaned against him, glad of his sturdy support in this painful moment, but couldn't quite manage to stop her tears as Anne waved out of the window and Martin drove off down the street.

And then they were gone, the sound of the car's

engine fading into the distance until there was silence again.

Jim gently steered her back into the house and closed the door. 'It's all right, Peg,' he said, his own voice unsteady. 'This war will soon be over, and then we'll have all our chicks home again.'

Peggy nodded, but she had the darkest dread in her heart that this war was far from over, and that it could be years before she saw them again.

As June ended, all the war news concerned Germany's shocking invasion of Russia, and their capture of Minsk. In the first week of July Stalin called for a 'Scorched Earth' policy, but seven days later the Germans crossed into the Ukraine and Britain made a pact of mutual assistance with Russia.

The heavy bombing raids in Cliffehaven lessened, although there were a few tip-and-runs that caught everyone on the hop, and the noise of British aircraft taking off and landing at the nearby base had become such a familiar background to everyday life that no one noticed it much any more.

Julie was busier than ever on her rounds, for there was still no sign of another district nurse joining the practice, and Jess had left to begin her training at the hospital. Eunice was unhelpful as usual, Michael continued to keep his distance, and his father was spending more time in his garden than in his consulting room. However, William's health was improving by the week, and his last check-up had shown that his heart rhythm had steadied, the murmur almost inaudible. It seemed the prognosis was correct, her hopes fulfilled, for his heart was quietly mending itself.

It was now the middle of July and she returned to Beach View Boarding House after another long day, aching for a cool soak in the bath before supper. But William seemed to have other ideas. He was fretful and stubborn, refusing his food and wriggling away from her when she tried to soothe him. 'Do you think he feels a bit warm, Peggy?' she asked.

'He is a bit,' she replied, feeling his forehead. 'But it's been a hot day and all that crying won't have helped. I'd give him a cool bath and move the cot under the open window, if I were you. It's going to be a sticky night.'

'Yes,' Julie murmured, still not really convinced. Yet there was no rash, no cough, no wheezing in his chest or runny nose. She was probably just making a fuss over nothing.

Having shared a cool bath with him, she gave him a bottle of formula to soothe him further and laid him in the cot in just a vest and nappy. She didn't leave him under the window as Peggy had suggested, since the night air could quickly turn cold, and she didn't want to risk him getting a chill. She kissed him goodnight, left the nightlight glowing on the bedside table and went back downstairs.

'I'm going to Eileen's for an hour or so,' she said as she ate her supper of sausage, potato and tomatoes. 'But I won't be late back. William's still rather warm, and I have an early start in the morning.'

'That's fine, dear,' said Peggy. 'I'll keep an ear open for him.' She regarded Julie over her teacup. 'You and Eileen seem to be getting on better now,' she said casually.

Julie nodded. 'It was a bit tricky at first, but we had a long talk and cleared the air. I feel sorry for her, really,' she sighed, pushing back her empty plate. 'She's awfully lonely, and I don't think her councillor friend is about to propose. He's too stuck in his ways.'

'It can't be easy for her,' murmured Peggy. 'But then, if you don't mind my saying so, she only has herself to blame.'

Julie acknowledged her comment with a smile. 'She can be daunting, I grant you. But I think that under all that gloss there's a woman just crying out to have a home and family of her own.'

Julie looked at Peggy and saw something in her expression that told her she knew about Eileen's baby. 'She told me about what happened all those years ago,' she said softly. 'And I think that, as time has gone on, she's frightened she won't get another chance of being a mother.'

Peggy sipped her tea and lit a cigarette, her expression guarded. 'I knew something of what happened back then, but of course one never learns the full story, just snippets of gossip here and there.'

Julie decided it wouldn't hurt to tell Peggy, for she knew it wouldn't go any further, and wanted to put the record straight so she'd see Eileen in a better light.

'So, you see,' she finished some time later, 'she understood completely how I felt when I thought William would be taken away, and I'll always be grateful to her for being so supportive.'

Peggy mashed out her cigarette. 'I'm glad you've made it up with her,' she said. 'Family is so important – especially these days.'

Julie washed and dried her supper things, collected a cardigan in case it got cold later, and hurried off with a cheery wave.

Peggy eased her back as she pushed up from the table and headed down the cellar steps to the garden, where Mrs Finch was dozing in one of the elderly deckchairs Jim had resurrected from the shed at the first sign of a proper summer.

The early evening was warm and scented with lavender, rosemary and thyme, which Ron had planted in a big pot by the back door, and she could hear music coming from a nearby wireless. Ron was at the Anchor, Jim was in his projection room at the Odeon, and the girls had arranged to meet Cissy for a drink in the town. Cissy would be coming home for the night, which was a rare occurrence these days – and although she was delighted to have her home, she was rather nervous about it, for she and Jim had decided it would be the perfect opportunity to tell everyone about the baby.

She sank into one of the other deckchairs and stared up at the sky, wondering what Cissy's reaction would be to her news. Jim had promised to be with her when she told her, but she had a nasty feeling Cissy would blow a fuse.

Mrs Finch snorted in her sleep and Peggy smiled. The old dear seemed able to doze off at the drop of a hat, and she envied her. This baby was a lively one already, especially at night when she was just aching for sleep. She ran her hand softly over the small, neat swell of her stomach which still lay hidden beneath her voluminous wrap-round apron, her thoughts turning to Julie and Eileen.

It was clear that Eileen had been liberal with the truth, telling Julie only the things that would put her in a good light and evoke sympathy. In fact there was a whole lot more to that story, a much darker side that revealed how cunning and self-seeking Eileen Harris really was. And poor Rosie Braithwaite had been caught right in the middle of it.

Eventually Peggy roused Mrs Finch from her doze and they went indoors as the warmth seeped away from the evening. Switching on the wireless so it would warm up in time for the nine o'clock news, she went upstairs to check on William.

He was still rather warm, and his sleep was restless, but his breathing was even, so it seemed it was just the weather getting to him. She drew the thin blanket over him and checked the window and the blackout curtains were closed before leaving the door ajar and returning to the kitchen.

'I still can't get over not having Rose Margaret asleep in the pram,' she said to Mrs Finch as they settled down with a cup of tea after listening to the news. 'The house seems empty without her, and I'm sure little William misses her.'

Mrs Finch raised a grey brow and regarded her over the top of her glasses. 'By my reckoning,' she said dryly, 'the spare pram won't be empty for long.'

Peggy put her hand protectively over her stomach and blushed.

Mrs Finch chuckled. 'I might be a bit deaf,' she said, 'but I'm not blind, Peggy Reilly. When is it due?'

'Early December,' she breathed. 'But how did you guess?'

'I caught sight of you and Jim one morning around the time Anne left for Somerset. You both had a look of intensity about you, and he rested his hand on your stomach so tenderly that it left little doubt.' She smiled happily. 'I was waiting for you to tell everyone, but when you didn't, I thought it best not to say anything.'

'I wanted to keep it to myself for a bit,' Peggy admitted.

Mrs Finch cocked her head, her expression concerned and kindly. 'How do you feel about it, Peggy? Must have come as a bit of a shock?'

Peggy giggled. 'You can say that again,' she spluttered. 'But once I'd got used to the idea, I realised how lucky I am. There's not many women my age who get another chance at this, and I aim to enjoy every last moment of it.'

'What's all this about getting a second chance, Mum?' Cissy appeared in the doorway and plonked herself down in a kitchen chair, shedding her gas-mask box and handbag on the floor beside her. 'What have you done? Won a sweepstake or something?'

Peggy was startled by Cissy's arrival and immediately worried about just how much she'd heard. 'You're home early,' she said dazedly. 'Where are the others?'

'On their way,' Cissy replied impatiently. 'Come on, Mum. Spill the beans. You're obviously excited about something, and you and Grandma Finch look like cats that have swallowed a canary.'

Peggy glanced at Mrs Finch, who gave a small shrug. 'It's up to you, dear, but it would probably be best if you told her first. She is family, after all.'

Peggy licked her lips as Cissy leaned towards her, her face alight with curiosity and excitement. 'Your father and I—' she began.

'Yes,' said Cissy impatiently.

Peggy couldn't look at her daughter, for she was suddenly terrified of what her reaction might be. She placed her hand on the swell of her belly. 'I'm having a baby,' she said.

There was a stunned silence, and when Peggy

445

dared to look at Cissy, she saw nothing but horror in her expression. 'It was as much a surprise to me as it obviously is to you,' she said hurriedly, reaching for her hand. 'But there's nothing I can do about it. Please be happy for me, Cissy.'

Cissy pulled away and stood up. 'I can't believe you could do something like that at your age,' she snapped. 'It's disgusting. And what will all my friends think? I'll be the laughing stock of the office when they find out.'

'Cissy, dear, do pull yourself together and think of someone other than yourself,' ordered Mrs Finch in a tone that brooked no argument. 'Your mother has enough to deal with, without you having hysterics.'

'But she's too old to be in the family way,' Cissy stormed, the angry tears glistening in her eyes. 'She's a grandmother, for heaven's sake, and it's not decent.'

'Now you're sounding like your Aunt Doris,' said Peggy firmly. 'Sit down, Cissy, and stop behaving like a four-year-old.'

Cissy slumped back into her chair, all the careful elegance and contrived maturity draining out of her as she folded her arms and looked petulantly at her mother. 'You've spoiled everything,' she muttered. 'James won't want me now, and my friends will laugh at me.'

'Then they're not worth the effort,' Peggy said mildly. 'Real friends will understand and support you – and if James is half the young man I think he is, then he'll stick around too.'

She leaned across and took Cissy's hands again, determined to get through to her. 'I'm sorry if you find all this embarrassing, but there's nothing I can do about it. Come December you'll have a baby brother or sister, and I'm hoping by then you'll accept the situation and learn to love it as we will.'

'She's told you then,' stated Fran as she came into the room, followed by Rita and Suzy.

Cissy lifted her reddened eyes, the accusation clear in her expression. 'You've already told them? How could you do that, Mum? I'm your daughter and—'

'Of course she didn't,' interrupted Suzy firmly. 'But we're nurses, Cissy. Me and Fran and Julie have known for ages and were just waiting for Peggy to say something.'

Rita came and sat down next to her childhood friend. 'Your mum's probably just as confused and shell-shocked as you, Cissy,' she said quietly. 'But we all think it's wonderful news, and hope that you will too.'

Cissy gripped Rita's fingers as her gaze took in all three girls. 'Really?' she breathed. 'You're not just saying that to be kind?'

Rita pushed back the halo of dark curls from her face and laughed. 'Of course not. We're your friends, and we love and admire Peggy as if she was our mother. Don't make it harder for her, Cissy. She's going to need all the support she can get over the coming months.'

Peggy watched the different expressions flit across her youngest daughter's face, and blessed Rita for her common sense and kindness.

Cissy sniffed back her tears and carefully blotted her face with a handkerchief before giving Peggy a wavering smile. 'I suppose I'll get used to the idea,' she said, 'but it's all a bit much to take in at the moment.'

'That's all right, darling,' Peggy said softly. 'It's taken me a while too, but as long as you think you can come to terms with it, then I'm sure we can find some way of getting through this together.' She looked round at the happy faces. 'How about we all have a cup of cocoa to celebrate?'

Cissy nodded and pursed her lips. 'Can we run to an extra spoon of sugar in it, do you think, and perhaps the cream off the top of the milk?'

Peggy laughed. Cissy would never change, but at heart she was a kind, loving girl who would no doubt love this baby as much as she adored her young brothers. 'I think we can manage that,' she replied happily.

Julie returned from Eileen's to discover a party was going on in Peggy's kitchen. It seemed she'd finally decided to tell everyone about the baby, and Jim was waxing lyrical about how clever and proud he was.

She smiled as she accepted the cup of cocoa and the rather stale digestive biscuit. Peggy's pregnancy had been the worst-kept secret in the house, what with Jim strutting about like a cockerel, and Peggy swathed in loose dresses and that voluminous apron of hers. Ron was the only one who hadn't cottoned on to the situation, but then he was so taken up with Rosie at the Anchor, that a bomb could drop right through the roof and he wouldn't notice.

She sipped the hot, sweet cocoa, noting that Cissy looked a bit put out by the whole thing, but then she had an idea that Peggy's youngest daughter enjoyed being the centre of attention, and that her little nose had been knocked rather out of joint by it all.

'I'll just go and check on William,' she murmured to Peggy. 'Has he been all right?'

Peggy nodded. 'He was still a bit warm when I looked in on him earlier, but he hasn't stirred all evening.'

Julie left the kitchen and hurried upstairs. In the dim light of the nursery lamp, she tiptoed over to the cot and peeked in. William was lying on his back, arms and legs splayed, the light blanket kicked away.

She felt his head and frowned. He was still a bit too warm for her liking, and his breathing sounded slightly laboured. Perhaps he was going down with a summer cold – there were plenty of them about at the moment.

She went and fetched the thermometer from her

nursing bag and tucked it under his arm. Checking his pulse as she waited, her concern rose, for it was far too rapid. Retrieving the thermometer, she felt her own pulse stutter. He definitely had a temperature, and although it wasn't dangerously high, it would need monitoring through the night.

Leaving the bedroom, she hurried into the bathroom, grabbed his flannel, and filled a metal basin with cool water. He was stirring as she returned to him, his eyelashes fluttering against his cheeks as he squirmed and whimpered in his sleep. 'Shhh. It's all right, darling,' she murmured, gently placing the cool flannel on his forehead. 'Mummy just needs to cool you down.'

Peggy came into the bedroom some time later and approached the cot where Julie was still bathing him with the cool flannel. 'You've been gone a long time,' she whispered. 'Is something the matter?'

Julie told her about his temperature. 'If I can't get it down, I'll have to phone the doctor,' she whispered back. 'His breathing's not good either, and I suspect he's got a cold coming.'

'Do you want me to sit with him while you get ready for bed?'

'Thanks, Peg.' She handed her the flannel and bowl. 'I won't be long.' Julie hurried into the bathroom, washed and changed into her nightclothes and hurried back. William had had colds before and they hadn't had any lasting effect, but this felt different somehow, and it worried her.

'You get off to bed, Peggy. I'll take over here,' she whispered.

'If you need me in the night . . .'

Julie nodded. 'I know. Go to bed, look after yourself and that baby you're carrying, and stop worrying about everyone else,' she said rather sternly. 'I'm sure your doctor told you to take things easy.'

Peggy grinned. 'He's an old fusspot, and I'm sure he means well, but you know me, Julie. I can't bear not to be at the centre of things.'

Julie gave her a swift hug and then turned her towards the door. 'Go to bed,' she ordered. When Peggy had reluctantly closed the bedroom door behind her, Julie went back to William.

His breathing was definitely laboured, and his temperature, although stable, was still too high. She put a pillow beneath the mattress so he wasn't lying flat, peeled off his vest and drew a chair up to the side of the cot. It could be a long night, she thought as she squeezed out the flannel and began to wash him down gently, but she didn't dare sleep.

It was two in the morning, and Julie must have dozed off. She opened her eyes, startled awake by the sound of William's rasping breath and phlegmy cough. Taking his temperature, she checked his pulse. Both gave her cause for alarm, and she ran swiftly downstairs and dialled the surgery.

The ringing seemed to go on for hours, and she

was about to abandon the call and ring the hospital when, finally, someone picked up at the other end.

'Cliffe Surgery. Dr Michael speaking,' said the sleep-heavy voice.

'It's Julie Harris,' she said urgently. 'William isn't at all well. He has a cough, his breathing is irregular, his pulse is rapid, and his temperature is creeping up.'

'I'll be about ten minutes.'

Julie replaced the receiver and ran back up the stairs to find Peggy standing by William's cot. 'Michael's on his way,' she said.

'I'll make a pot of tea and wait for him downstairs.' Peggy buttoned her dressing gown. 'Is there anything else I can do?'

Julie shook her head, unable to speak for the terror that was threatening to swallow her. William was clearly a very sick baby, and with his heart condition, it could even be fatal. The thought of losing him now was something she didn't dare contemplate.

She swiftly changed into a cotton dress and cardigan, and was just lacing her shoes when she heard Michael's car pull up outside. Julie finished tying the laces as he and Peggy exchanged words in the hall, and was standing in the bedroom doorway waiting for him as he reached the landing.

'Thank you for coming so quickly,' she whispered, not wanting to wake the rest of the house.

'No problem,' he muttered as he strode into the bedroom and made straight for the cot. Despite her terrible anxiety, she noted he must have dressed quickly, for his shirt was hanging out of his trousers, and he was wearing odd shoes. His face was haggard with weariness, his hair flopping over his eyes as he swiftly examined William and fired a barrage of questions at her.

Julie was on tenterhooks as she waited for him to finish, and when he turned from the cot and looked at her, she knew her worst fears had been realised.

'He seems to have a chest infection,' he said, folding his stethoscope into his medical bag. 'Best I take him straight to the hospital in my car. Would you get him ready while I phone and warn them we're coming?'

She stared up at him, unable to move or speak for the fear that tore through her.

'It's all right,' he said, his brown eyes kindly as he looked down at her. 'The infection isn't serious, but with William's heart condition, it's best not to take any chances.' He edged towards the door. 'Wrap him up warmly,' he advised. 'It's quite chilly out there.'

Julie heard him run down the stairs. Heard him say something to Peggy and the single 'ting' of the telephone as he lifted the receiver and asked the operator to put him through to hospital admissions. She moved as if in a dream – a nightmare – and began to prepare William for the short drive to the hospital.

As she carried him downstairs she was all too aware of how floppy he'd become, and how dry and hot his skin was. The infection had clearly taken hold and was now rampaging through him.

With only a hint of a smile at Peggy, she almost ran out of the house after Michael. He gunned the engine as soon as she'd shut the door, did a screeching three-point turn and then put his foot down and raced them down a deserted Camden Road.

They came to a skidding halt on the gravel outside the main doors and, before Julie could clamber out, Michael had snatched William from her arms and was running up the steps to where Mr Watson was waiting.

She slammed the car door and ran after them, but the two men were already almost out of sight as they headed down the long corridor to the special baby ward. Her heart was in her mouth, her fear a terrible, clawing thing in her gut as she tried to catch up with them.

They clattered through swing doors and disappeared into the special side ward, and as Julie finally managed to reach them, they were already surrounded by nurses, busy at work on William.

Michael turned. 'Wait outside, Julie,' he said sternly. 'You can see him when we've finished here.'

'He's not going to . . .'

'Not if I can help it,' smiled Mr Watson. 'Now, please, leave us to get on.'

Julie slowly backed away through the doors and stood watching them through the window until the nurse drew the curtains around the bed. She sank onto one of the hard chairs in the long corridor and stared at the blank wall in front of her, determined not to shed a tear or lose control. William needed her to be strong, needed her to fulfil the promise she'd made on that awful day when Franny had died. She was all he had, and she couldn't fail him now.

Time stretched interminably as she sat there in that almost deserted corridor. Nurses went in and out of the ward, each giving her a cheerful smile and encouraging her to drink tea while she waited. But none of them would tell her what was happening inside that little room, saying only that the doctors would tell her as soon as they'd finished.

She'd set aside the third cup of unwanted tea when she heard the tap of familiar footsteps approaching. 'Oh, Peggy,' she sighed. 'I'm so glad you're here. But you should be in bed resting.'

Peggy patted her hand and sat down. 'I couldn't possibly rest knowing how worried you must be.' She dug into her string bag and pulled out a flask. 'I made tea, but I see you've already had some,' she said, eyeing the discarded cup and saucer. 'Never mind. We'll have it later.' She took Julie's hand and gave it an encouraging squeeze. 'Do you know anything yet?'

Julie shook her head. 'No one is telling me anything, and I haven't seen either of the doctors since they went in there.' She gave an exasperated sigh. 'I hate hospitals,' she hissed. 'They're like gentlemen's clubs, the doctors all ganging up on us, thinking we're just silly women and don't know our arse from our elbows.'

Peggy giggled. 'That's it, Julie. You let off some steam, girl. It'll make you feel better if nothing else.'

Julie grinned shamefacedly. 'You can take a girl out of the East End, but you can never take the East End out of the girl,' she said softly.

'Do you miss it?'

'More than I like to admit sometimes,' she replied. 'It's where I was born, what I know and understand. Being down here is like being on holiday – not real, somehow.'

'Do you think you'll go back?'

'Once I know it's safe to take William. He's a Londoner, too, and he should know where he came from.'

The doors swung open and Julie shot to her feet as Michael and Mr Watson came into the corridor. 'How is he?'

'He has a mild chest infection which we can clear with medication,' said Mr Watson. 'But his heart is definitely struggling with the build-up of fluid in his lungs, so we need to monitor him closely over the next few days.'

'But he will get over this?' she asked anxiously.

'We have every reason to believe so,' he replied. 'You may see him for a few minutes, and then I suggest you go home and come back during visiting time tomorrow afternoon.' He looked at his watch and smiled. 'Or rather, this afternoon.'

Michael stepped forward and smiled down at her rather stiffly. 'Do as he says, Sister Harris, and don't worry about your rounds. I'll get Eunice and Fay to take them over while I sort out the two surgeries with Father.'

Julie and Peggy watched as the two doctors strode down the corridor. 'I'll wait here until you're ready to come home,' said Peggy quietly. 'Go and see that boy, and give him a kiss from me.'

Julie went into the side ward, smiled wanly at the sister in charge and went to William's cot. He was in an oxygen tent, just as he'd been when he was born. Propped up by bolster pillows into almost a sitting position, he had a drip feed in his arm, and a huge machine by the side of his cot monitored his heartbeat. She couldn't touch him, couldn't kiss him – not while he was encased in the oxygen tent – so she had to satisfy herself by just gazing down at him, willing him to find the strength to fight the infection and get better.

Peggy was waiting for her as she'd promised and, as the first light of a new day began to filter over the horizon, they slowly walked arm-in-arm in companionable, thoughtful silence towards Beach View.

Chapter Twenty-one

As Peggy mopped the hall floor on that hot August morning, her thoughts drifted over the last three traumatic weeks. Julie had been spending every spare moment she had sitting by William's bedside, for the little chap had rallied at first, and then faltered to the point when they'd all thought they might lose him. His recovery had been slow and painful, but he seemed finally to be on the mend, and poor Julie was so exhausted, she barely knew what day it was.

Peggy had been most relieved to hear that Dr Sayers had at last found another two volunteer medical aides, and a retired local nurse who was willing to step in during this crisis and share the workload. However, Julie's midwifery skills were still in demand, and both Peggy and Julie dreaded the telephone ringing in the middle of the night, for it meant another few precious hours of sleep were lost.

Peggy was very proud of how everyone at Beach View had rallied round and supported Julie. Even Fran and Suzy, who worked long hours at the hospital, had given up their days off to cover Julie's rounds when it was thought William might not pull through. Poor Julie, it had been a roller-coaster ride and Peggy's heart went out to her – and to dear little William. Life could be cruel, she thought with a sigh. You never knew what lay in store until it bit you on the bum, and Julie had definitely had more than her share of heartache and worry this year.

Peggy continued to mop the tiles on the hall floor without much enthusiasm, for the baby was squirming restlessly and pressing on her bladder, and she felt hot, tired and fat. Finally abandoning the mop and bucket, she traipsed upstairs to the bathroom for the umpteenth time that morning. She'd forgotten the inconveniences of pregnancy – how tired and ungainly it made her feel, what with the need to pee every five minutes, and the difficulties involved with cutting her toenails or bending to pick anything up.

Coming back down minutes later she heard the rap of the front door knocker and stumbled on the loose stair carpet in her hurry to answer it. She grabbed the banister and stood for a moment to quell the rush of fear that made her heart pound. She could have gone from top to bottom, and with the house deserted . . . It wasn't something she wanted to contemplate.

'Damn thing,' she muttered as she plodded on. 'I've told Jim time and again to fix it – but will he listen? Men!'

The rap came again, more commanding and insistent. 'All right, all right, I'm coming, for goodness' sake,' she shouted as she reached the hall and wrenched the door open.

Her snooty sister Doris was standing on the doorstep, her expression stony beneath the broad brim of her white hat, and Peggy was sorely tempted to slam the door in her face and run for the hills. But Peggy was made of sterner stuff and she'd known this moment would come sooner or later. 'I wondered when you'd turn up,' she muttered.

Doris was resplendent in a beautifully cut linen dress, high-heeled two-tone shoes and a matching handbag. Gold jewellery glistened at her neck and wrist and in her ears, and it was obvious she'd just been to the hairdresser's. Her make-up was flawless as usual, and her nails freshly manicured. For a woman fast approaching her fiftieth birthday, she looked very well indeed, but then Doris was a pampered wife who lived in a big house in Havelock Gardens with a girl to do the rough work and a husband with an open wallet.

She stepped into Peggy's hall, her silence eloquent as her gaze flitted over the swell beneath Peggy's wrap-round apron.

Peggy saw that look and steeled herself. Doris had a way of making her feel inferior, but today, she vowed, she would not let her get under her skin. 'We've run out of storage space, so the dining room's a bit of a glory hole at the moment,' she said. 'You'll have to put up with sitting in the kitchen.'

'I have no wish to sit in your kitchen,' Doris

replied haughtily. 'What I have come to discuss can be said here without your dubious household listening in.'

Peggy dug her hands into her apron pockets. 'Everyone's out, so just say your piece, Doris, and get it over with.'

Doris drew herself up to her full height and looked down her patrician nose. 'I think it's disgraceful that a woman of your age should parade herself about in that condition,' she said coldly. 'It's unseemly and has caused me no end of embarrassment.'

Peggy adopted the same tone. 'Why should it embarrass *you*? You're not the one who's pregnant.'

'I should think not,' Doris snorted. 'The idea is appalling.'

Peggy held her gaze. 'Appalling? How can something so natural be appalling?'

'It's not decent to be carrying on with Jim at your age,' Doris muttered.

Peggy laughed. 'What Jim and I do in the privacy of our bedroom is none of your business, Doris.' She saw the look of distaste on her older sister's face and couldn't resist taunting her. 'Jim's a lusty man, and we enjoy a good cuddle.'

Doris actually shuddered. 'It's disgusting,' she hissed. 'Edward and I gave up that sort of behaviour years ago.'

'No wonder poor old Ted looks so miserable all the time,' Peggy retorted.

She waved Peggy's words away with a sweep of

her manicured hand. 'So, what are you going to do about this?'

Peggy frowned. 'I'm going to give birth to it, what else do you expect?'

'Of course you are,' Doris said sharply. 'What I mean is, are you going to continue flaunting yourself around Cliffehaven, or will you do the decent thing and stay at home until it's born?'

'I've got too many commitments to be shut away like a nun,' replied Peggy firmly as she opened the front door. 'Now, if you've quite finished, I have better things to do than stand here being talked at by you.'

'I have spoken to my friend Lady Chalmondley, and she agrees with me that it might be better if you didn't continue with your work at the WVS centre until after you've had it.'

Peggy stared back at her in amazement. 'Your Lady Chalmondley might think she's in charge, but she's just a small cog in a very big wheel. I'll carry on until Head Office tells me otherwise.'

Doris sniffed and stepped out of the door. 'You will live to regret being so rebellious, Margaret,' she said sternly. 'One has to be careful what one does in such a small town, and I do not appreciate you bringing my family into ill-repute.'

Peggy had had enough. 'Do you know what, Doris? I don't care. Go home and put your own house in order before you come round here sticking your oar in.' She took a step towards her. 'And while you're at it, give Ted some attention for a change instead of using him as your private bank. A man needs his comforts, Doris, and if he doesn't get them at home, he'll look elsewhere.'

'How *dare* you?' Doris hissed. 'Edward is an honourable man who wouldn't dream—'

'Goodbye, Doris.' Peggy slammed the door and immediately regretted her outburst. It had been unkind to say those things about poor old Ted. He was a nice, rather boring man who'd been middle-aged before he'd reached thirty, and probably hadn't got the wit or the inclination to seek that sort of comfort at home, let alone elsewhere. But if the boot had been on the other foot, Doris wouldn't have hesitated to say such things, and Peggy was almost able to justify her instant of nastiness.

'Oh, well,' she sighed. 'Perhaps after today she'll cut me off completely and leave me in peace.' But as she made the long trek back to the bathroom yet again, she knew she wouldn't. Doris delighted in her one-upmanship, and simply couldn't resist flaunting her money and so-called status every time she came round. Rich, she might be, and well connected with all those seats on charity commissions run by snooty women like Lady Chalmondley, but she had nothing else to occupy her. There were no grandchildren to spoil, her son had left home to work for some government office, and Ted was either immersed in his work as manager of the big Home and Colonial Stores in the High Street, or out on the golf course. Peggy suspected that, beneath all that powder and paint, Doris was an unhappy and unfulfilled woman and, despite everything, she couldn't help feeling rather sorry for her.

Rosie had packed a picnic basket and, once she'd closed the pub for the afternoon, she and Ron had tramped up the hill with Harvey to sit on the headland and enjoy the lovely weather.

They had spread out the moth-eaten tartan blanket and eaten well, for there were paste sandwiches, tomatoes from Ron's garden, a couple of sausages, a bit of cheese, some crackers and a handful of ripe plums they'd picked from Lord Cliffe's abandoned fruit trees on the way up here. Bottles of beer washed it all down delightfully, and now they were leaning back on the blanket, sated and at ease while Harvey dashed about chasing things in the long grass.

'It's lovely up here,' she murmured, taking in the bleached blue of the sky and the way the sun glittered on the sea. 'I don't know why I've never come before.'

'You've been too busy running that pub,' he said round the stem of his pipe. 'Besides,' he added with a smile, 'those high heels you usually wear aren't exactly the best footwear for hiking.'

She laughed and wriggled her feet in the sandshoes Ron had bought her that morning from the little shop that still stocked buckets and spades and anything else one might need for a day at the seaside.

Made of white canvas and rubber, they laced up to the ankle and were the sort of thing children wore on the beach and in the rock pools. They were a far cry from the glamorous shoes she usually wore.

'I never thought I'd see the day,' she replied. 'But although they're hardly the height of fashion and not terribly flattering to a girl's legs, they are extremely comfortable.'

'Your legs look good in everything,' he said, admiring them stretched out on the rug beside him. Rosie was wearing white shorts, a checked shirt, sunglasses and a big sun hat. With the sun warming her skin to a golden tan, and the soft breeze ruffling her hair, she looked young, beautiful and carefree.

He gazed down past his own baggy khaki shorts to the sturdy knees that stuck out above long brown socks and boots. He'd seen worse during the summers before the war, when the tourists came and flaunted their skinny white bodies to all and sundry, their legs like bits of celery sticking out from under their shorts.

Rosie leaned back on her elbows and watched Harvey flop panting in the shade of vibrantly yellow gorse bush. 'I wish I had a dog,' she murmured. 'They're good company, aren't they?'

'I'll get you one, if you want. There's always pups needing good homes.'

She shook her head. 'It wouldn't be fair to take one on. I don't have time to exercise it, not with the pub and everything – and I'd want a big dog, not one of those tiny yapping things.'

He stretched out beside her and tipped the brim of his hat over his eyes to shield them from the sun. 'What made you take on the pub in the first place? It's unusual for a single woman to get a licence.'

She rolled onto her stomach and began to pluck at a loose thread in the blanket. 'James and I took over his parents' pub in Chippenham when they decided to move up to Scotland and open a small hotel. I was given the licence to run it on my own after he'd been admitted to the asylum, but it wasn't the same.'

She gave a little sigh. 'Too many memories, I suppose – lost dreams, and plans that would never be realised. But I was still young, only in my thirties, and knew I didn't want to give up the life – it was something I was good at, and enjoyed. So when someone made me a more than fair offer on the place I came down here and was lucky enough to find the Anchor for sale.'

'But why here, when you could have had the pick of places?'

'I used to spend my childhood holidays here and thought it would be nice to live by the sea for a change.'

His admiration grew. Rosie was a tough wee woman, and no mistake – it was little wonder that he loved her. 'That was a brave thing to do when you were still so young. It couldn't have been easy, with no family or friends to support you.'

'My dad died in the last war, but Mum helped a bit when I first came down. She's been crippled with arthritis for years, and I see her when I can, but it's difficult because she's had to move in with my brother's family along the coast, and I don't really get on with them.'

'I didn't realise you had a brother,' he said, looking at her from beneath his hat brim.

She rolled back over and sat up, hugging her knees, her expressive face hidden by the dark glasses and dipping hat. 'We aren't close and he rarely bothers to call in unless he's after something,' she replied flatly. 'It's best I keep him at arm's length, anyway. He's always been the black sheep of the family, and a liability for someone in my line of business.'

Ron sat up abruptly and pushed his hat back so he could see her properly. 'Have I ever met him?' he asked quietly.

She lit a cigarette and blew smoke into the warm, still air, her gaze fixed to the panorama of sea and cliff spread before them. 'Once or twice.'

Ron's suspicions were roused. Surely it couldn't possibly be true, not his Rosie linked to that particular worm? He dreaded asking the question that rang in his head – dreaded what the answer might be – but he had to know. 'What's his name, Rosie?'

She remained silent for a long while and then

looked at her watch. 'I think you already know, Ron, and I've said enough. It's time we were getting back.' She reached for the hamper.

Ron stilled her by taking her hands. 'Rosie, darlin' girl, there's no shame in it, and although I've never been one to hide my abhorrence for that man, I want you to know that I would never let it come between you and me.'

She sank back onto her heels and hung her head. 'But I am ashamed, Ron,' she murmured. 'He's done some terrible, wicked things in the past, and as far as I know, is still up to no good.'

'You're not responsible for your brother, Rosie,' he said urgently. 'You're a fine, respectable, beautiful woman and should hold your head up with pride.'

She finally looked back at him, her lovely smile tremulous as she kissed his cheek. 'I do love you, Ron,' she murmured. 'And thanks for being so understanding. Having Tommy Findlay as a brother has never been easy, but I feel I can cope with anything now I have you.'

Julie had dashed straight to the hospital when she'd finished her round and, although she was sticky and uncomfortable in this heat after cycling all over town, she didn't want to waste time going back to Beach View to wash and change out of her uniform.

The ward was hushed as usual as she pushed

through the double doors, but she'd got to know the nurses very well over the past three weeks, and they greeted her with friendly smiles. 'How's he doing today?' she asked.

Sister Dora Black grinned as she looked up from her patients' notes. 'He's holding his own, and his temperature's almost back to normal. Why don't you go and sit down, and I'll get one of the nurses to make you a cup of tea?'

'That would be lovely,' Julie sighed. 'You're ever so kind, Dora.'

'We look after our own in here,' Dora said softly. 'Go and sit before you fall down. You look all in.'

'It's been a busy day, and I was up half the night delivering twins.'

'In that case you deserve a biscuit to go with that tea,' she said before bustling away.

Julie sank into the chair beside William's cot. His tiny hand lay like a budding water-lily on the white blanket, and she gently placed her finger in the palm, feeling his fingers curl round it as if he knew it gave her comfort.

The oxygen tent had been removed at the beginning of the week, but there was still a drip feed going into his arm which supplied the drugs necessary for his recovery, and the heart monitoring machine continued to beep reassuringly. He'd lost weight since being in here, the glow of health dimmed by the fever he'd fought so courageously, but the chart at the end of the cot showed he was indeed holding his own, and for the first time in weeks, Julie began to believe he would get through this.

She always felt a bit useless, just sitting here hour after hour while the other nurses tended their small patients, for there was nothing much she could do. But she was grateful they turned a blind eye to her coming in outside visiting hours and staying for as long as she wanted.

'Here's the tea I promised,' murmured Dora. 'And I managed to pinch a couple of custard creams from the packet Nurse Giddings hides in the cupboard.' She shot a glance at the overweight nurse. 'Think of it as saving her another few inches,' she added with a gleam of humour in her eyes.

Julie smiled back at her and guiltily ate the biscuits, savouring their creamy sweetness. She hadn't had a custard cream since the outbreak of war, and she wondered fleetingly where on earth Nurse Giddings had managed to buy them.

The bell for visiting time echoed through the hospital and the doors opened to admit a stream of parents and grandparents into the ward. Julie watched them pour in and returned their greetings, for over the weeks she'd come to know most of them, and the atmosphere in the ward, although tense, had a family feel about it.

She was about to turn her attention back to William when she saw Peggy come through the doors and waddle towards her. Her expression was businesslike, and there was no warm smile. Julie was at once alert.

'What's the matter, Peggy?' she asked as she gave up her chair.

'You're not going to believe it,' she panted as she settled her gas-mask box and handbag on her lap. 'Let me get my breath back, and I'll tell you.'

'I hope you didn't walk all the way here,' said Julie sternly. 'You know what the doctor said about overdoing things.'

'Don't fuss. Alf the butcher gave me a lift in his truck,' Peggy replied impatiently.

Julie waited anxiously for her to get her breath back, but her alarm wasn't eased by Peggy suddenly gripping her hand.

'Now I don't want you to get upset, Julie,' Peggy said quietly, 'but something happened today, and I wanted to warn you so it wouldn't come as too much of a shock.'

'Peggy, you're frightening me. I have no idea what you're on about. It's not the baby, is it?'

'Nothing like that,' Peggy said dismissively. She gripped harder on Julie's fingers. 'Listen, I haven't got much time and they'll be here any minute . . .' Her voice faded into silence as her gaze was drawn to the opening doors and three people who hovered there.

Julie followed her gaze and felt the world stop spinning as she watched the man separate from the middle-aged couple, and navigate his awkward way down the ward on crutches. His left leg had been amputated above the knee, his face was lined and

471

much older than she remembered, and there were streaks of grey in his brown hair – but she would have recognised him anywhere.

She stood frozen to the spot as his dark gaze held her. 'Bill?' she gasped through her fingers. 'Bill, is it really you?'

His smile was warm and slightly mocking as he grabbed a spare chair and sank into it. 'Aye, lass,' he murmured, 'it's me reet enough, though bits of me are still buried somewhere in North Africa.'

Julie didn't know what to say. She was still in shock.

He laid the crutches on the floor and leaned towards the cot. 'And this must be William,' he sighed. 'Eee, lad, I've waited a long while to see thee.' He reached out a broad hand and placed the tip of a finger in William's palm as his eyes filled with tears. 'I can see Franny in him,' he said hoarsely.

'Yes,' she managed. 'He has her smile too.'

There was a long moment of silence, and Peggy struggled out of the chair. 'I'll leave you to it,' she murmured, and hurried off before anyone could reply.

Bill looked up at Julie and reached for her hand. 'Sit down, lass, afore ye drop.'

'It's such a shock seeing you,' she said as she plumped down into the chair Peggy had just vacated. 'We were told you were dead.'

'Aye, I know. Didn't you get my letter?' As Julie shook her head he gave her a sympathetic smile.

'Never mind, I'm here now, and there's plenty of time to catch up on things.' He looked down at the crutches, his smile fading. 'Happen I'm not going anywhere in a hurry.'

Julie's gaze drifted to the large, manly finger still coiled into William's tiny fist. The pain in her heart was almost unbearable as she realised she was about to lose the baby she had come to think of as her own. Tears pricked as all the hopes and dreams of their future together died.

He must have read the agony in her expression, for he patted her hand. 'Eee, lass,' he said gruffly. 'I'm reet sorry if I've caused you trouble, but he's my son – mine and Franny's. He's what I fought for, what I lost me leg for. Happen it's only reet he comes back with me to Yorkshire where he belongs.'

She understood, of course she did, but that didn't make it any easier. 'Who will look after him there?' she asked tearfully. 'I don't want that Charity going anywhere near him.'

'No need to mither, lass,' he said reassuringly. 'I heard what she said, and told her to say nowt more.' His brown eyes twinkled with humour. 'I'm not like me mam, Julie. I speaks me mind and won't tek Charity's bullying. She'll not be looking after babby.'

'Who then?' she persisted.

'Me, and me mam and dad. We'll bring him oop on farm and teach him to be a good Yorkshireman.' He looked down with a soft smile as William stirred in his sleep. 'We'll soon have him fit and strong again, and he'll grow oop knowing he's loved.'

'I love him too,' she said. 'From almost the moment he was born, and I can't bear the thought I might never see him again.'

His eyes widened in surprise. 'Why, lass, you'll always be welcome to visit. We won't let him forget you, you can be sure of that.'

Julie knew she was clutching at straws, but she couldn't stop herself. 'But will your parents be able to cope with such a young baby? His health is delicate and—'

'There you go, mithering again,' he said softly. 'And there's nowt to fret thee, lass. You'll see.' He looked over her shoulder and beckoned. 'Me parents come down with me on train. Happen they've waited long enough to be introduced to their grandson.'

Julie turned as the middle-aged couple walked hesitantly towards her. He was tall and broad-shouldered, his face weathered by the elements. She was small and round like a cottage loaf, with apple cheeks and bright eyes. They both looked a little self-conscious in what Julie suspected were their best clothes, but they certainly bore no resemblance to the dreadful Charity.

'How do,' said Bill's father. He was clearly a man of few words, and he turned away, clasped his roughened hands behind his back and leaned over the cot. He nodded with approval. 'Seems a right little bobby dazzler,' he muttered.

This was clearly regarded as huge praise, for Bill's smile lit up his face.

Bill's mother turned from the cot and placed her hand on Julie's arm. 'You're to call me Edith,' she said softly, 'and you're not to fret, lass. I'll look after babby as if he were me own. I promise thee that.'

Julie looked into her sweet face and knew that William would indeed be loved and cared for by these good people. Yet the agony of knowing her time with him would soon be over was too much to bear, and she was finding it almost impossible to control the tears that threatened to fall.

'Eee, lass, I know how painful this be,' Edith crooned as she stroked her arm. 'I thought I'd lost my boy too – but by some miracle he survived, and although 'tis hard for you to let babby go, our Bill has earned the right to raise his son.'

Julie's battle with her tears was lost when Edith put her arm about her and drew her to her motherly bosom. The dam broke and she sobbed against her, her heart breaking.

Chapter Twenty-two

From that day on Julie began to withdraw from William. She found it almost impossibly distressing not to go to the hospital and sit with him, but she knew that if she faltered, it would only make their parting harder. She had to learn to live without him – but every hour of the day felt like forever, and her dreams were full of him.

Peggy, bless her, had understood what she was going through, and had quietly removed the cot from her room while she was at work, and placed the lovely pram out of sight in the dining room. The bedroom and hall seemed so empty without them, but it was the next step towards accepting that William was already gone.

'I'll take the pram back to the WVS centre,' said Peggy. 'Bill won't be able to take it with him on the train, and I'm sure someone will appreciate it.'

'Why don't you keep it, Peg?'

Peggy smiled. 'The old pram's still got a lot of use in it, and it's a bit of a family heirloom. It was good enough for the others, so it will do for this little one.'

Julie folded her arms tightly round her waist,

resisting the overwhelming need to rush into the dining room and touch the pram one last time. The memories of wheeling William along the prom and down the High Street were almost too hard to bear, and she realised then that every corner of Beach View Boarding House was redolent with the echoes of the few happy months she'd spent with him here.

'You've decided to go back to London, haven't you?' asked Peggy quietly.

Julie nodded. 'I need to go home now I'm on me own again.' She regarded Peggy through her tears. 'You've been a diamond, Peg, and I couldn't have managed without you and all the others. You gave me a home and loving support when I needed it most, and I'll always be grateful to you for that. But London's where I belong, and where I know I can learn to put all this behind me and begin again.'

Peggy put her arms round Julie and gave her a hug. 'We'll miss you,' she murmured, 'and I was hoping you'd be here when this little one arrives. I was rather counting on having the best midwife in the district.'

'Don't worry, Peg,' said Julie, sniffing back her tears. 'I think you'll find me replacement will be just as reliable.'

Peggy frowned. 'You've already started making plans to leave?'

Julie nodded. 'But it'll be a while yet, so you won't get rid of me that easily.' She pulled on the navy blue cardigan over her striped cotton uniform and picked up her medical bag. 'I'll see you tonight,' she said and gave a watery smile before heading down to the basement to fetch her bicycle.

Julie cycled along the seafront towards the surgery, grateful for the sea breeze that chased away the shadows of another restless night and dried her tears. She came to the end of the promenade and stood watching the sea roll in glassy waves against the shingle as the gulls hovered and glided effortlessly on the breeze.

Once Bill's father had returned to the family farm in the Dales, Peggy had found rooms for Bill and his mother in a nearby private hotel, realising that having them at Beach View would be much too painful for Julie. However, the mother and son had become regular visitors to the house, and Julie still found it difficult to sit and listen as they talked about William's progress and their plans for the future. They had been here for almost two weeks now, and the time was fast approaching when William would be well enough to make the long journey north.

She gave a trembling sigh and tried very hard to see the positive side of things, for Edith was motherly and capable, and Bill was a good man, his every word and gesture proving that he would be a kind and loving father to precious little William, despite his crippling injuries.

She looked out to the horizon, remembering Bill's almost dismissive account of how he'd sustained those injuries. Like so many men who'd been through the horrors of war, he was reluctant to go into any real detail, but he'd said enough to paint a very stark picture of what had happened.

He'd been in the desert on reconnaissance with two others when they'd been mown down by enemy fire. His comrades were dead, but despite having a bullet in his thigh, he'd managed to hide among the rocks of a nearby escarpment. With the Germans camped in the dunes below him, he was trapped for several days before he could try and make his way back to his battalion. Then he'd slipped and fallen, breaking his leg so badly he'd passed out with the pain, his identification papers fluttering away to be lost among the desert sands.

The Bedouin had found him some time later, delirious and badly dehydrated. They'd tended his wounds and revived him enough to make the long trek across the desert to an Allied camp where the medics had had little option but to amputate his leg, for gangrene had set in. It was weeks before he was coherent enough to tell anyone who he was.

After a long and difficult recovery in a military hospital in Cairo, he'd finally been repatriated, to find a stack of returned mail waiting for him – and the news that his beloved Franny was dead, but that his son had survived.

Julie gave a deep sigh and turned away from the seafront. Bill had certainly earned the right to be a father to his son, and she knew in her heart that he would make sure William knew who she was, and what she'd done for him in his precious first few months. It was time to accept that and move on.

It was still early and hardly anyone was out, but as she arrived at the surgery, she could see that Maud was already on her knees scrubbing the floor.

'Morning, ducks,' she said brightly, glad of the excuse to stop work. 'Up with the lark, as usual, I see.' She tilted her head towards Michael's consulting room. 'Doc's already in, if you were wanting a word,' she said with a knowing smile.

'Thanks, Maud.' Julie tiptoed across the damp floor, tapped on Michael's door and went in.

'Hello, you're early,' he said, standing up as she closed the door behind her. 'There isn't a problem with William, is there?'

'No. His father tells me he's coming along a treat.' She adjusted her apron and sat down. 'Firstly, I wanted to say how grateful I am for all the care you and Mr Watson have taken with him. I don't think he would have pulled through without you both.'

His dark eyes became watchful as she hesitated. 'What is it, Sister Harris?'

'I've come to give you me notice,' she replied. 'Of course I won't be leaving immediately, but I've been offered the chance to take up a post at me old place in London. They'll need me to start in four weeks.'

'But we need you here,' he blurted.

'No, you don't,' she replied softly. 'You have three

volunteers, Mrs Clough who's only too delighted to use her nursing skills again, and Eunice. I also heard that another district nurse is starting in three weeks.'

He reddened and couldn't meet her gaze. 'That's true,' he admitted, 'but there's no guarantee she'll be suitable.'

Julie grinned for the first time in days. 'Oh, I think you'll find she is,' she replied. 'Alison Chenoweth is an extremely good nurse and midwife, and although you may find her difficult to understand with that Cornish accent of hers, she'll be an asset to the practice, I promise.'

His eyes widened in astonishment. 'How on earth do you know so much?'

'Alison worked with me in London and we've stayed in touch. I told her about the post here and she jumped at the chance. She's a country girl at heart, and this place will suit her just fine.' She didn't add that Alison was an imp, and would probably sum up Eunice in a trice and see to it that she was kept on her toes.

'When I said we needed you here,' he began hesitantly, 'it wasn't the practice I was talking about.'

She regarded him warily as he leaned forward, his arms resting on his desk.

'You see, I realise now that I shouldn't have let others influence how I felt about things,' he continued awkwardly. 'I know I've been somewhat distant and rather formal of late, but I wasn't at all sure about . . .' He gave a helpless smile and shrugged his shoulders. 'Well, you know.'

Julie took pity on him and gave him a warm smile. 'I understand completely, Michael. You were led to believe that I was a young, single woman with a baby in tow who was looking for some poor sap of a man to give her a bit of respectability.'

'That's not quite how it was put,' he protested.

'I bet it's close enough,' she replied mildly. 'But I was never looking for anything more than friendship from you, Michael – and if only you'd come to me and talked it over, I could have set things right between us.'

'I see,' he murmured.

'I'm sorry,' she said, leaning towards him. 'You're a lovely man, with a deep sense of responsibility and care for your patients. But you shouldn't judge a book by its cover, Michael.'

'I never presumed—' he protested.

'I'm sure you didn't,' she said dryly, 'but if you look at things from where I see them, you might find it easier to understand my feelings on the matter.' She stood up and smoothed down her apron. 'I like you, Michael, but I'm not the one who's in love with you. You need to look closer to home than that.'

She let herself out of the consulting room and bumped straight into Eunice. 'Dr Michael would probably appreciate a cup of tea,' she said brightly. 'And while you're at it, why don't you ask him to that fund-raising garden party? I know you happen to have a spare ticket.'

She left the surgery feeling lighter somehow, and as she set off on her rounds, she could feel the tug of London calling her home, and the first stirring of hope that she would come through this time of trauma a stronger, better person.

Julie took up her position on the platform at Cliffehaven Station. It was strange to think how much had happened since she'd arrived there all those months ago. Now the first of September had arrived, and Bill would be taking William to Yorkshire the following morning. She tamped down on the feeling of dread as she waited for the London train to arrive.

Alison Chenoweth emerged from the cloud of steam with a bright smile, dropped her cases and threw herself into Julie's arms, her words of delight at seeing her again tripping over one another in her excitement.

Julie tried to translate what she was saying, and gave up. It was just lovely to see her again, and to catch up on all the news. She took one of her cases and they set out for Kath Carter's house, where Alison would be lodging in the spare room.

Kath's mother was out at work, but the three girls soon settled down in deckchairs to make the most of the end of summer in the pretty garden and to catch up on the gossip. Julie elicited a promise from

Alison that she'd take very great care of Peggy, and then put her wise to the ways of the surgery and the budding romance between Eunice and Michael, warning her that Eunice could be tricky.

Kath promised to introduce her to her friends and show her round Cliffehaven, and they both listened as Alison talked about life at the hostel, Lily's latest young man, Sister Preston's engagement to a Canadian soldier, and the surprising news that Matron seemed to be getting rather close to one of the senior doctors at the hospital.

'I be 'earin' that Stanley you were engaged to got 'is call-up papers and 'e be gorn to be a soldier,' said Alison some time later. 'I 'ope ye be none too upset, Julie.'

Julie shook her head, surprised at her lack of caring one way or another. She'd hardly thought about Stan these past months. 'I thought his job was considered a reserve occupation.'

'That's as maybe,' muttered Alison. 'But I heard tell he blotted his copybook, and were about to be kicked out of the force. Reckon he jumped afore he were pushed,' she said with an impish grin.

Julie made no comment, even though she did wonder what Stan had done to get himself the sack. Then all thoughts of Stan were dismissed as she heard the grandfather clock in the hall chime half past seven. 'I've got to go,' she said reluctantly.

Kath and Alison went with her to the door, and as she stepped onto the path, they gathered her into a tight embrace. 'I'm going to miss you, Kath,' Julie managed through her tears. 'You've been such a good friend.'

Kath returned her hug. 'I'll write often, and don't forget us down here.'

'I won't.' She grinned through her tears at Alison. 'And try not to wind Eunice up too much – she's not really that bad.'

Alison pulled a face. 'I'll make me own mind up on that.' She hugged Julie and then gave her a nudge towards the gate. 'Get you gone, Jules, or I'll be blabbering.'

Julie closed the gate behind her, gave them one last smile and wave, then hurried down the road. Reaching the entrance to the park, she turned, saw they were still watching, and waved again before she turned away and almost ran through the leafy gardens. It was a day of goodbyes – a day when she had to close the door on this chapter of her life, and steel herself for the next. But it wasn't quite over – for the hardest goodbye was yet to come.

The ward was quiet, for visiting hour was long over, but Sister Black understood her need to be with William tonight, and kindly agreed to her having some time alone with him.

Julie stood by the cot and watched him play with his fingers. He'd filled out again, she noticed, and seemed to have grown in the long weeks since she'd seen him last. He was changing, she realised, his features becoming more defined, his hair darkening to his father's brown. But his smile was still Franny's.

She lifted him from the cot and he grabbed her hair, gurgling with delight as she held him. He filled her arms so perfectly, and his baby skin was soft and sweet-smelling. He had more teeth now, and his eyes were a much darker brown. Soon she wouldn't recognise him at all.

She kissed his little face, breathed him in for the last time, then put him back in the cot. 'Goodbye, my darling boy,' she whispered. 'You were never really mine, but you'll be in my heart always.'

Julie did not go to the station the following morning to see Bill and his mother take William away from Cliffehaven, but spent most of the day with Eileen. Then she returned to Beach View Boarding House to pack her cases and prepare for her last night with the Reilly family.

The next morning found her standing on the platform at Cliffehaven Station yet again, her cases beside her as she waited for the train. Peggy had offered to come with her, as had Eileen, but she had no wish to prolong the agony of parting, for it felt as if she'd spent the past few days severing all ties to Cliffehaven and the people who'd come to mean so much to her.

She and Eileen had parted tearfully, but she knew they wouldn't lose touch again, and that once the war was over, Eileen would probably return to London. The knowledge that William and Bill were probably already in the Yorkshire Dales, and therefore out of reach, made her heart ache. But one day she would see William again, she vowed, and in the meantime she would keep in touch with Bill.

As the train chugged into the station and a great cloud of steam rolled along the platform, Julie took her last look down the High Street to the glint of blue sea and then climbed aboard. The last few weeks had been filled with sadness, but now she felt a surge of excitement. The tug of London was ever stronger, drawing her home – home to where her heart lay, and where she could begin again.

Epilogue

Peggy's baby was born just in time for tea at a quarter to six in the evening of 7th December 1941. Jim was cock-a-hoop, and although Peggy was exhausted after a long labour, she too was euphoric over the safe delivery of her beautiful new daughter. They called her Daisy.

The Reilly family didn't realise, until they heard the news on the wireless the following day, that Daisy had been born at the very moment Japan had launched a deadly dawn attack on the American Naval Fleet in Pearl Harbour.

The Americans were now very much involved in the war, and soon they would be arriving in their thousands to help defend this small island and its embattled people.